I0803138

IMAGES
of America

SANTA FE ART AND ARCHITECTURE

ON THE COVER: This 1930 photograph shows the annual Fiesta Parade looking across East San Francisco Street to Santa Fe's oldest hotel, the landmark La Fonda, which sits at the end of the legendary Santa Fe Trail across from the St. Francis Cathedral Basilica. (Courtesy of the Palace of the Governors Photograph Archive, 118249.)

IMAGES
of America

SANTA FE ART AND ARCHITECTURE

Lyn Bleiler and Charles Strong,
The Martin Foundation for the Creative Arts

ARCADIA
PUBLISHING

ISBN 978-0-7385-9598-6

Published by Arcadia Publishing
Charleston, South Carolina

Printed in the United States of America

Library of Congress Control Number: 2012940163

For all general information, please contact Arcadia Publishing:
Telephone 843-853-2070
Fax 843-853-0044
E-mail sales@arcadiapublishing.com
For customer service and orders:
Toll-Free 1-888-313-2665

Visit us on the Internet at www.arcadiapublishing.com

This book is dedicated to the artists and photographers who made this book possible, especially those who so diligently documented the Southwest: Jesse L. Nusbaum, Carlos Vierra, and John Collier.

Contents

Acknowledgments

Special thanks to Anita McDaniel at Taos Historic Museums, Daniel Kosharek and Mark Scharen at Palace of the Governors Photograph Archive, Sibel Melik at the New Mexico State Records Center and Archives, Terry Martin-Hart, and Cris Pulos.

Unless otherwise noted, all images are from the Library of Congress.

INTRODUCTION

The oldest capital city in North America, with the oldest public building still in use in America, Santa Fe has a rich and varied cultural history. Evidence indicates that Ancestral Puebloan Indians inhabited the area as early as 500 A.D. Spanish explorers led by Francisco Vasquez de Coronado arrived in Santa Fe in the early 1540s and found Indian villages consisting of flat, often multi-storied dwellings made of mud and wood beams, or *vigas*.

By 1610, the Spaniards had founded what they called Villa Real de Santa Fe, or "Royal City of Holy Faith." When Mexico gained independence from Spain, Santa Fe became the capital of the Mexican province of Nuevo Mejico. In 1846, following 25 years of Mexican rule, the United States claimed Santa Fe and the surrounding region as a US territory. In 1912, New Mexico achieved statehood.

The arrival of Anglos was hastened by the building of the transcontinental railroad and Santa Fe became a tri-cultural community. In the late 1800s, the Southwest became a haven for tuberculosis patients, and a number of sanatoriums were built in Santa Fe. Many creative individuals—including poets, artists and architects—who came to Santa Fe for health reasons stayed on, significantly contributing to the city's cultural development. At the forefront of art, folk art, crafts, and design, Santa Fe received the distinction of being the first American community to be designated a "Creative City" by the United Nations Educational, Scientific, and Cultural Organization (UNESCO) in 2005.

One

Early Santa Fe Architecture

Early Puebloan architecture predates the arrival of Europeans in North America. Santa Fe and northern New Mexico were settled by ancestors of Anasazi Indians, who had built intricate villages between 1050 A.D. and 1300 A.D. in the Four Corners area—where the state lines of New Mexico, Colorado, Arizona, and Utah meet. The Anazasi people migrated to the Rio Grande Valley, breaking off into 19 smaller tribal pueblos, including Zuni, Acoma, Taos, Santa Clara, San Ildofonso, Sandia, Tesuque, and others.

The grandest, most ambitious buildings of the Spanish settlers were their Catholic churches. The simple yet monumental Acoma Pueblo Mission Church was the inspiration for the Fine Arts Museum complex (see pages 22 and 43). Even the smaller, more modest churches possessed a grandness of scale not seen in even the largest haciendas of the day.

The design and ingenuity of Puebloean architecture was adopted by Spanish colonial settlers and ultimately by the artists and architects who worked to achieve a unified Santa Fe identity. *Kiva* fireplaces, *latilla* (wooden) ladders, Pueblo step corbels, *vigas* (log) roof beams, and keyhole doorways are among the architectural details adopted by both the Spanish and Anglos. By 1915, thanks to the efforts of artists and architects, many of whom arrived in Santa Fe in search of a cure for tuberculosis, these elements became signature components of the new/old Santa Fe style that Santa Fe is known for today.

The Anglo influence first made an imprint through architecture. The Cathedral Basilica of Saint Francis of Assisi was commissioned by the archbishop in a Romanesque revival style. In this period, numerous Victorian buildings were built on three sides of the Santa Fe Plaza. On the north side is the block-long Palace of the Governors, the oldest public building in the United States. This building once suffered the addition of a Victorian parapet, which was removed in the early 1900s. Many of the Victorian buildings were later covered in stucco and their gingerbread trim was removed or torn down completely as the movement for new/old Santa Fe style gathered momentum. The flagships of this movement are the Museum of New Mexico (formerly the Fine Arts Museum) and the La Fonda Hotel, which was rebuilt and expanded in 1926.

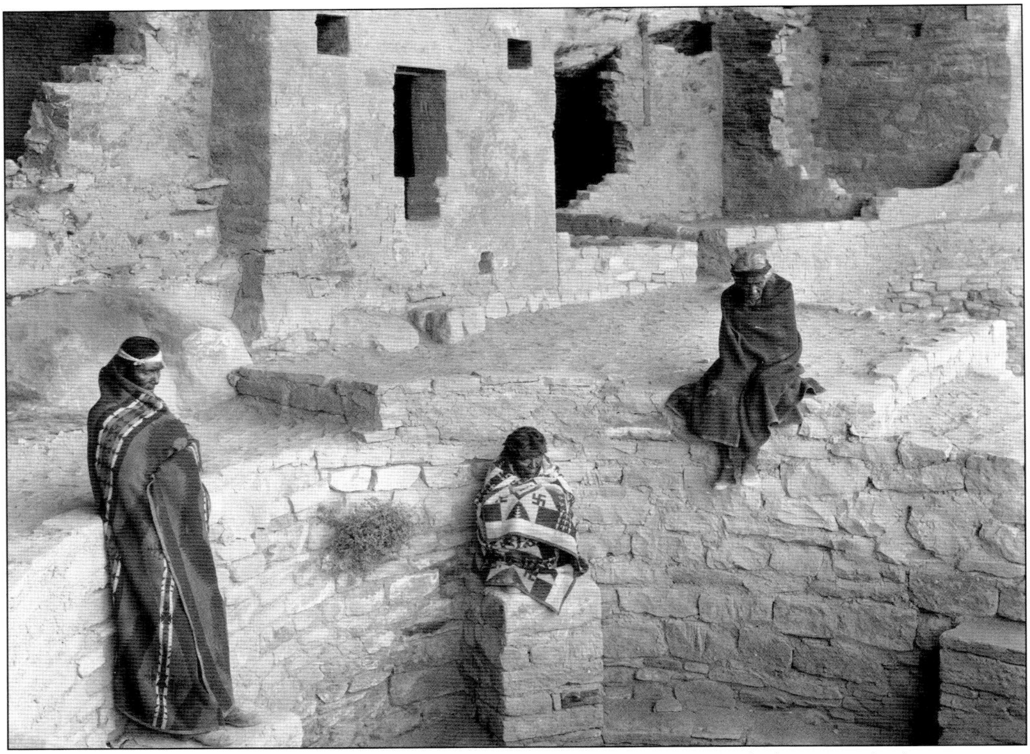

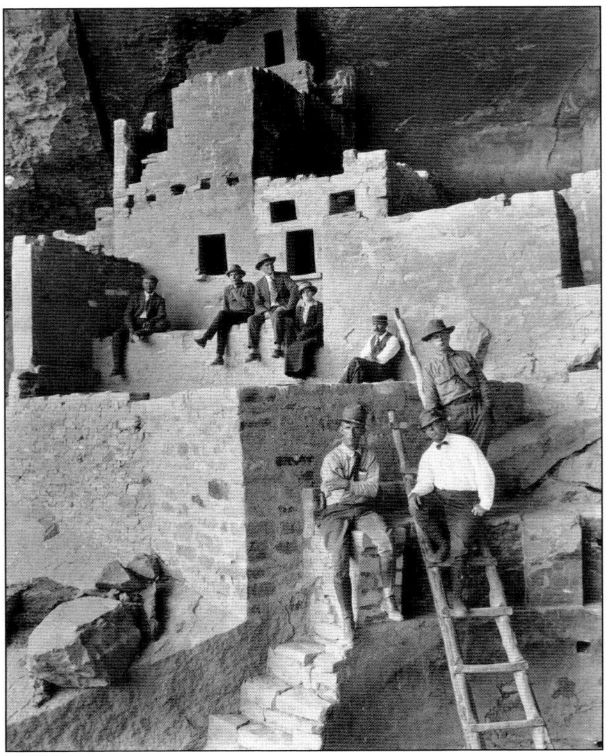

The staged photograph above, taken by George L. Beam around 1920, shows Native Americans wrapped in tribal blankets posing around a reconstructed kiva at the Balcony House ruins in Mesa Verde National Park. The Balcony House is accessed by climbing a 32-foot ladder and crawling through a short tunnel.

A group of tourists pose with their park service guide in the Cliff Palace, a structure with more than 150 rooms at Mesa Verde National Park. This photograph was taken by George L. Beam between 1916 and 1925.

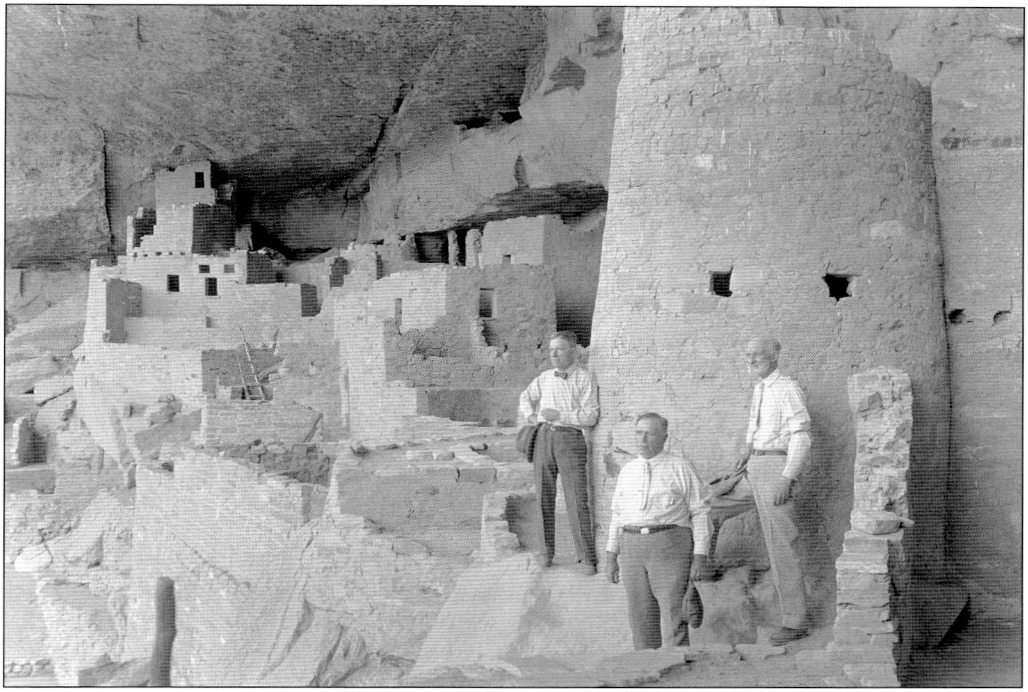

The caption written on the back of this photograph identifies these men as John D. Rockefeller Jr. with Dr. R.W. Corwin and Bert Mattison standing in front of the Round Tower building at Cliff Palace in Mesa Verde National Park. The photograph was taken by Jesse L. Nusbaum around 1925.

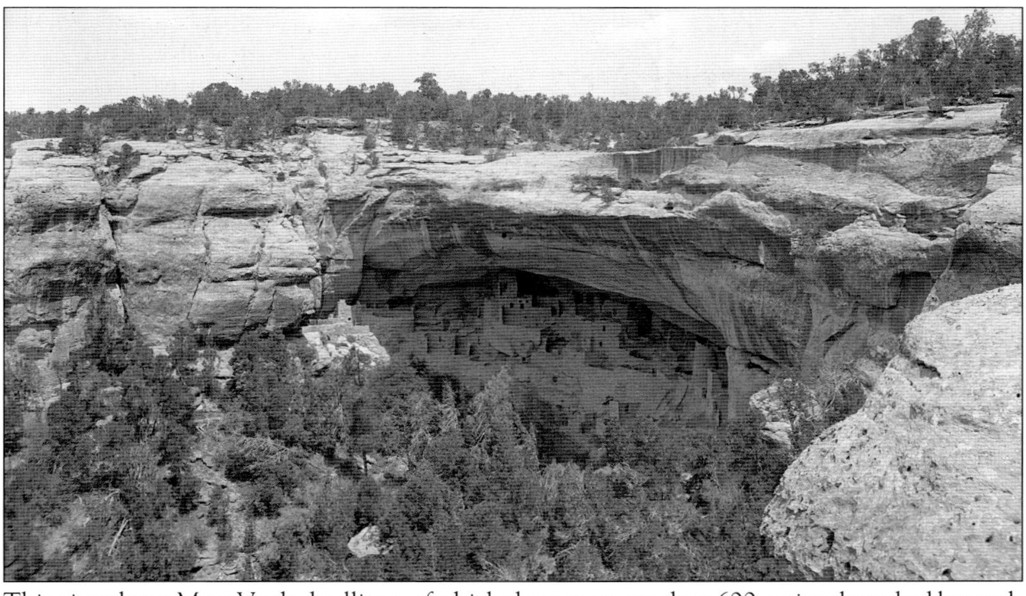

This view shows Mesa Verde dwellings, of which there are more than 600, uniquely tucked beneath the overhanging sandstone cliffs. Inhabitants of these dwellings ultimately migrated south and established pueblos throughout the Southwest. Mesa Verde National Park is a designated United Nations World Heritage site.

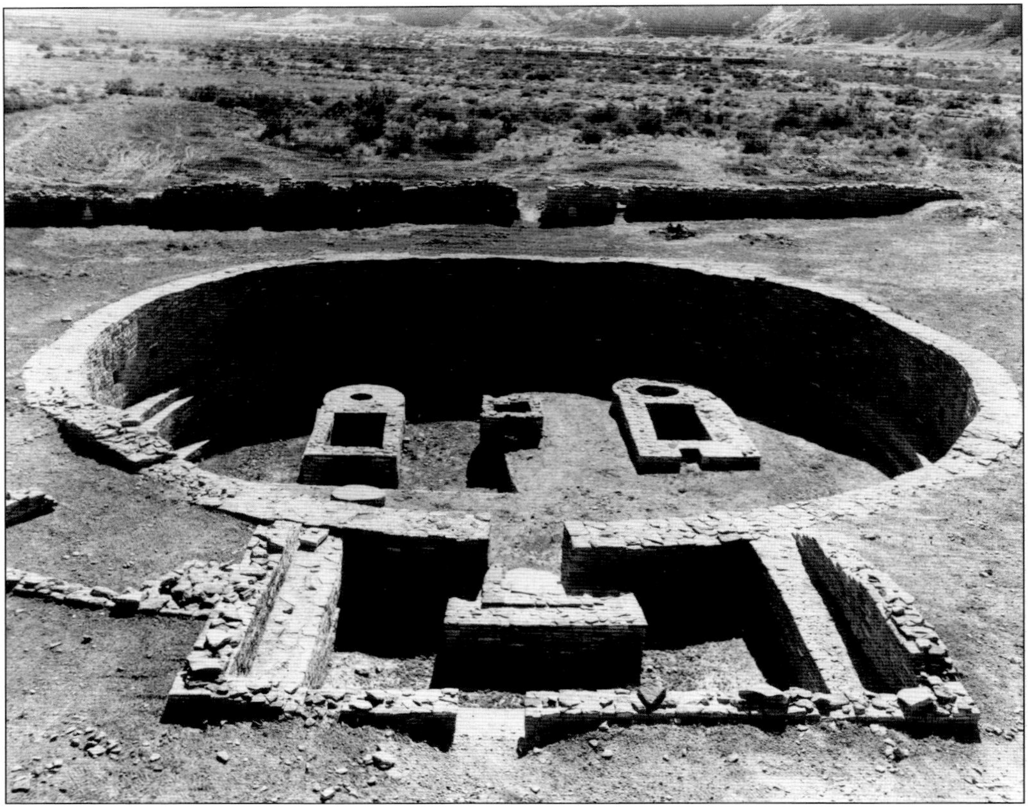

This photograph of the Chaco ruins gives the viewer a sense of the artistry employed in constructing these large-scale stone buildings. Several of these "Great Houses" were connected by a system of roadways to dozens of others throughout the region. It is believed that they were used as an early form of public architecture to accommodate ceremonial and trading visitors.

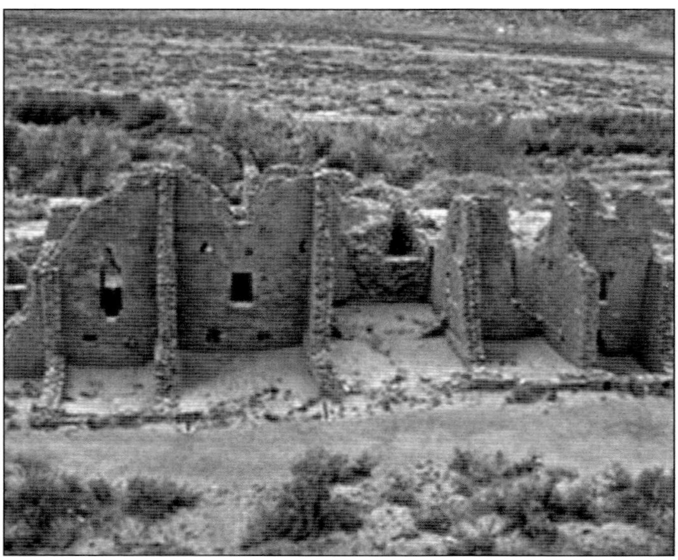

Once the ceremonial and economic center of the San Juan Basin, the complex architectural village of Chaco Canyon was home to a thriving ancestral Puebloan culture established in the mid-800s and lasting for more than 300 years. Massive multi-storied stone structures known as Great Houses contained hundreds of separate dwellings. The "houses" were oriented to solar and astrological markers and purposely situated within what inhabitants believed to be a sacred landscape surrounded by mesas and mountains, which had deep-rooted spiritual significance for them.

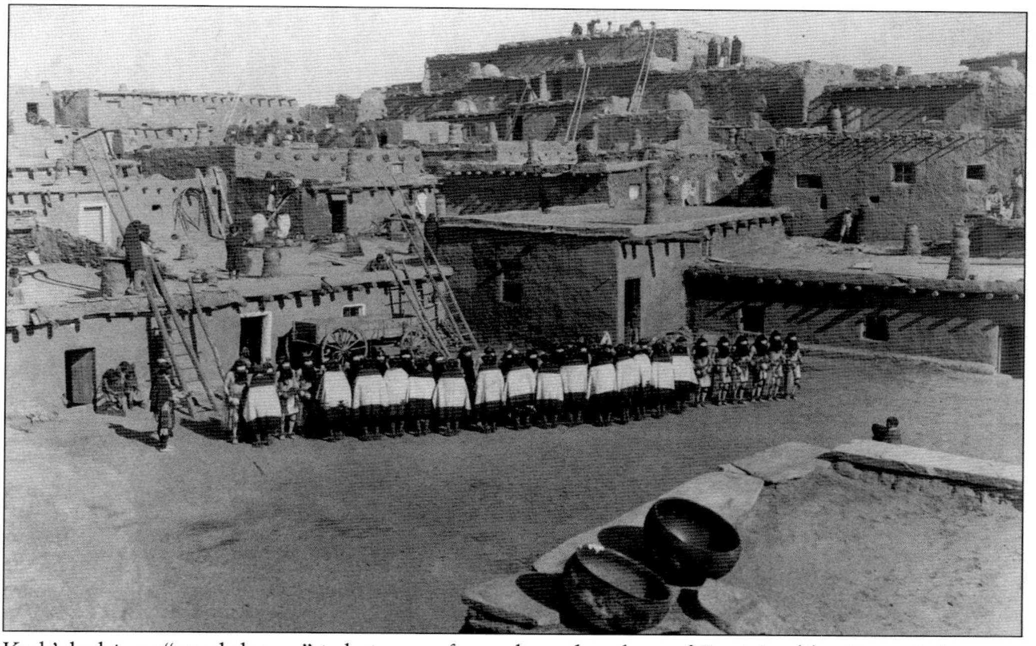

Ka-k'ok-shi, or "good dance," is being performed on the plaza of Zuni Pueblo. One of the most famous of the Kachina dances, Shalako, is still held every December in the Zuni Pueblo to celebrate the end of the old and the beginning of the new year and to bless all of the houses of the pueblo erected during the year. Ben Wittick took this photograph on June 19, 1897.

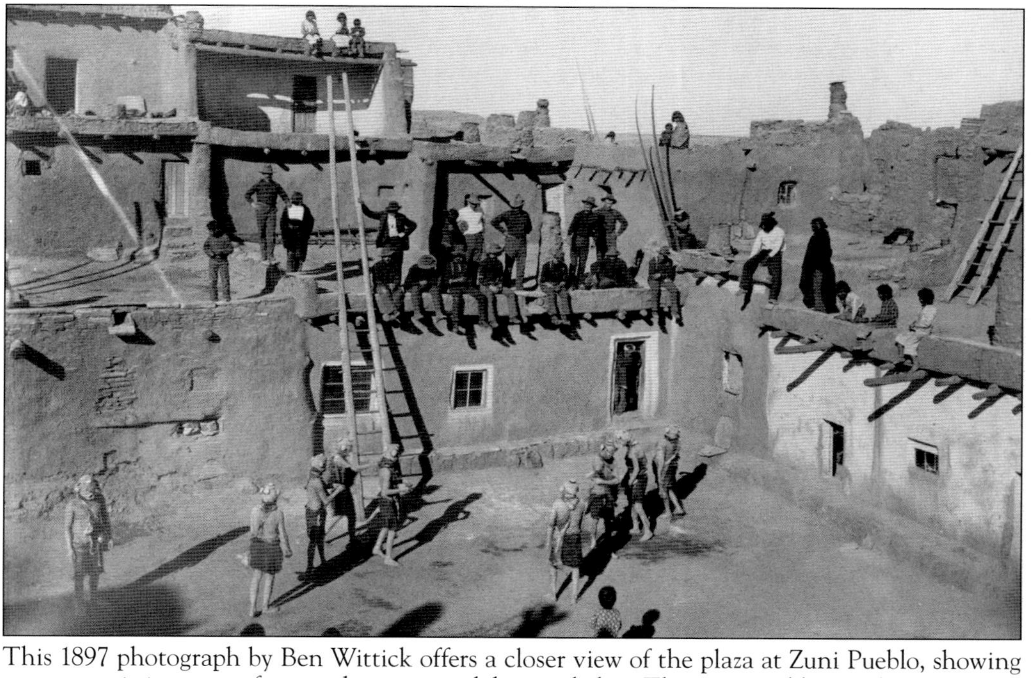

This 1897 photograph by Ben Wittick offers a closer view of the plaza at Zuni Pueblo, showing spectators sitting on rooftops with ceremonial dancers below. The Zuni Pueblo was the first native settlement Spanish explorers visited on their search for what they believed were the Seven Golden Cities of Cíbola, also known as the Seven Cities of Gold, in 1540.

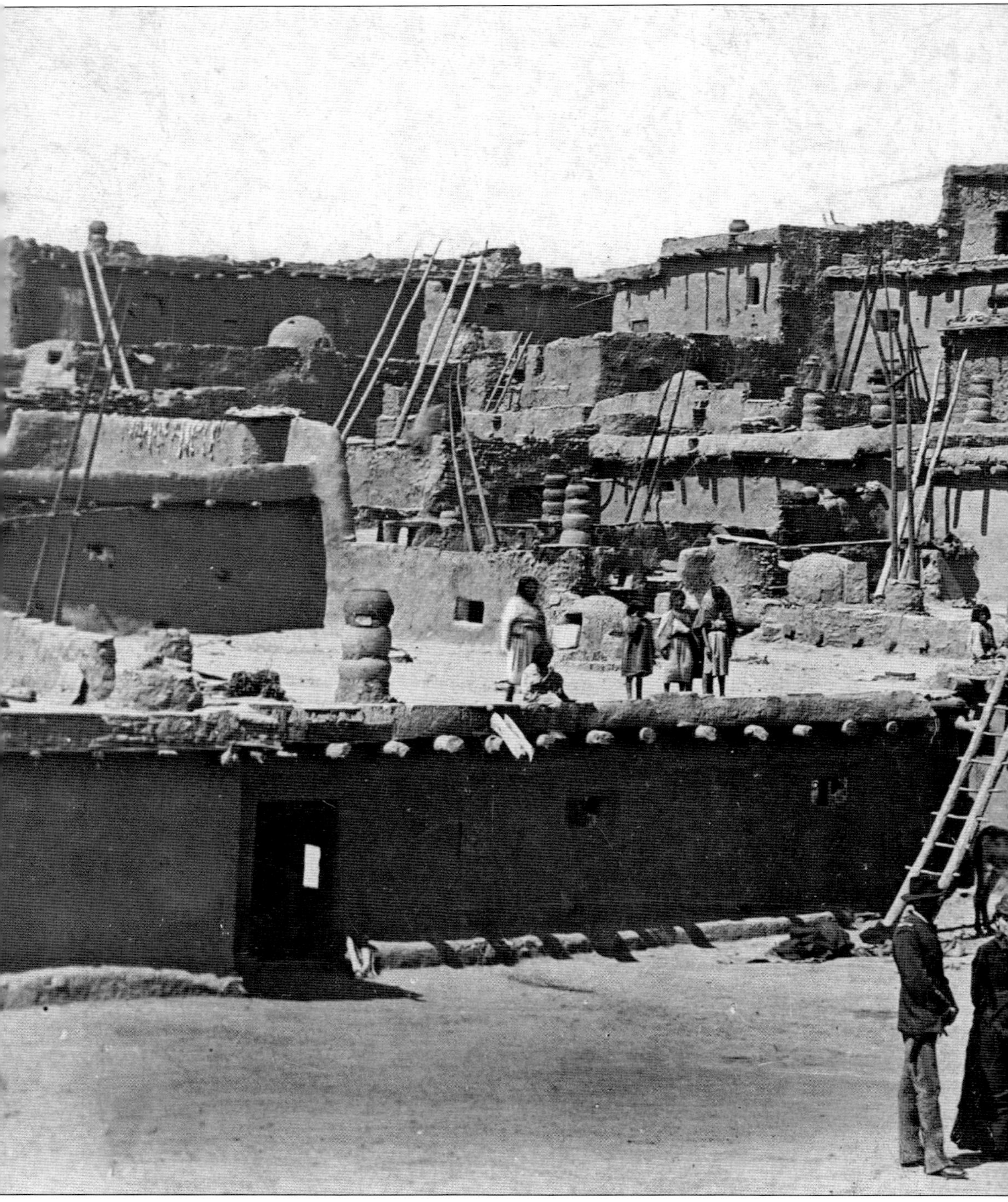

The caption on this photograph identifies "General John A. Logan and party" at Zuni Pueblo. These adobe and flagstone structures are an example of early, multi-storied tribal housing. Like Ben Wittick, who took this photograph in September 1882, Carlos Vierra became fascinated by Pueblo and Hispanic architecture and, along with Jesse Nusbaum, extensively documented the

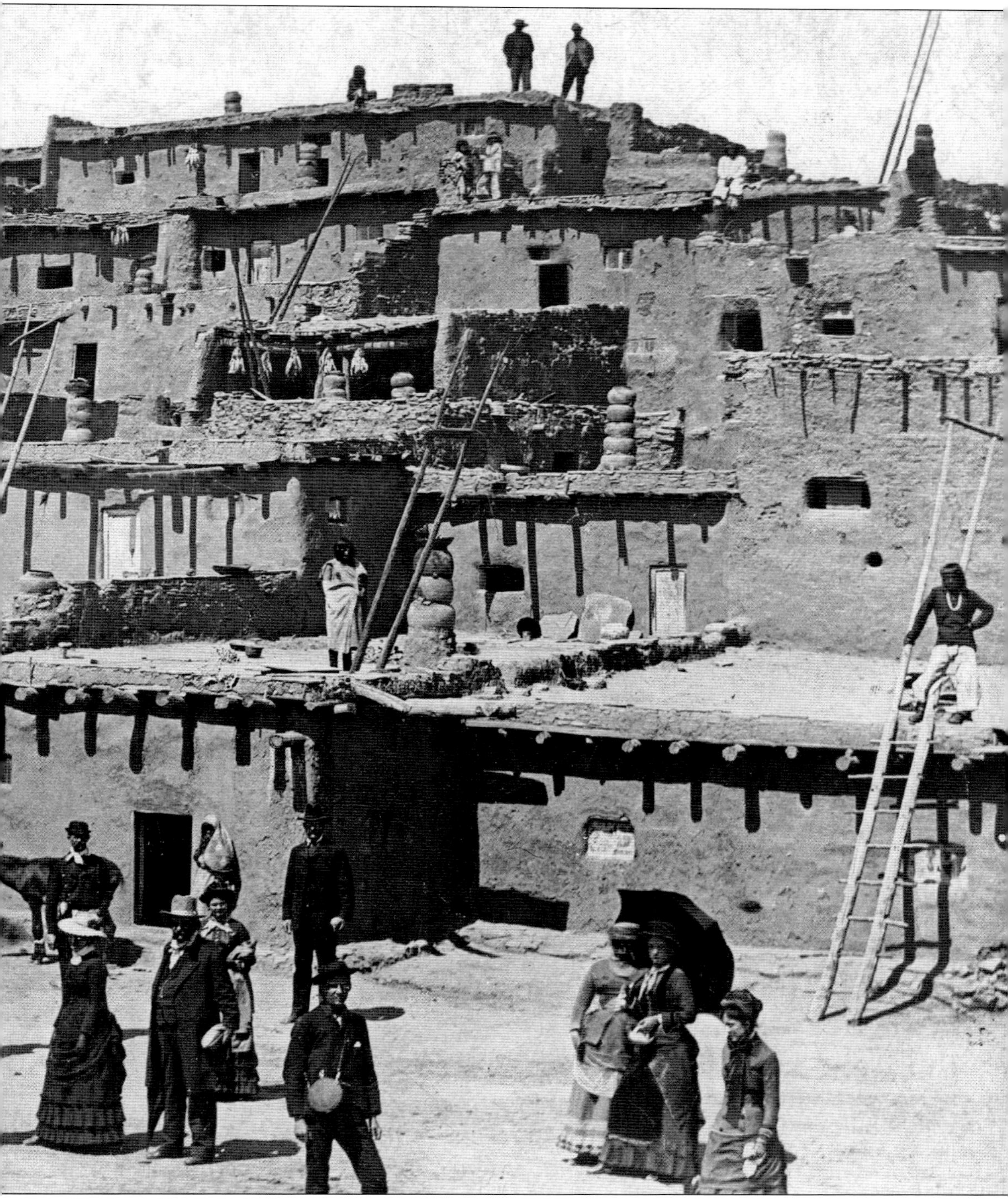

region's Pueblos. By the late 1910s, a collection of Vierra's photographs housed at the Museum of New Mexico had become seminal to the development of the Santa Fe style. (Courtesy of Palace of the Governors Photograph Archive, 016054.)

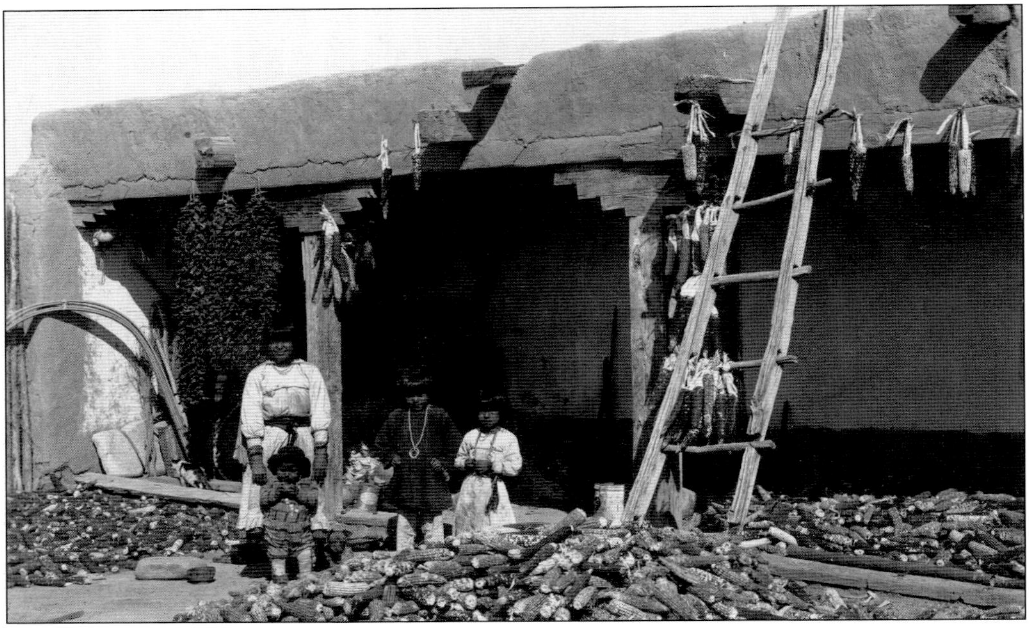

The caption on this photograph reads, "Agrapina Quintana and children, wife of Marcial Quintana, with drying corn and chili, Cochita Pueblo." It was taken around 1920 by Carlos Vierra. The covered portal, Pueblo step corbels, and kiva-style ladder details would later be integral components to what would be known as the new/old Santa Fe style. (Courtesy of Palace of the Governors Photograph Archive, 041532.)

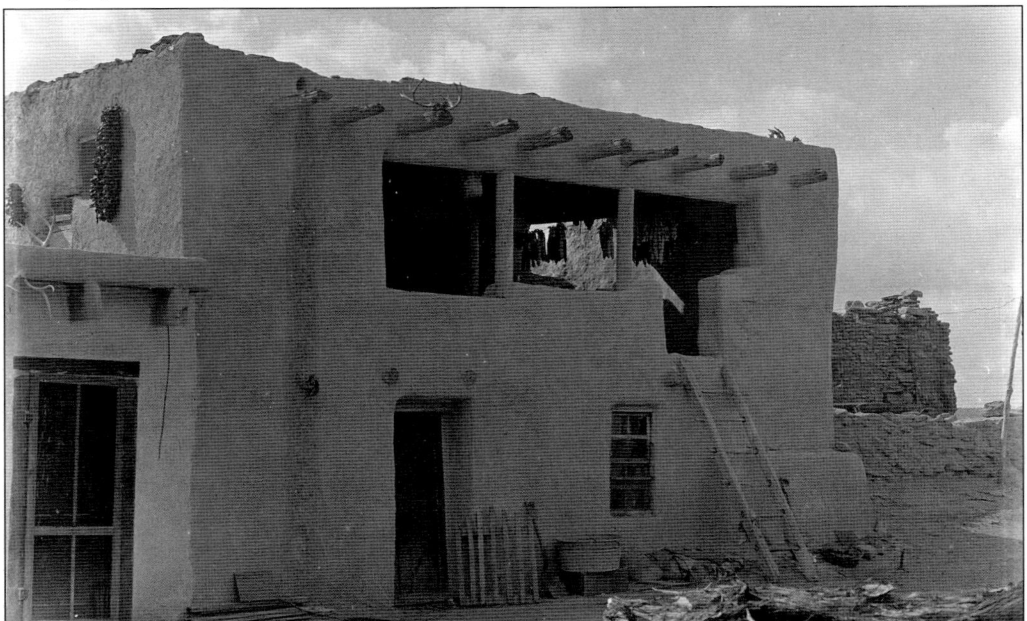

Located on the south side of the Laguna Pueblo plaza, this building has a keyhole-type doorway as well as *vigas* and a *latilla* ladder, features that would be incorporated into the Santa Fe style. (Courtesy of the Palace of the Governor's Photograph Archive, 042133.)

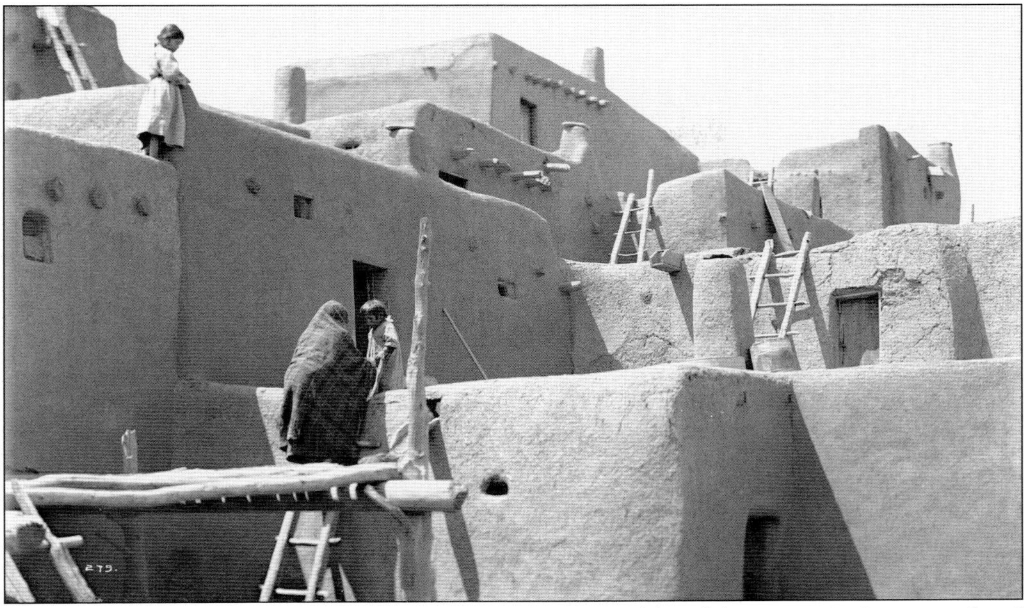

This photograph of the Taos Pueblo shows a condominium-like adobe structure. It is considered to be one of the oldest continuously occupied buildings in America and is an official UNESCO historic site. This structure would greatly influence the Santa Fe style and Southwest architecture. As shown here, living quarters were entered through rooftops to allow for the security of inhabitants against outside attack. This 1912 photograph was taken by either Carlos Vierra or Jesse Nusbaum. (Courtesy of the Palace of the Governor's Photograph Archive, 042977.)

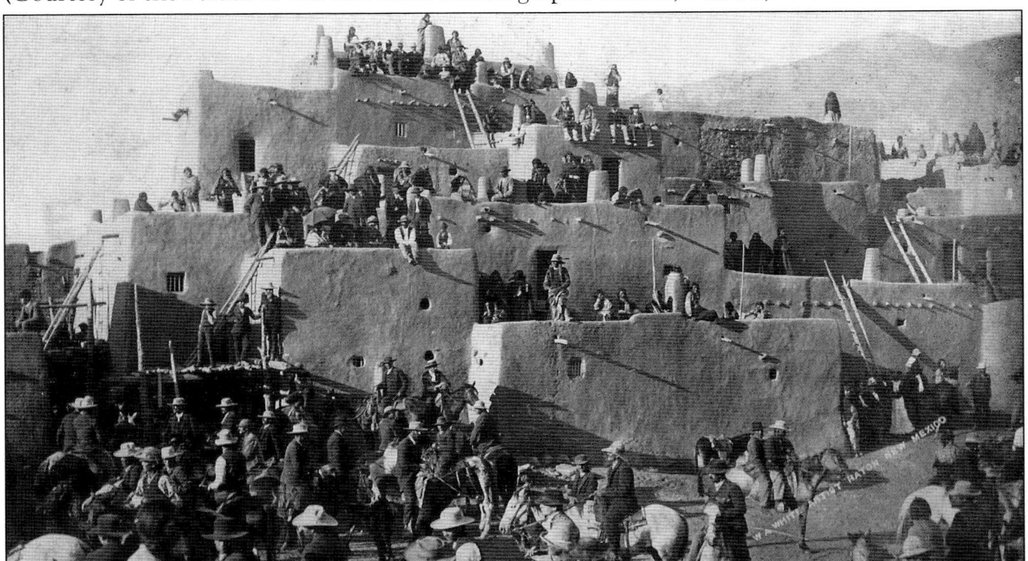

Taken by photographer W.A. White of Raton, New Mexico, this fascinating photograph captures visitors and Taos Pueblo residents awaiting the start of San Geronimo, an annual celebration named for St. Jerome, the patron saint of Taos Pueblo. Originally a day for trading with neighboring tribes, after Spanish colonization, San Geronimo Day began incorporating religious ceremonies as well. (Courtesy of Charles Strong.)

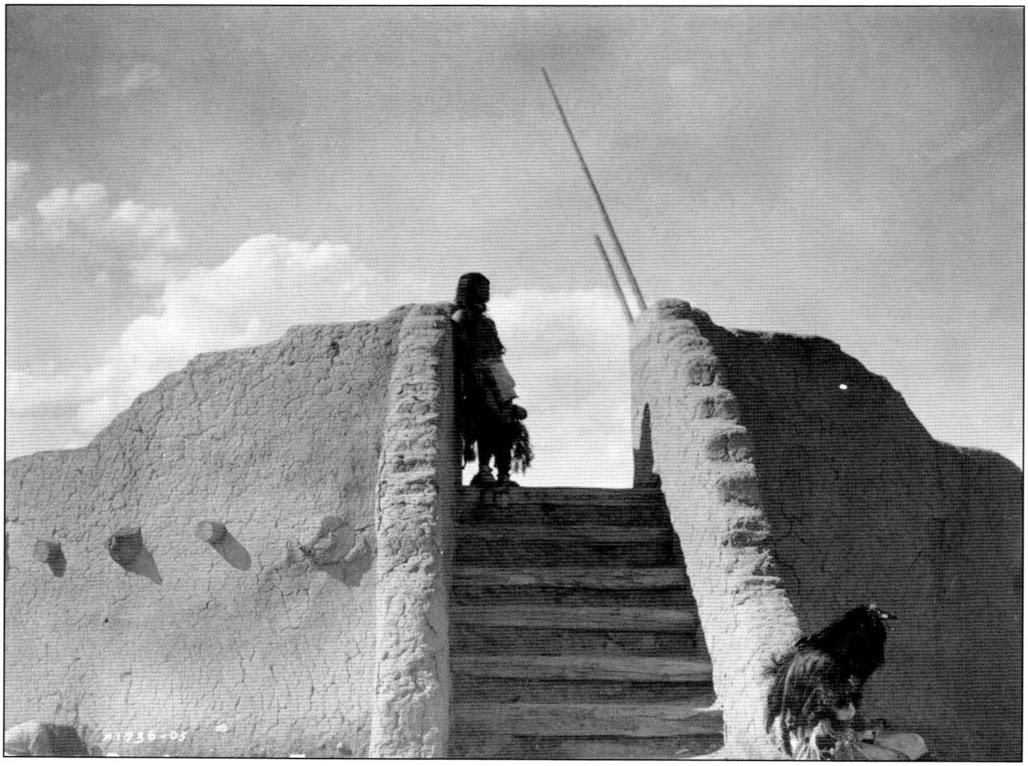

These round Pueblo structures accessed by a staircase to a rooftop entry are known as kivas and are sacred buildings used for religious instruction and ceremonial purposes. Above, a Tewa guard stands at the top of the stairs of the San Ildefonso Pueblo, traditionally known as Po-woh-ge-oweenge, or "Where the water cuts through." Below is the curved exterior of the Nambe Pueblo kiva.

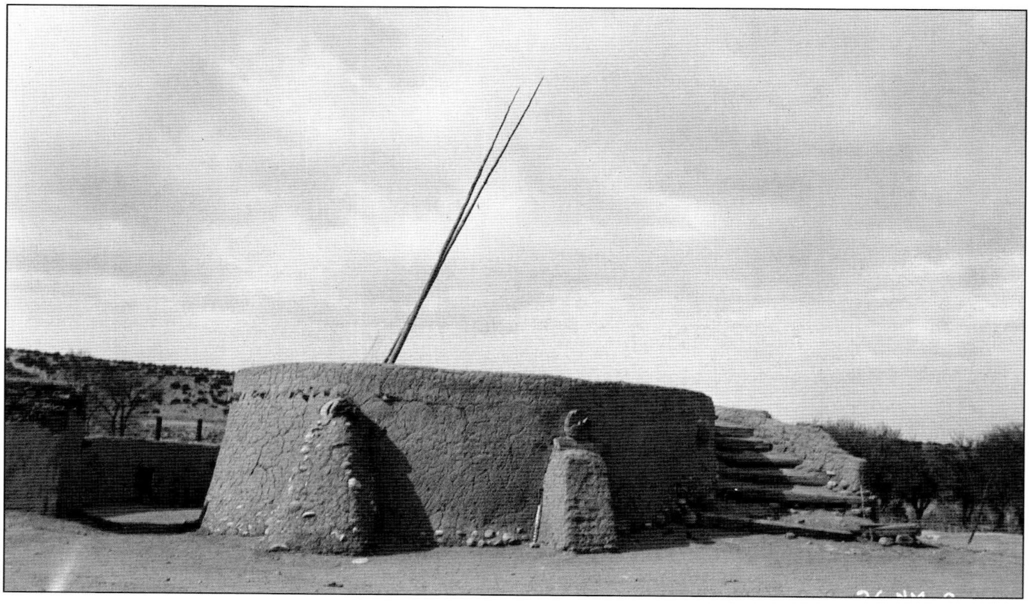

Accessed through ceiling openings, this Acoma Pueblo has a traditional corner kiva fireplace. The photograph gives the viewer a sense of Pueblo living spaces.

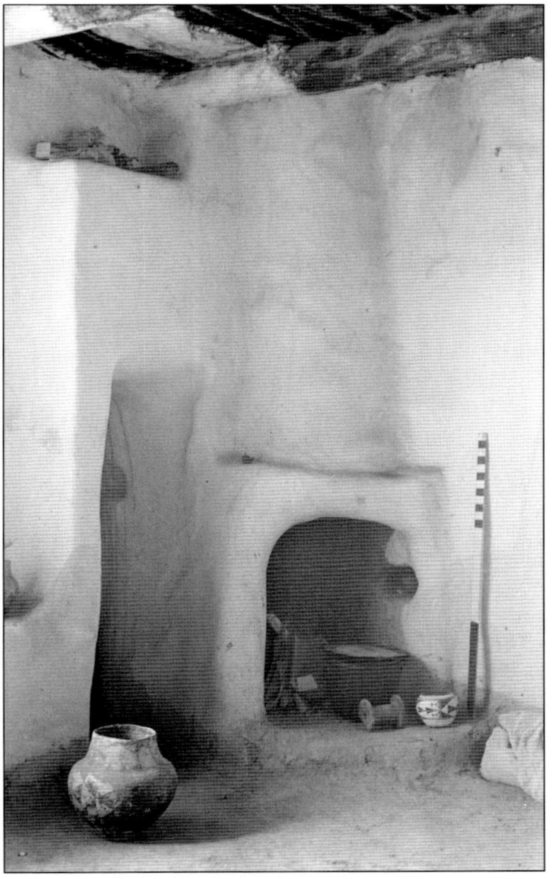

With the San Ildefonso Pueblo in the background, the photograph below shows a ceremonial dance in the plaza. Occupied since the 14th century, San Ildefonso Pueblo contains several ceremonial kivas, a central plaza, and a church built in 1905 at the remains of a 17th-century mission church.

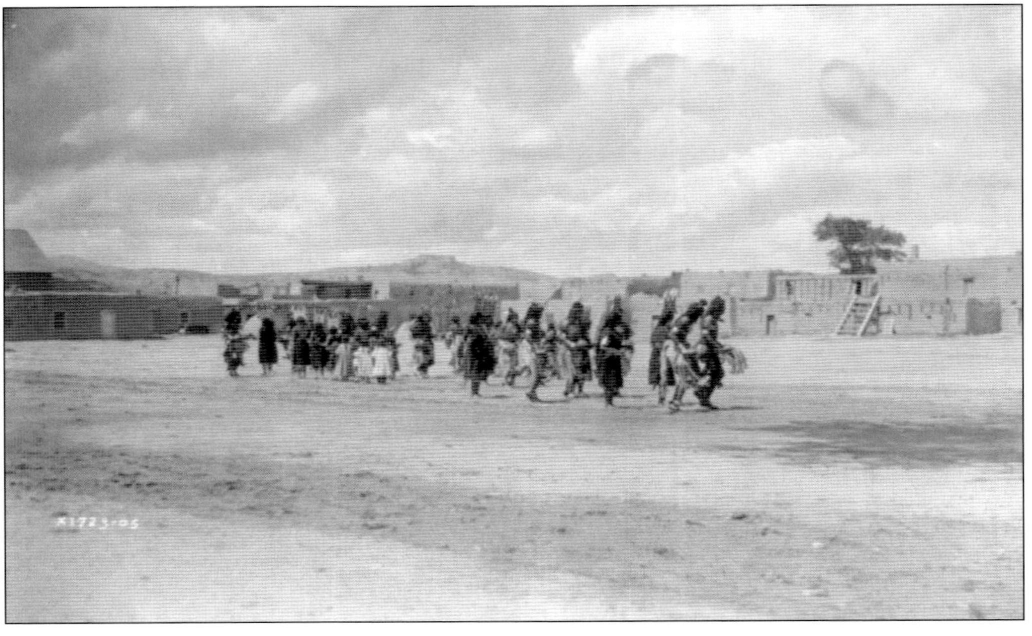

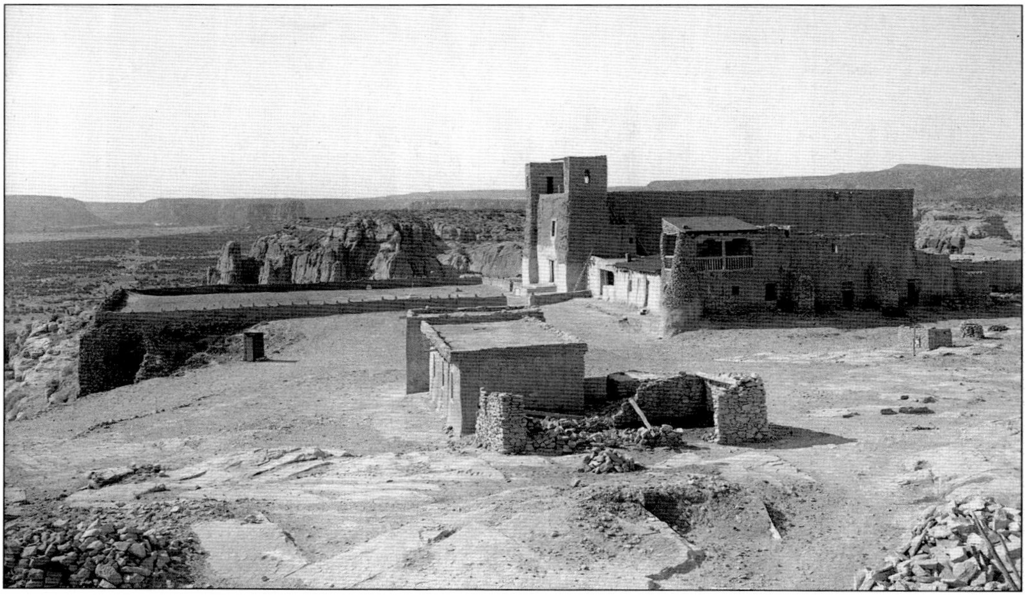

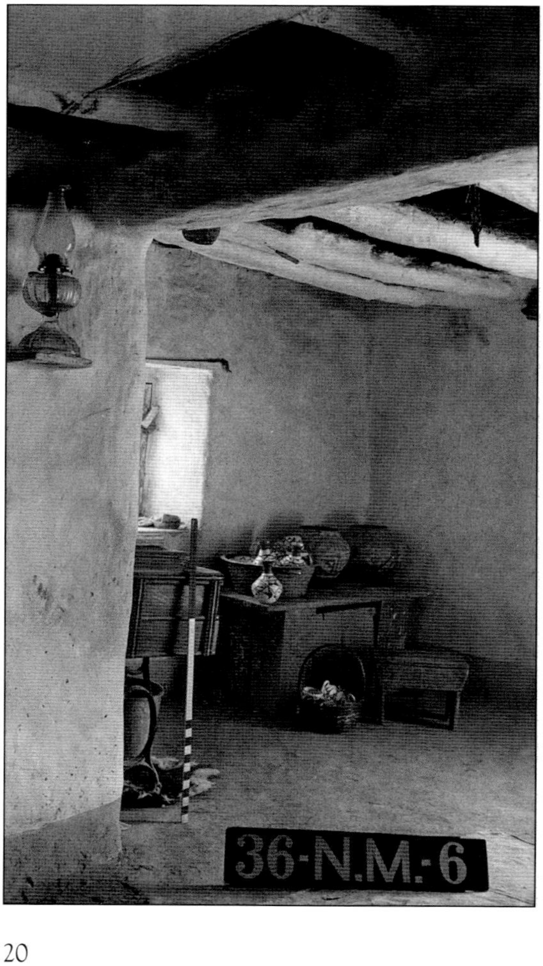

This view of Acoma Pueblo, which has been occupied since 1150 A.D., illustrates why Acoma is often called "Sky City," as it sits atop a 367-foot sandstone bluff mesa in a valley of sacred, towering monoliths. The Acoma Mission (seen in detail on page 22) is on the right in the background.

This interior photograph shows an adobe-walled Acoma Pueblo dwelling with a trundle foot sewing machine and a kerosene lamp. Note the ceiling entry, though which the latilla ladder would be dropped to gain entrance.

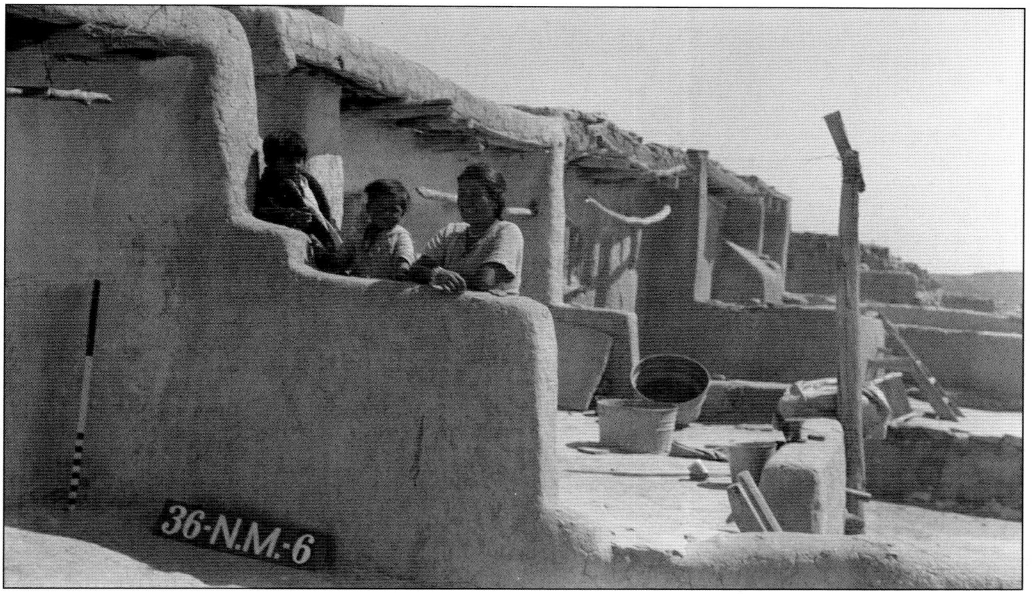

The word "Acoma" is from the Acoma and Spanish word "Acoma," or "Acú," meaning "the place that always was" and "people of the White Rock." Here, an Acoma family enjoys a rooftop view. The ceiling beam construction and the latilla ladders leading down through the roof into the dwelling are seen here.

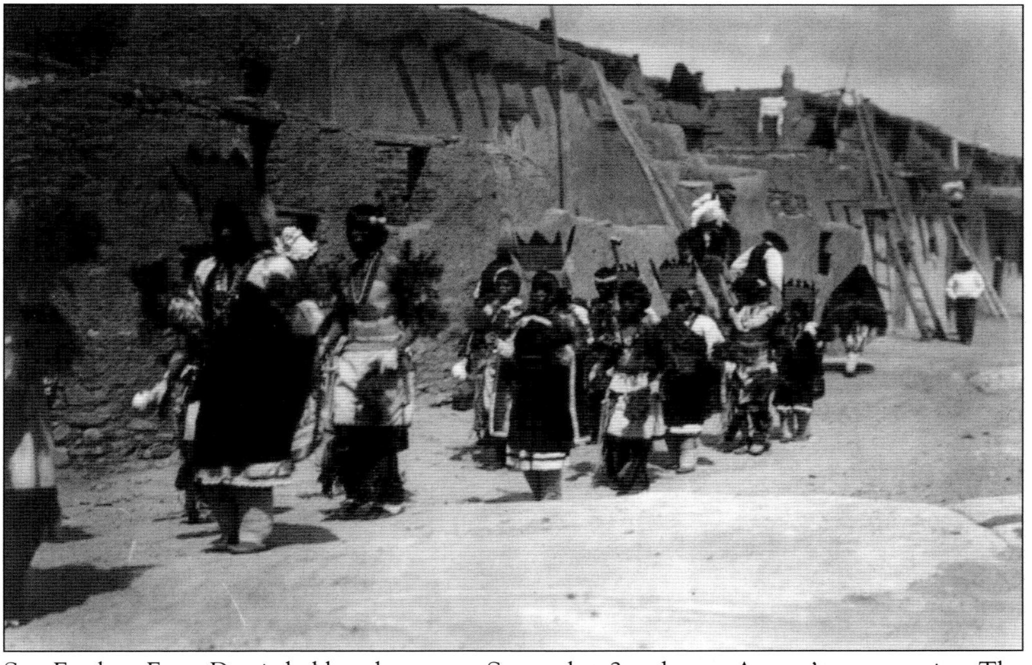

San Esteban Feast Day is held each year on September 2 to honor Acoma's patron saint. The celebration includes a mass followed by a procession led by a figure of San Esteban and a colorful harvest dance.

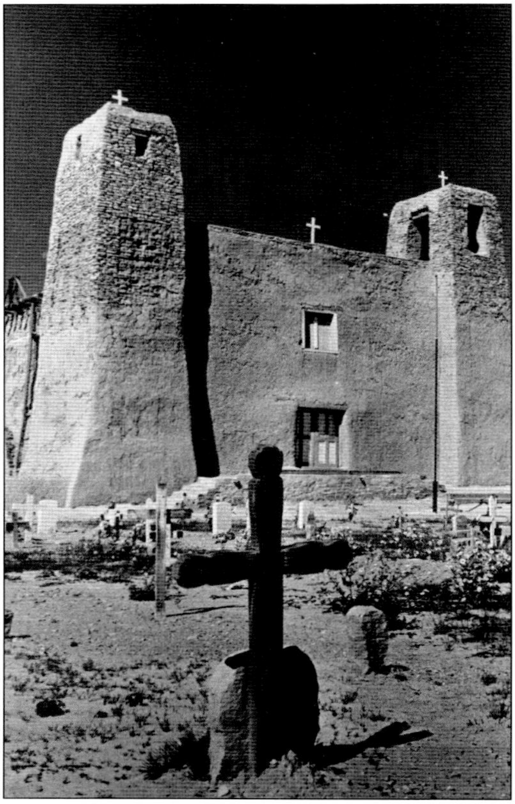

This adobe mission church established in 1629 at Acoma Pueblo served as the inspiration behind the 1915 Pan America-California Exposition's New Mexico Building, designed by the architectural firm of Rapp and Rapp. Also featured in the Panama-California Exposition, which celebrated the completion of the Panama Canal, were several other Southwest installations encompassing a five-acre compound called the Painted Desert, with interpretations of pueblo structures, kivas, and cliff dwellings. It was sponsored by the Santa Fe Railway. Twenty-eight San Ildefonso Pueblo families, led by acclaimed potter Maria Martinez and her artist husband, Julian, were brought to the Expo to demonstrate pottery making. The Acoma Pueblo Mission Church also became the prototype for Rapp and Rapp's design of the Fine Arts Museum (page 43), completed in 1917. The photograph below of the interior of the church, taken by Ben Wittick between 1880 and 1890, shows Pueblo parishioners with the beautifully carved altar piece in the background. (Left, courtesy of Palace of the Governors Photograph Archive, 053197.)

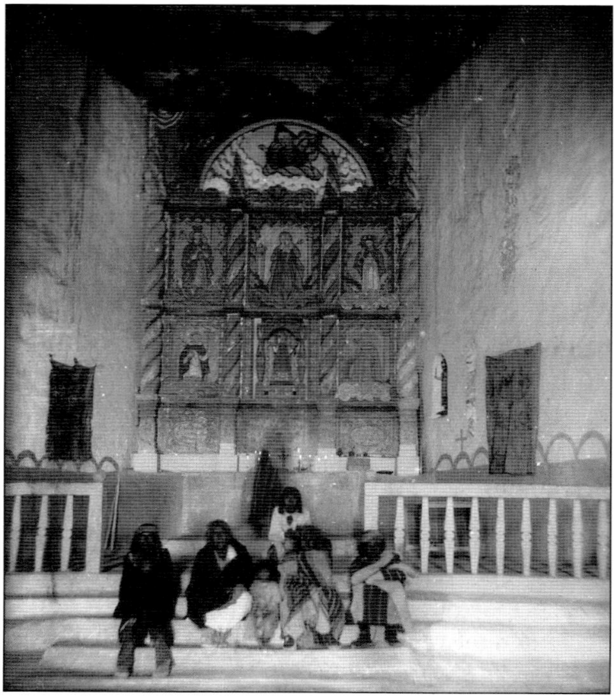

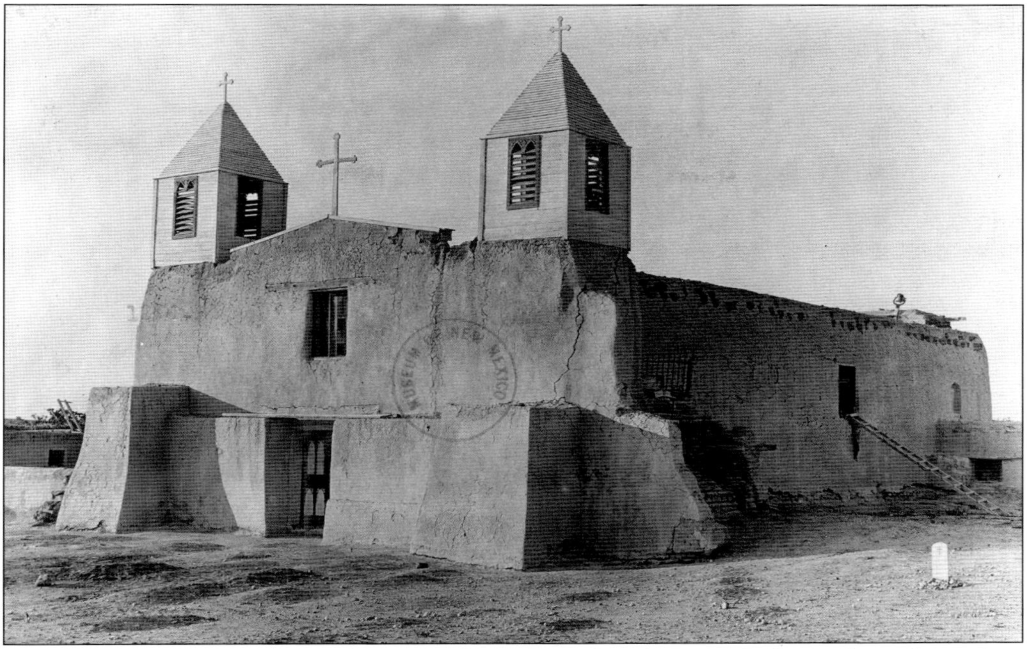

Taken in 1912 by artist and architect Carlos Vierra, this photograph shows the still-standing San Agustin de la Mission at Isleta Pueblo, which was established in 1612. In 1923, the mission went through an extensive restoration thanks to Father Anton Docher, who was affectionately known as "the Padre of Isleta" and is buried near the church altar. (Courtesy of the Palace of the Governors Archive, 012322.)

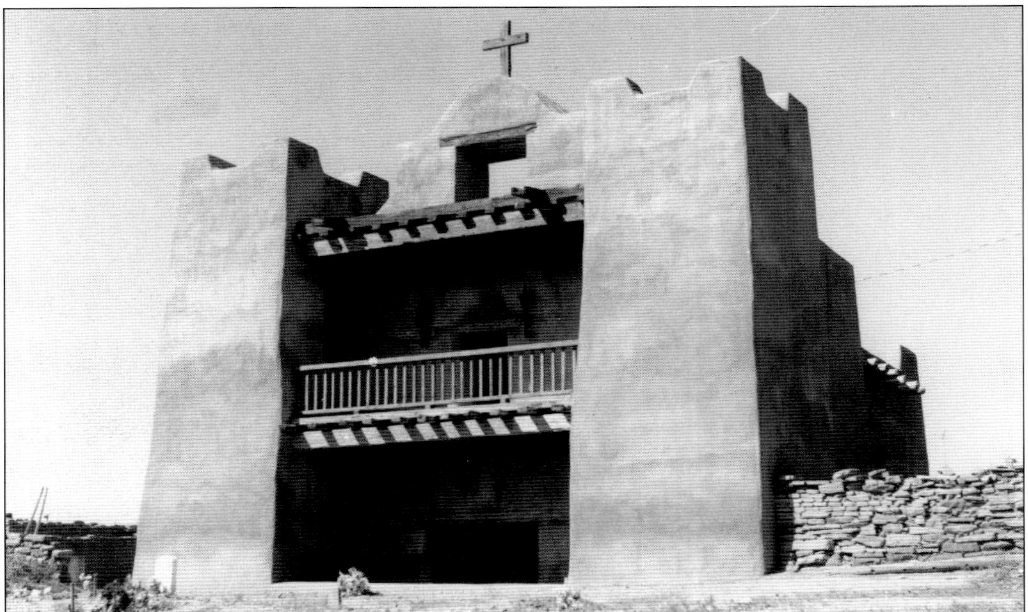

Located in the center of the Zuni Pueblo, the Our Lady of Guadalupe mission church was built in 1629. Many of the architectural features of this and other mission churches greatly influenced the creation of the Santa Fe style.

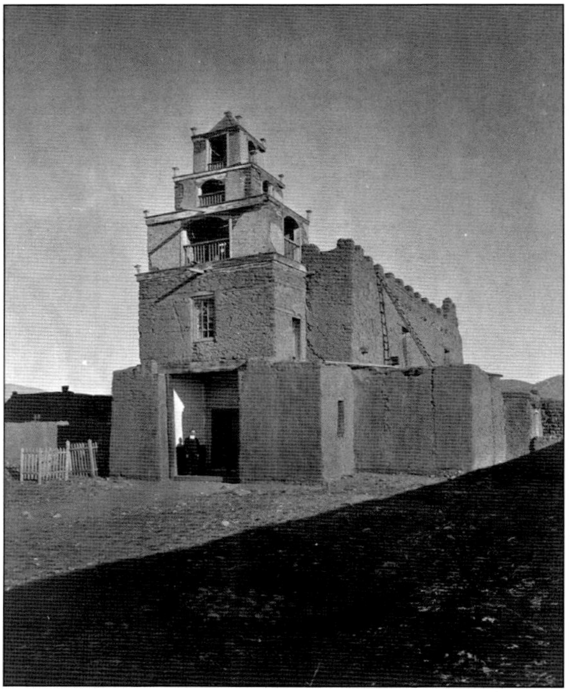

The San Miguel Chapel was damaged in the 1680 Pueblo Revolt and rebuilt in 1710 following the Spanish re-conquest, after which it served as a chapel for Spanish soldiers. It has been restored and modified several more times over the years. The chapel is pictured at left, with drawings of the north and south elevations below.

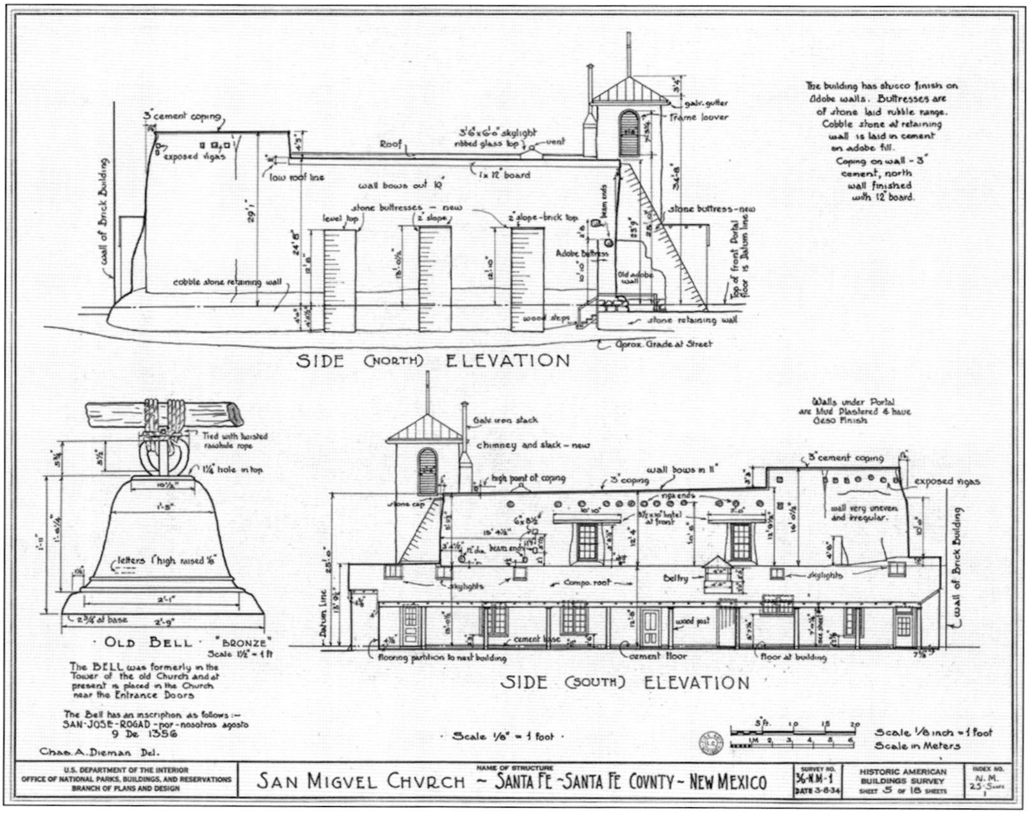

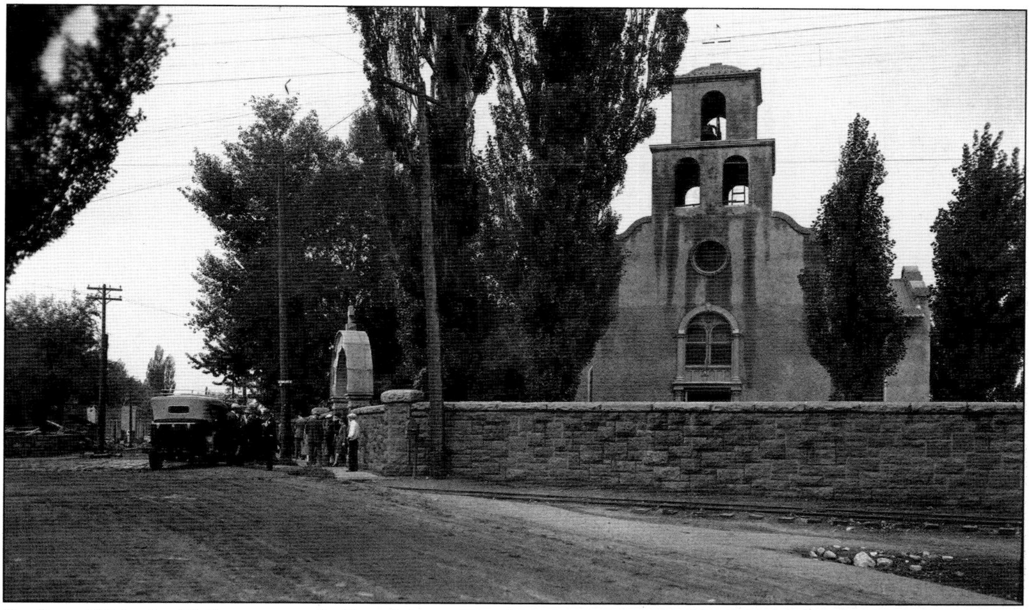

Built in 1781, the El Santuario de Guadalupe, also known as Our Lady of Guadalupe, now serves as an art and history museum, housing the Santa Fe archdiocese's collection of Mexican baroque paintings, Italian Renaissance paintings, New Mexican carved images of saints, and a painting by Jose Alzibar of Our Lady of Guadalupe dated 1783. (Courtesy of the Palace of the Governors Archive, 010038.)

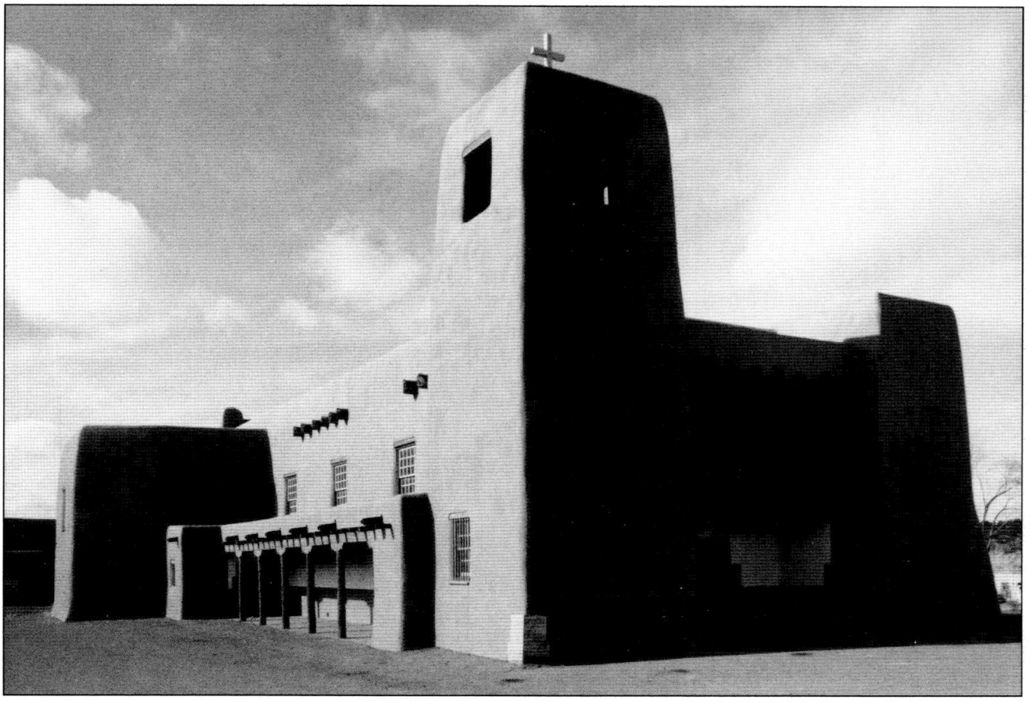

Located at the corner of Canyon Road and Cristo Rey Street, the adobe Cristo Rey Church is an example of New Mexico mission architecture. Inside are examples of Spanish Colonial religious art and decorative altar screens known as *reredos*. This photograph was taken in 1943 by John Collier.

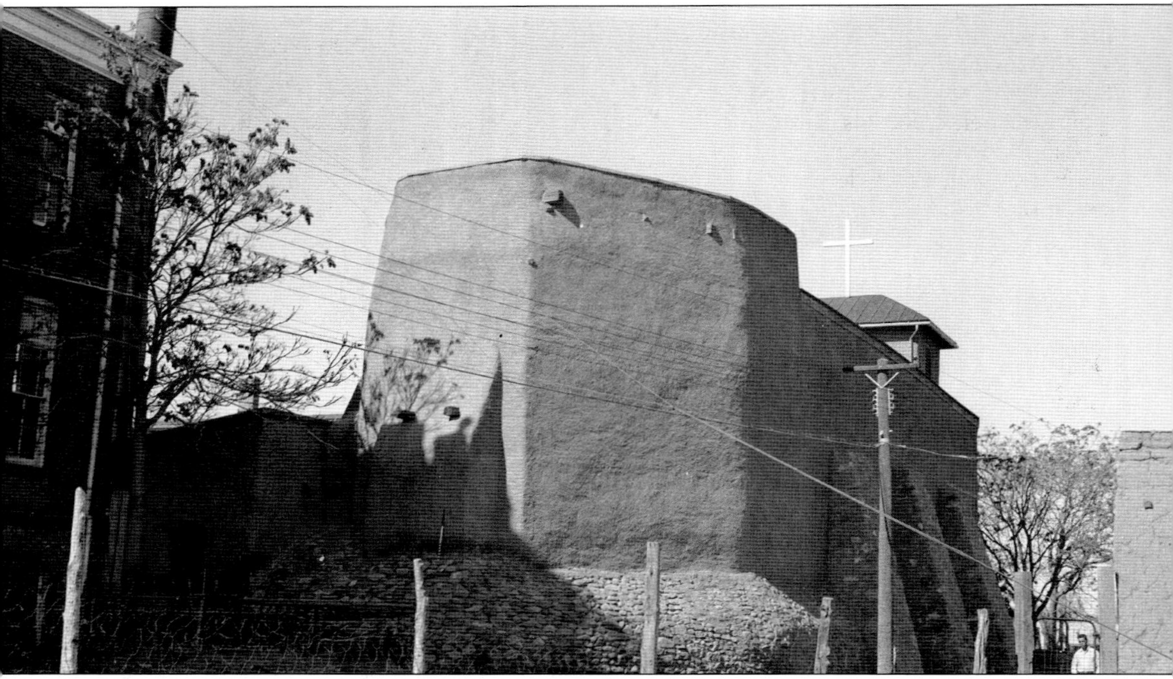

Taken in 1934 by James M. Slack, this photograph shows the rear of Santa Fe's historic San Miguel church from the northeast. The church contains the oldest decorative altar reredos, dating back to 1798, as well as a carved statue of St. Michael illustrating his victory over Satan.

This is a view of the altar at San Miguel Church, also known as the Chapel of San Miguel. Constructed in approximately 1610, this church was built for Santa Fe's poor parishioners, which included mostly Mexicans and Native Americans.

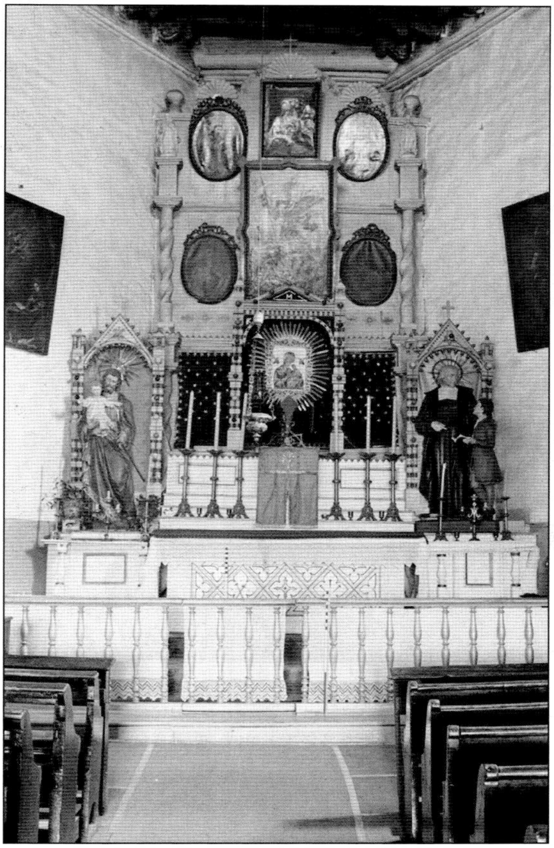

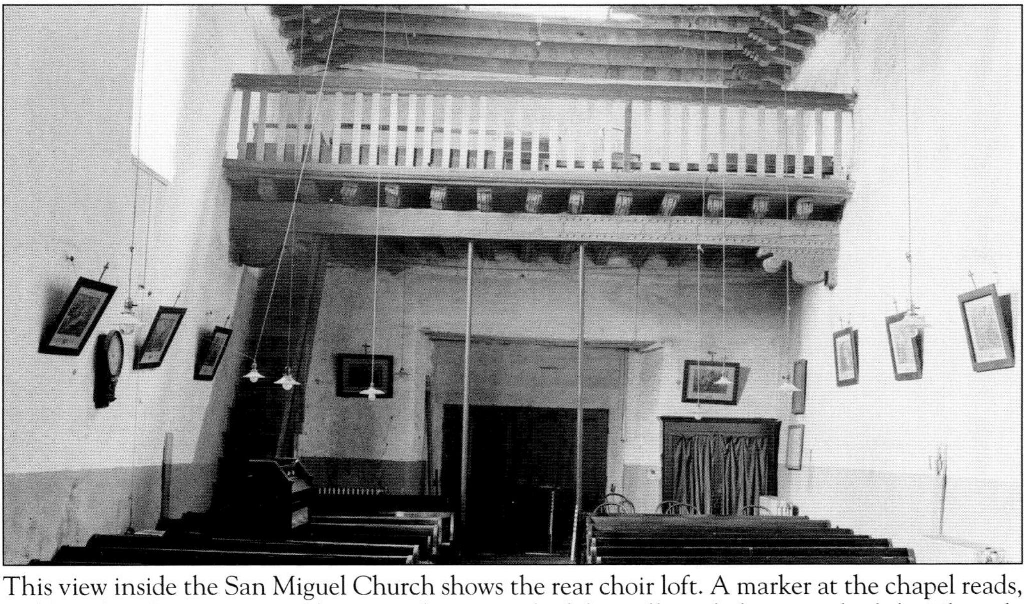

This view inside the San Miguel Church shows the rear choir loft. A marker at the chapel reads, "Oldest church structure in the U.S. The original adobe walls and altar were built by Tlaxcala Indians from Mexico under the direction of Franciscan Padres, circa 1610."

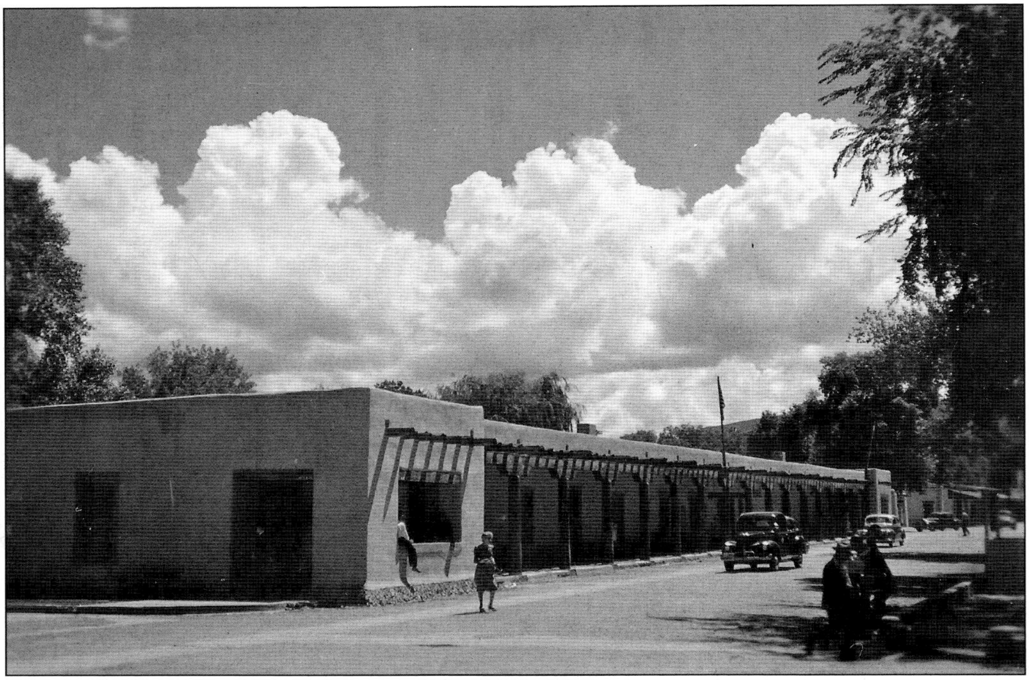

The Palace of Governors was designated a National Historic Landmark in 1960 and an American Treasure in 1999. The adobe structure is the oldest public building in the Unites States, dating to 1610. The building has served many purposes over the years. It was commissioned by Pedro de Peralta, then the governor of the Spanish territory, but changed hands when New Mexico did, reverting back to Spanish control during the 1693–1694 re-conquest, becoming the property of Mexico in 1821, and in 1846 falling to the possession of the United States. Below, Indians sell their wares in front of the Palace of Governors, just as they do today. (Both courtesy of the Taos History Museums.)

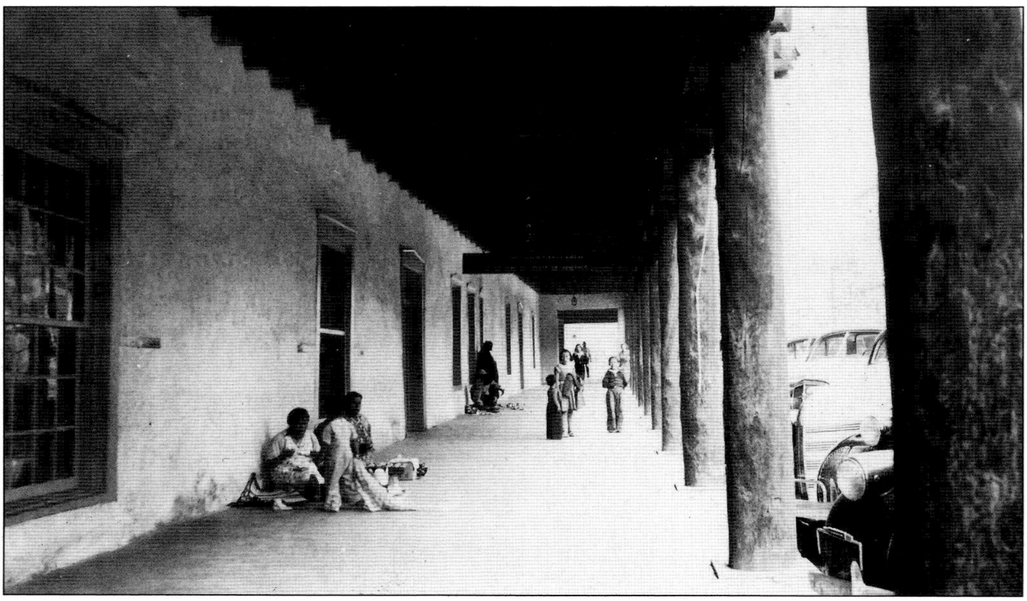

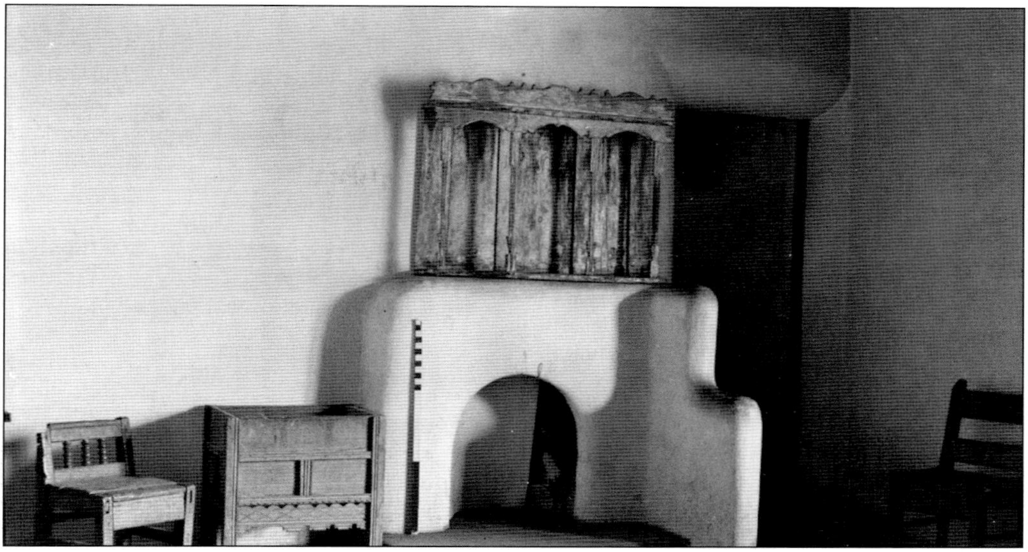

Among its many incarnations, the Palace of Governors briefly served as the Confederate army's regional headquarters during the Civil War. In 1909, it became a state history museum, and with the addition of a new adjacent building, it is currently home to the New Mexico History Museum. The above image shows an interior adobe fireplace and furnishings; the courtyard is shown below.

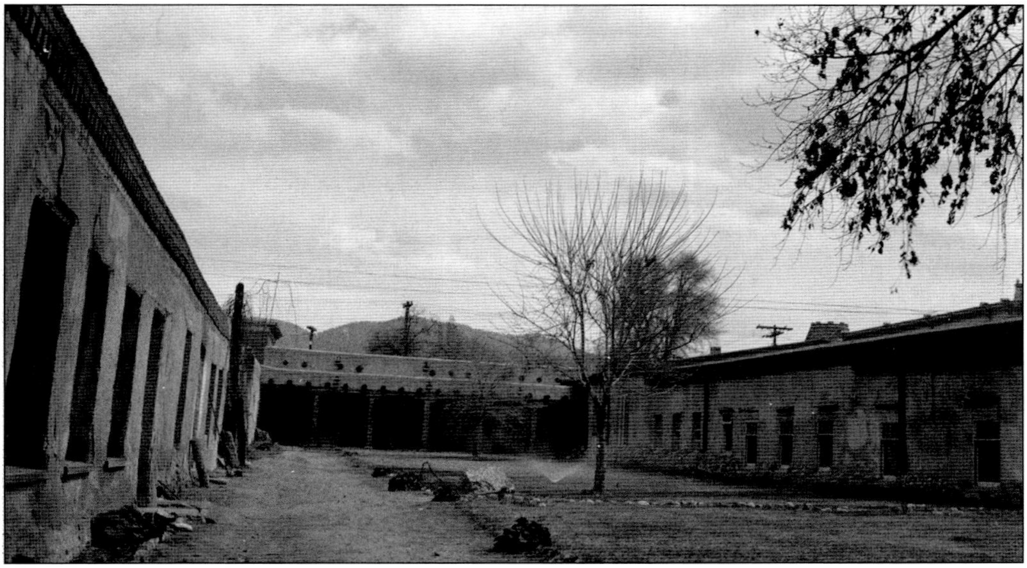

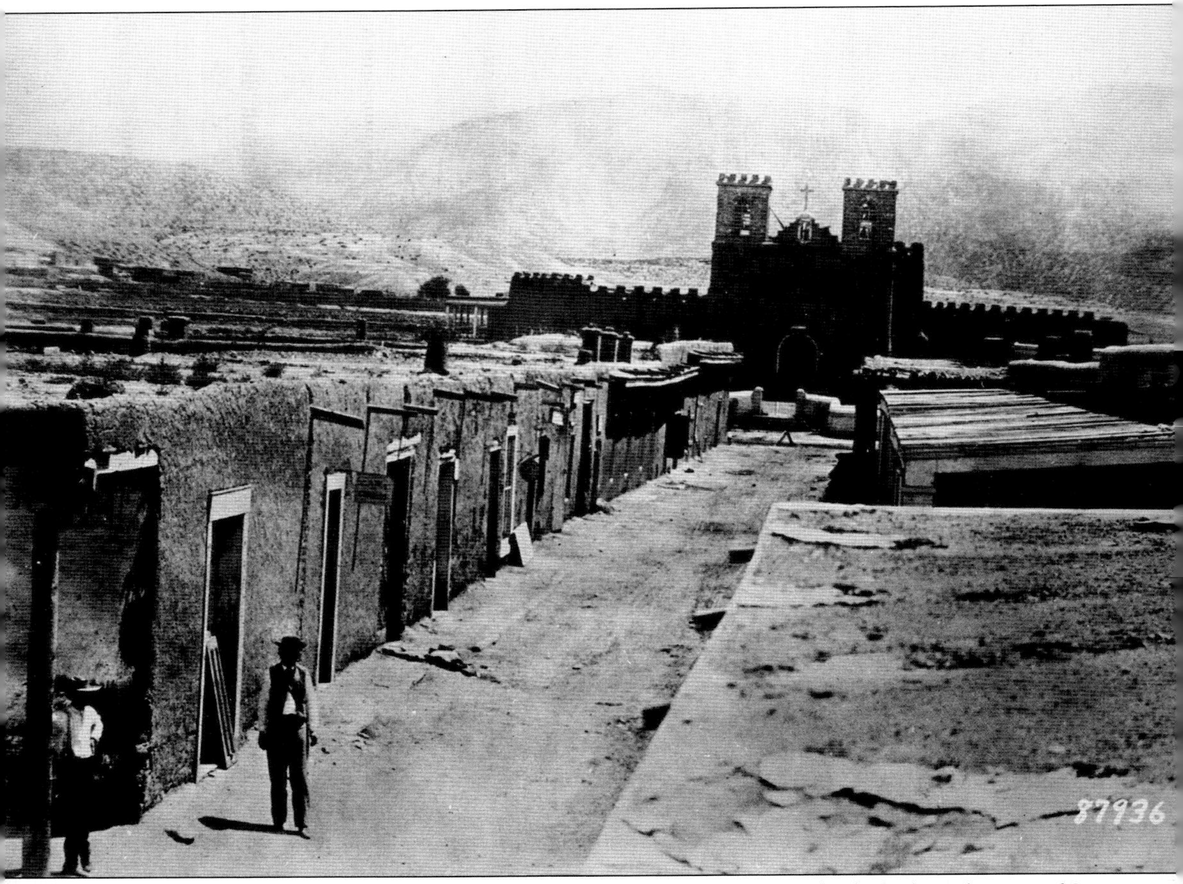

An adobe church was built on the site of the current St. Francis Cathedral when the city of Santa Fe was founded in 1610. It was later replaced by a larger church in 1630, which was destroyed in the Pueblo Revolt of 1680. Only a small adobe chapel that had been brought from Spain in 1625 survived. Dedicated to Our Lady La Conquistadora, it still exists today. A new adobe church was built in 1693 named in honor of Santa Fe's patron saint, Saint Francis of Assisi, but known as La Parroquia. This is a very early view of the plaza leading to La Parroquia. (Courtesy of Taos Historic Museums.)

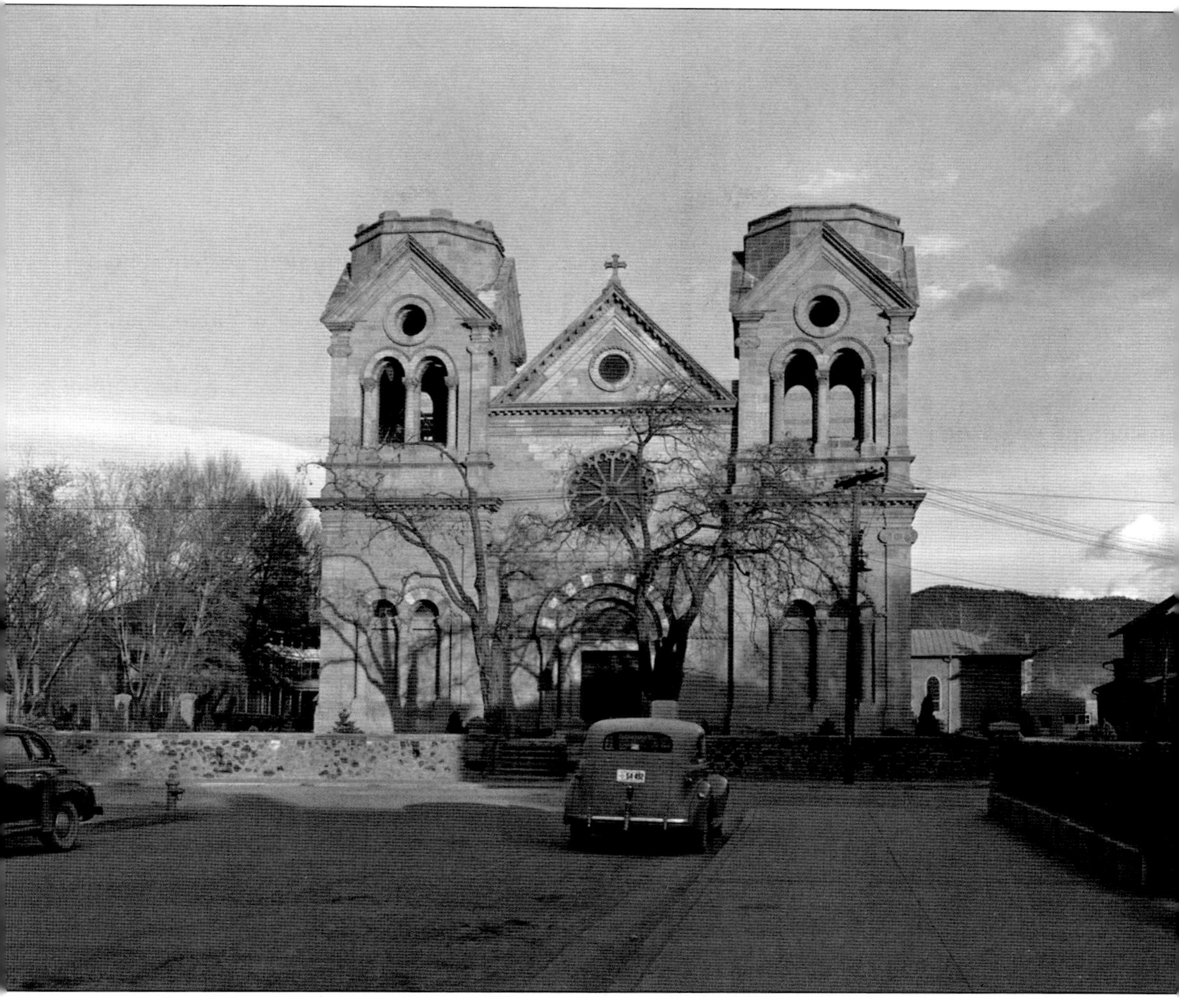

In 1850, Father John Baptiste Lamy came to Santa Fe from France to be the city's first bishop—he later became archbishop. He commissioned a new Romanesque church to be built in place of the existing adobe structure of La Parroqia. From 1869 to 1887, French architects and Italian stonemasons constructed the church, complete with stained-glass windows from France depicting the 12 apostles, seen in this 1943 photograph by John Collier. When construction was completed, the original La Parroquia was dismantled and taken out through the front door. Archbishop Lamy and six other archbishops are buried in the church's sanctuary. Many improvements have been added to the church in recent years, and in 2005, the cathedral's status was elevated to a basilica by Pope Benedict XVI.

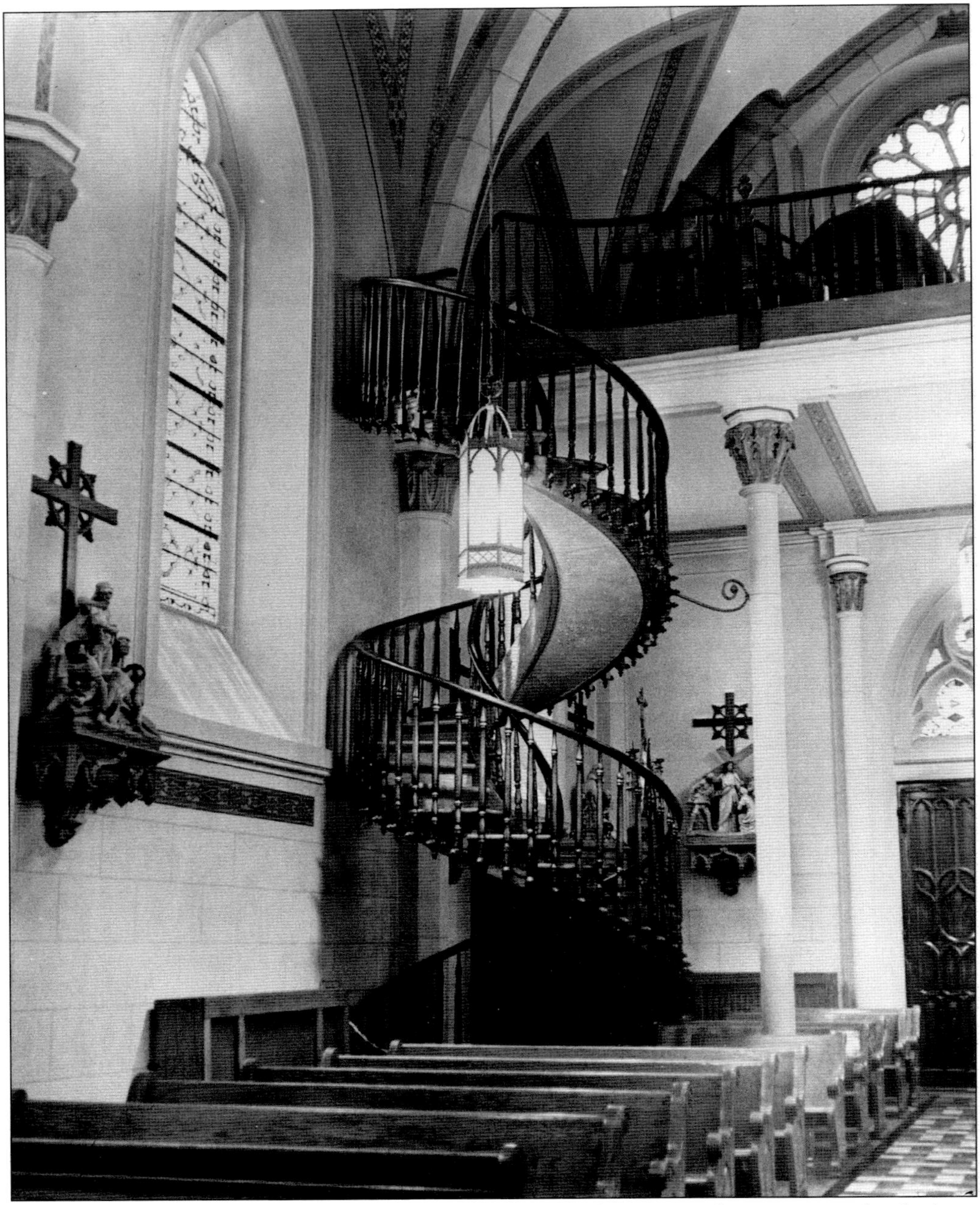

In 1852, Archbishop Lamy was successful in encouraging the Sisters of Loretta to make the long journey to Santa Fe to establish an educational system. The Sisters opened the Academy of Our Lady of Light in 1853, and with Parisian architect Antoine Mouly and his son, Projectus Mouly, they oversaw the building of a Gothic revival–style chapel to accompany the school based on King Louis IX's Sainte-Chapelle in Paris. The Loretto Chapel houses a famous spiral staircase known as the "Miraculous Stair."

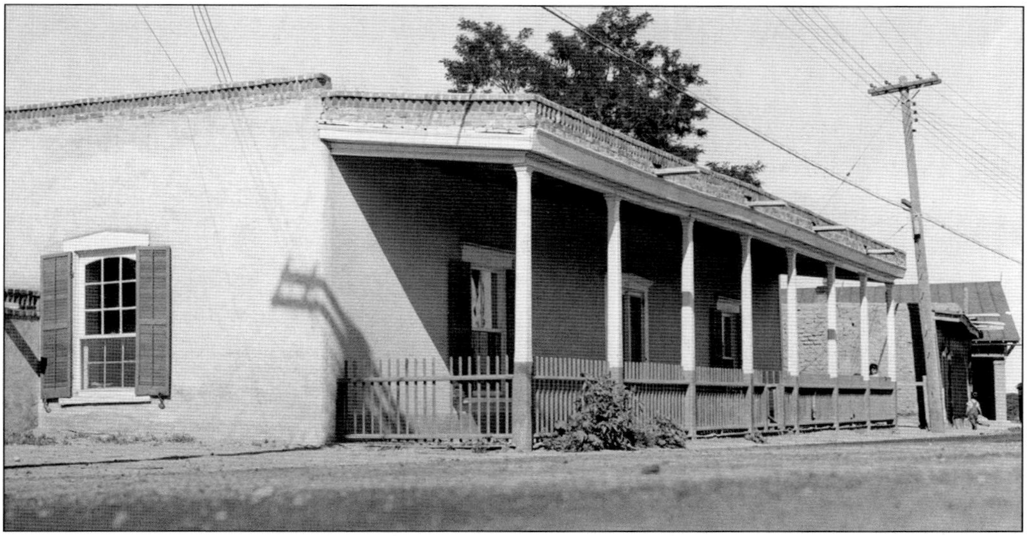

Located at 724 Canyon Road, the one-story Borrego House, with its long front portal and triangular pediments topping the exterior windows and the door, is a classic example of Territorial-style architecture. For 75 years, the home belonged to the Borrego family, who were prominent members of Santa Fe society. In 1928, it was purchased by women's rights activist and socialite Margretta Stewart Dietrich, who, along with Frank Applegate and writer Mary Austin, helped establish the Spanish Colonial Arts Society of Santa Fe. Dietrich won a 1930 competition for the best proper restoration of a residence in the Santa Fe style, receiving a $100 award.

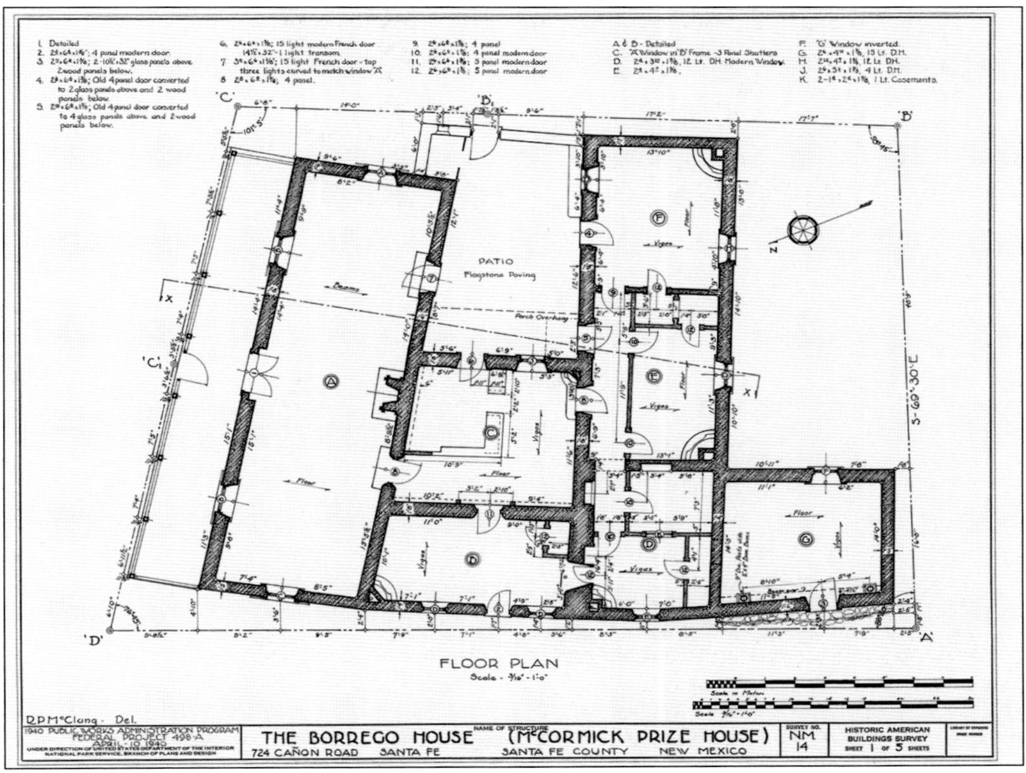

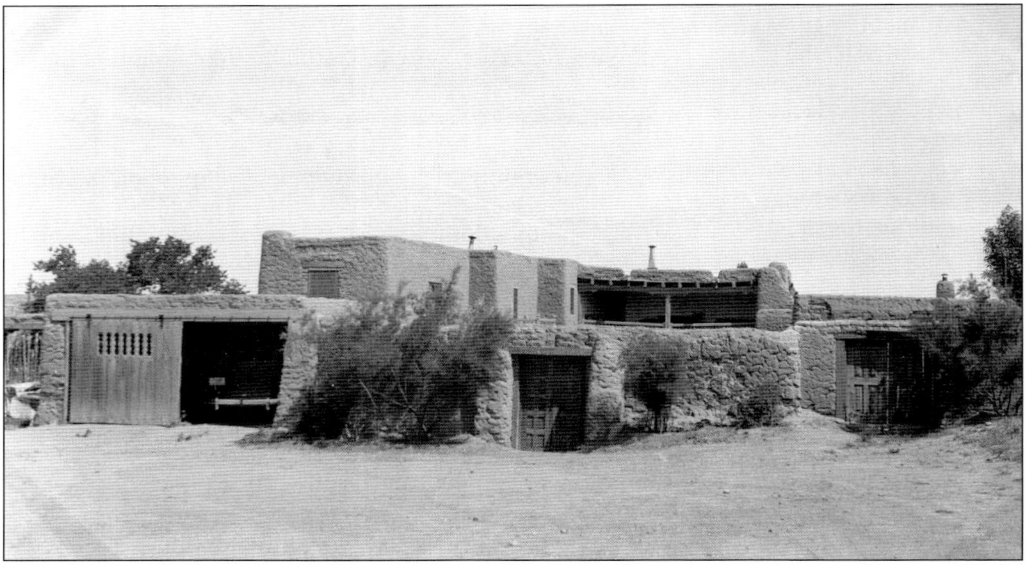

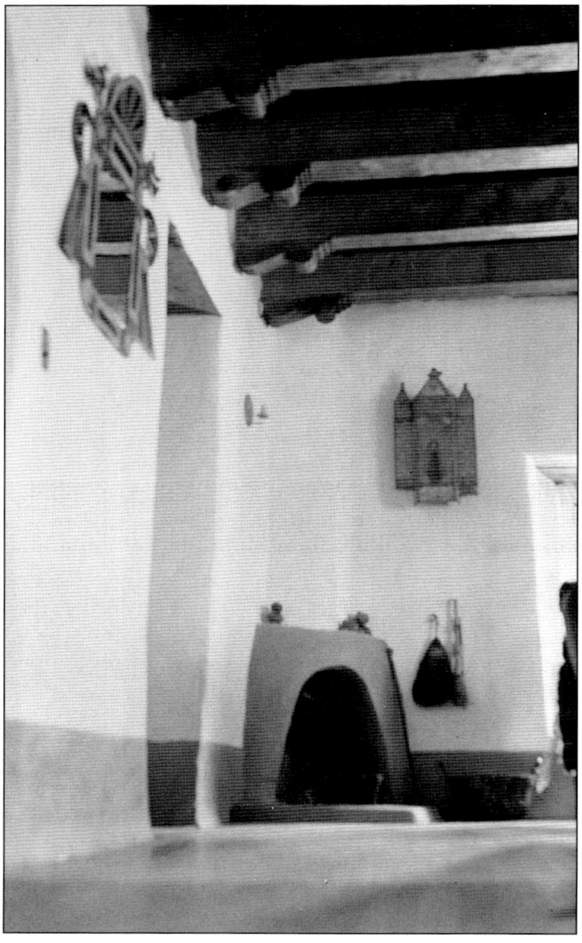

Teacher, painter, ceramicist, and sculptor Frank Applegate, along with his wife, Alta, and their daughter first ventured to the Southwest from New Jersey in 1921 to investigate native clay. After a weeklong camping adventure on the Canyon Road property of painter Gerald Cassidy and his wife, Ina, the family decided to move to Santa Fe. In 1926, Applegate purchased a large one-story, flat-roofed adobe residence considered by the *Santa Fe New Mexican* as "perhaps the largest hacienda in the city." Dedicated to honoring the home's original integrity, Applegate used recycled building materials to match architectural details as much as possible when adding additional rooms, a second story, and Spanish Colonial balconies. At left is an interior shot of the kiva fireplace and massive ceiling beams and corbels.

This portrait of Frank Applegate (1881–1931) was taken around 1920. Applegate was an important member of Santa Fe's artist colony, and along with his friend, writer Mary Austin, was instrumental in establishing the Spanish Colonial Arts Society, which has grown to become Santa Fe's internationally recognized annual Spanish Market. (Courtesy of the Palace of the Governors Archive, 185034.)

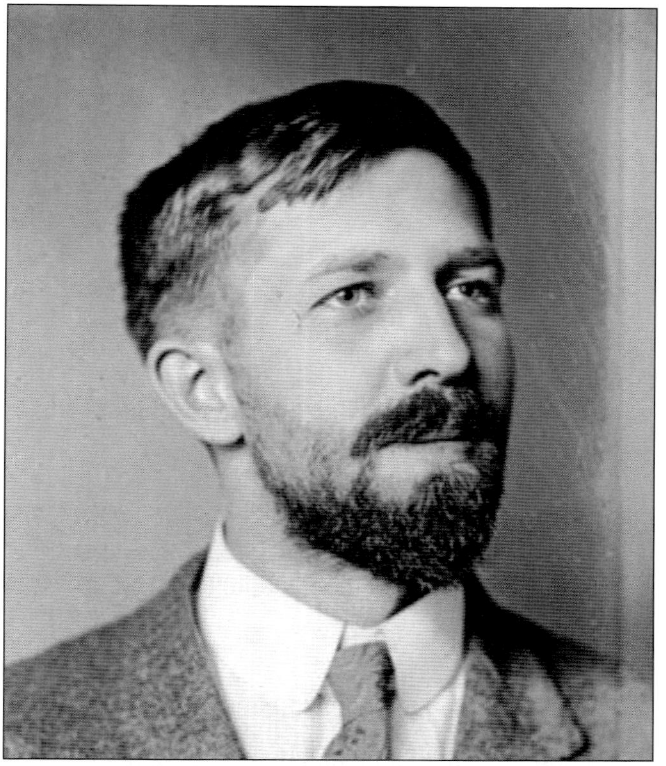

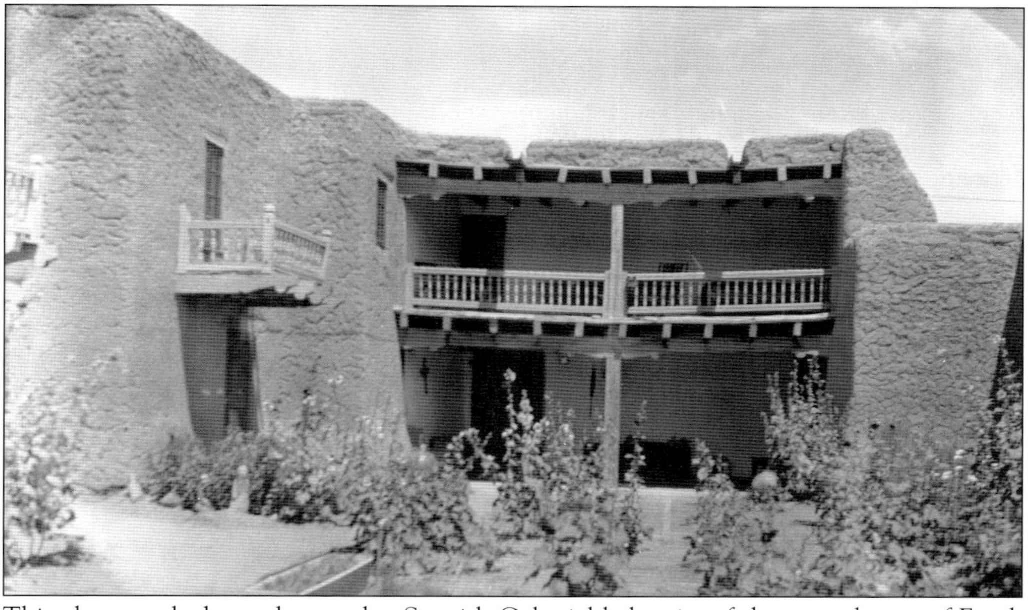

This photograph shows the wooden Spanish Colonial balconies of the second story of Frank Applegate's residence. The house became well known as a perfect example of Spanish Pueblo Architecture. In 1929, it was featured in *House and Garden* magazine, and photographs taken by legendary photographer Ansel Adams accompanied an article on the residence in a 1930s issue of *Ladies Home Journal*. (Courtesy of the Palace of the Governors Archives, 133158.)

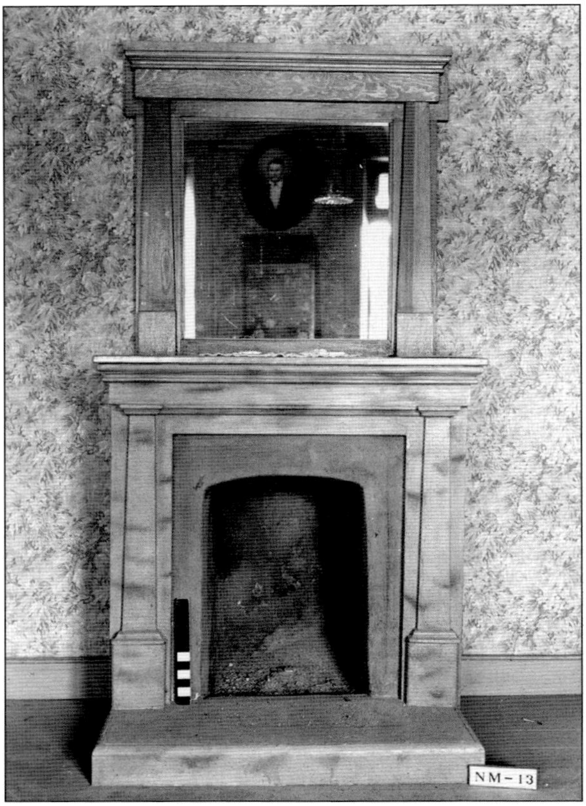

The stone fireplace in this interior shot of the Garcia residence shows that a number of architectural styles had converged in Santa Fe by 1900. When city visionaries later established a unified architectural identity, wallpaper, Victorian elements, and traditional fireplaces such as these would be replaced by the adobe kiva fireplaces first introduced in Pueblo architecture.

Here, the exterior of the Garcia residence shows adobe construction and stepped corbels borrowed from Pueblo architecture in this courtyard portal.

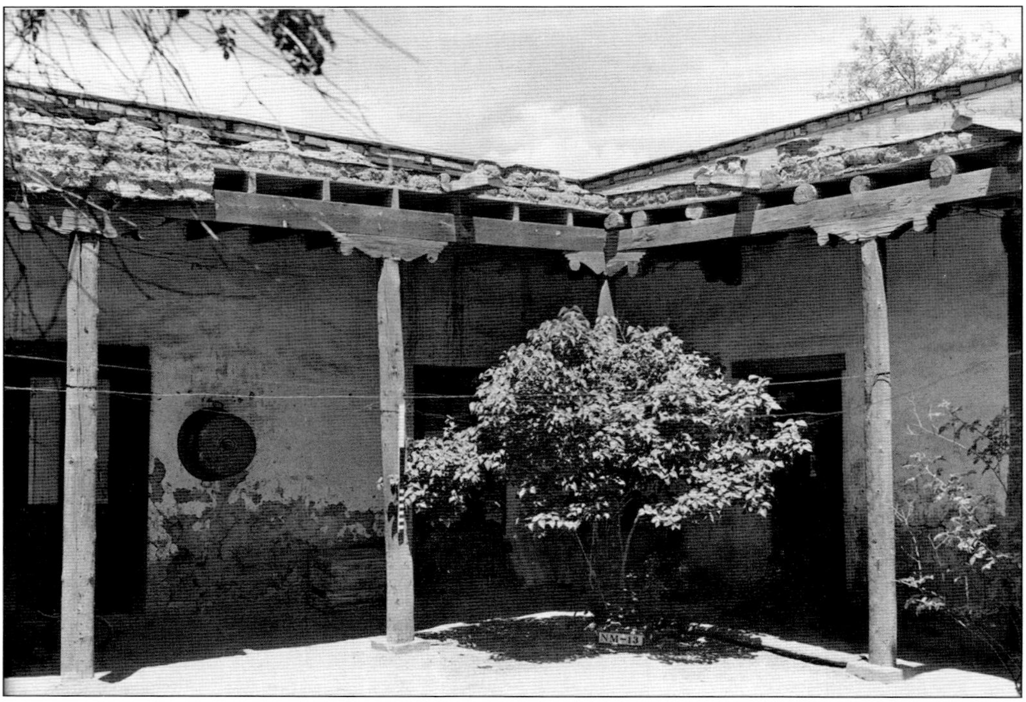

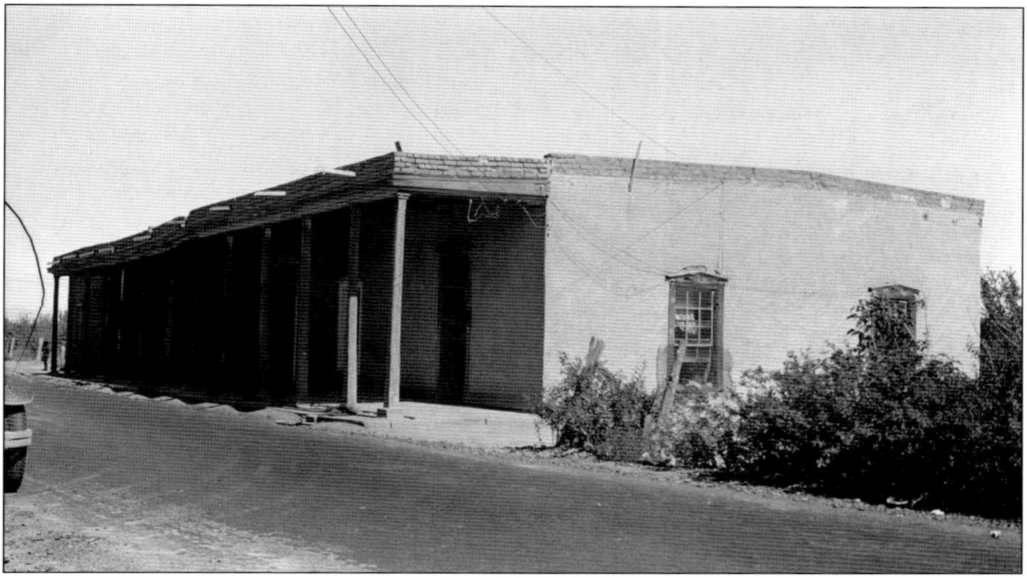

Spanish Colonial houses adopted Pueblo architecture's construction but tended to be one-story residences with additions built as families grew. The rear view of the Rael residence shown here illustrates how the building was added on to over time.

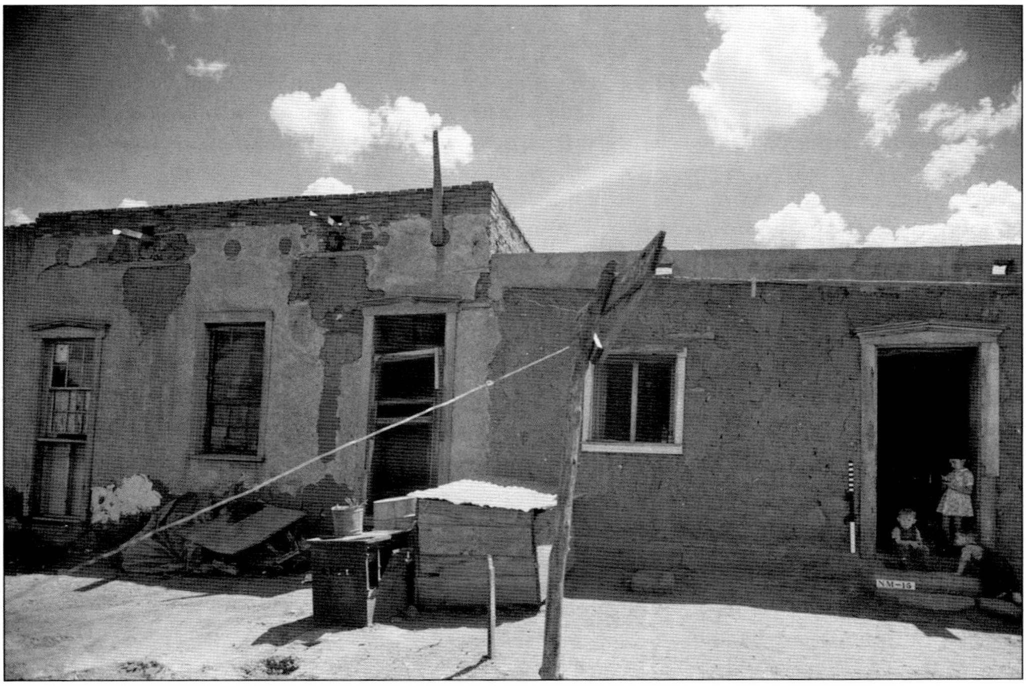

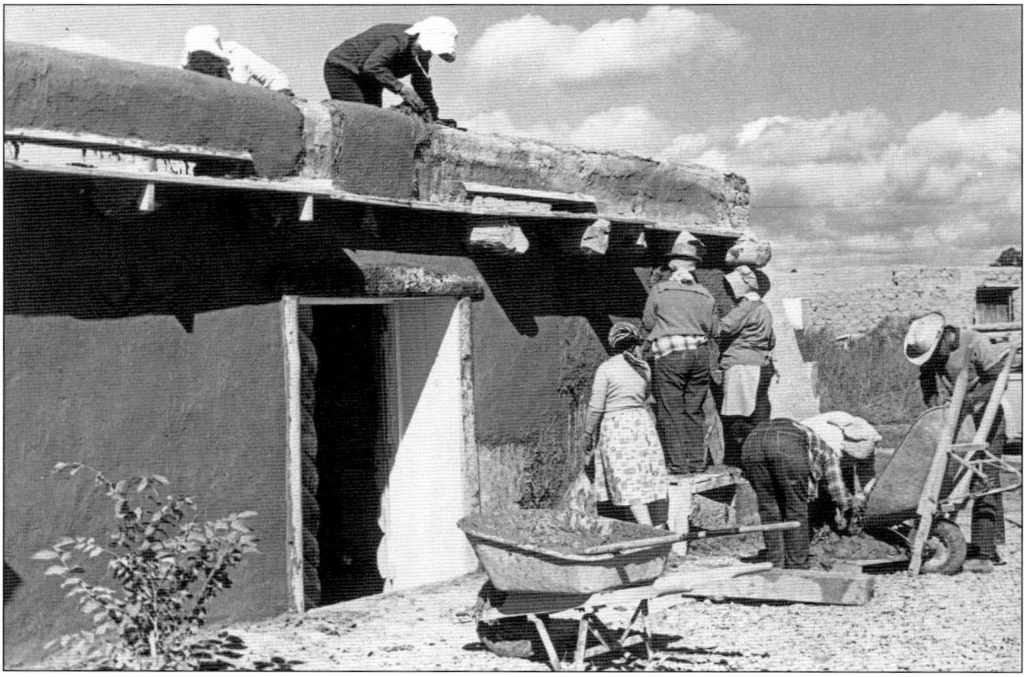

This Spanish-American family stuccoes the exterior of a home with mud. Annual "mudding" is critical to the preservation of adobe structures. This photograph was taken by Mildred Tolbert Crews around 1940. (Courtesy of Palace of the Governor Archives, 06644.)

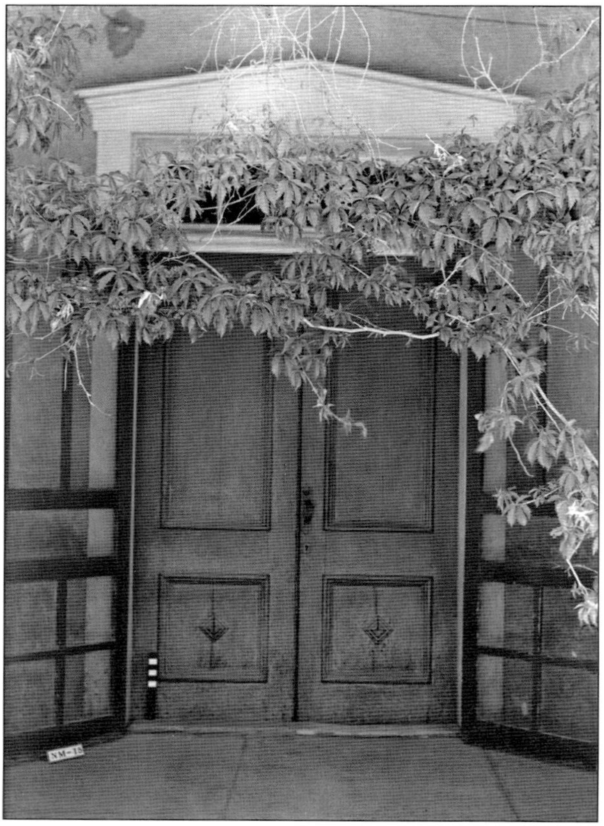

The wood pediment detail over the front entry door of the Rael residence is a classic Territorial-style architectural detail.

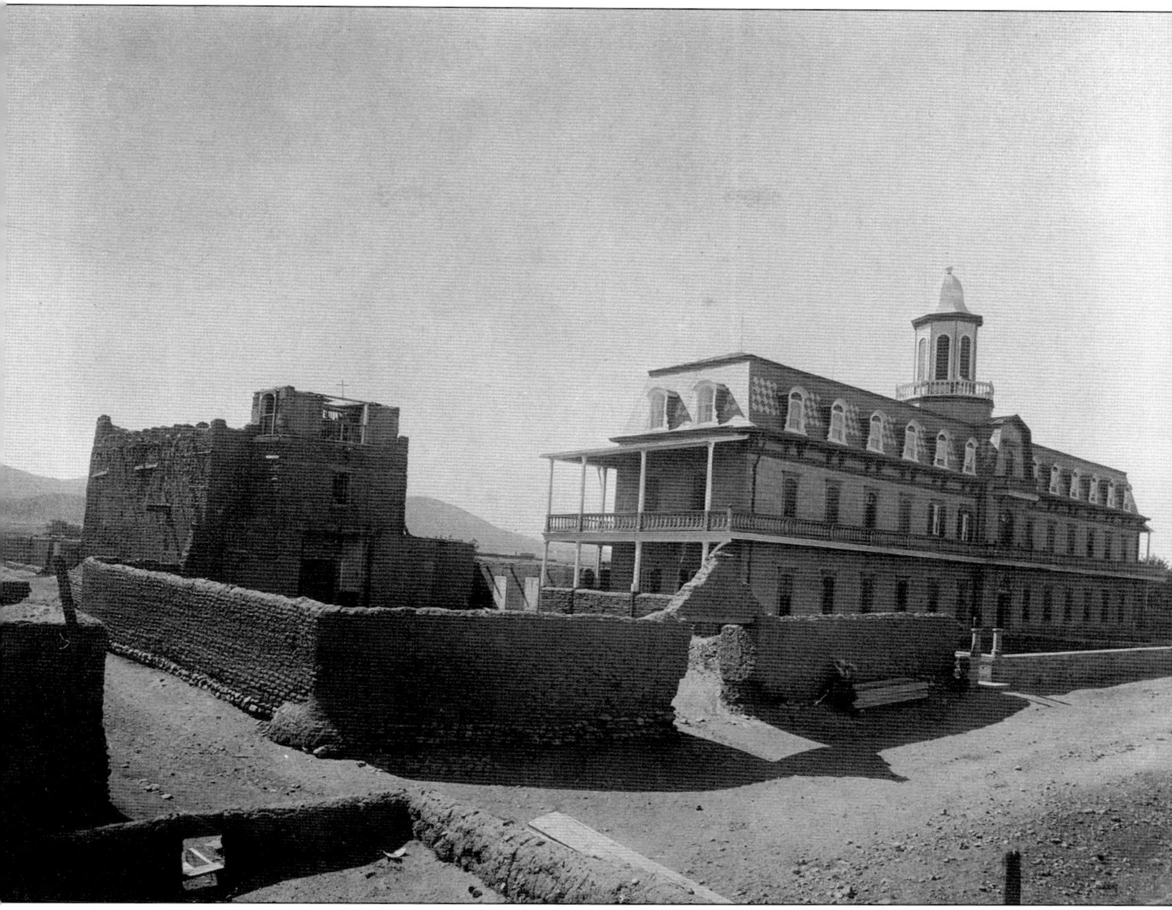

This view shows the juxtaposition of architectural styles, with Santa Fe's San Miguel Chapel next to Saint Michael's College as they appeared in 1881. Built in 1879, the mansard roof and decorative ornamentation of the three-story French Second Empire–style college built by the Christian Brothers sharply contrasts with the humbleness of San Miguel Church. In the mid-1800s, Archbishop Jean Baptiste Lamy brought the Christian Brothers to Santa Fe to start a school for boys and to manage the San Miguel Chapel, which served as the school's chapel. (Courtesy of the Palace of the Governors Archives, 001403.)

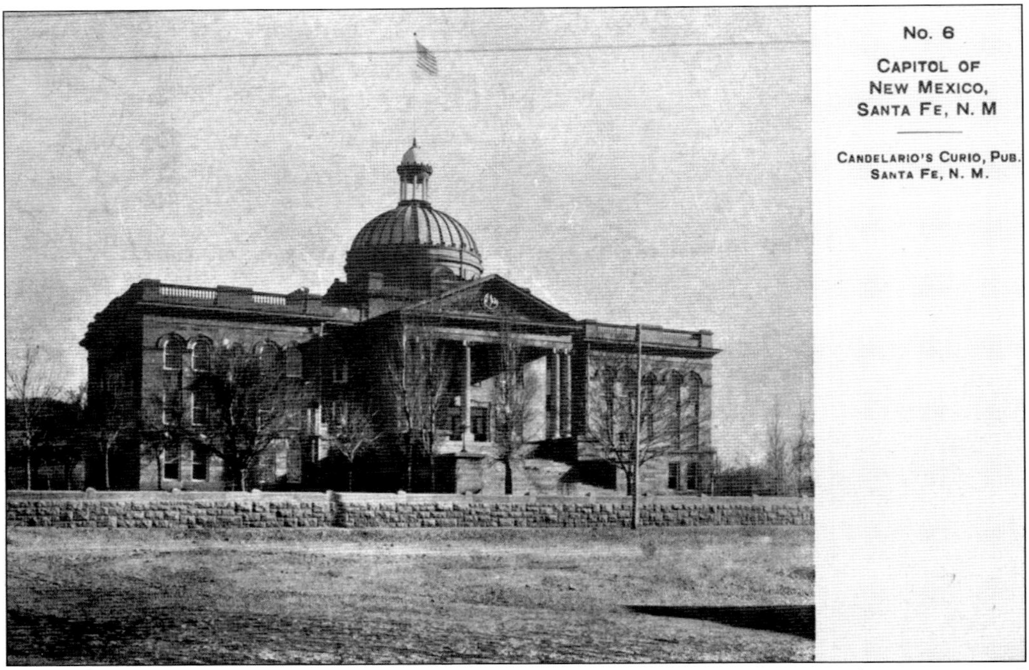

Architect Isaac Rapp designed the Santa Fe capitol building in 1900. Over the next several decades, a number of additions were added, and in 1950, amid the fervor of unifying the Santa Fe style, the building's dome was removed and replaced with a 105-foot tower and the pedimented portico was removed. The building, which bears little if any resemblance to the one seen here in a 1943 John Collier photograph, is now known as Bataan Memorial Building.

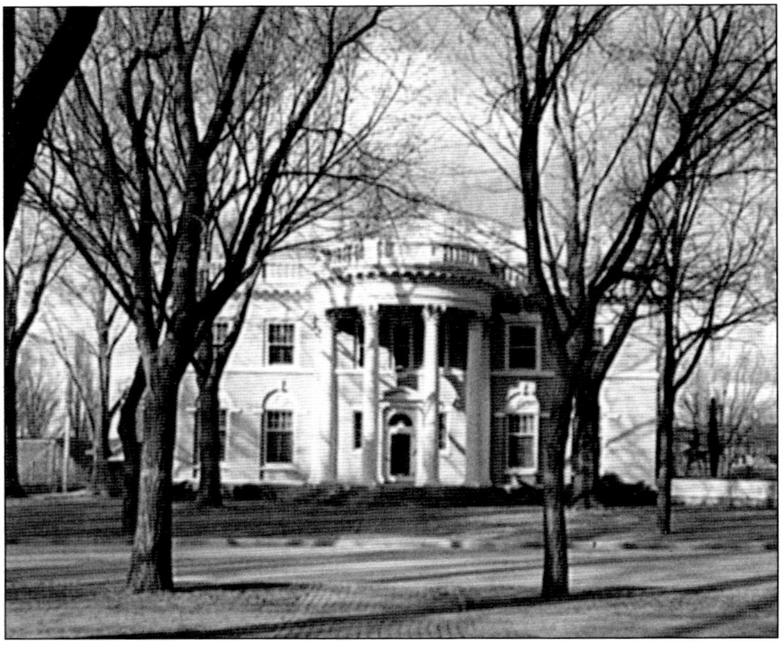

Built to resemble the White House, this neoclassical mansion housed Santa Fe governors from 1870 to 1940. The mansion included expansive gardens and a fishpond. In 1954, the building was in disrepair and out of step with the Santa Fe style of the city. It was replaced with the current governor's mansion. This photograph was also taken by John Collier in 1943.

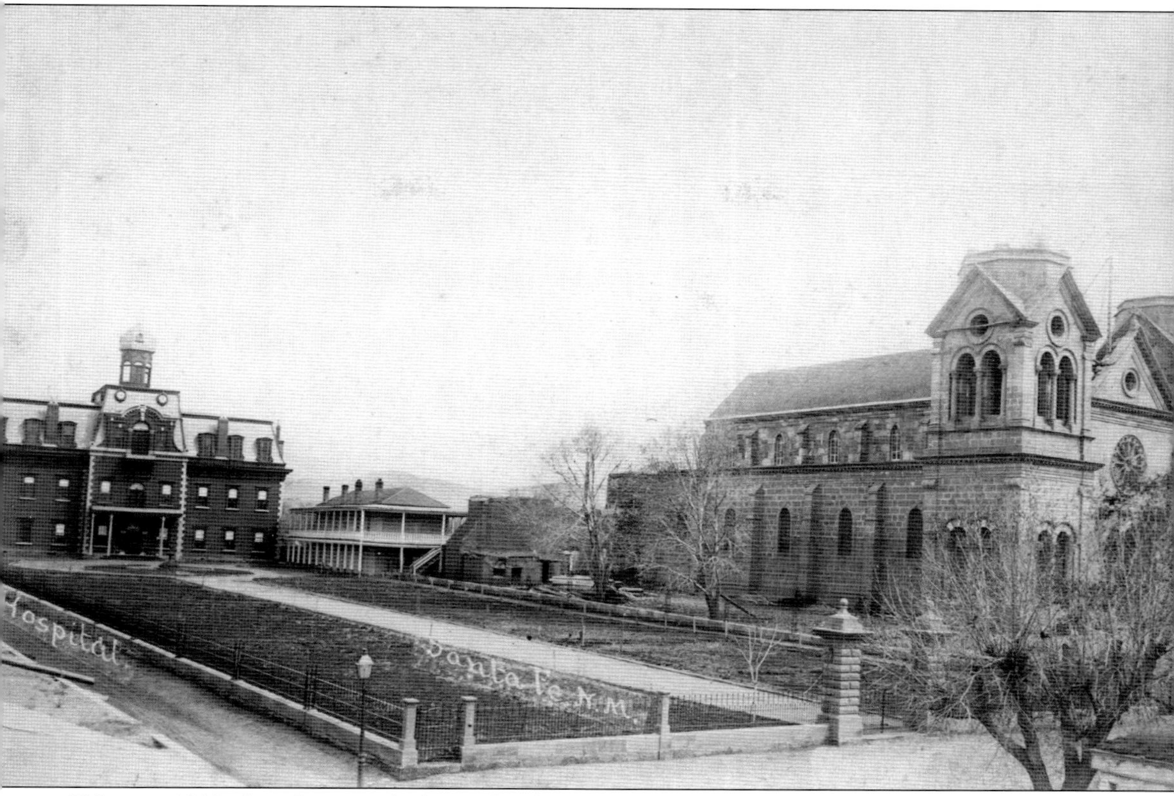

Taken in 1888, this photograph shows the close proximity of Saint Vincent's Sanitarium and St. Frances Cathedral Basilica. One of Santa Fe's earliest sanitariums, St. Vincent's is an example of the French Second Empire style. (Courtesy of the Palace of the Governors Archives, 105949.)

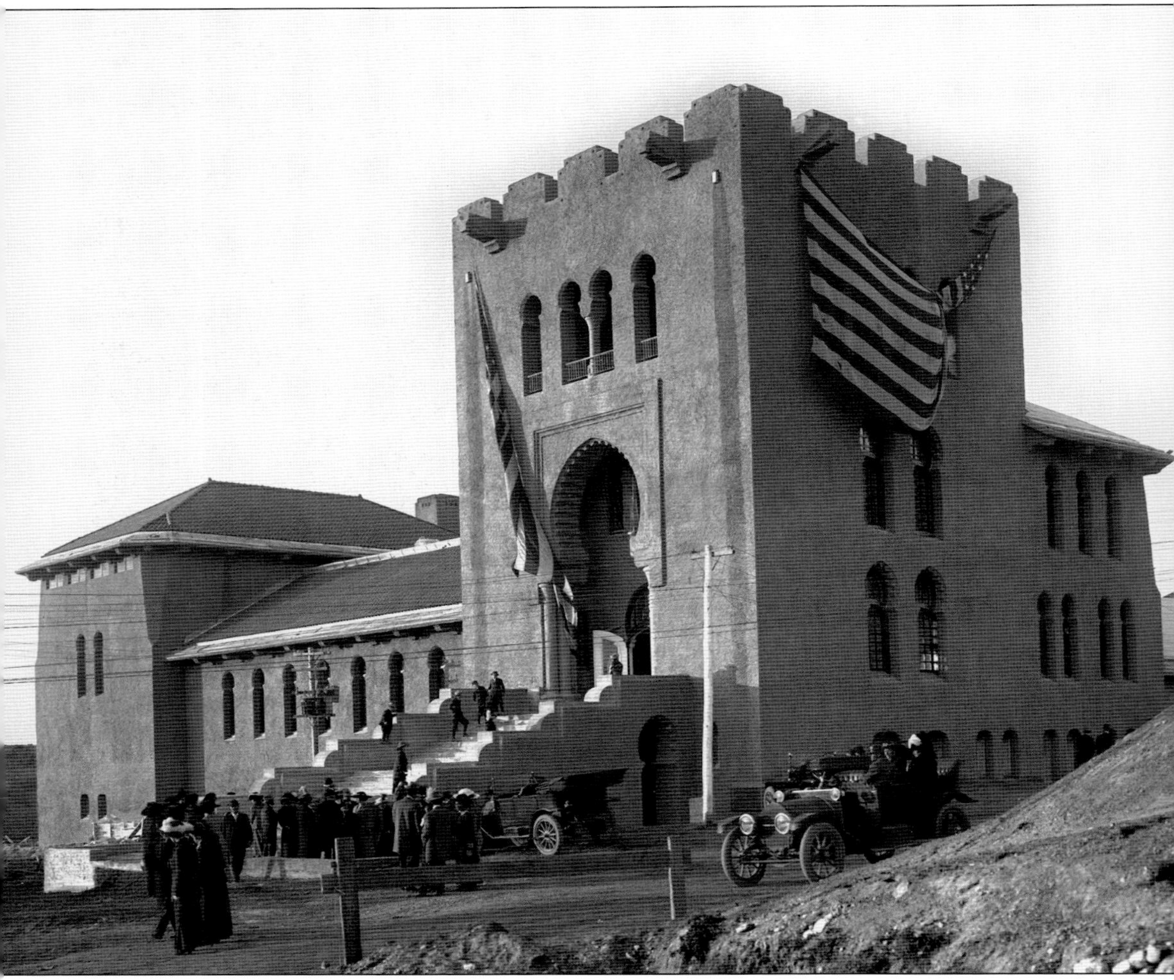

The Moorish Revival–style Scottish Rite Masonic Temple was designed by the Los Angeles architectural firm of Hunt and Burns and built in 1911. The building, which still stands today, was listed in the National Register of Historic Places in 1987. Jesse. L. Nusbaum took this photograph in 1912. (Courtesy of the Palace of the Governors Archives, 061379.)

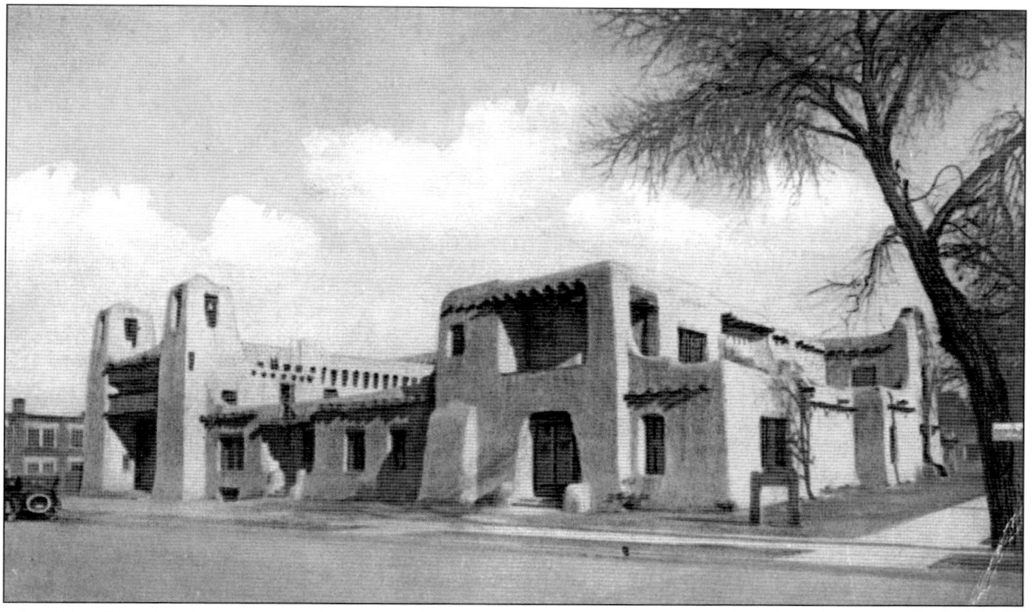

The New Mexico Museum of Art (above) on the plaza was founded in 1917 as the Fine Art Gallery of the Museum of New Mexico. The museum is housed in a spectacular Pueblo Revival building designed by I.H. and William M. Rapp. It was based on their New Mexico Building at the 1915 Panama-California Exposition, which in turn was based on the Acoma Pueblo church below. The museum's architecture inaugurated what has come to be known as the Santa Fe style. (Above, photograph by John Collier; below, courtesy of the Palace of the Governors Archives, 148154.)

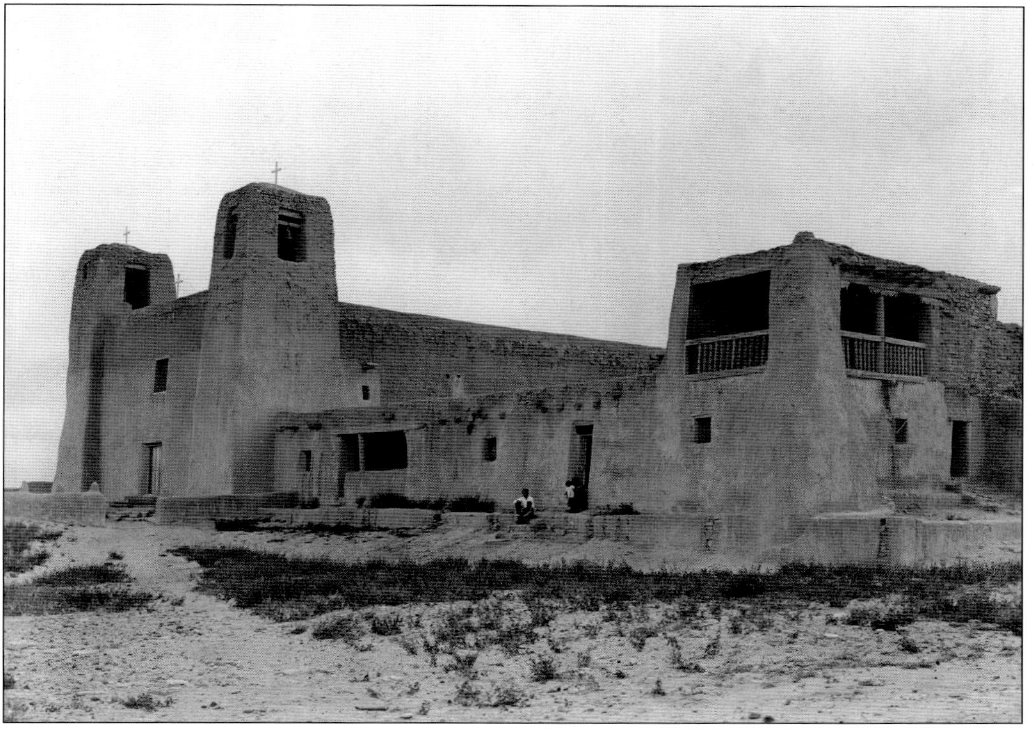

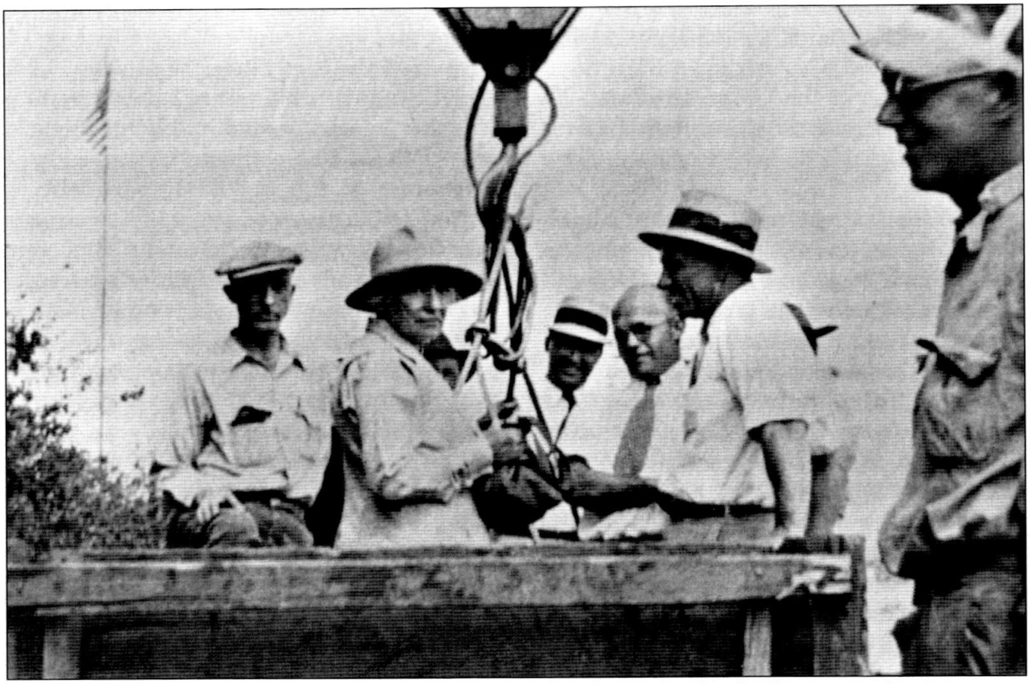

Mary Elizabeth Jane Colter (1869–1958) attended the California School of Design in San Francisco and in 1901 was commissioned by the Fred Harvey Company to design the interior of the Alvarado Hotel in Albuquerque. She was hired by the company on a full-time basis in 1910, and over the next 30 years, she completed 21 projects for Fred Harvey, including the design of the interior renovation of Santa Fe's landmark La Fonda Hotel. On that project, she worked directly with local artists and craftsmen to create a distinctive Southwest interior, much of which remains the same today. Taken in 1932, this photograph shows Colter with a building crew at the Indian Gardens project.

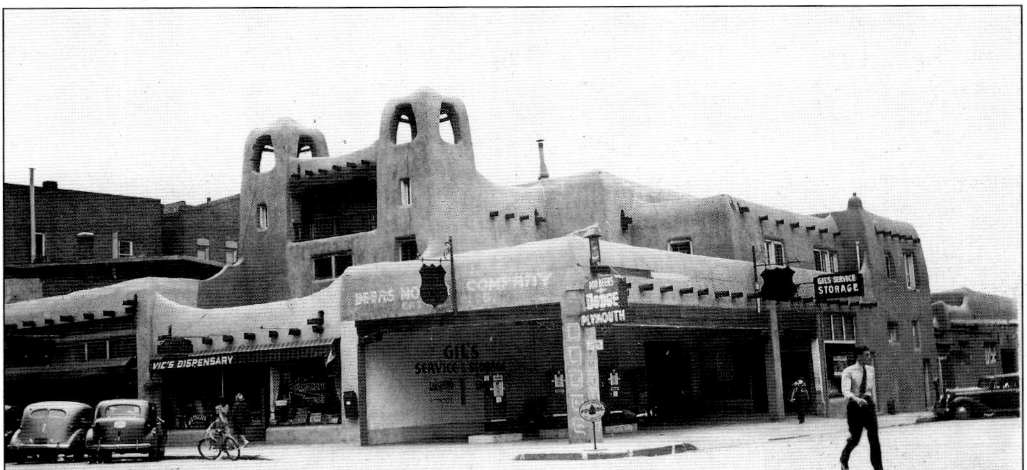

The La Fonda Hotel, which remains one of Santa Fe's most popular inns and local gathering spots, was designed by architect John Gaw Meem (page 60) in collaboration with interior designer Mary Colter. (Courtesy of Taos Historic Museums.)

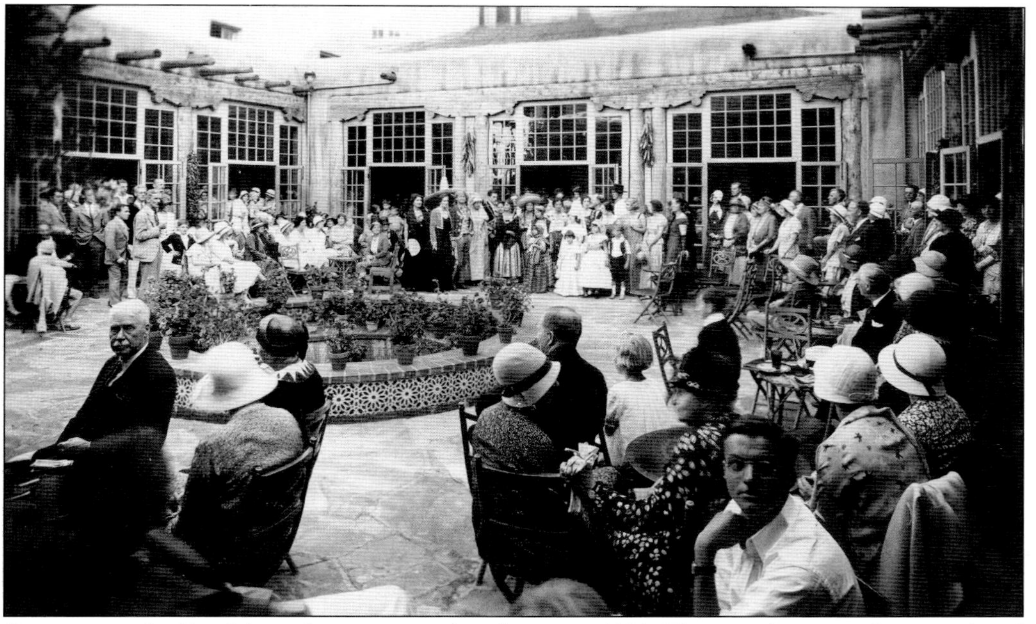

Guests enjoy La Fonda's outdoor courtyard and patio in 1930. This area has since been enclosed and is now a restaurant. (Courtesy of the Palace of the Governor's Archives, T. Harmon Parkhurst Collection, 023098.)

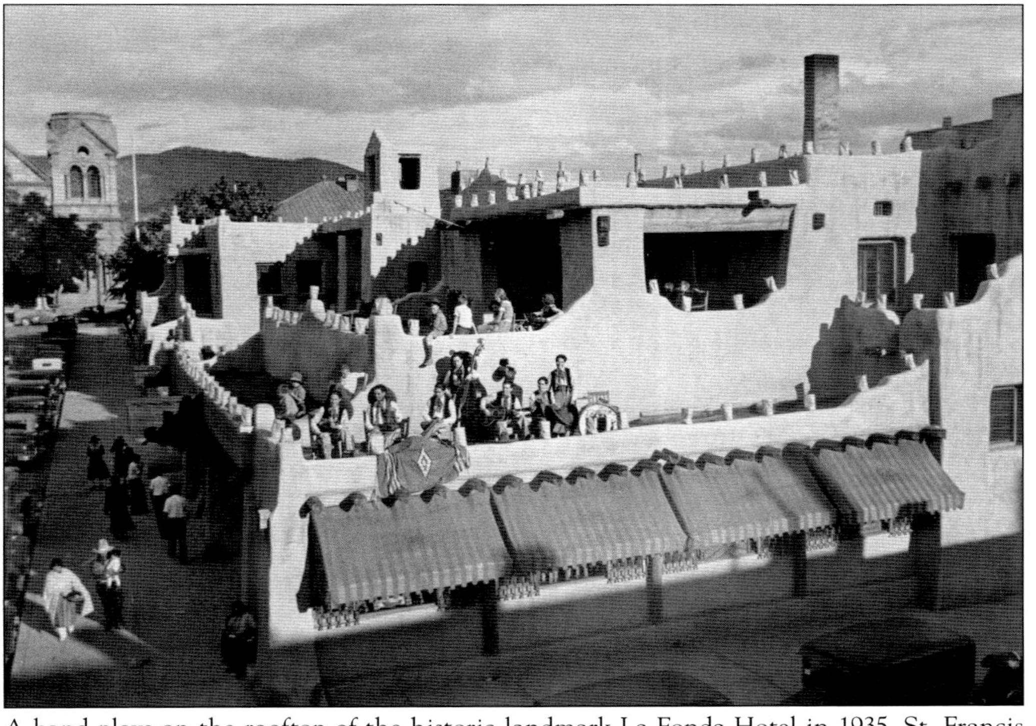

A band plays on the rooftop of the historic landmark La Fonda Hotel in 1935. St. Francis Cathedral Basilica can be seen in the background on the left. (Courtesy of Palace of the Governor's Archives, 046953.)

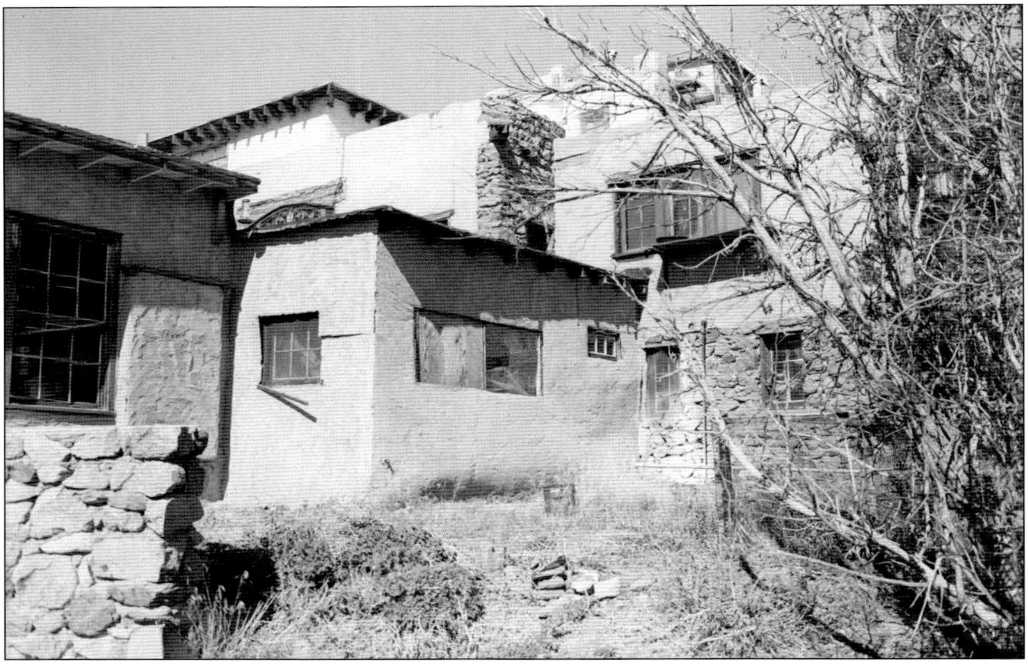

Ernest Thompson Seton (1860–1946) was born in England, lived for a time in Canada, studied art in Paris, and showed with the Impressionists in a New York exhibition. He came to New Mexico to hunt wolves for ranchers, but upon reflecting on the killing of wolves, became an ardent environmentalist. In 1910, Seton was the chairman of the founding committee of the Boy Scouts of America. He was the head of the scouts from 1910 to 1915. However, he did not agree with the military emphasis of the Boys Scouts and resigned. He developed the Woodcraft League of America, moved to Santa Fe in 1931, and built a residence called Seton Village (above). The image below shows Seton with three Blackfoot Indians.

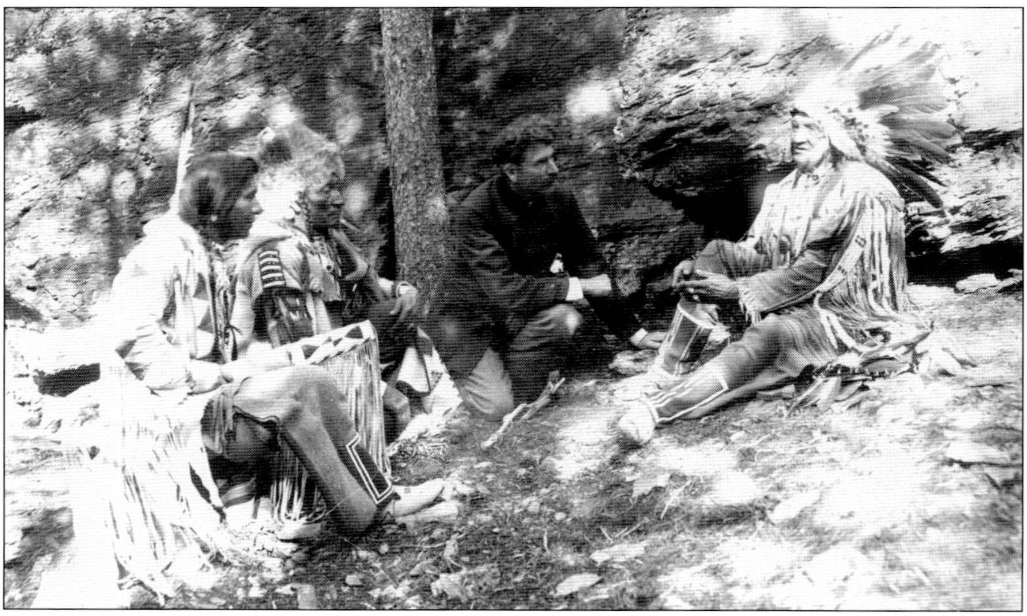

Seton incorporated many Indian and Southwestern carved motifs throughout the residence. The photograph at right shows an Indian figure painted on an interior door; below is the carved and embellished exterior of the Seton residence's front door.

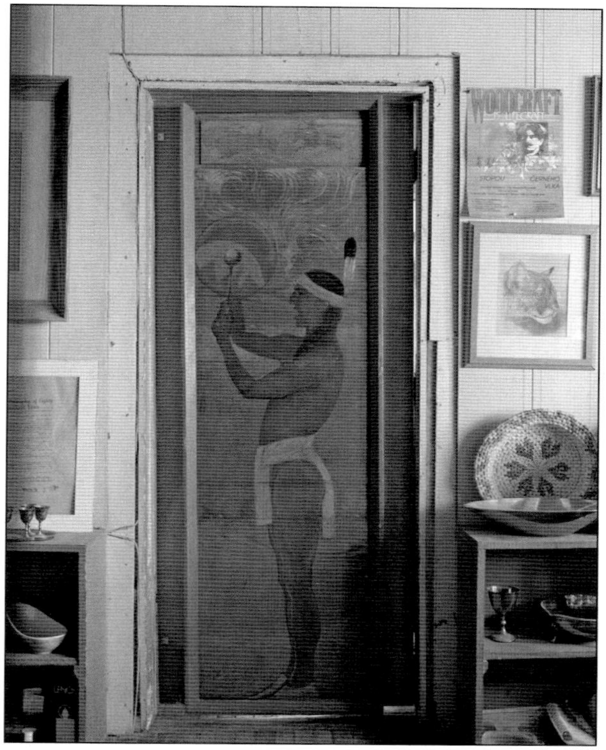

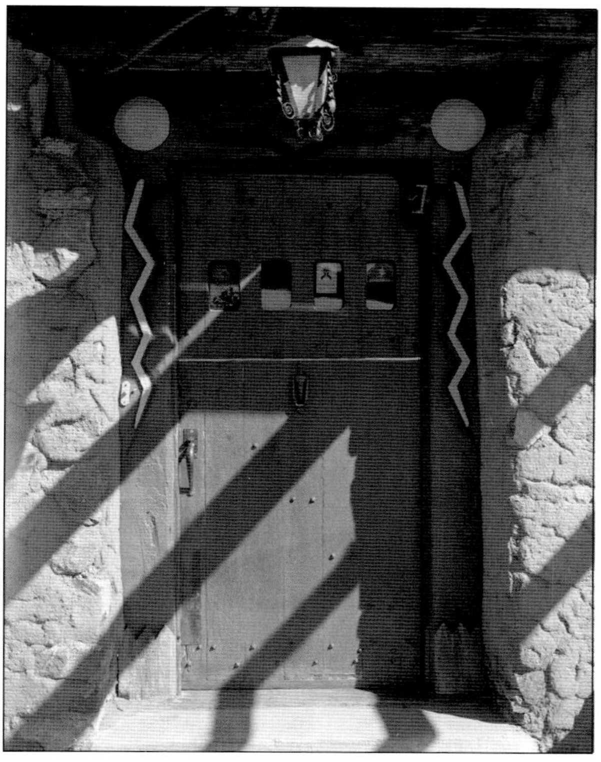

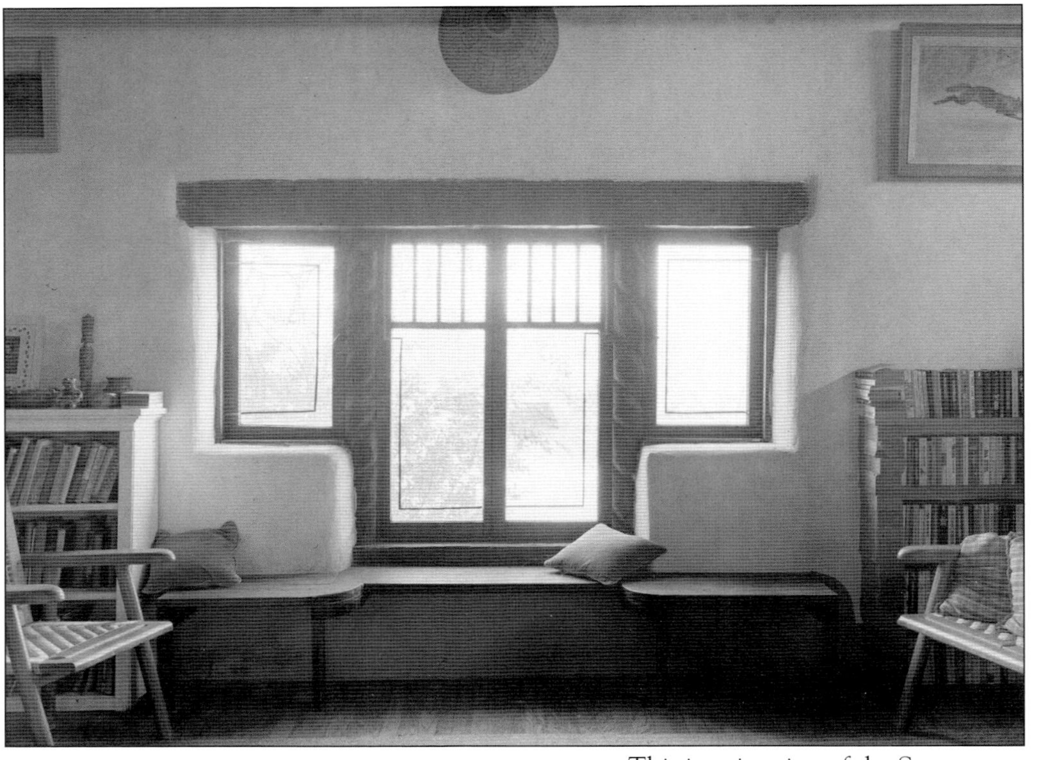

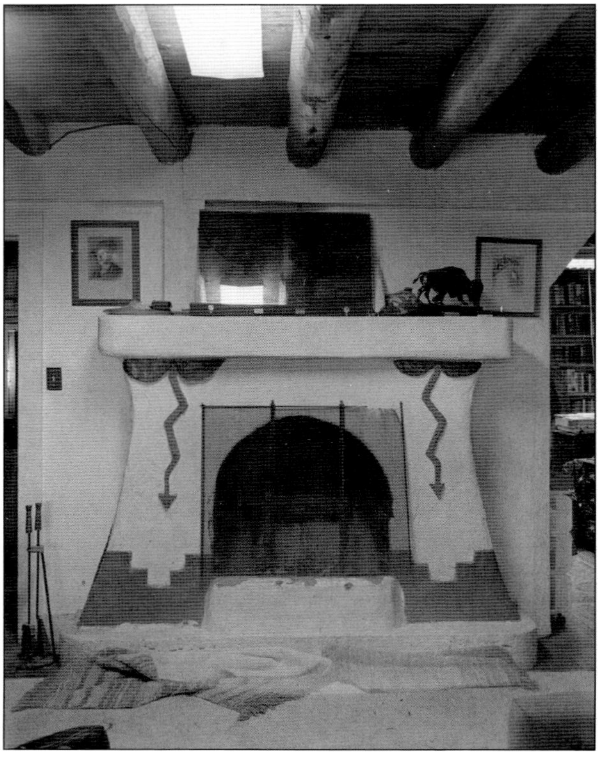

This interior view of the Seton residence looks through windows that mimic the keyhole shape seen at Mesa Verde and on Laguna Pueblo.

The Seton residence's embellished fireplace and the vigas on the ceiling are indicative of his attention to detail throughout the home.

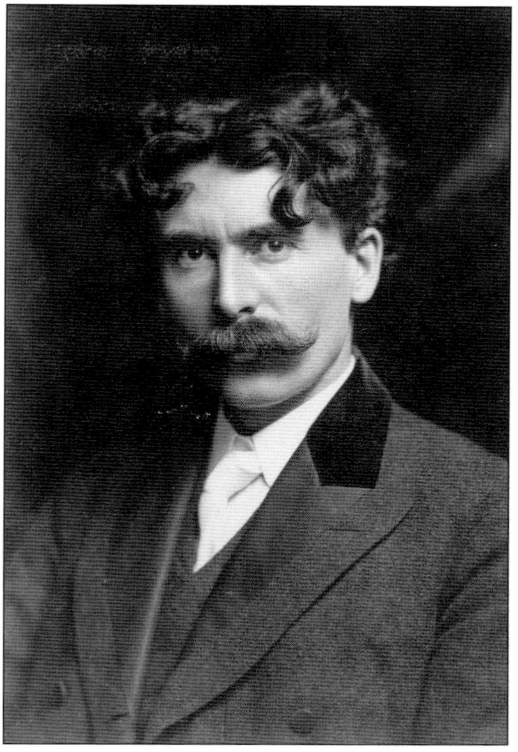

Ernest Thompson Seton and his wife, Julia Buttree Seton, had these portraits taken in 1901.

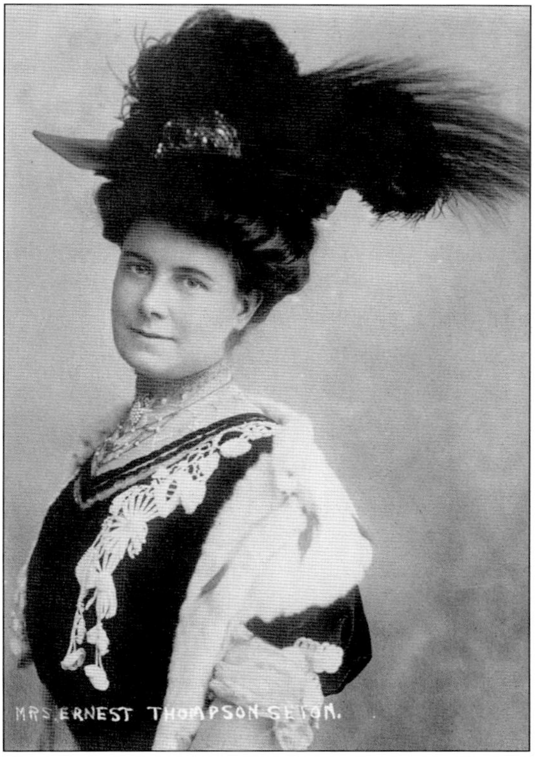

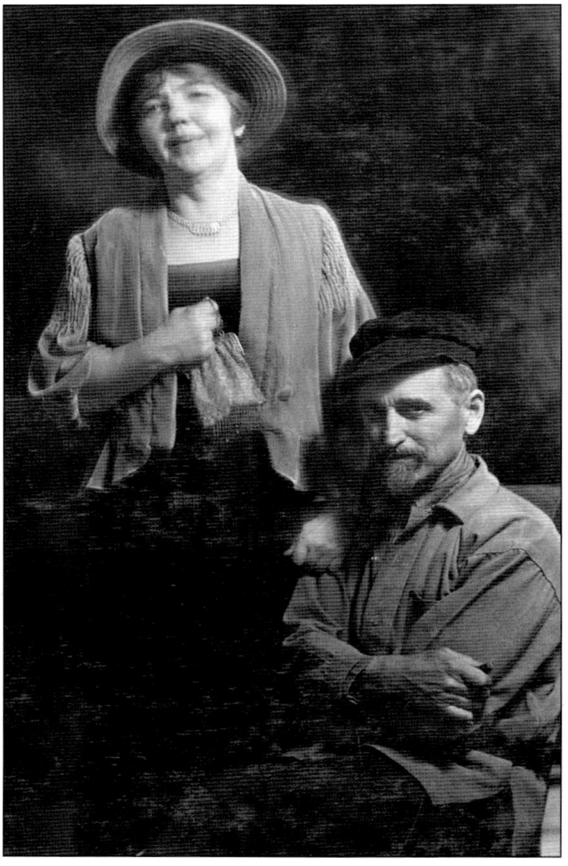

Carlos Vierra (1876–1937) was born in Moss Landing, California. He studied art with Gottardo Piazzoni at Mark Hopkins Institute, which became the California School of Fine Art and is currently called the San Francisco Art Institute. He contracted tuberculosis and moved to Santa Fe in 1904 for treatment. Vierra worked for Edgar L. Hewett photographing area pueblos and was commissioned by benefactor Frank Springer to paint the pueblos. Native architecture became Vierra's passion and he believed it should become the architectural style of Santa Fe. Working with local businessmen, artists, and architects, the new/old Santa Fe style was born. Vierra also painted murals for the 1915 exposition in San Diego. Vierra is seen at left with his wife, Ada. Their Santa Fe residence is pictured below. (Left, courtesy of the Palace of the Governors Archive, 059762; below, courtesy of the Palace of the Governors Archive, 030856.)

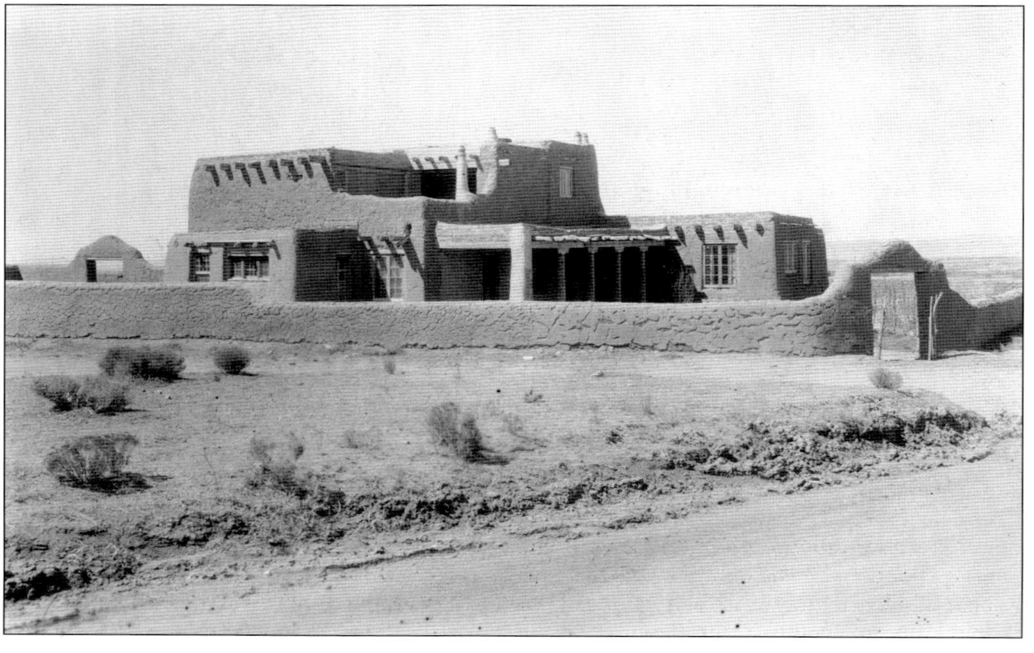

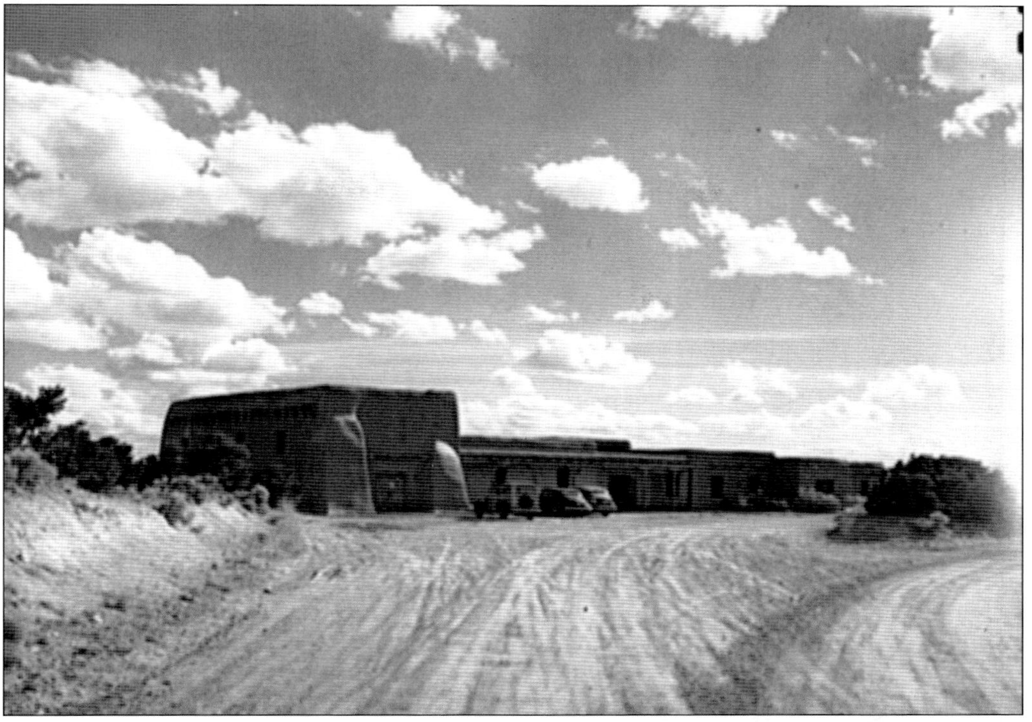

The Laboratory of Anthropology was designed by William Penhallow Henderson and opened in 1913. Henderson and his wife, Alice Corbin Henderson, came to Santa Fe in search of a cure for Alice's tuberculosis and became vital members of the Santa Fe art community.

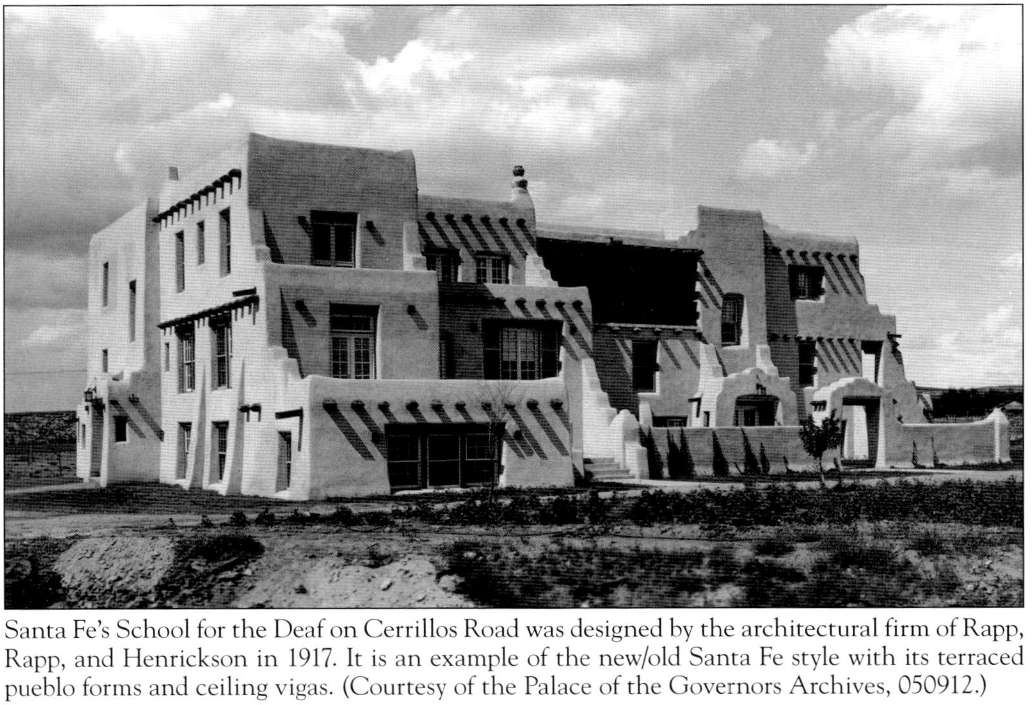

Santa Fe's School for the Deaf on Cerrillos Road was designed by the architectural firm of Rapp, Rapp, and Henrickson in 1917. It is an example of the new/old Santa Fe style with its terraced pueblo forms and ceiling vigas. (Courtesy of the Palace of the Governors Archives, 050912.)

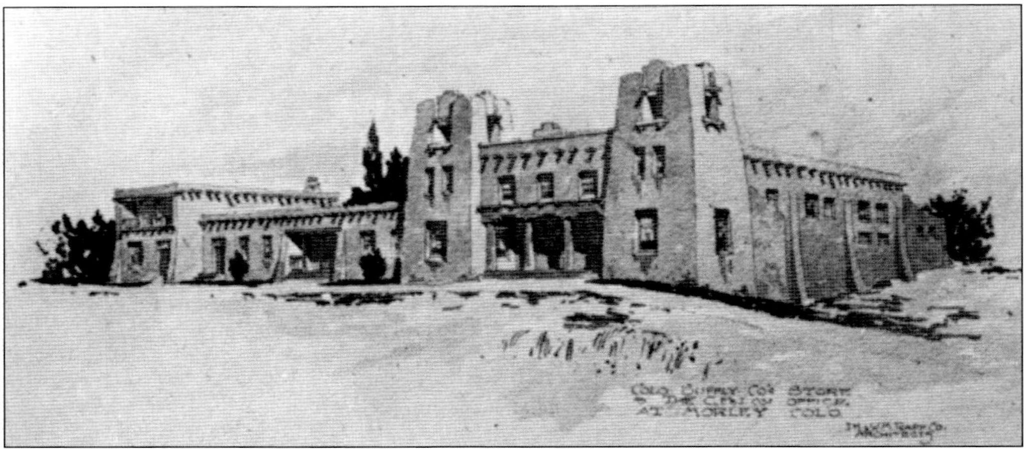

This architectural rendering by Rapp & Rapp of the Colorado Supply Company Store in Morely, Colorado, shows the early incorporation of the new/old Santa Fe style in the firm's building designs. (Courtesy of the Palace of the Governors Archive, 061210.)

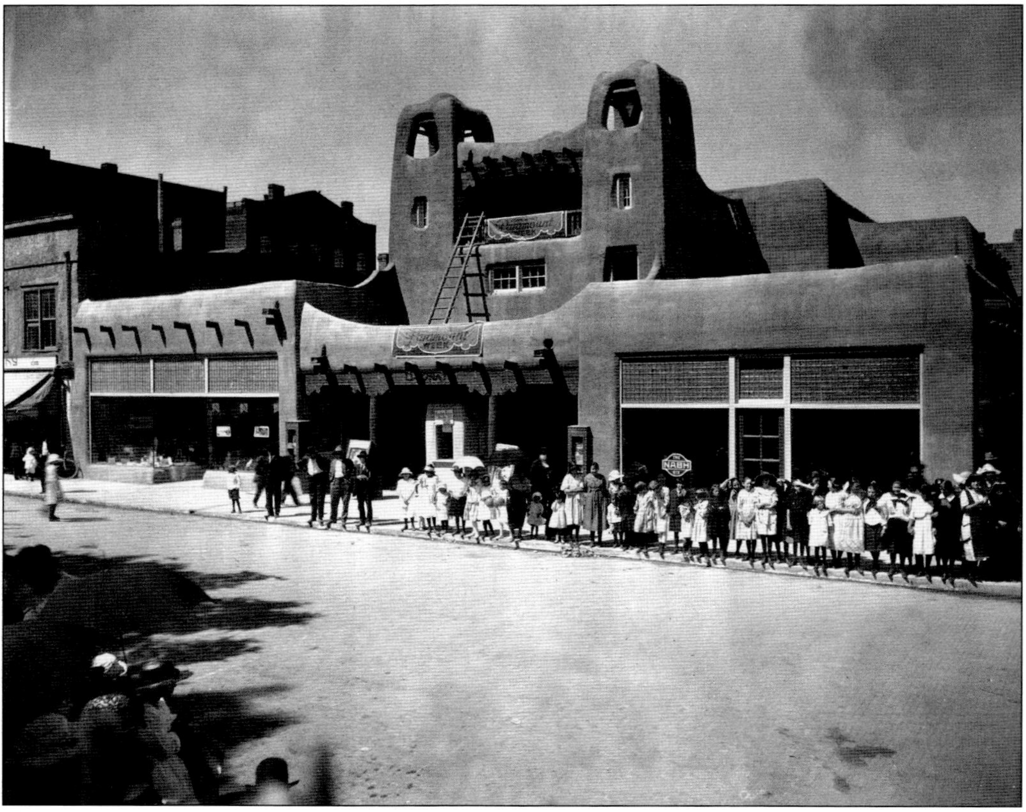

This crowd lines the streets in front of the El Onate Theater in the Cassell Building at Lincoln and Palace Avenues around 1921. One of the earliest movie theaters in Santa Fe, it is a good example of Spanish Pubelo style. Its time as a theater only lasted until 1924, when it was converted into retail space. (Courtesy of Palace of the Governors Archive, 010661.)

Two

The Tuberculosis Influence

As the tuberculosis epidemic swept the United States in the late 1800s and early 1900s, many "lungers"—as sufferers were called—were drawn to the Southwest in search of a cure. Many sanatoriums sprang up in and around Santa Fe offering fresh air, sunshine, and sweeping vistas to the visiting city folks, among them poets, writers, artists, and architects. Enchanted by the landscape, climate, and multiple cultures, many of these talented people chose to stay in Santa Fe permanently and, as a result, the new/old Santa Fe architectural identity emerged, establishing Santa Fe as a popular tourist destination that would ultimately become widely known for Santa Fe style.

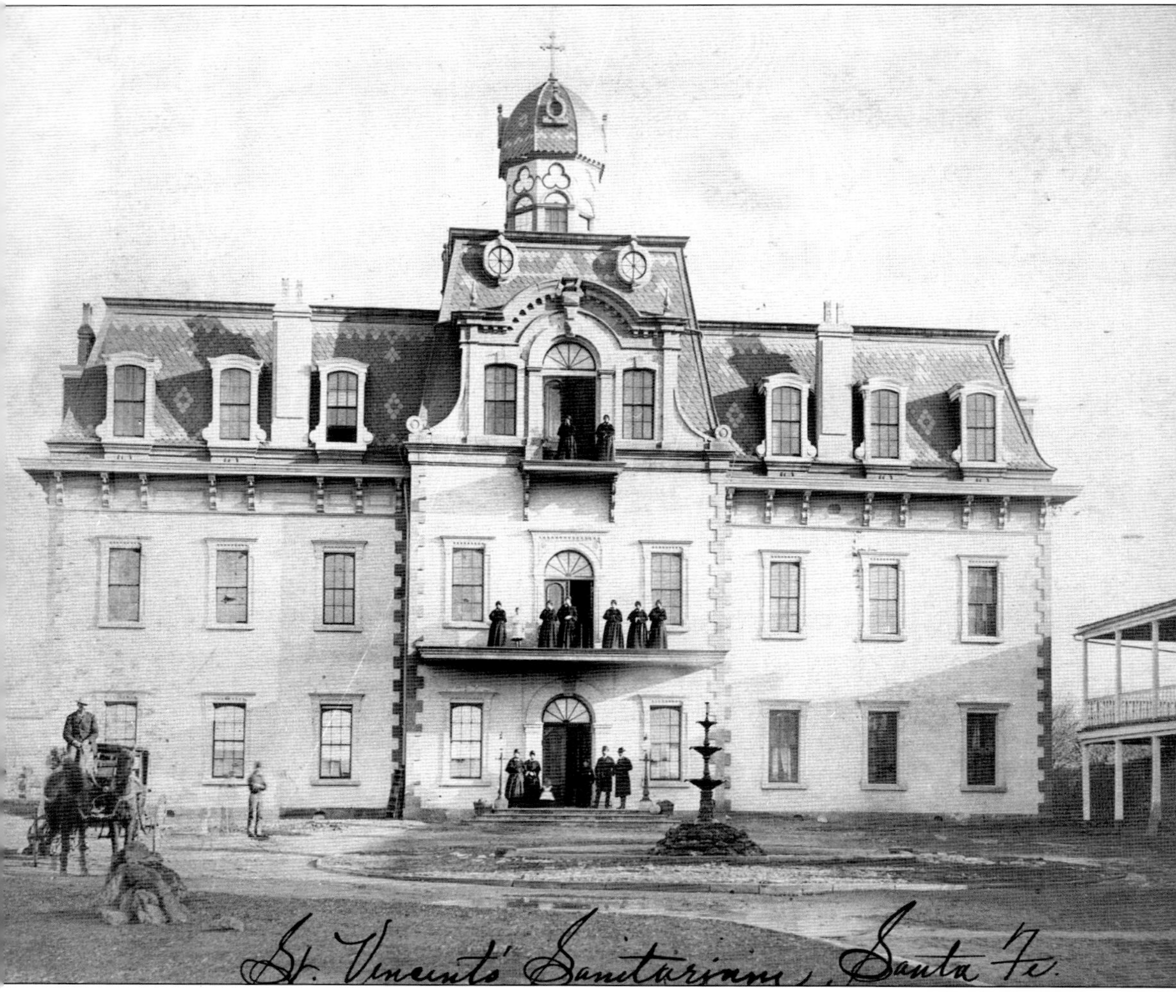

Saint Vincent's was one of Santa Fe's earliest sanatoriums. Located on the plaza next to the St. Francis Cathedral Basilica on property granted by Archbishop Lamy, this Second Empire–style building included patients' dining rooms and parlors, dormitories and a ward on the second floor, and a large chapel and stage for entertainment and community events on the third floor. (Courtesy of Palace of the Governor's Archives, 067744.)

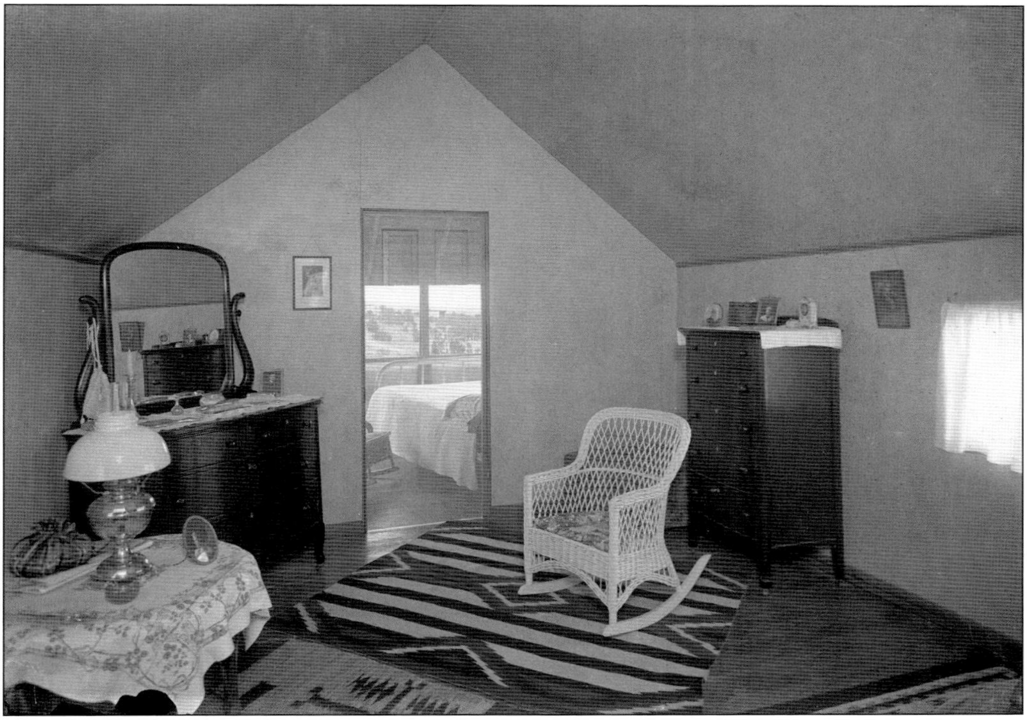

This early patient cottage at Santa Fe's Sunmount Sanatorium shows the comfort and ease offered by these restorative facilities. Many tuberculosis patients chose to settle in Santa Fe once they were cured, and as a result, craftsman-style bungalows were built throughout the city. (Courtesy of Palace of the Governor's Archives, 061398.)

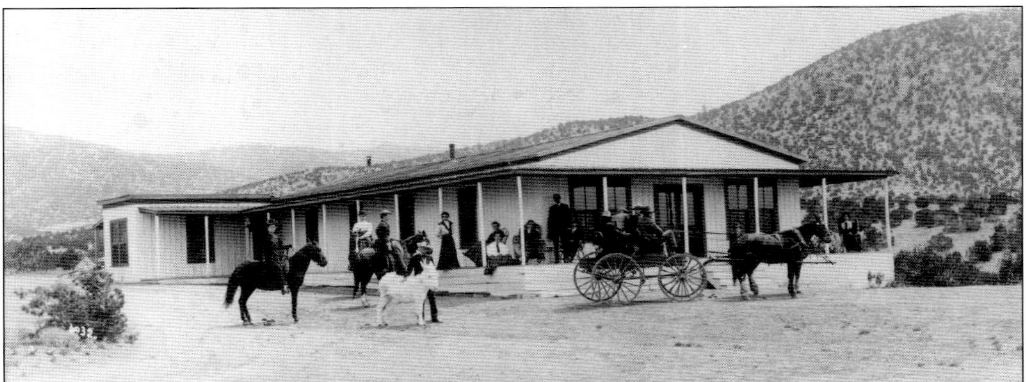

With the influx of tuberculosis patients and the popularity of the facility, Sunmount Sanatorium grew substantially over the years. This view of an early public building shows patients relaxing on the porch. (Courtesy of New Mexico State Records Center and Archive, the John Gaw Meem Photograph Collection.)

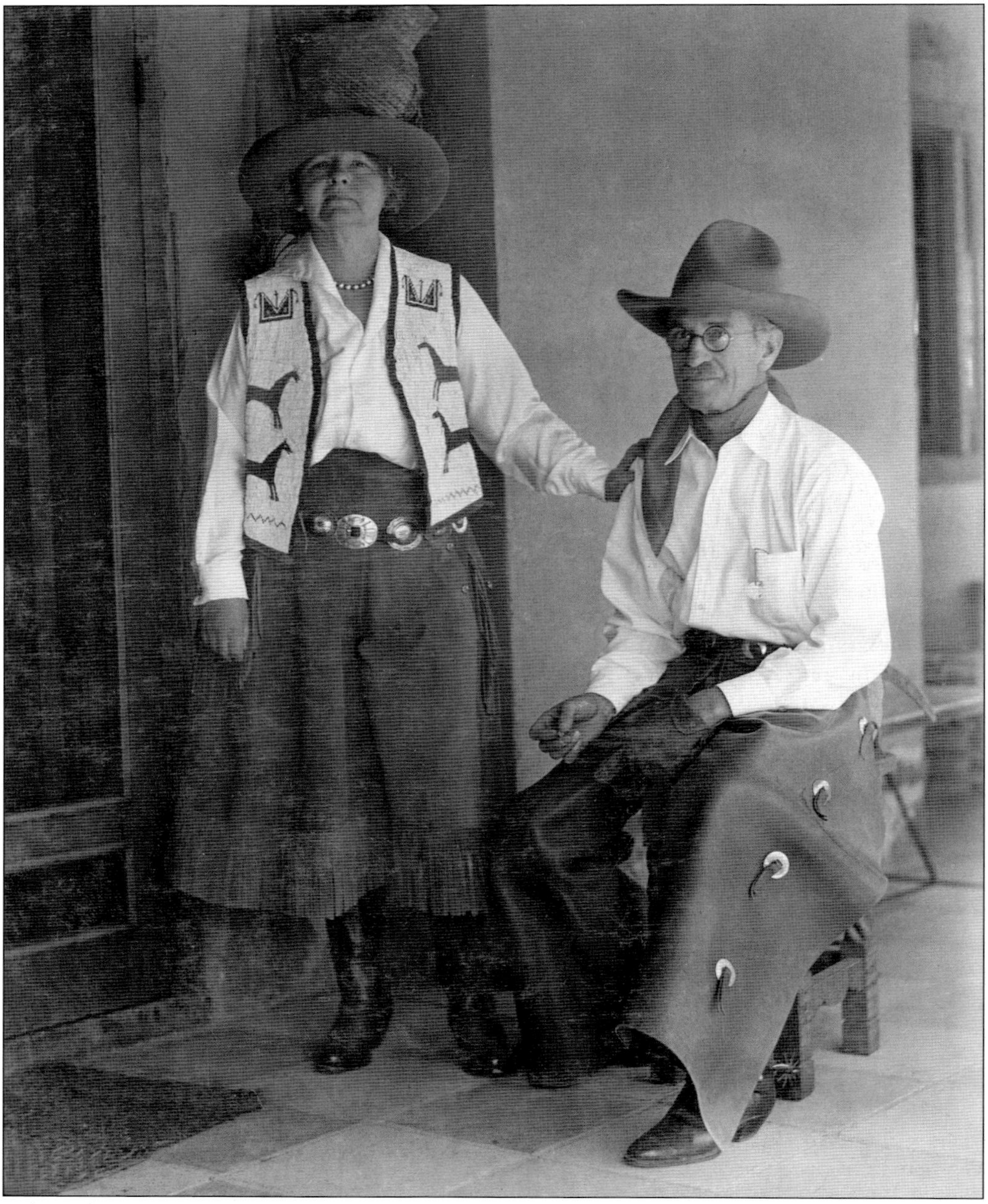

Tuberculosis patient Alice Corbin Henderson, a poet, author, and editor, is seen here with her architect husband, William Penhallow Henderson. They came to Sunmount seeking a cure for Alice and while they were there, Alice coordinated weekly salons for creative folks from the facility and the surrounding Santa Fe community. These salons were the basis for what would ultimately result in a unified effort to establish a new/old Santa Fe style to attract tourism. (Courtesy of the Palace of the Governors Archive, 059757.)

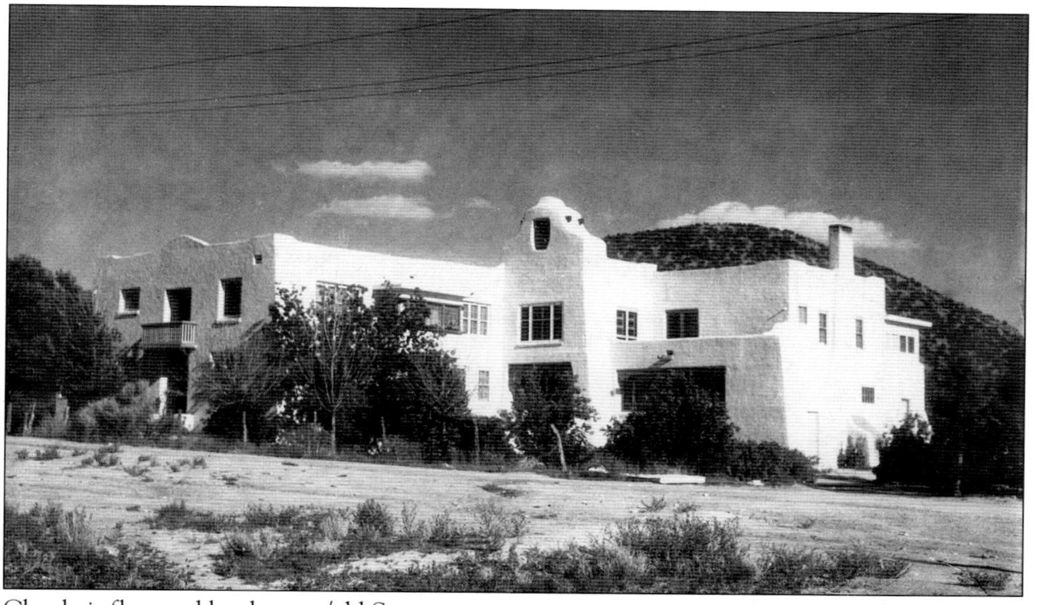

Clearly influenced by the new/old Santa Fe architectural movement, this later version of Sunmount Sanatorium's main building, seen here in 1925, is a far more substantial structure than the first building. (Courtesy of Palace of the Governors Archive, 155710.)

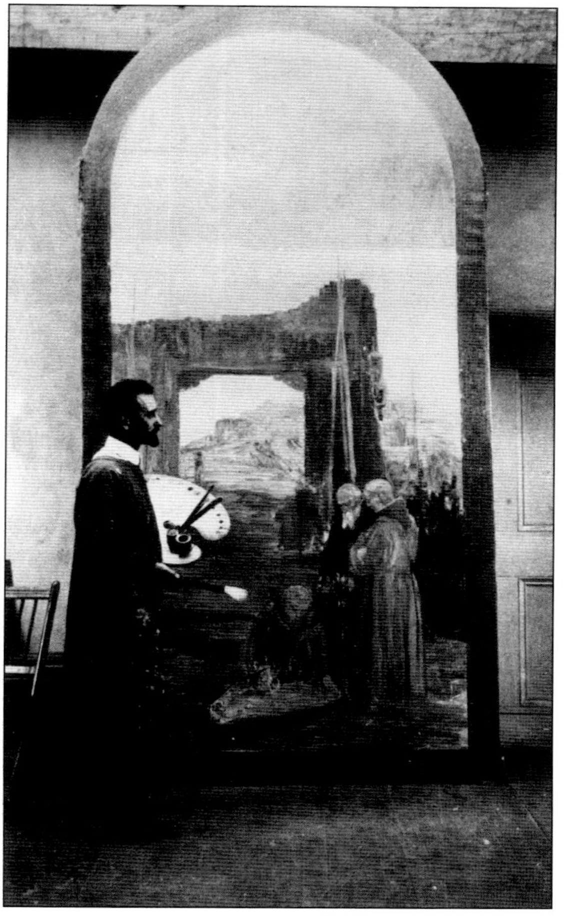

Artist and architect Carlos Vierra, seen here in front of one of his paintings, came to New Mexico seeking treatment for tuberculosis and was an active participant in Alice Corbin Henderson's weekly Sunmount Salons. Vierra was instrumental in establishing the new/old Santa Fe architectural identity and also diligently documented Pueblo and Mission architecture in photographs. (Courtesy of Palace of the Governors Archive.)

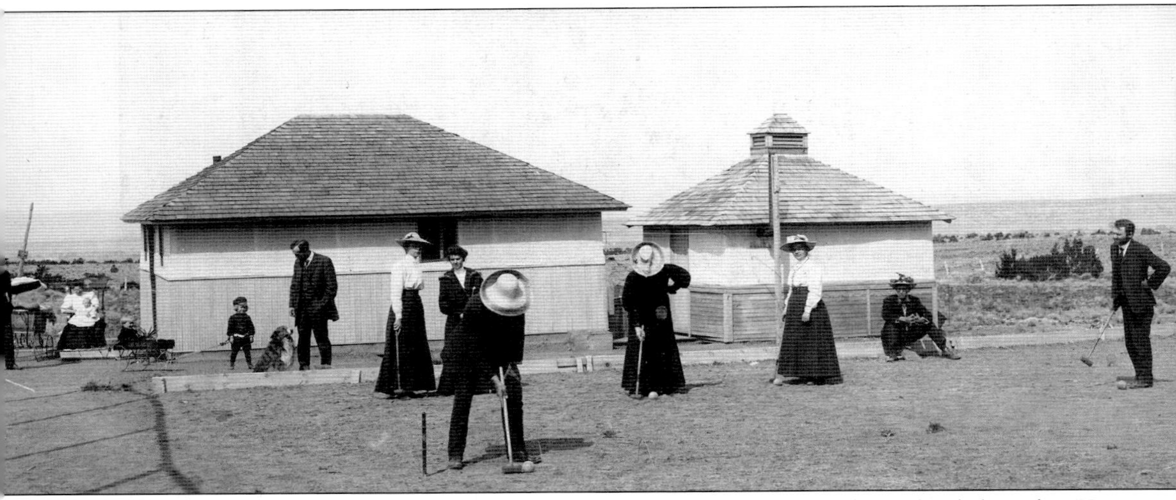

Outdoor and social activities were key to the sanatorium's healthy lifestyle philosophy. Here, Sunmount patients enjoy both as they engage in a game of croquet. (Courtesy of New Mexico State Records Center and Archive, the John Gaw Meem Photograph Collection.)

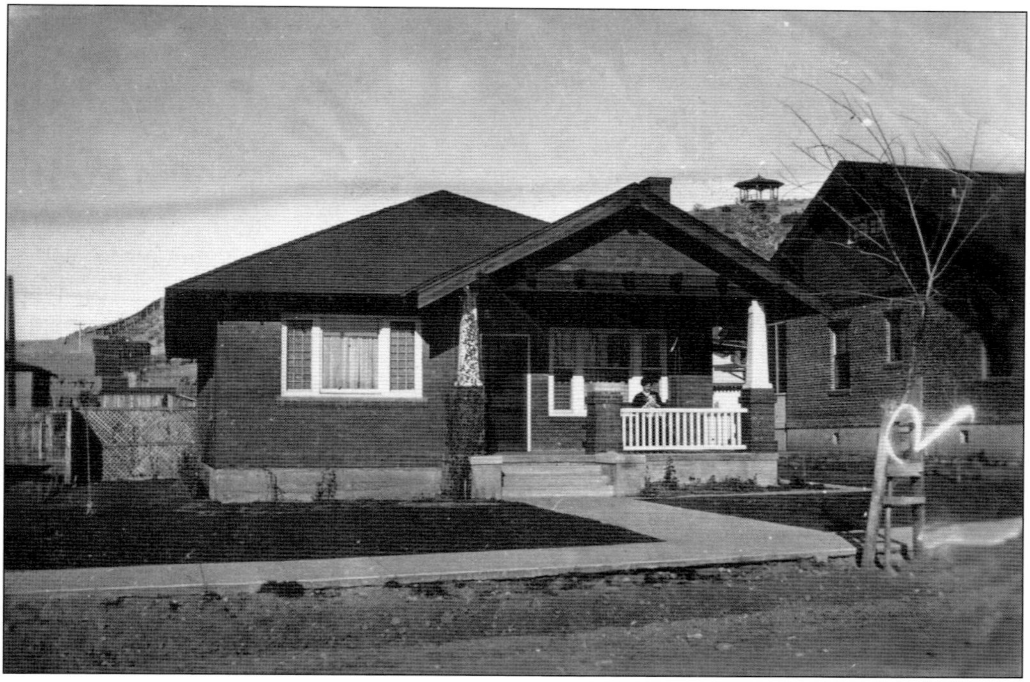

After tuberculosis patients stayed in the area following their treatment, "lunger's bungalows," as they were called, like the one above, cropped up all over the city. Below is an early view of the Sunmount patient cottages. (Above, courtesy of Palace of the Governors, 01520; below, courtesy of the Palace of the Governors Archives, 061390.)

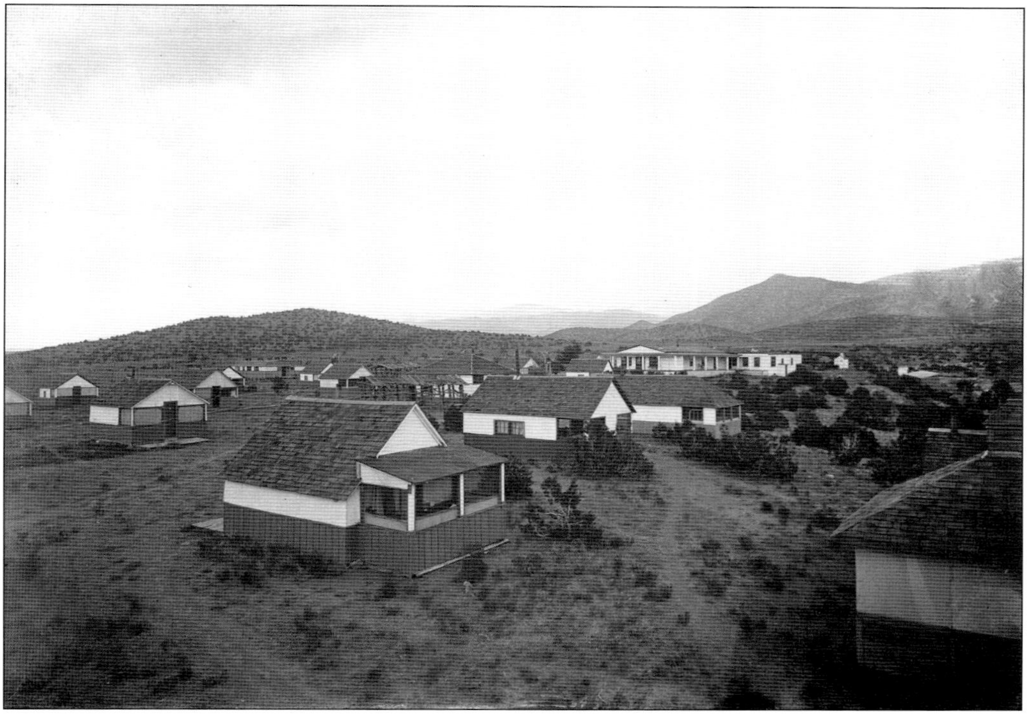

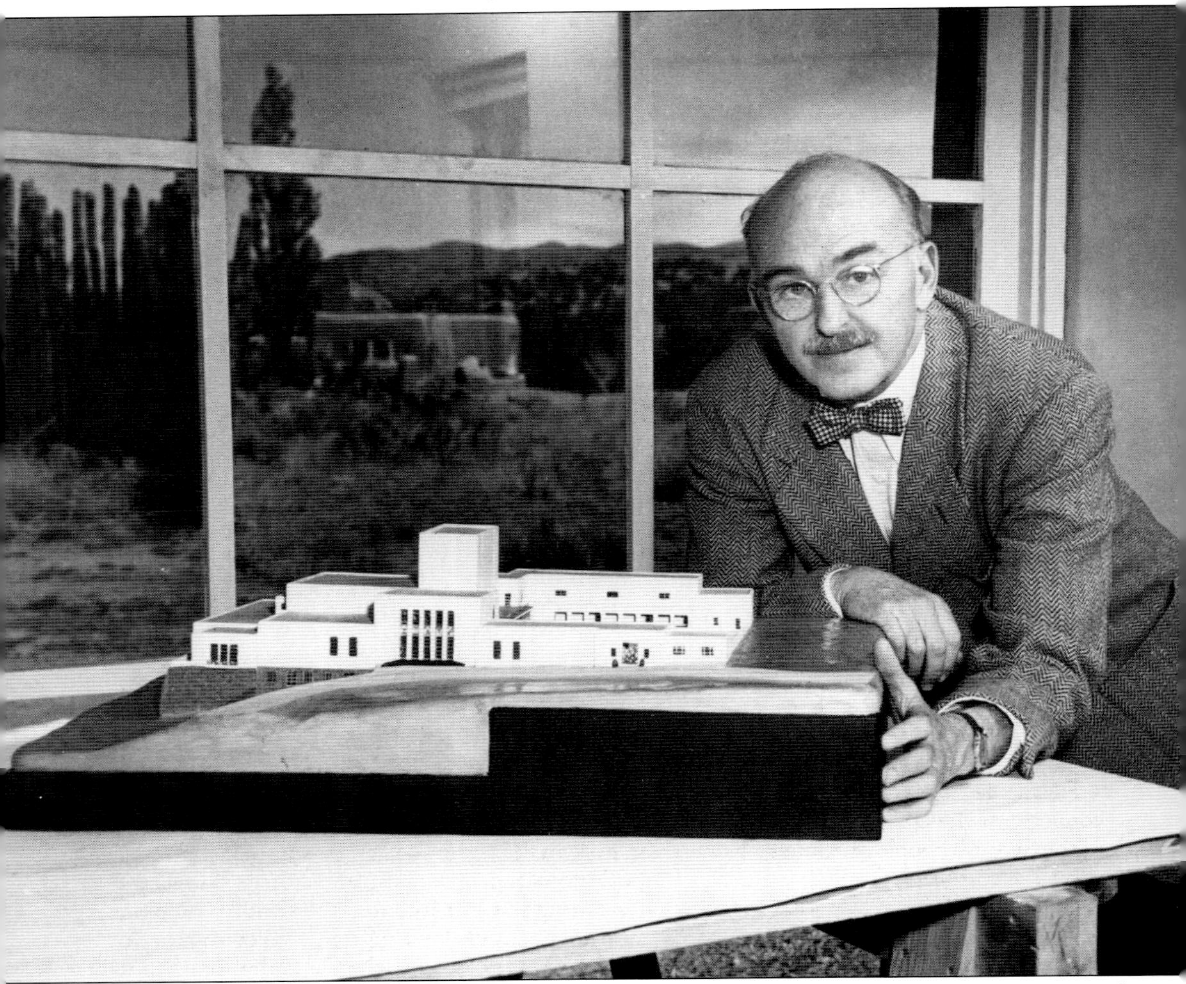

Architect John Gaw Meem (1894–1983) was born in Brazil to missionary parents. He earned a degree in civil engineering in Virginia. While working for the National Bank of New York, he was sent to Rio de Janeiro, where he was diagnosed with tuberculosis. Meem arrived at Sunmount Sanatorium, where he participated in Alice Corbin Henderson's weekly salons. It was at Sunmount that Meem developed an interest in architecture and shared Carlos Vierra's passion for pueblo buildings. He and fellow patient and businessman Cassius McCormick opened an architectural practice, which was housed in an extra building at Sunmount. Gaw Meem's building designs became paramount to the transformation of Santa Fe's unified architectural identity. (Courtesy of Palace of the Governors Archive, 019646.)

Three

Fiestas and Celebrations

The Fiestas de Santa Fe tradition began in 1712. This annual celebration commemorates the re-conquest of the city by Spanish colonists led by Gen. Don Diego de Vargas in 1692. Prior to that, the Spanish people of Santa Fe had been in exile in El Paso del Norte, now known as Ciudad Juarez, Mexico, during the Pueblo Revolt of 1680. Appointed by the king of Spain, de Vargas and his men surrounded the city with cannons, threatening resident Indians with death. The fiesta begins with Novena masses that start during a reenactment of the knighting and coronation of Don Diego de Vargas and La Reina de Santa Fe in a procession from the Cathedral Basilica to Rosario Chapel. Nine masses follow through the rest of Fiestas Week, and culminate in the return of La Conquistador from Rosario Chapel to the Cathedral Basilica. The beginning of the Fiestas is marked by the burning of Zozobra, also known as "Old Man Gloom," a 50-foot-tall marionette designed by artist Will Shuster representing the ridding of oneself of the challenges and despair of the previous year. Other popular events include a children's pet parade, a historical/hysterical parade, and Fiesta Ball. Santa Fe Plaza takes on a carnival-like atmosphere, with music, food, crafts booths, and merrymakers. Fiestas de Santa Fe concludes with mass at the St. Francis Cathedral followed by a candlelight procession to the Cross of the Martyrs.

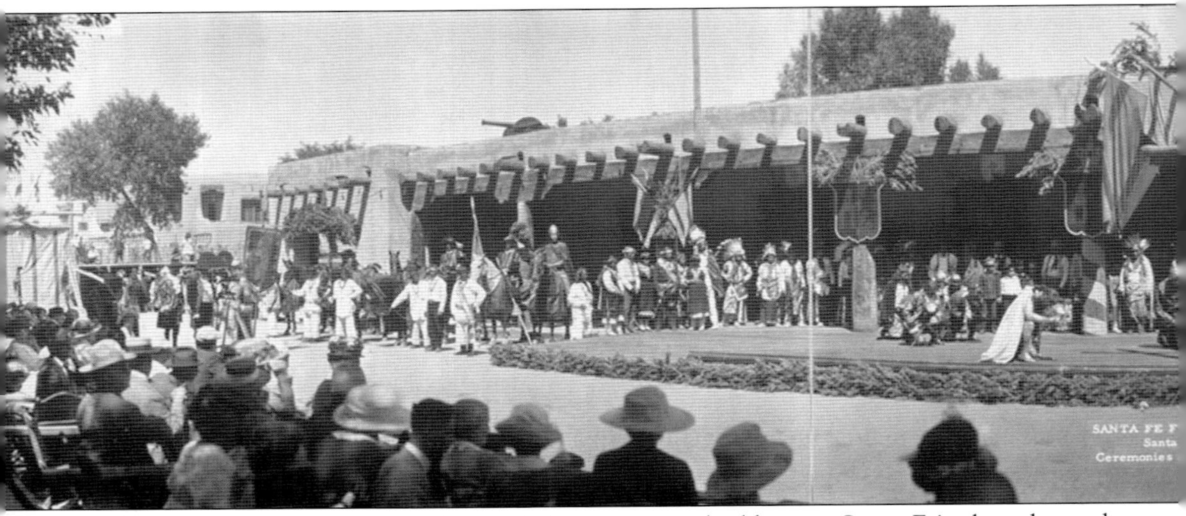

This spectacular view of the Palace of the Governors building on Santa Fe's plaza shows the annual reenactment of the knighting and coronation of Don Diego de Vargas by the king of

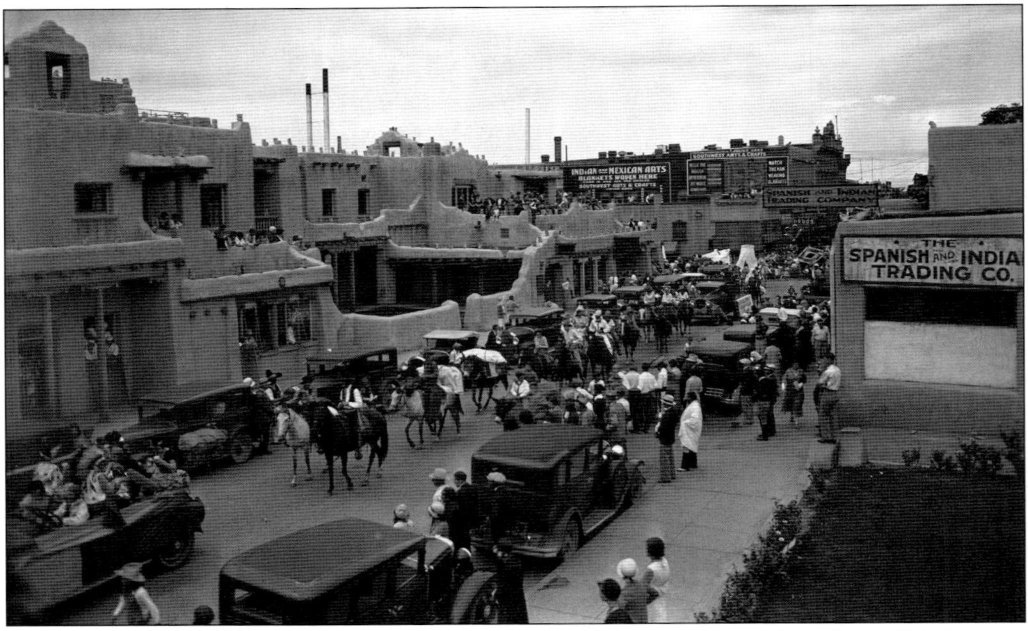

A 1930s Fiesta parade makes its way past the landmark La Fonda Hotel on Santa Fe's historic plaza. All three Santa Fe cultures—Indian, Spanish Colonial, and Anglo—are represented in this photograph. (Courtesy of Palace of the Governors Photograph Archive, 118249.)

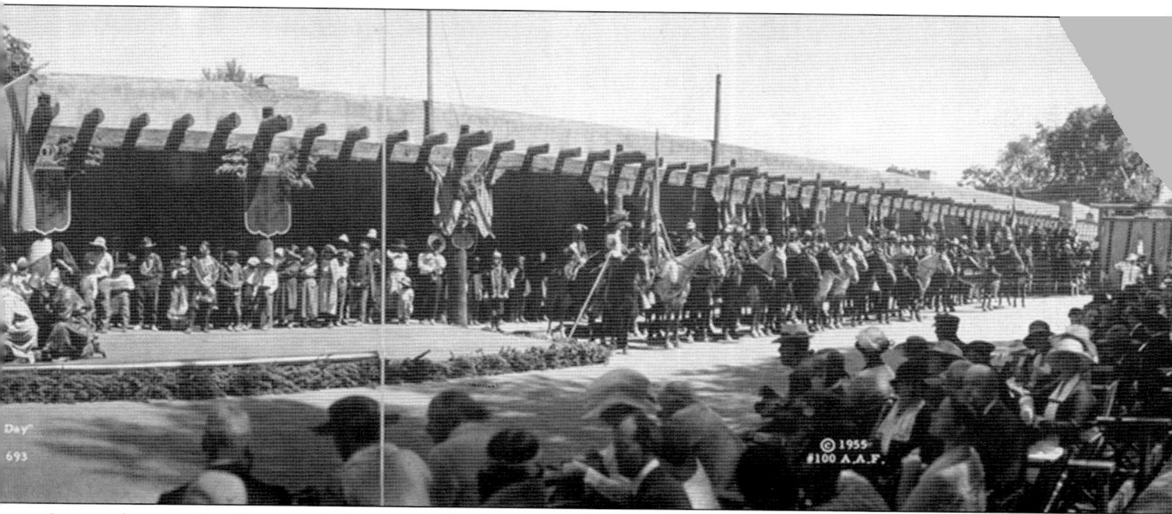

Spain during the Fiestas de Santa Fe.

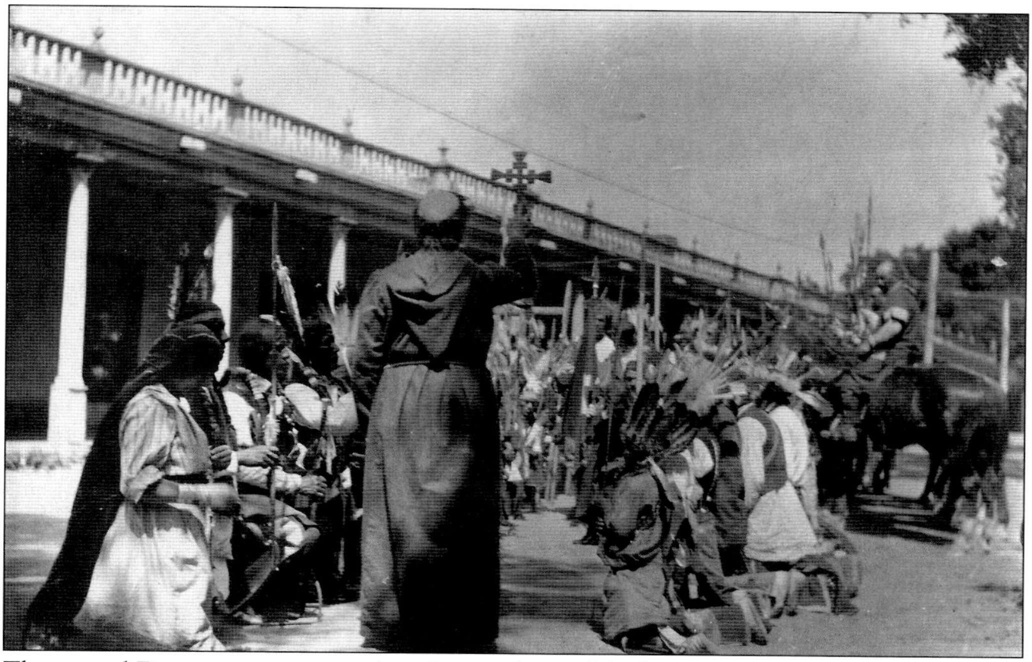

The annual Fiestas reenactment takes place in front of the Governor's Palace. While the exact date of this photograph is not known, it is interesting to note the Victorian wooden trim along the roof of the Palace of the Governors. This was later removed when Santa Fe embarked on a citywide effort to adhere to the new/old architectural style embracing Pueblo and Spanish Colonial influences. (Courtesy of Taos Historic Museums.)

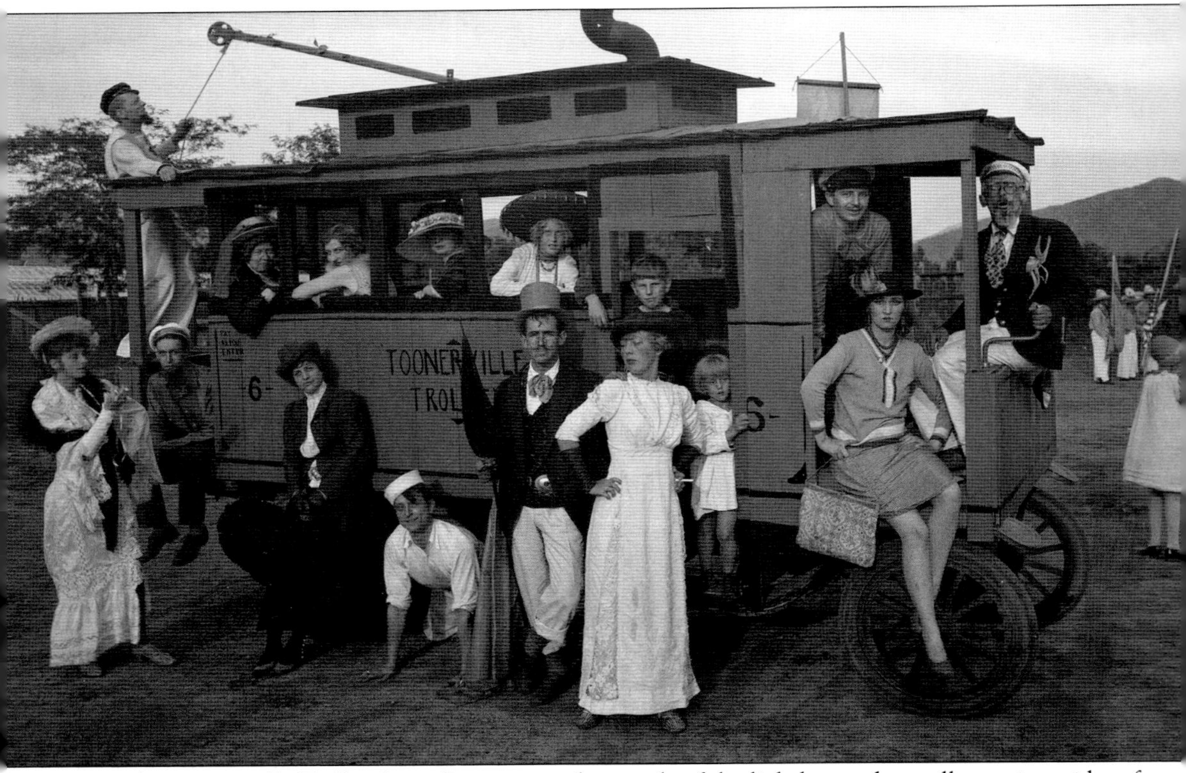

The Toonerville Trolley fiesta float is a good example of the lighthearted as well as serious sides of Fiestas celebrations. The float was inspired by the popular newspaper cartoon *Toonerville Folks* by Fontaine Fox. Also known as *The Toonerville Trolley That Meets all the Trains*, it ran from 1908 to 1955 and was nationally syndicated in 1913. This photograph was taken by T. Harmon Parkhurst between 1925 and 1945. (Courtesy of the Palace of the Governors Archives, 117681.)

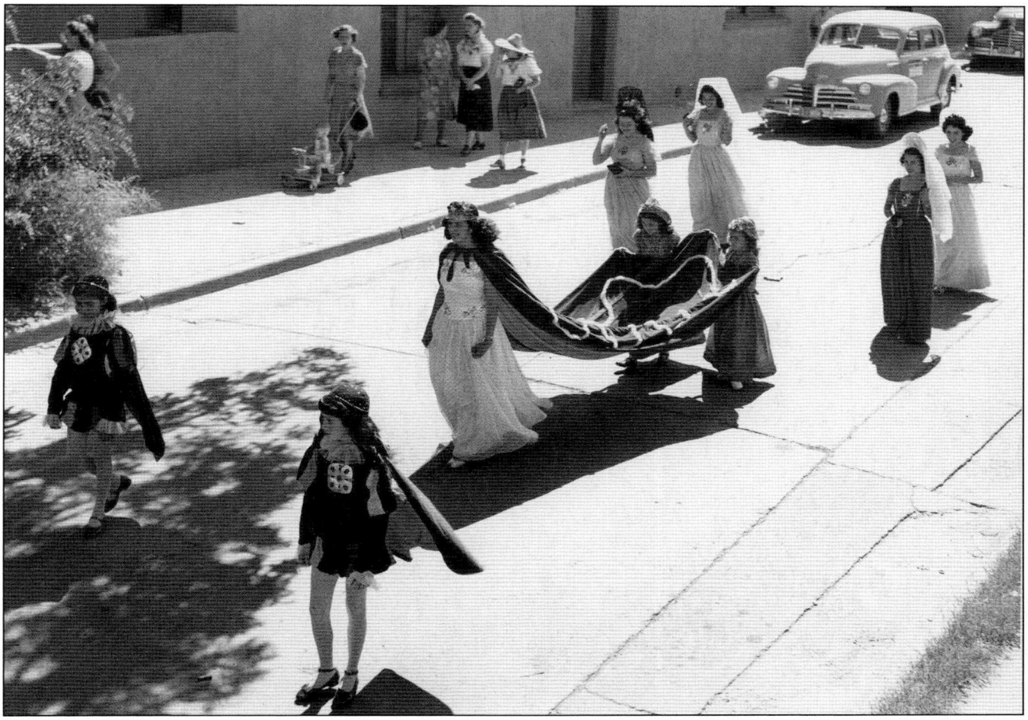

This 1948 Fiesta queen, possibly Elizabeth "Betty" Serna-Cardenas, is accompanied by her royal court in the annual Fiesta parade on Santa Fe Plaza. The photograph was taken by Robert H. Martin. (Courtesy of the Palace of the Governors Archives, 041384.)

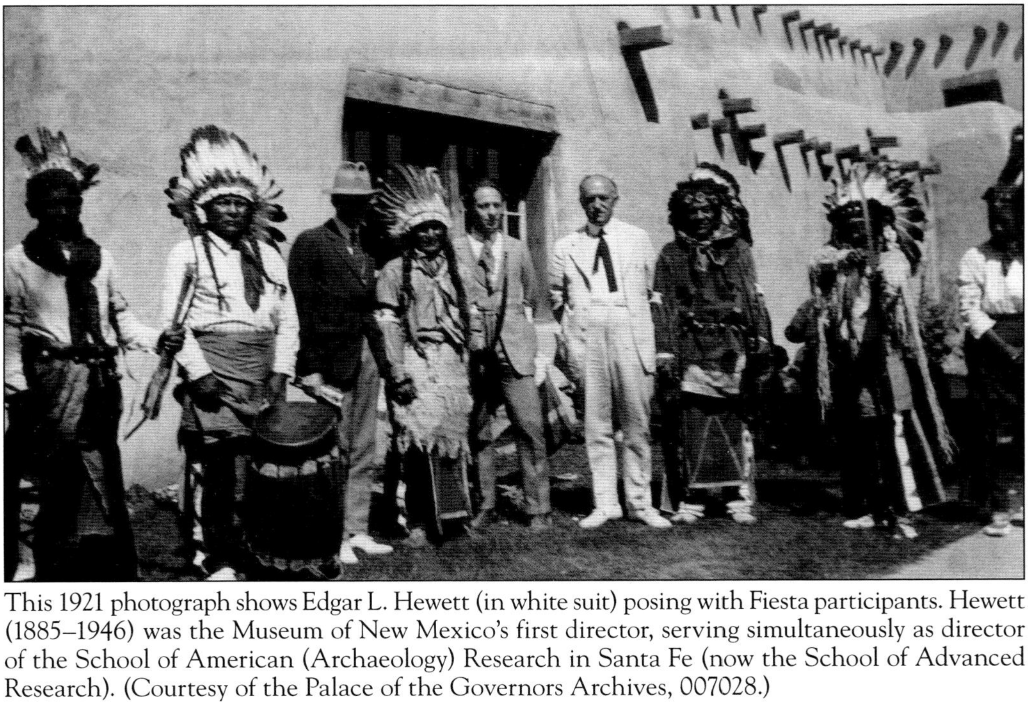

This 1921 photograph shows Edgar L. Hewett (in white suit) posing with Fiesta participants. Hewett (1885–1946) was the Museum of New Mexico's first director, serving simultaneously as director of the School of American (Archaeology) Research in Santa Fe (now the School of Advanced Research). (Courtesy of the Palace of the Governors Archives, 007028.)

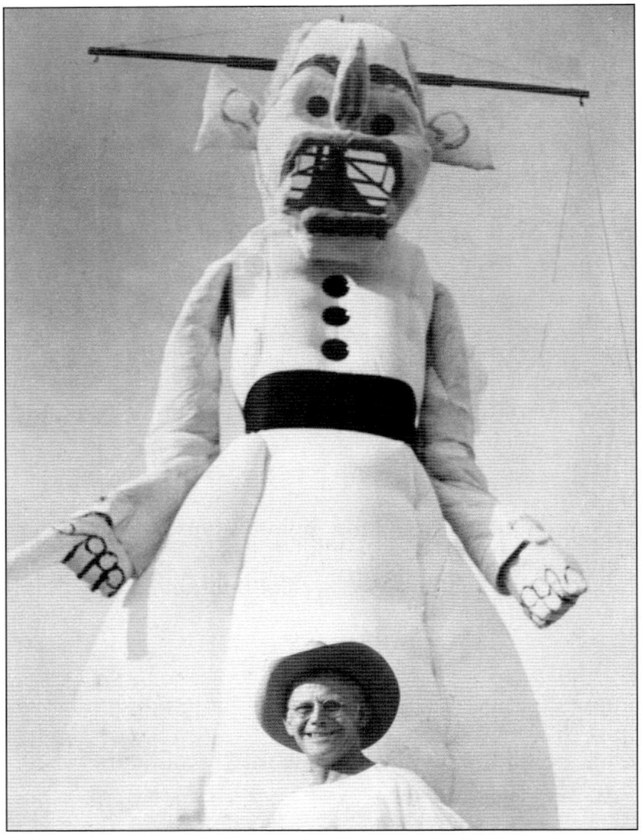

Santa Fe artist William Howard Shuster (1893–1969) poses with his creation, Zozobra, also known as Old Man Gloom, in 1942. Schuster originally conceived of the oversized and somewhat gruesome figure in 1924 for the entertainment of his artist and writer friends at a Fiesta celebration held at his home. He credited his inspiration to the Holy Week celebrations of the Yaqui Indians of Mexico. Theirs is an effigy of Judas filled with firecrackers, which is paraded through the village on a donkey, and ultimately burned. Shuster and his friend, newspaper editor E. Dana Johnson, chose the name Zozobra, which they defined as anxiety, anguish, and gloom. (Courtesy of the Palace of the Governors Archives, 027852.)

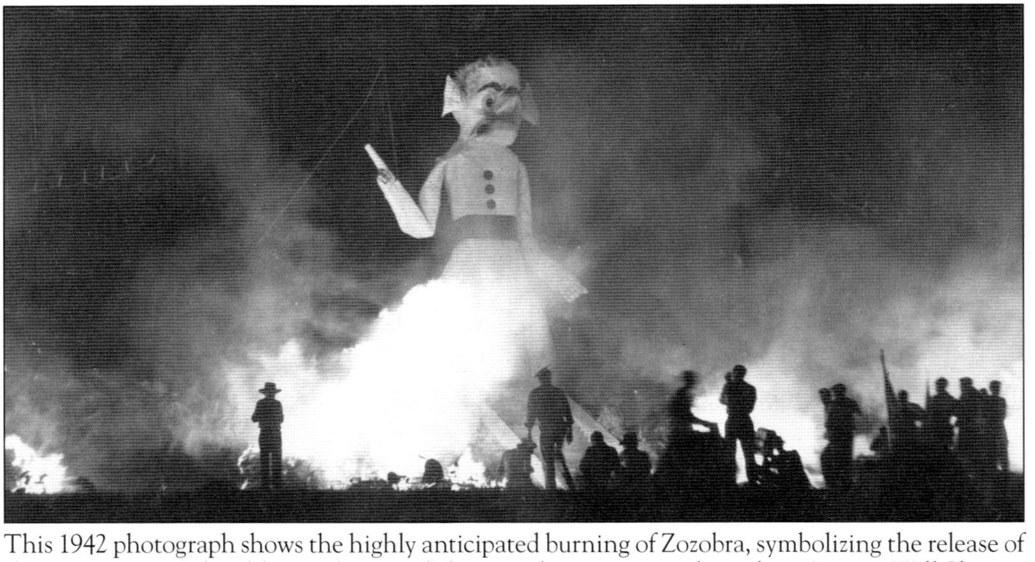

This 1942 photograph shows the highly anticipated burning of Zozobra, symbolizing the release of the previous year's hardship and pain, while an enthusiastic crowd watches. Creator Will Shuster assigned all rights, title, and interest of Zozobra to the Kiwanis Club of Santa Fe. This wildly popular annual kick-off to Fiesta Week generates a significant amount of funds that benefit the community. (Courtesy of the Palace of the Governors, Archives 047328.)

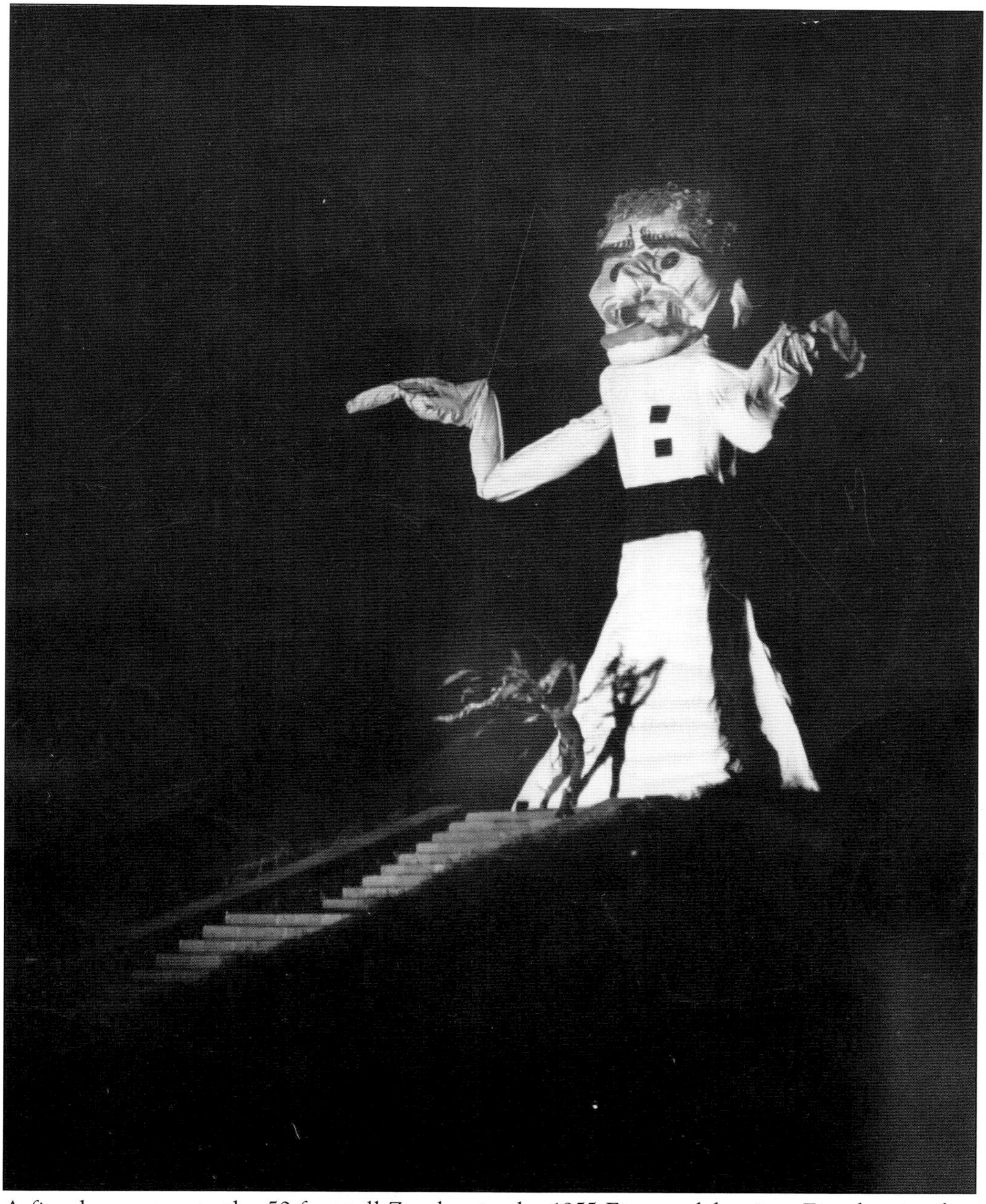

A fire dancer taunts the 50-foot-tall Zozobra in the 1955 Fiesta celebration. Fire dancing has become an extremely popular and highly choreographed element to the celebration of the burning of Zozobra. (Courtesy of the Palace of the Governors Archives, 177006.)

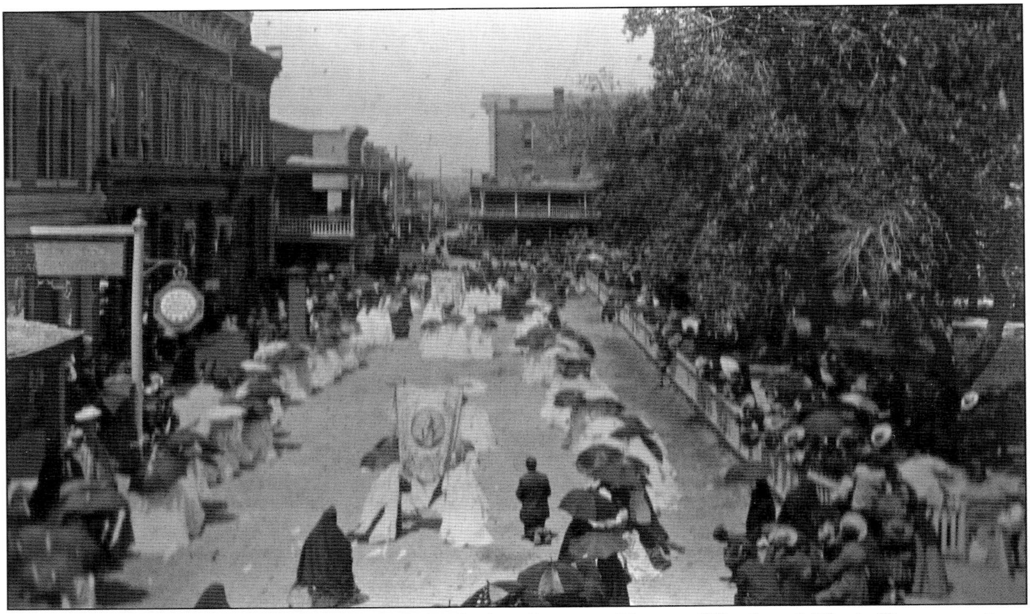

These photographs show the annual Catholic Corpus Christi ("Body of Christ") procession. The above image, from 1872, shows the historic Santa Fe Plaza, while the procession below was photographed by H.T. Heister in 1868 in front of the Palace of the Governors. (Above, courtesy of Taos Historic Museums; below, courtesy of Palace of the Governors Archives, 038022.)

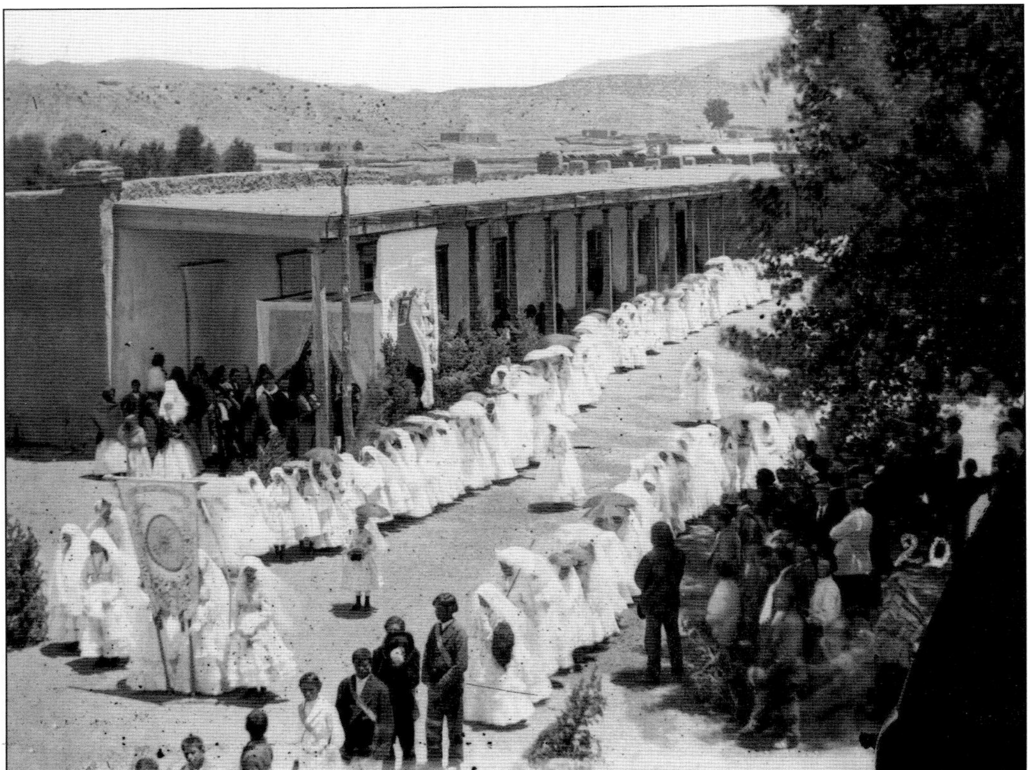

Four
Early Santa Fe Art

The Native American presence in the Southwest began some 9,000 years ago. In dry caves in the Grand Canyon, split-twig animal figures carbon-dated between 2,000 and 4,000 years ago are believed to be hunting fetishes used in rituals praying for a successful hunt. These earliest examples of animism are considered by many to be the beginnings of Native American art.

Pottery, a utilitarian craft, became an art form to be traded and sold. Painting was used to create religious images in kiva wall murals and on pottery, while pecked-rock images called petroglyphs are found throughout the Southwest. Early Pueblo jewelry was made with shells traded from other Native peoples, and turquoise, bone, and wood were also used. These traditions have traveled unbroken from the Anasazi people to today.

The early Spanish Colonial people faced a hard existence in the New Mexico Colony. With the realization that the Seven Cities of Gold was a myth, Spanish interest in the colony waned. Spoken language and the Catholic faith tied the colonists together. Religious images were of the utmost importance. The carving and painting of *bultos* and *retablos* for homes, churches, and *moradas* became an extraordinary and unique New Mexican art form. Due to space constraints, this chapter concentrates on this important Hispanic art form rather than other arts and crafts such as furniture making, metal work, and weaving.

Eastern painters like Albert Bierstadt and Thomas Moran traveled to the western territories. *Harper's* illustrations of New Mexico appeared in the late 1800s and created national interest in New Mexico and Santa Fe. The Santa Fe Railroad commissioned artists to do paintings for display in ticket offices and for reproduction on calendars.

Artists started coming here in the first years of the 20th century, but by 1915, the Anglo artists' and writers' community really began to grow after many came to Santa Fe for tuberculosis treatment. With the arrival of the Anglos, Santa Fe became the rich tri-cultural community it is today. It is one of the few places in the United States where Anglo culture never came to completely dominate. Instead, Hispanic and Indian culture continue to inspire the newcomers greatly.

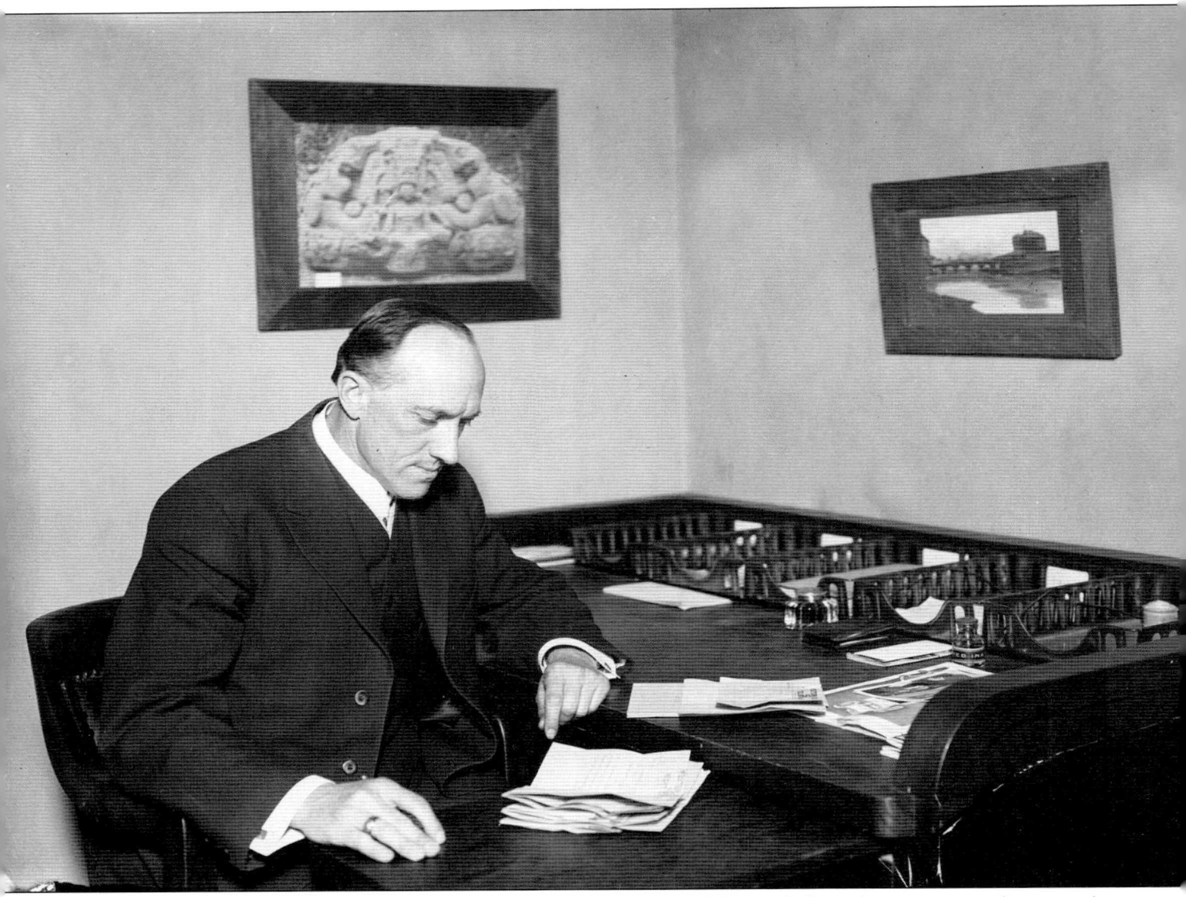

Edgar Lee Hewett (1885–1946) was the Museum of New Mexico's first director, simultaneously serving as director of the School of American (Archaeology) Research in Santa Fe. He was considered a preeminent scholar in Native American archaeology. He is quoted as saying, "In no other state of this union is the trend of life so clearly shaped by art as in New Mexico. Art has rescued this state from the commonplace and made it conscious of its own fine character."

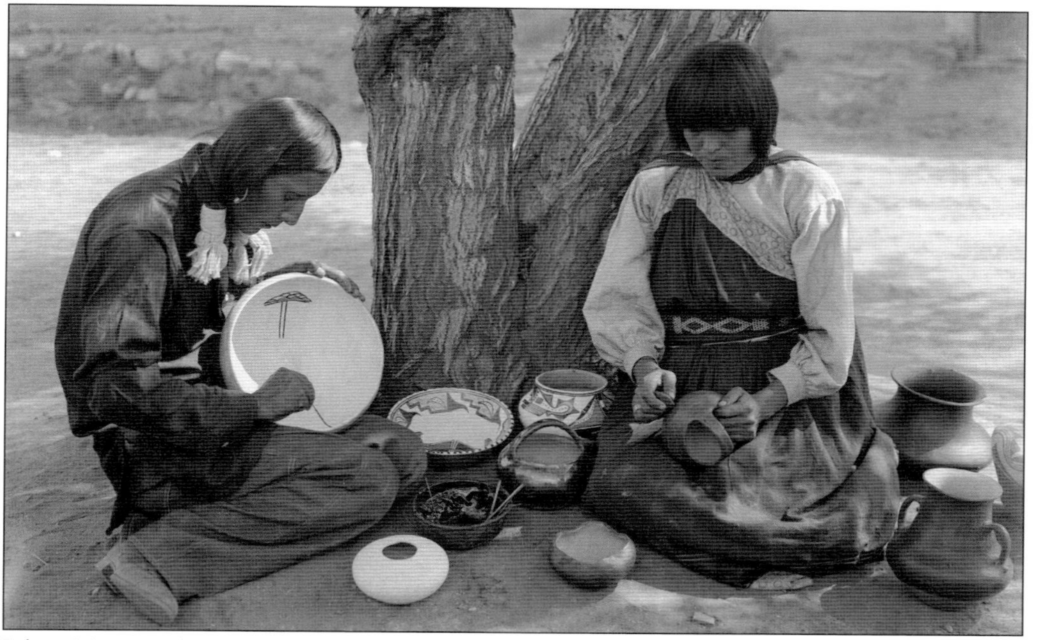

Julian Martinez (c. 1885–1943) and his wife, Maria Montoya Martinez (1887–1980), display their pottery at the patio of the Palace of the Governors. Both Maria and Julian are from the San Ildefonso Pueblo. The Martinezes and Edgar L. Hewett enjoyed a mutually beneficial relationship. This photograph was taken by Jesse Nusbaum in 1912. (Courtesy of Palace of the Governors Archives, 040814.)

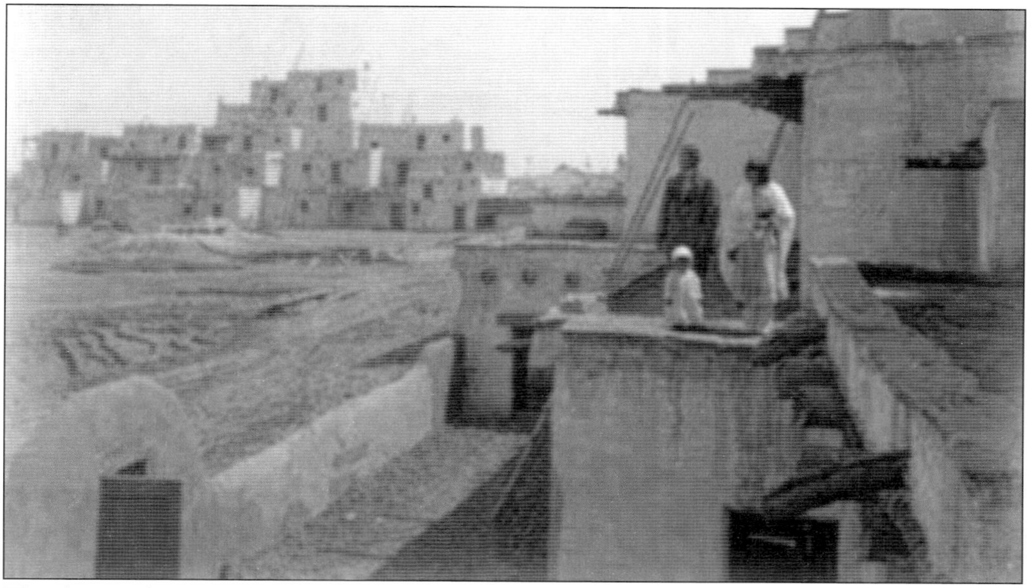

Thanks to Edgar L. Hewett, Julian and Maria Martinez, seen here with their young son, Tony, went to California to demonstrate the process of making their traditional pottery at the Indian Village as part of the Painted Desert Exhibit at the 1915 San Diego Exposition. The couple also participated in the 1904 St. Louis World's Fair and the 1934 Chicago World's Fair. This photograph was taken by Jesse Nusbaum. (Courtesy of Palace of the Governors Archives, 060411.)

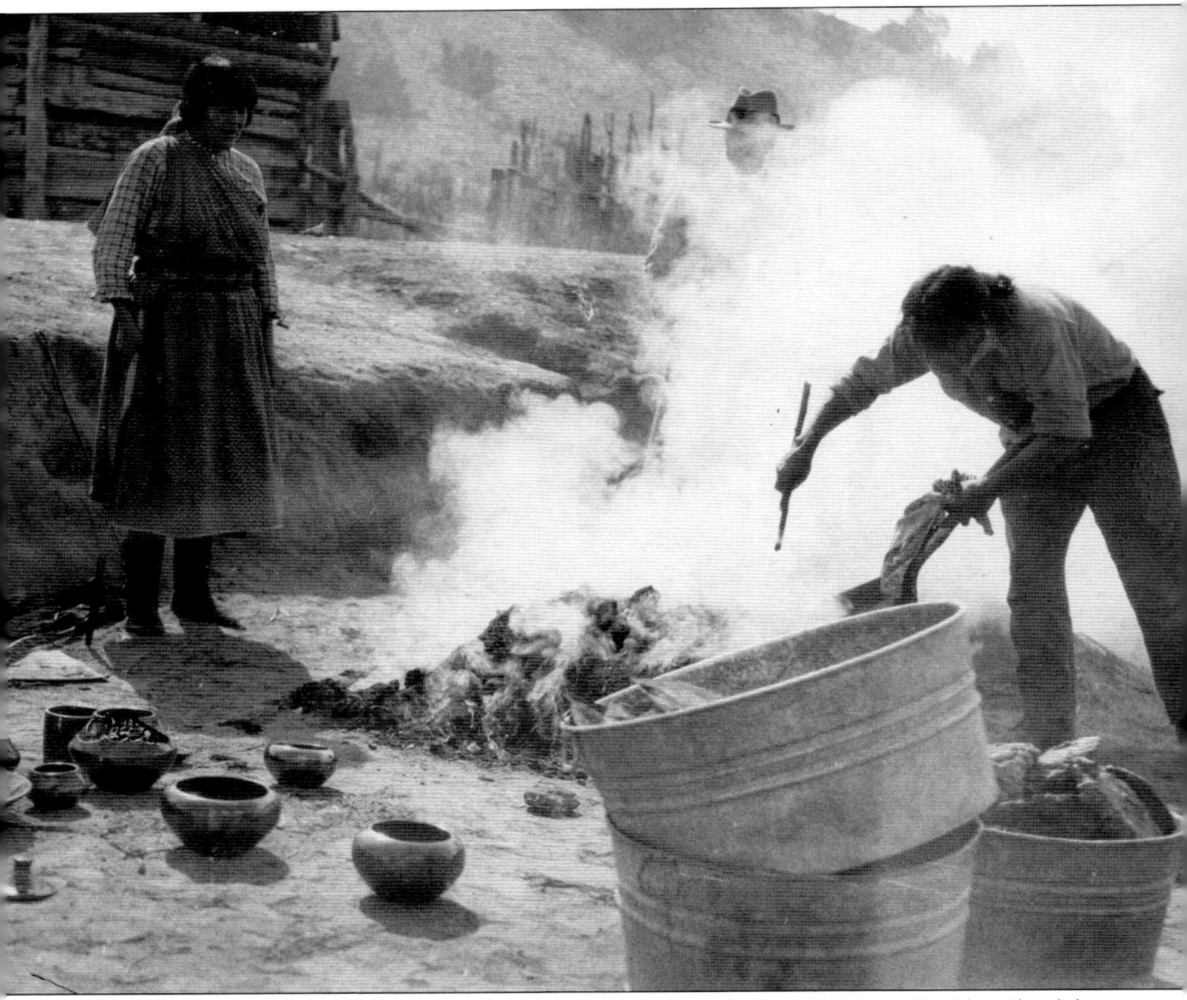

Maria and Julian Martinez demonstrate open-pit firing at the San Ildefonso Pueblo. This labor-intensive process occurs after the pots are formed. Pots are carefully stacked on top of an iron grill. Wood and dry cow manure are ignited, and once the fire has reached maximum heat, it is smothered using ash and/or cow manure. (Courtesy of Palace of the Governors Archive, 030467.)

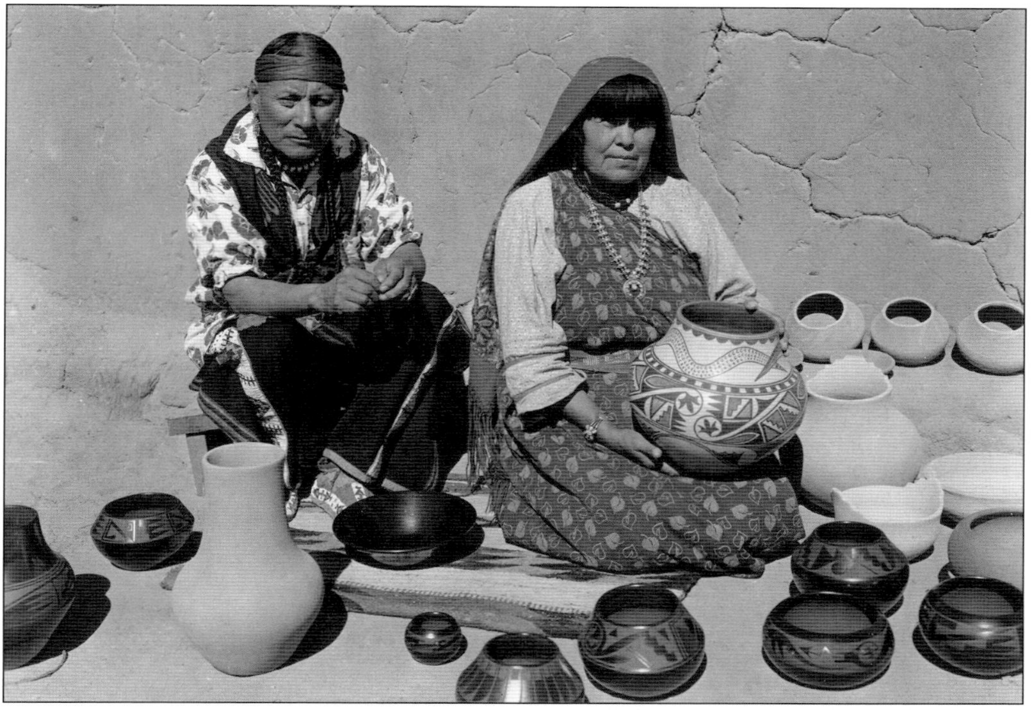

Julian and Maria Martinez are seen here displaying their traditional black-on-black pottery at the San Ildefonso Pueblo in 1938. (Courtesy of the Palace of the Governors Archive, 004591.)

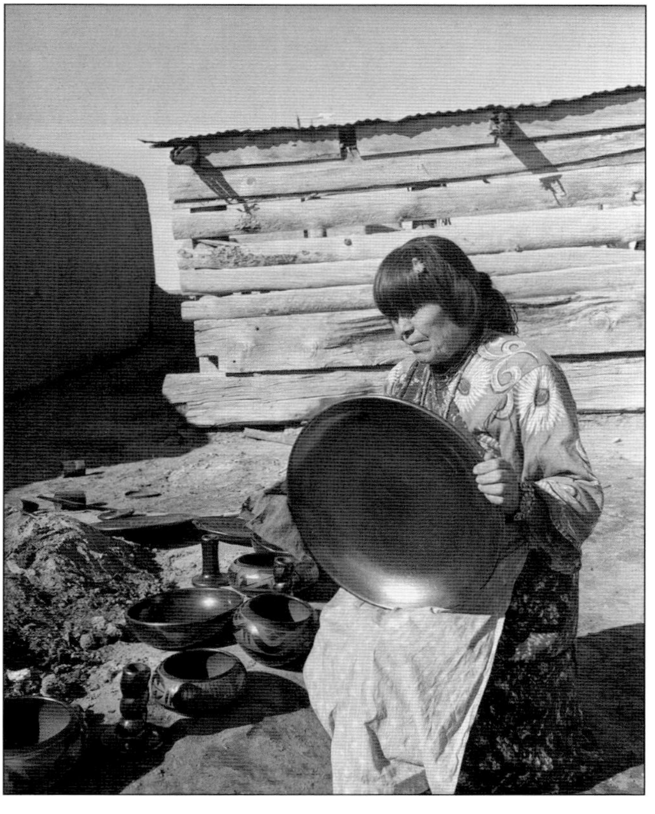

Maria Martinez holds a large pot at San Ildefonso Pueblo in 1950. (Courtesy of the Palace of the Governors Archives, 012180.)

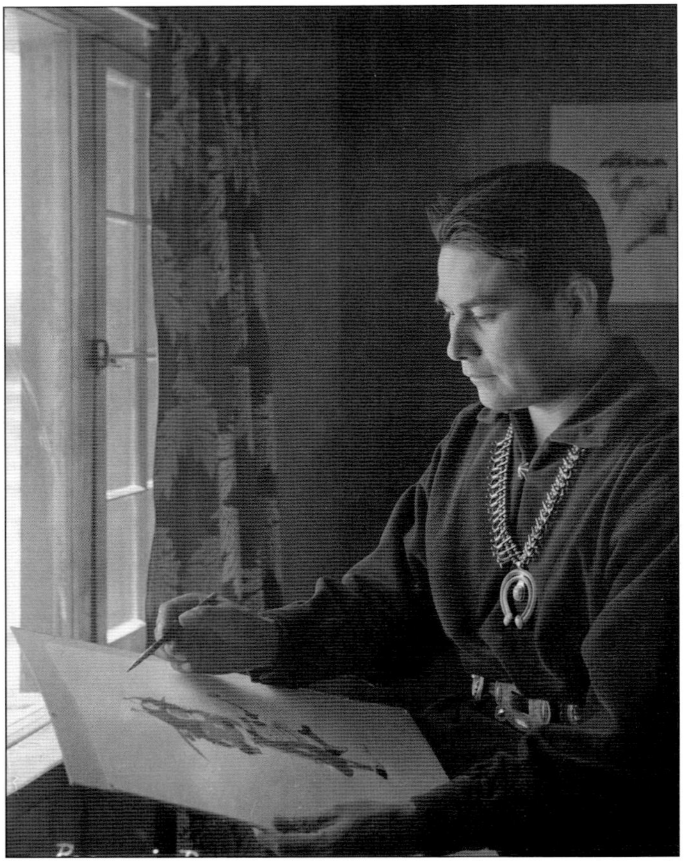

After Julian Martinez's death in 1943, Maria worked with her daughter-in-law, Santana, who assumed Julian's painted decorative work. In 1956, their son, artist and potter Tony Martinez—also known as Popovi Da—helped market her work by establishing a shop on the San Ildefonso Pueblo and lecturing throughout the country on the black-on-black pottery process.

Maria Martinez and her son, Popovi Da, teach pottery class at the San Ildefonso Pueblo in 1935. The Martinez family was instrumental in resurrecting this important art form, which benefited many Pueblo families culturally as well as financially. (From the T. Harmon Parkhurst Collection. Courtesy of the Palace of the Governors Archive, 001038.)

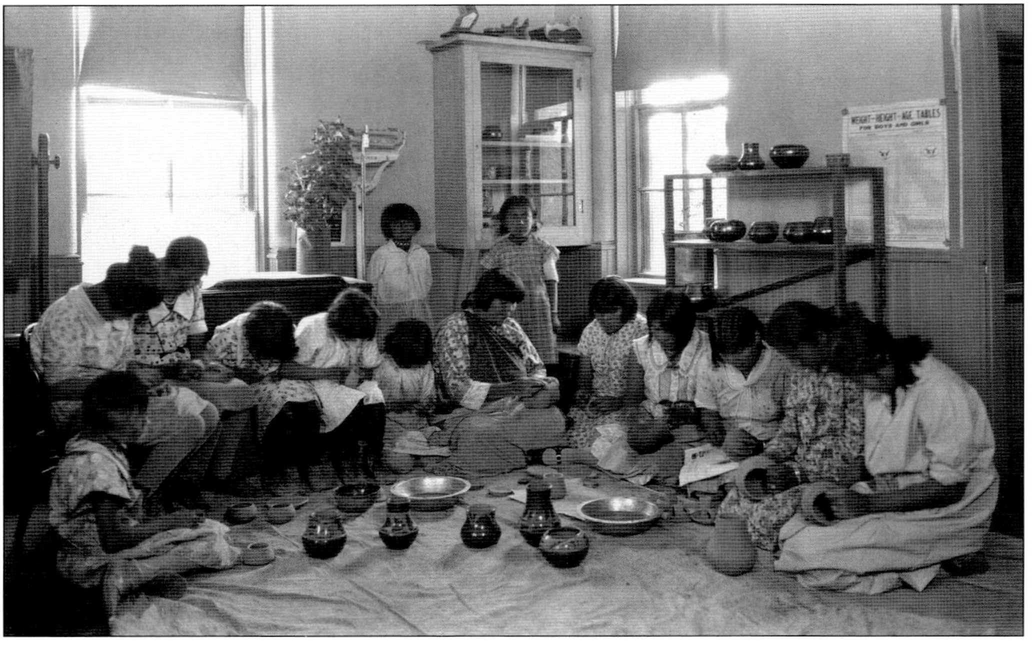

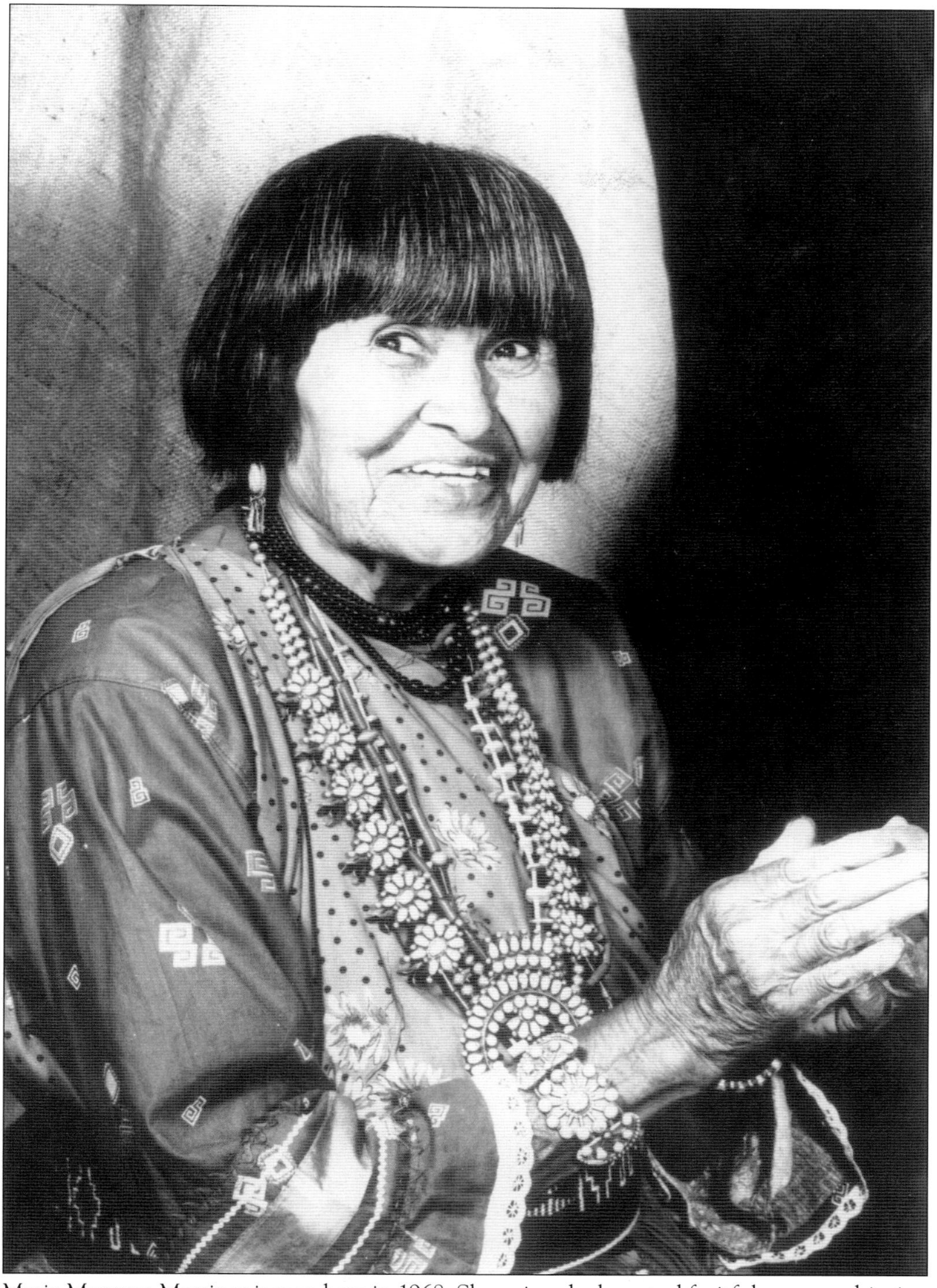

Maria Montoya Martinez is seen here in 1968. She enjoyed a long and fruitful career, achieving worldwide fame for her pottery. (Courtesy of the Palace of the Governors Archive, 131843.)

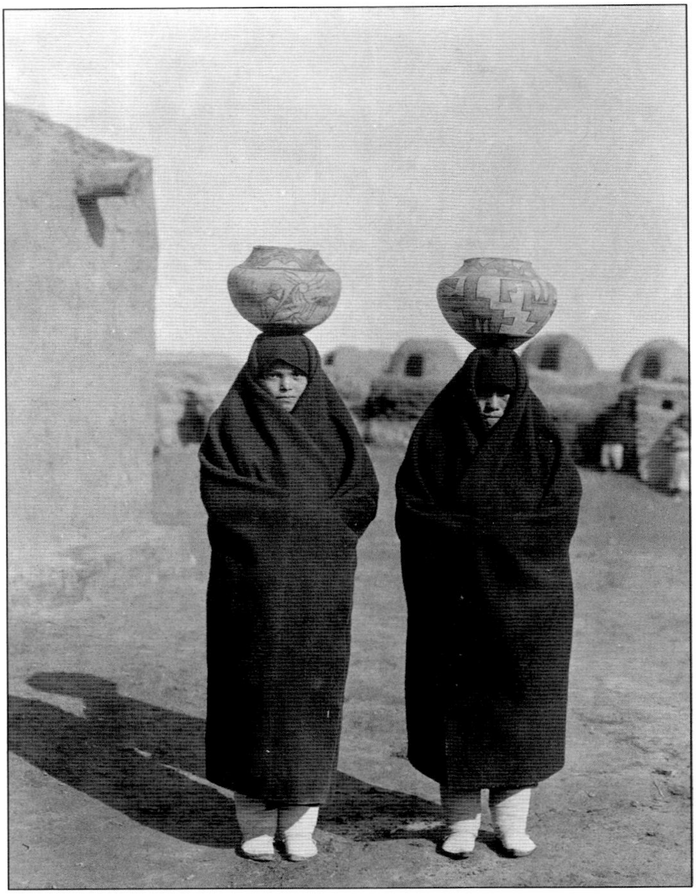

Two Zuni water carriers use beautifully decorated utilitarian pottery to transfer water skillfully on their heads. Zuni pottery is distinguished by the use of white to gray clay, which is then painted with a bright white slip, followed by black and brown mineral paint. Dark red is often used as an accent.

The Zuni woman below builds a traditional coiled clay pot. This process begins with rolling rope-like clay coils. Starting at the base and building up, the pot is formed with a cylinder of coils.

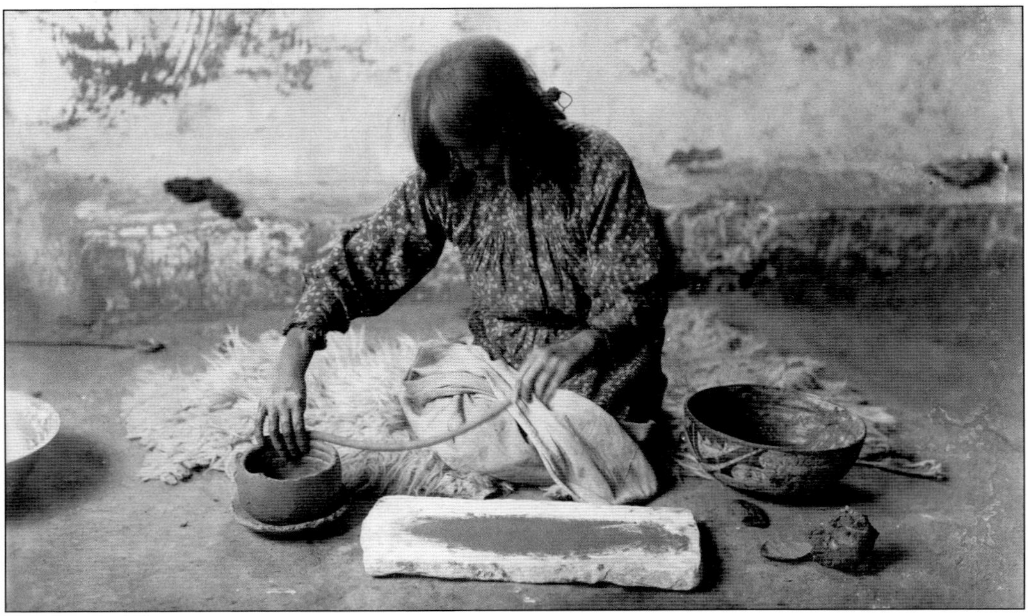

A Zuni woman skillfully balances a large ornate *olla* pot on her head. Zuni designs emphasize the function of their pottery, while still achieving beautifully artistic creations.

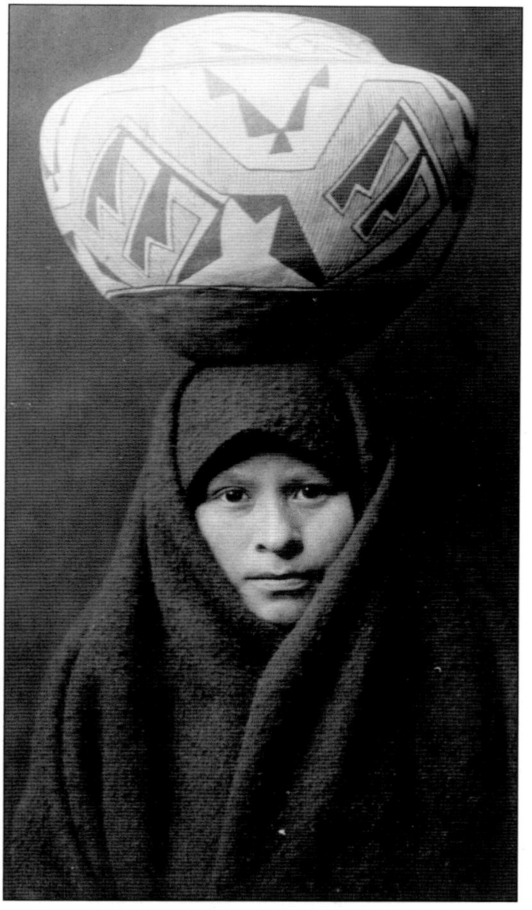

Below, a group of Anglos have pitched tents at Zuni Pueblo. Five examples of ollas, large water-storage pots, are on display.

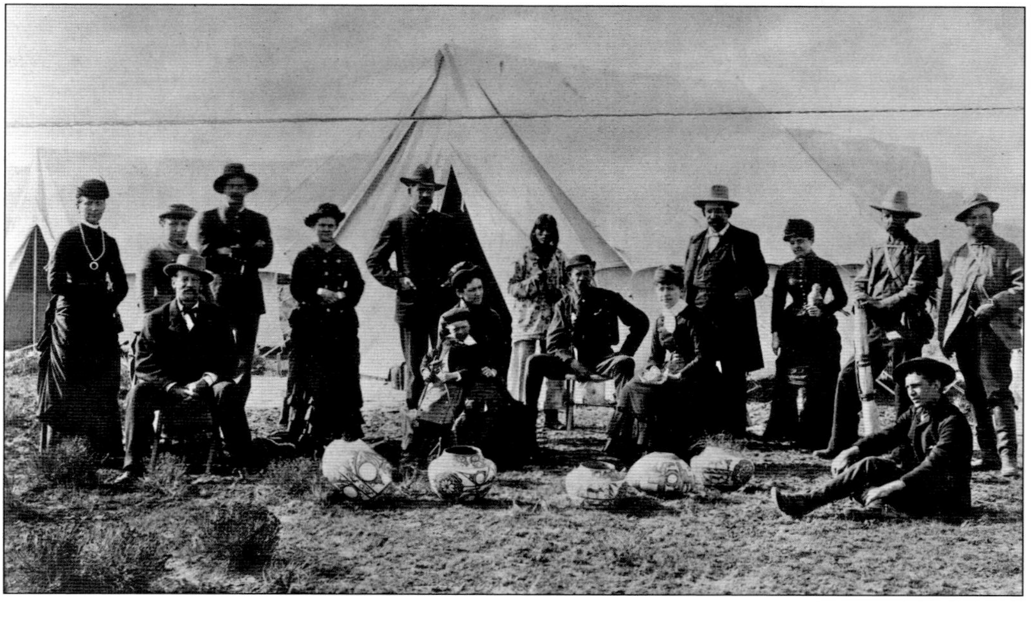

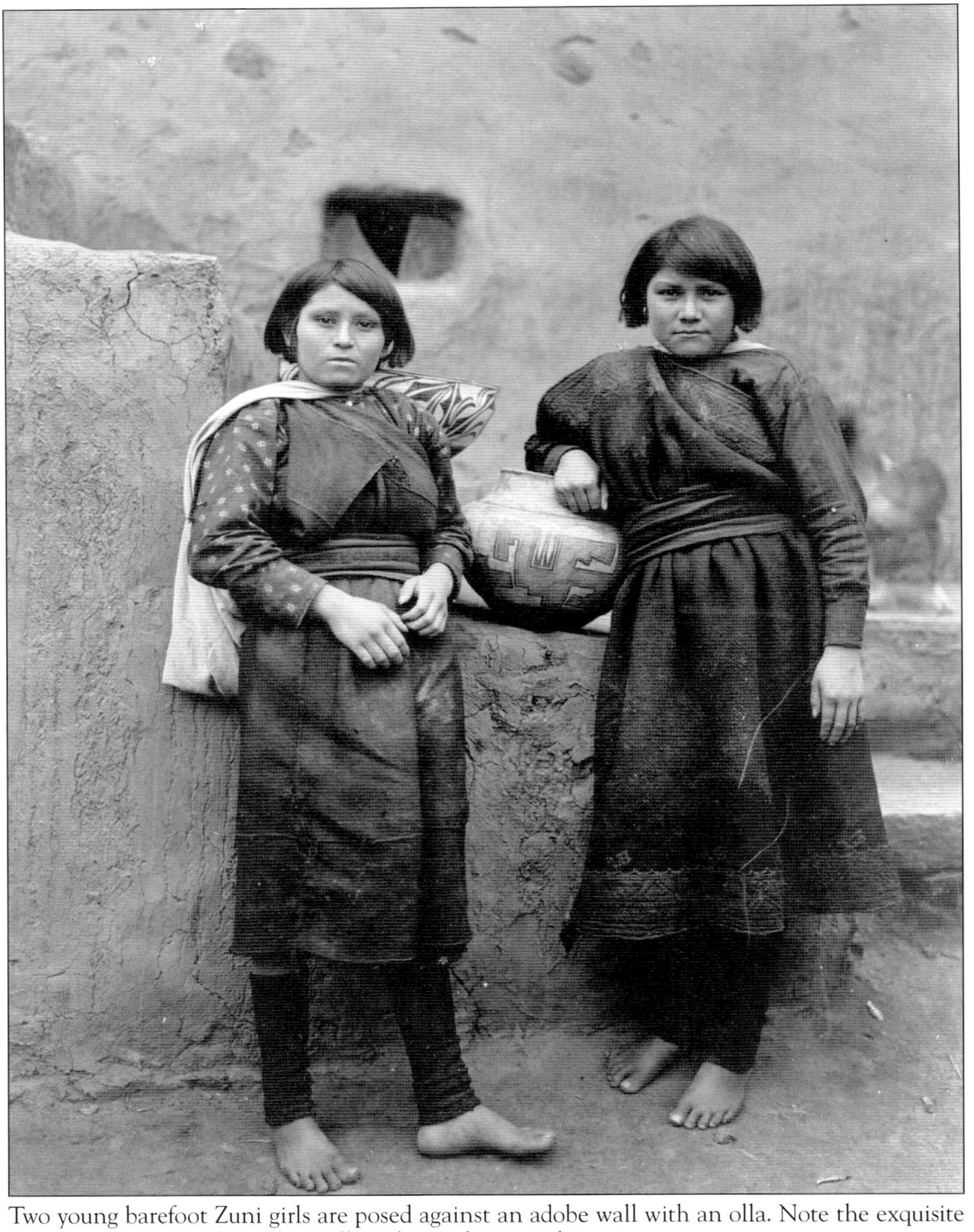

Two young barefoot Zuni girls are posed against an adobe wall with an olla. Note the exquisite detail of design on what is basically only a utilitarian object.

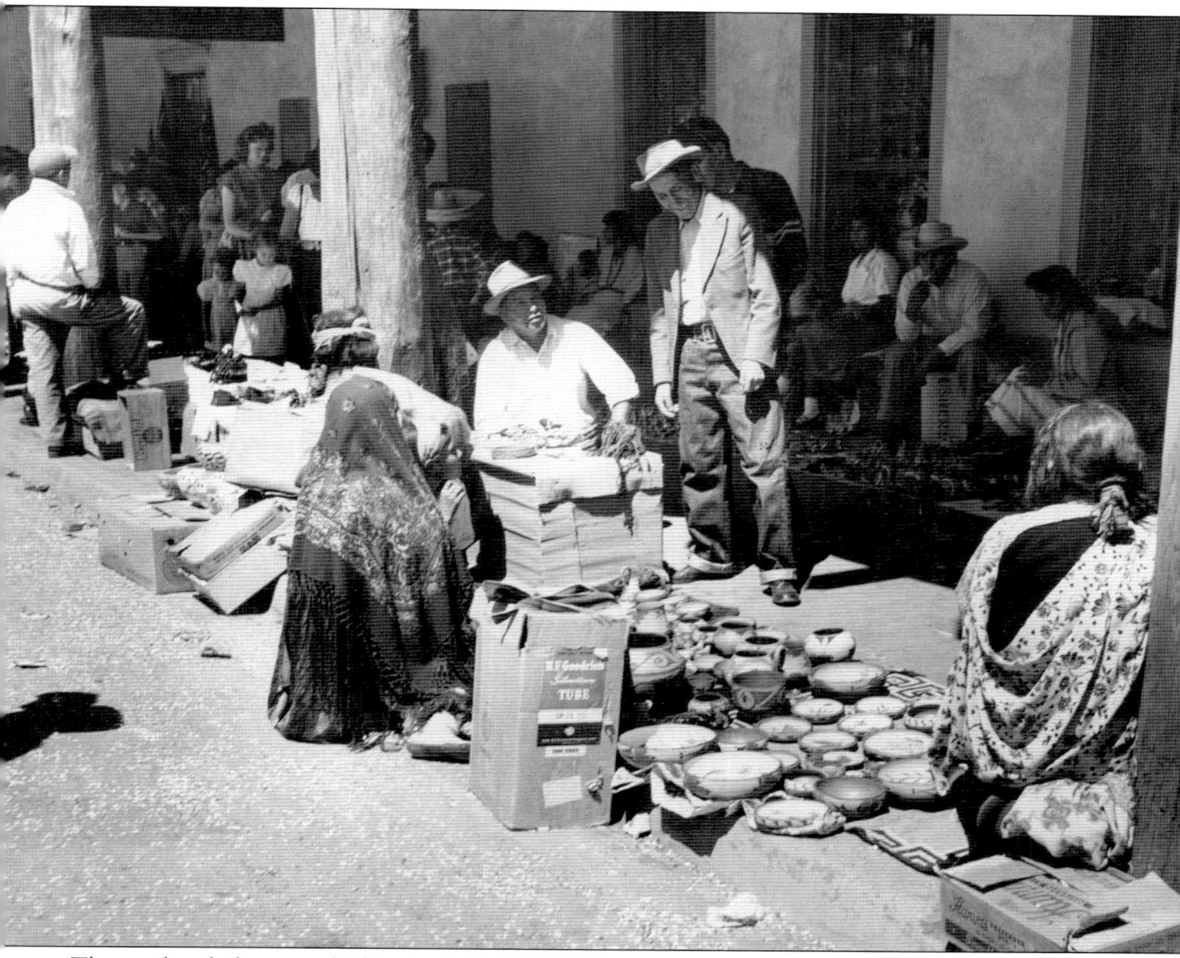

This undated photograph shows tourists looking at native pottery in a market-like atmosphere. Eventually, the popularity of Pueblo arts and crafts resulted in Santa Fe's internationally recognized annual Indian Market.

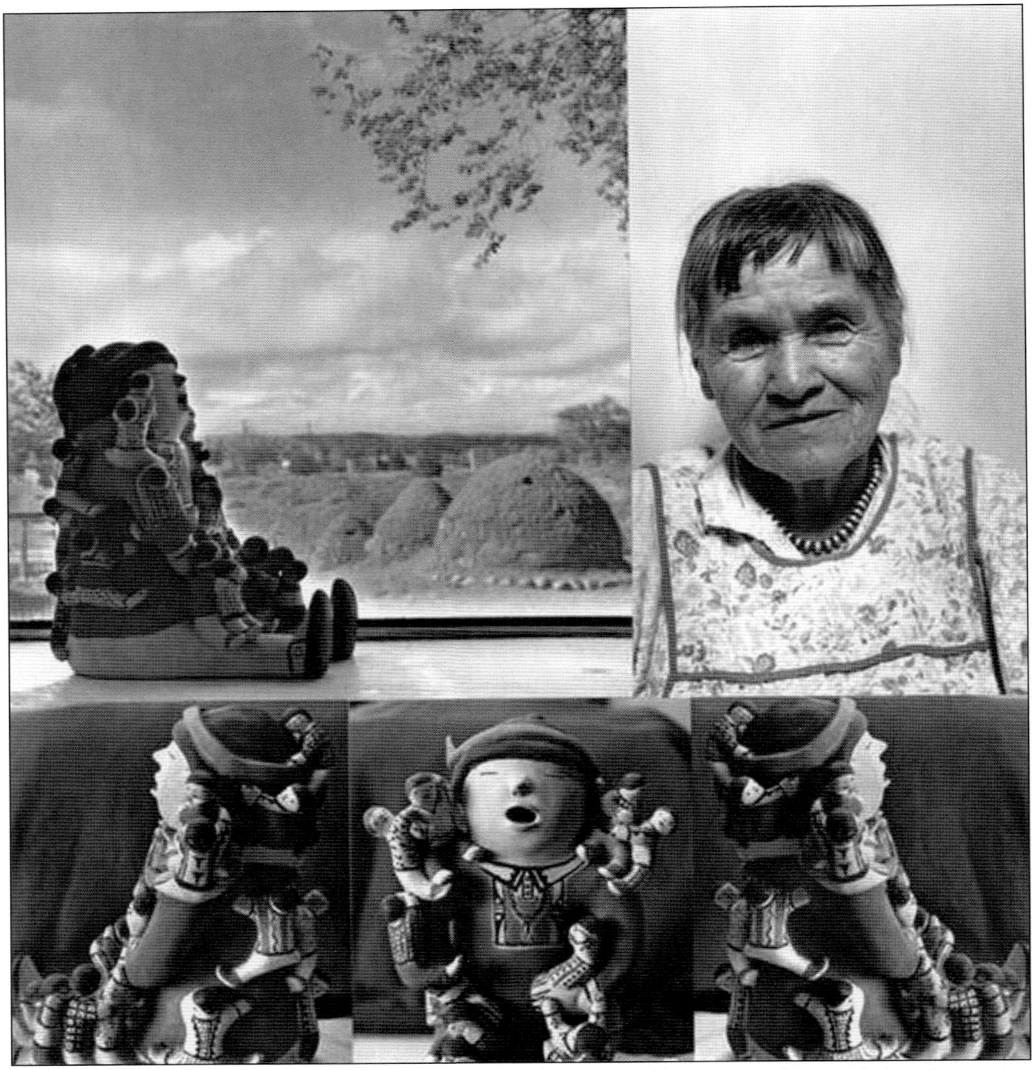

This collage shows legendary potter Helen Cordero from Cochiti Pueblo with her figurative storytelling images. Storytelling dolls are clay figures specific to New Mexico Pueblo people. Cordero is credited with creating the first contemporary storytelling doll, which she made of her grandfather, a tribal storyteller. (Courtesy of Palace of the Governor Archive, 189270.)

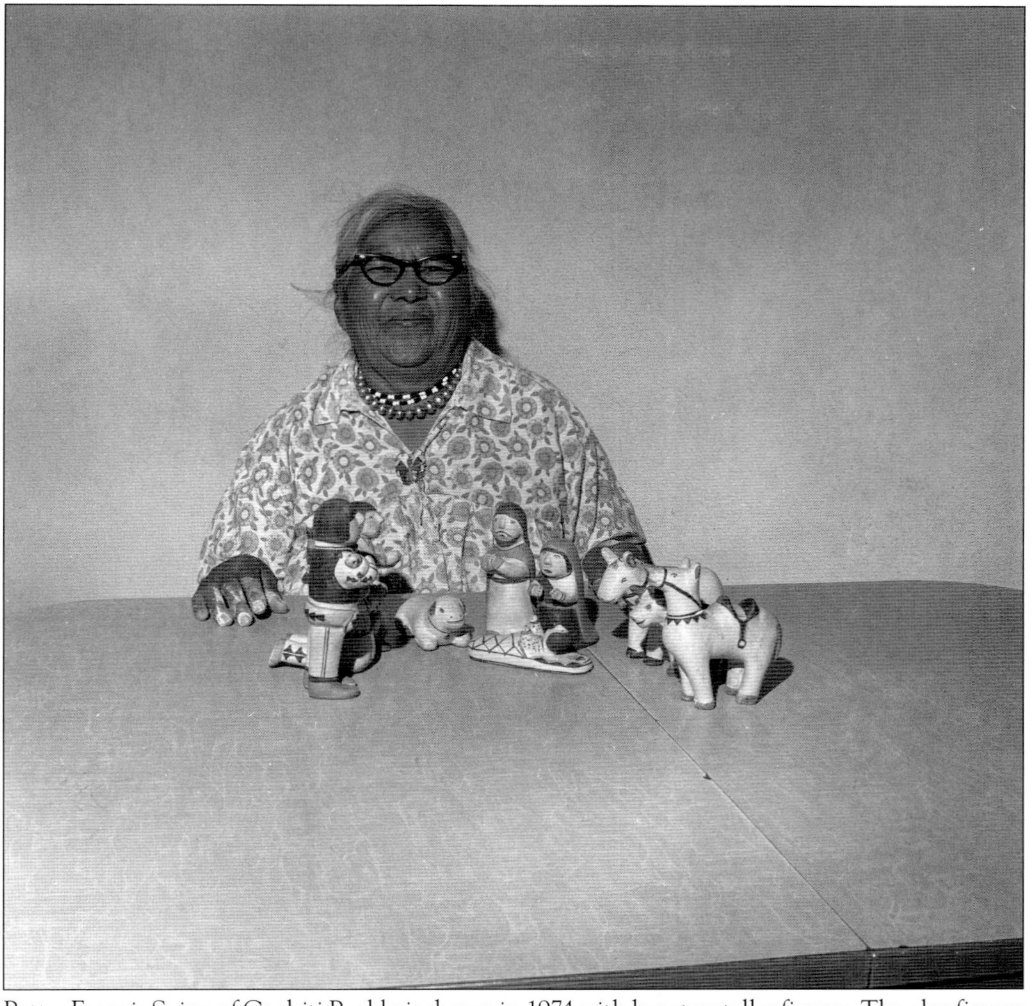

Potter Francis Suina of Cochiti Pueblo is shown in 1974 with her storyteller figures. The clay figures are often of a man or woman with their mouth open, surrounded by smaller figures of children to whom stories are being told. (Courtesy of Palace of the Governor Archive, 157155.)

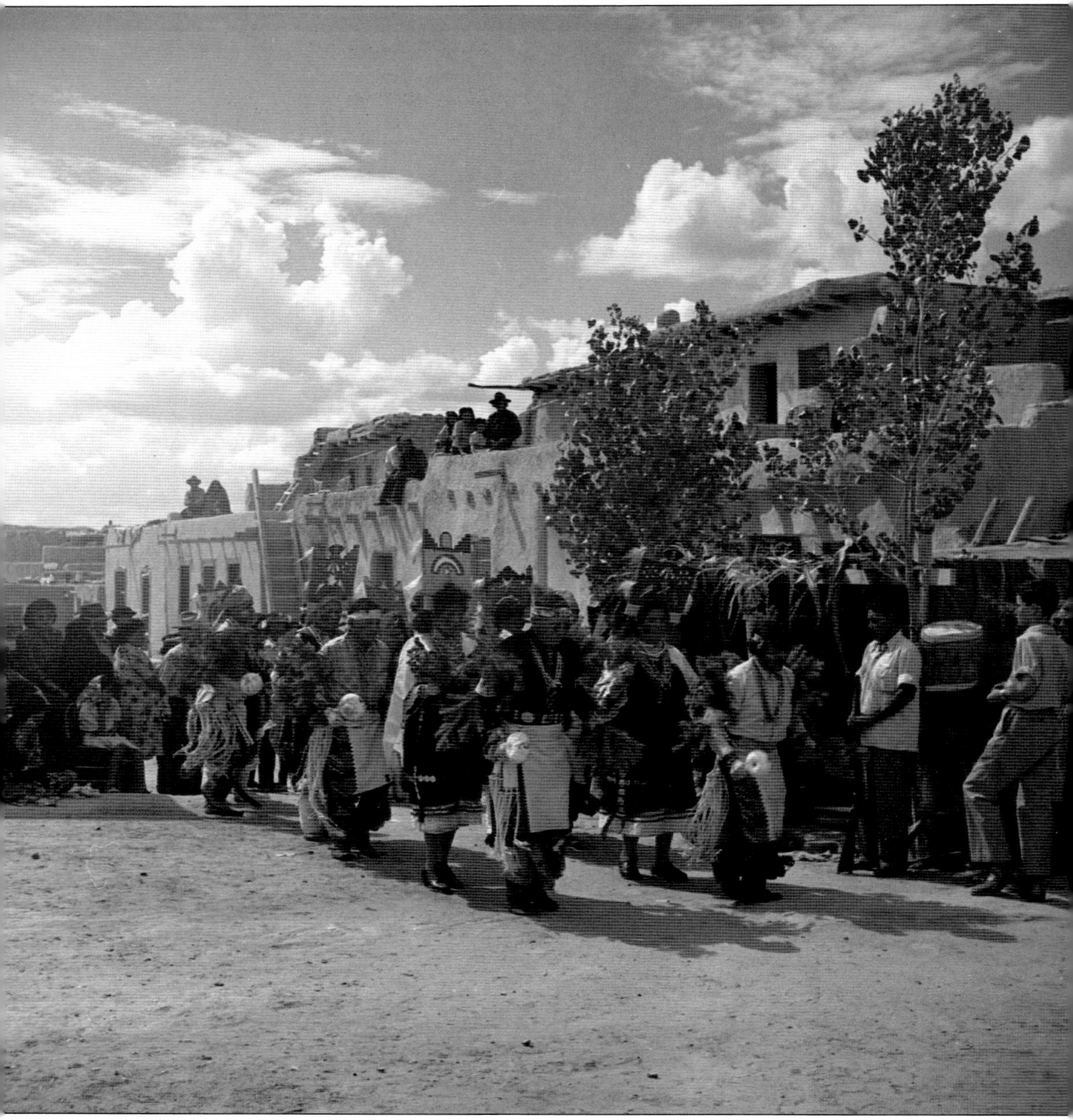

In this image of the Acoma Pueblo Feast Dance, women dancers wear *tablitas*, artfully painted wooden headdresses with designs reflective of their clan affiliation. All Pueblo tribes used tablitas for identification during ceremonies. Native costumes appear to have a transformative power for the dancers.

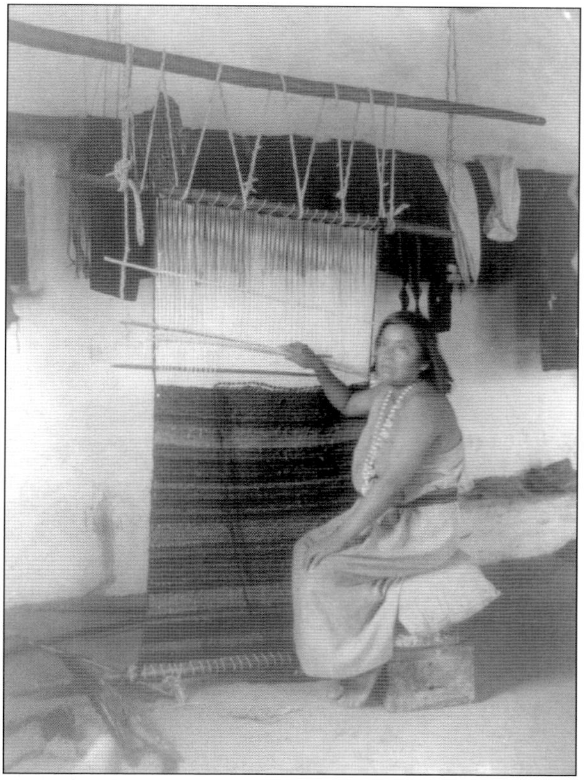

Although this photograph shows a female weaver creating a heavy-wearing blanket for warmth, at Zuni Pueblo, men are frequently weavers as well.

This photograph shows a Navajo artist working on a sand painting, also known in Navajo as a "place where the Gods come and go." Sand painting is used in religious rituals, including healing ceremonies.

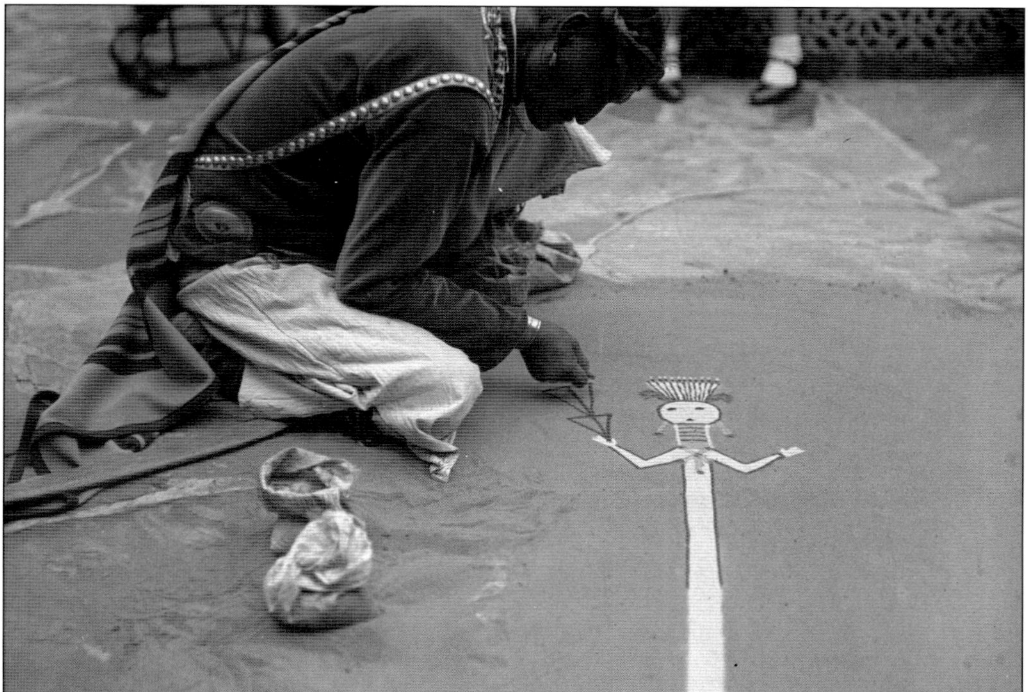

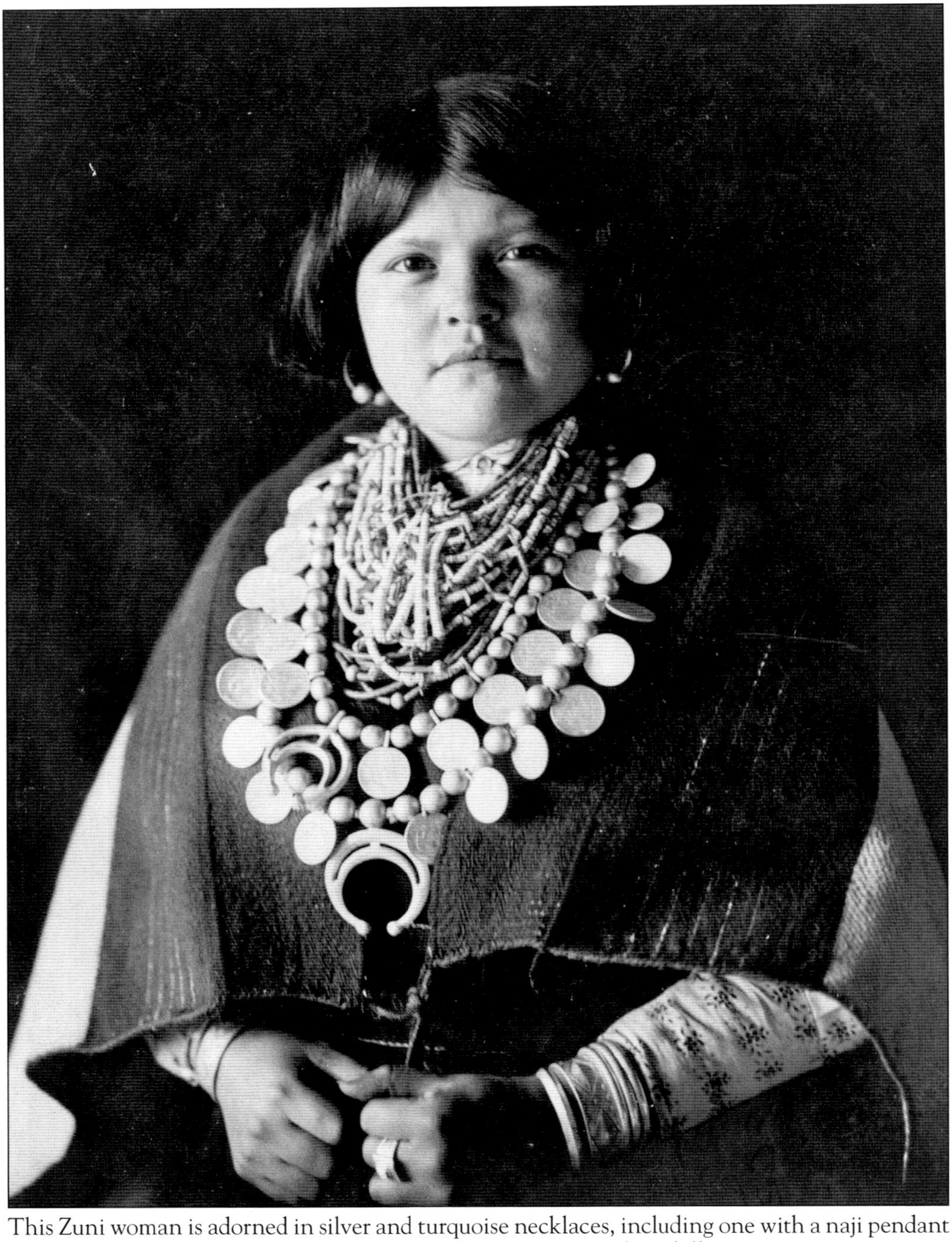

This Zuni woman is adorned in silver and turquoise necklaces, including one with a naji pendant and large silver coins—possibly Mexican pesos or American silver dollars.

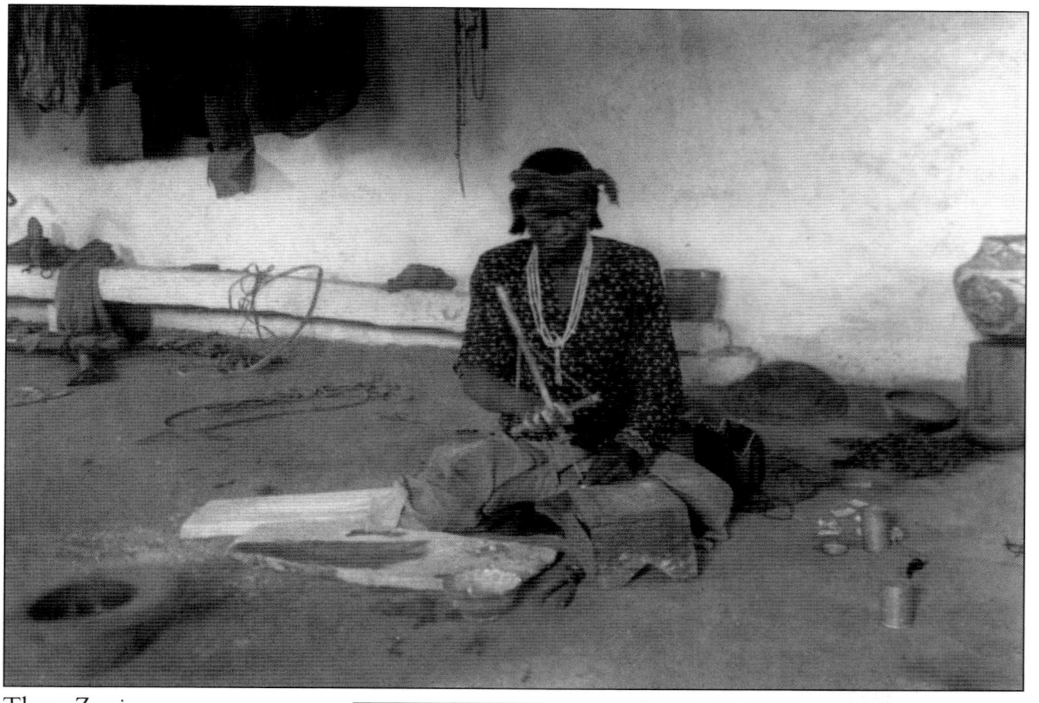

These Zuni men make turquoise beads using a hand drill.

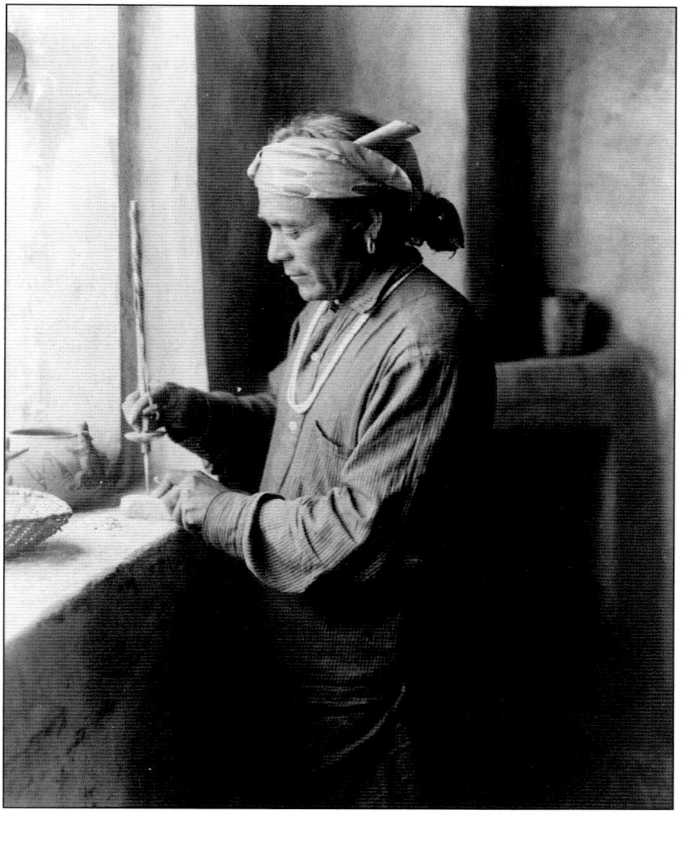

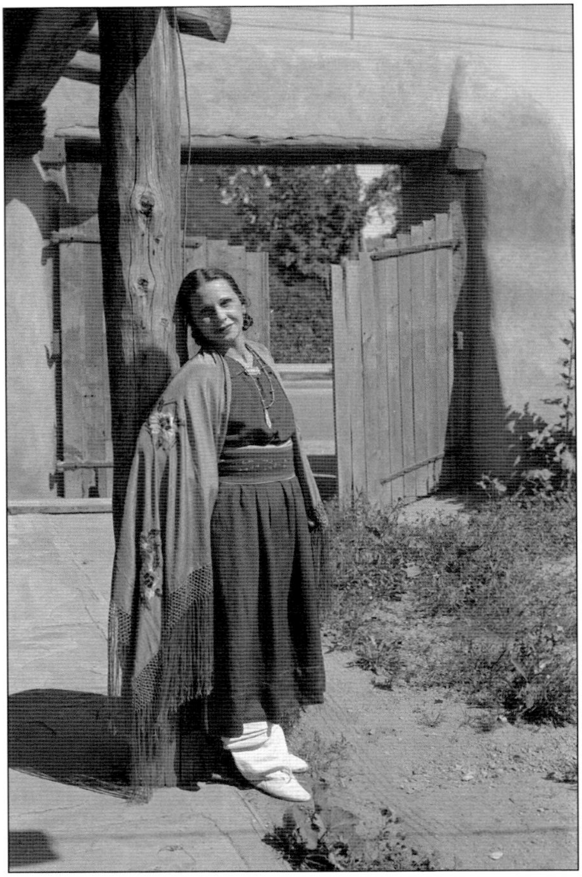

Pop Chalee (Tiwa for "Blue Flower"), also known as Merina Lujan (1906–1993), was a painter, muralist, singer, and performer whose father was from Taos Pueblo and whose mother was a predominantly Swiss Mormon. She studied art with Dorothy Dunn at the Santa Fe Indian School. (Courtesy of Palace of the Governors Archive.)

Zia Pueblo artist Velino Shije Herrera (1902–1973) attended the Santa Fe Indian School. His paintings were shown at the Museum of New Mexico in 1919 and at the New York Society of Independent Artists show in 1920. His work was widely exhibited in the United States and Europe. He and five other artists were commissioned to paint 2,200 feet of murals for the Department of the Interior's main building in Washington, DC. Herrera was awarded the French government's Ordre des Palms Academiques in 1954. (From the T. Harmon Parkhurst Collection, courtesy of the Palace of the Governors Archive, 094468.)

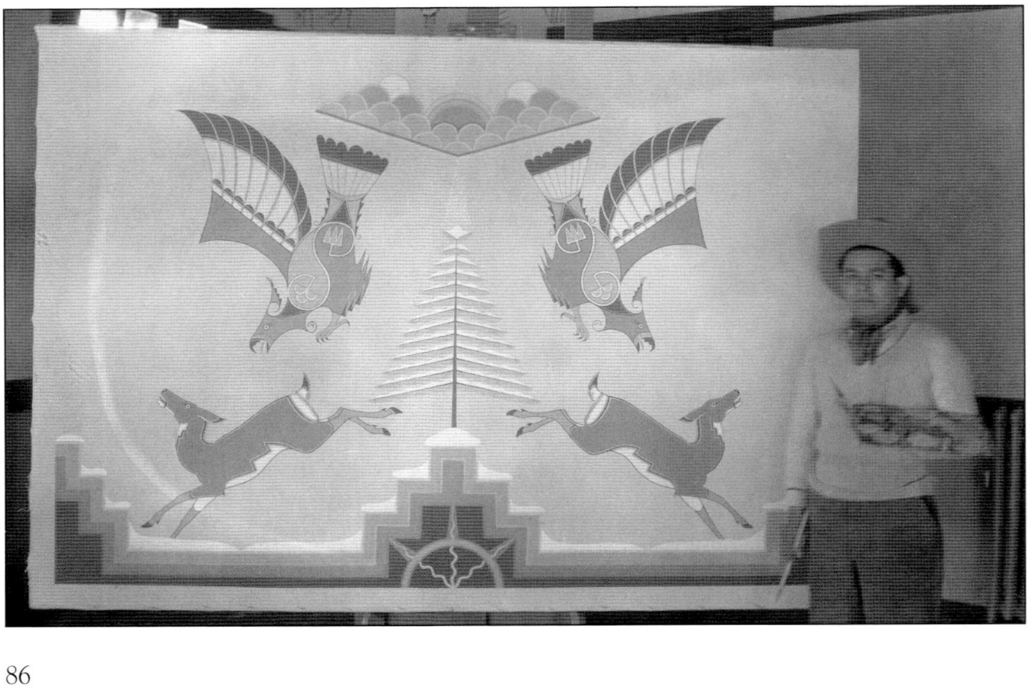

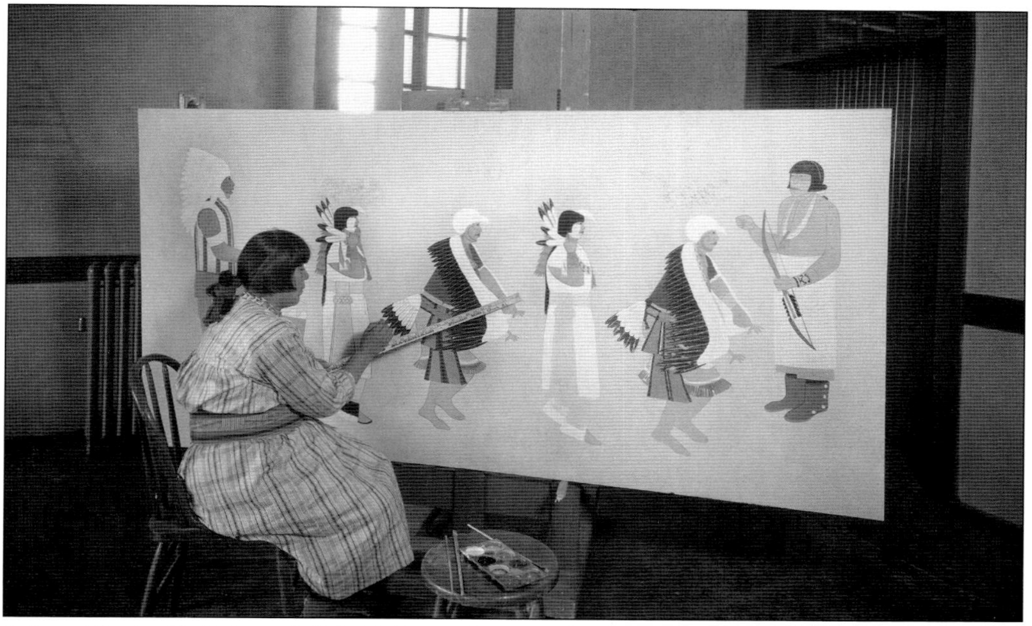

Painter Tonita Vigil Pena (1893–1949) was born at the San Ildefonso Pueblo and raised at the Cochiti Pueblo, where she lived for the rest of her life. She was a member of a group of self-taught painters along with Julian Martinez, Alfonso Robel, and Crecencio Martinez. Pena was considered one of the most important female artists of that period. (From the T. Harmon Parkhurst Collection, courtesy of the Palace of the Governors Archive, 073945.)

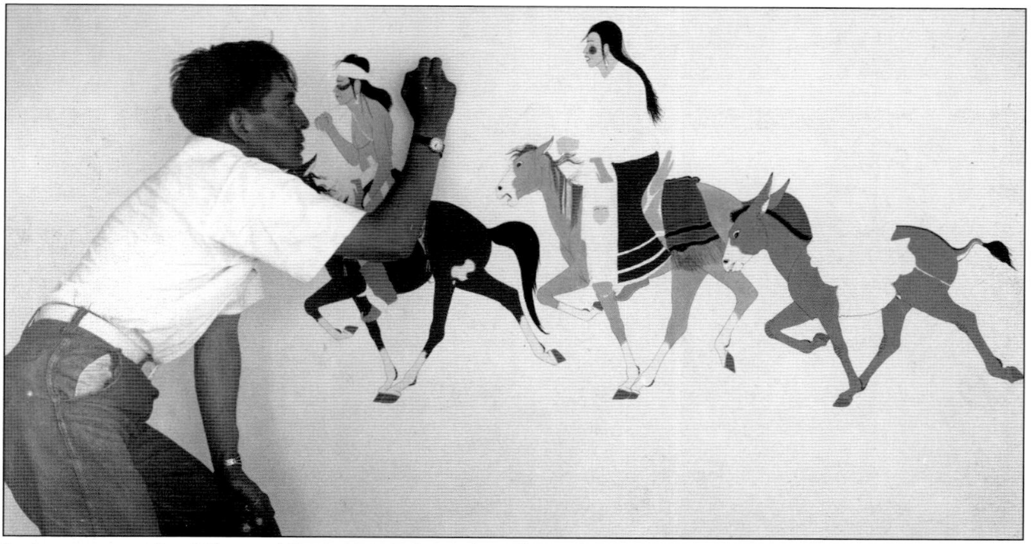

Indian artist Alan Houser (1914–1994), from the Chiricahua Apache tribe, became very well known as a sculptor. This photograph shows Houser at Santa Fe's Indian School, which he attended in the mid-1930s. He was in the 1939 World's Fair and at the Golden Gate International Exposition. Houser painted murals in the main Department of the Interior building in Washington, DC, and received a Guggenheim fellowship. Beginning in 1962, he taught for 13 years at the Santa Fe Institute of American Indian Arts (IAIA), and in 1992, he became the first Native American to receive a National Medal of the Arts. (Courtesy of the Palace of the Governors Archive.)

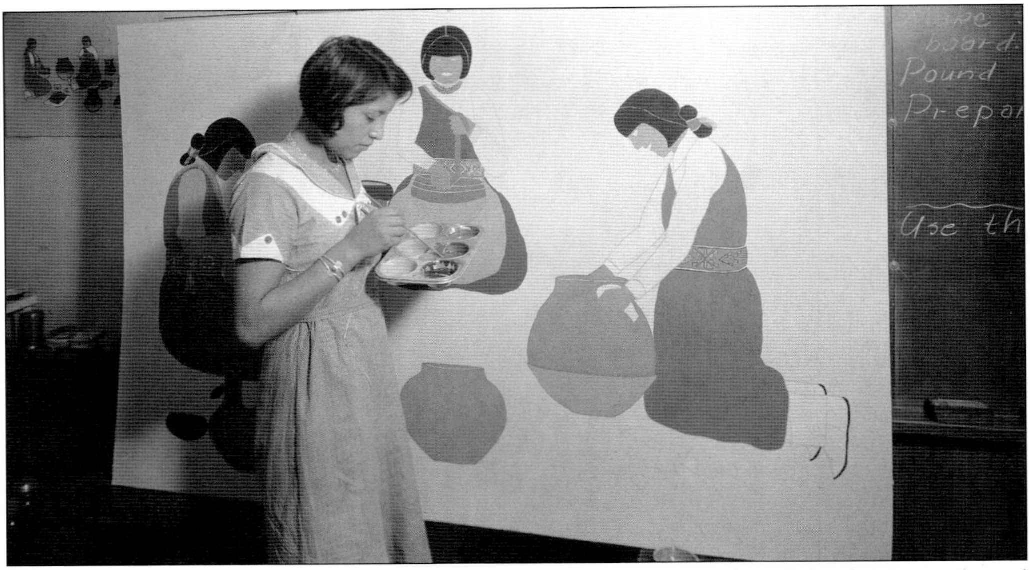

This photograph shows a young Indian art student at Santa Fe's Indian School. Many talented Pueblo Indians have attended this school. (Courtesy of Palace of the Governors Archive.)

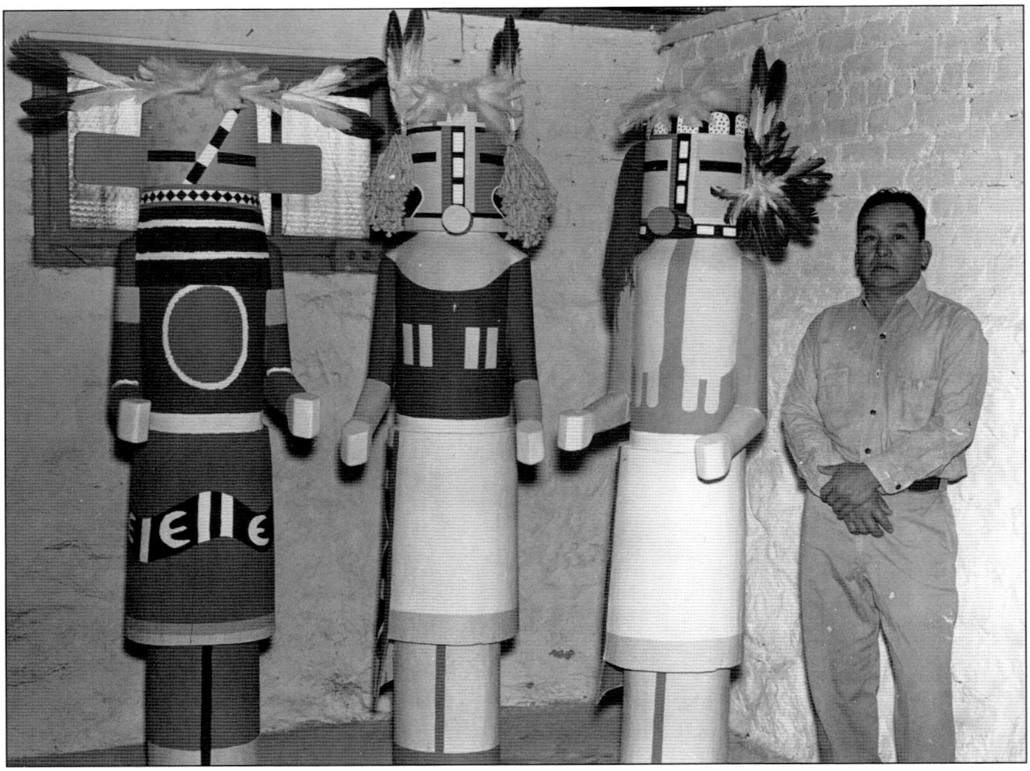

Hopi artist Aldred Puyesva poses with his unusually large-scale Kachina dolls at the Santa Fe Indian School in 1955. Kachina dolls are used in home altars and to teach the pantheon of gods to Hopi children. They became a source of art and income for many Hopi carvers. (From the Harold Hanson Collection. Courtesy of the Palace of the Governors Archive, HP.2009.90.11.)

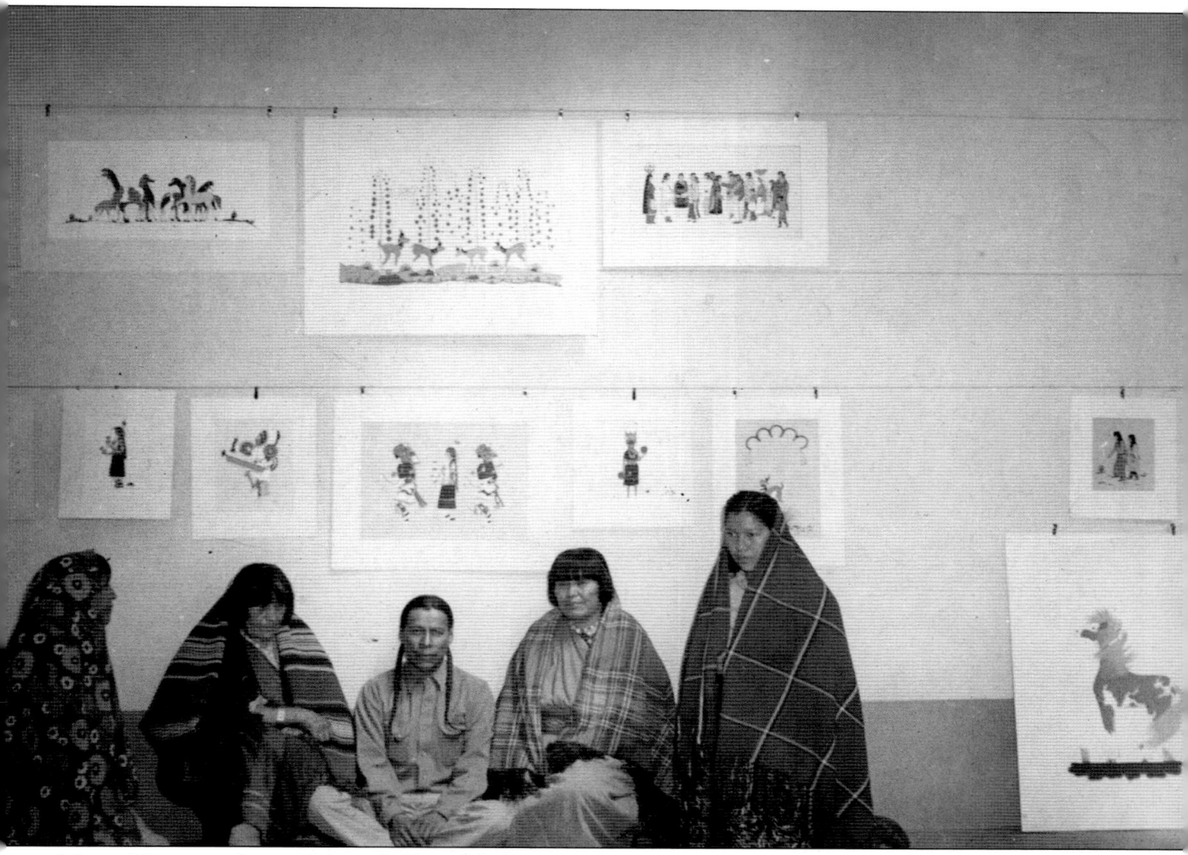

Maria Martinez (second from left) and her son, Adam (third from left), look at student artwork at the Santa Fe Indian School in 1944. The Martinez family was instrumental in reinstating the San Ildefonso Pueblo's art of black-on-black pottery. (Courtesy of Palace of the Governors Archive, 020792.)

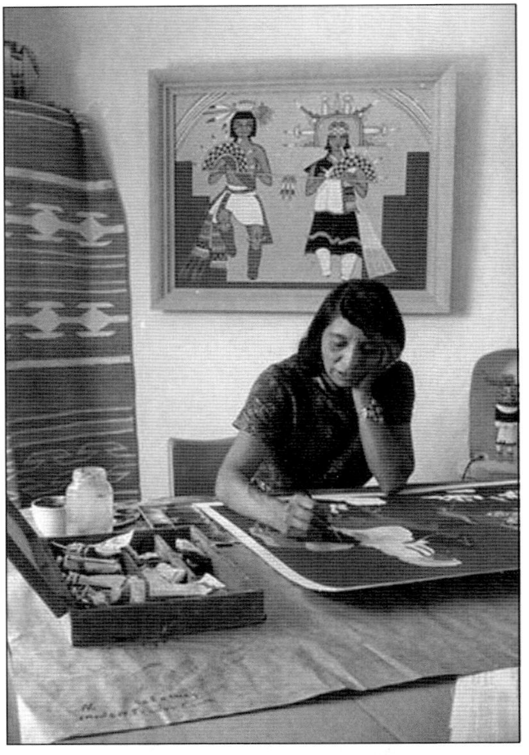

Painter Pabilta Velarde was born in 1918 at Santa Clara Pueblo. She painted a mural for the 1933 Chicago World's Fair at age 15. In 1935, she attended the Santa Fe Indian School and as a young artist toured with Ernest Thompson Seton. Velarde became a painter, illustrator, and author. Along with Velino Shije Herrera, she received the French government's Ordre des Palms Academiques. (Courtesy of the Palace of the Governors, 174201.)

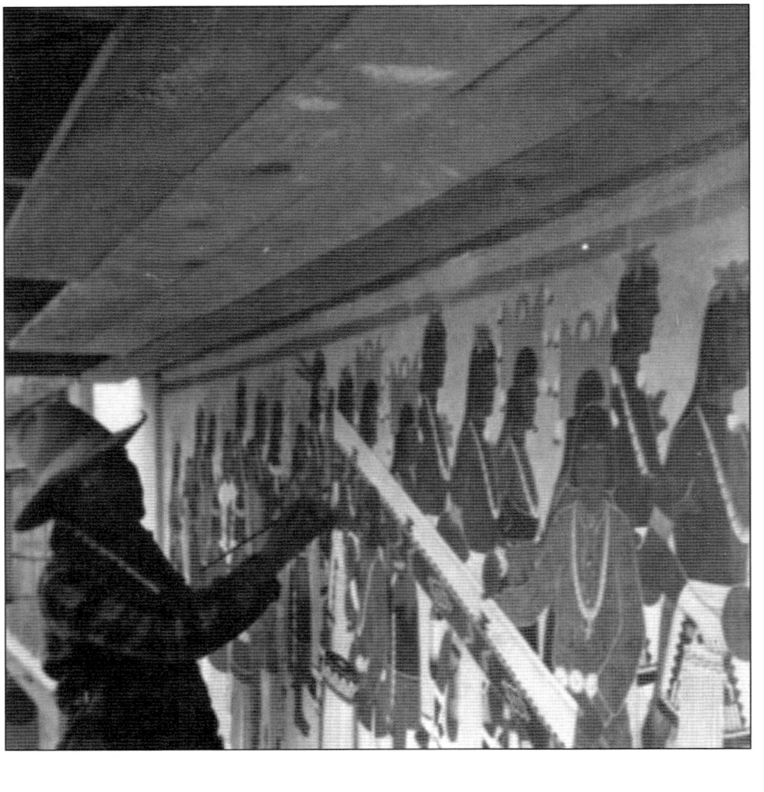

Muralist Alfonso Roybal (also known as Awa Tsireh) paints the corn dance for John Gaw Meem and Olive Rush in Albuquerque. Roybal was born in 1895 at San Ildefonso Pueblo, was closely associated with Zia Pueblo artist Velino Shije Herrera, and was one of the early-20th-century Santa Fe painters. His work is in the collection of the Museum of Modern Art in New York City. He died in 1955.

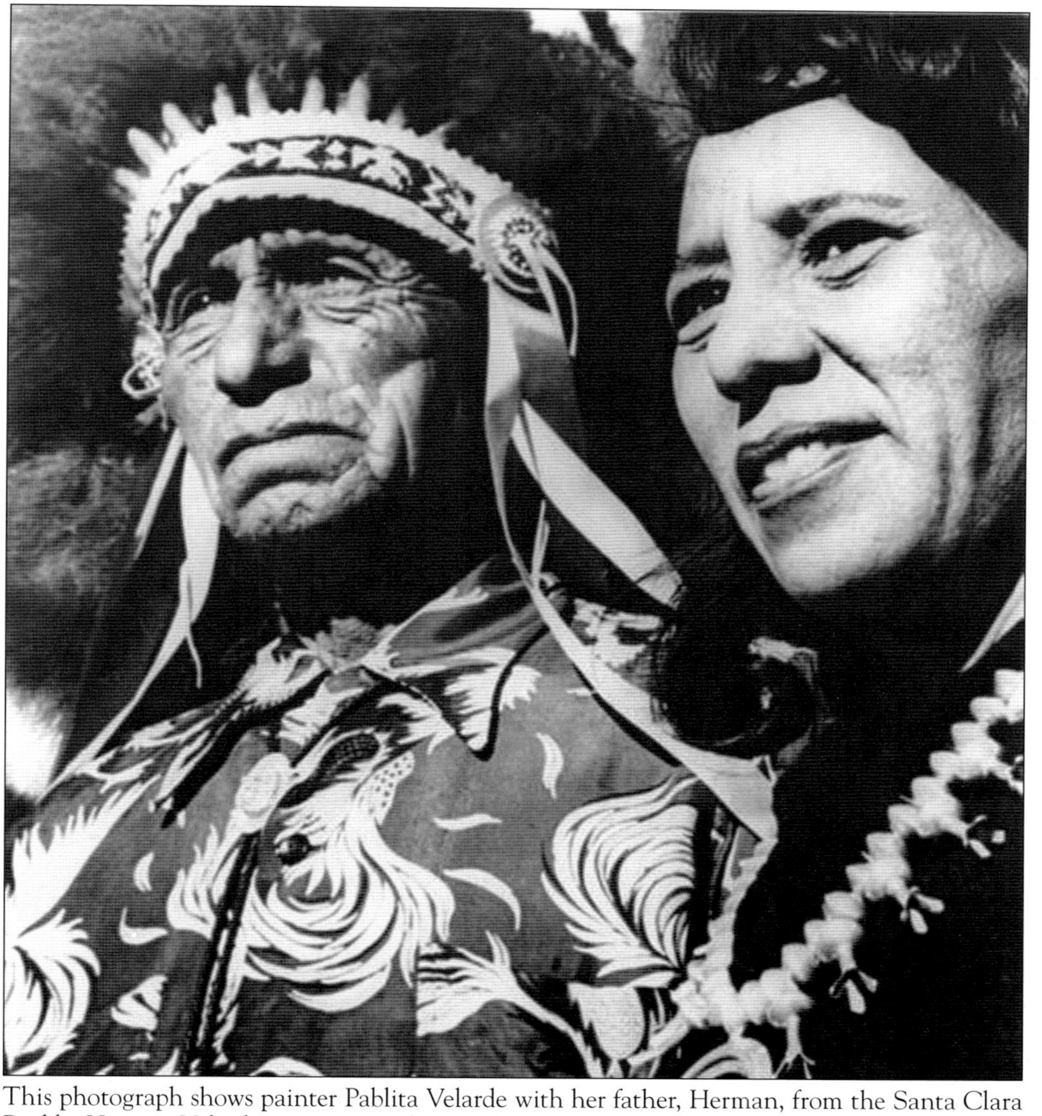

This photograph shows painter Pablita Velarde with her father, Herman, from the Santa Clara Pueblo. Herman Velarde is wearing a Plains Indian outfit and a shirt made of floral fabric, popular clothing among Pueblo Indians. (Courtesy of Palace of the Governors Archive, 151997.)

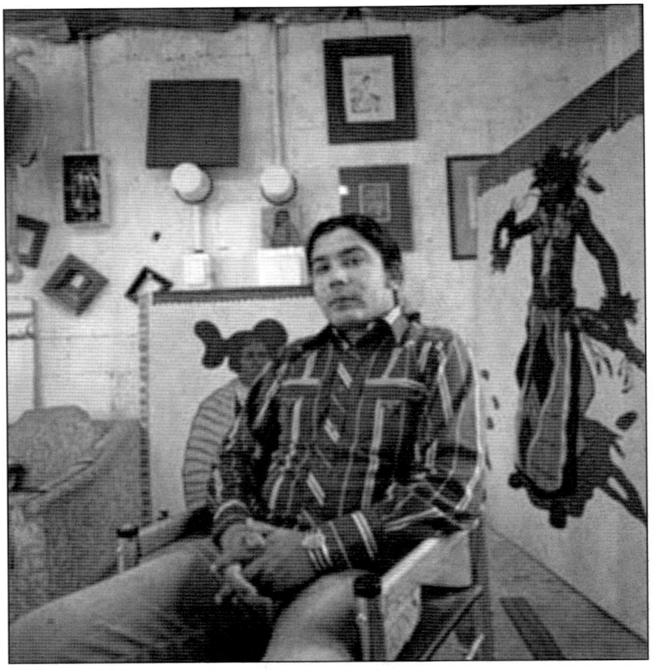

T.C. Cannon (1946–1978) was of Kiowa/Caddo heritage and was raised in Oklahoma. He attended Santa Fe's Institute of American Indian Arts. Later, he attended the San Francisco Art Institute for two months before quitting to join the army. He fought in Vietnam in 1967 and 1968, where he earned two Bronze Stars. In 1972, his work was shown along with Fritz Scholder's at the Smithsonian National Gallery. He died in an automobile accident at age 31. Cannon brought a sense of humor and irony to his portrayal of Native Americans in his colorful and well-crafted paintings. (Courtesy of Palace of the Governors Archive.)

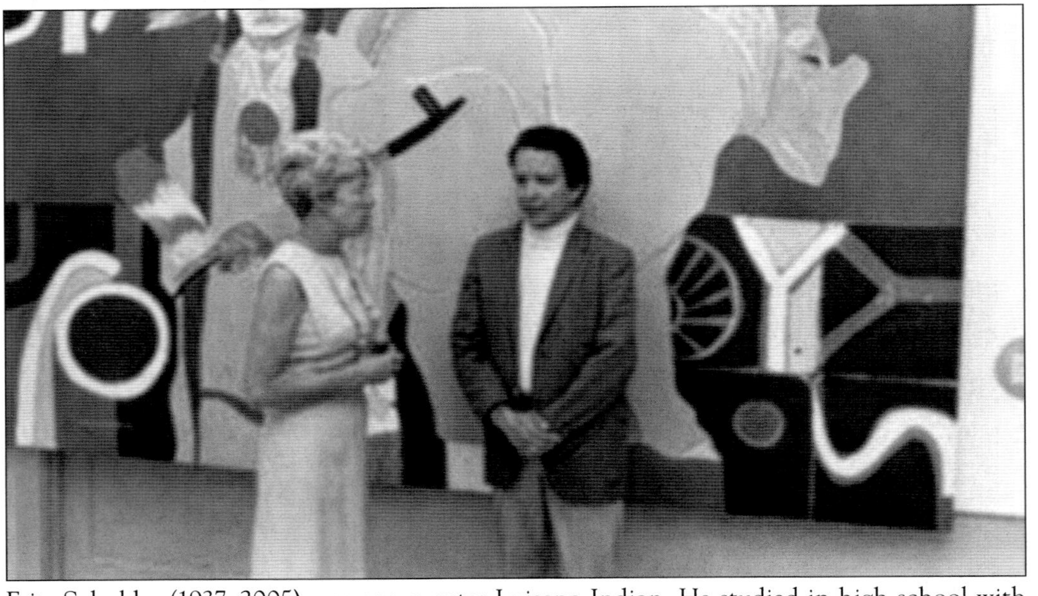

Fritz Scholder (1937–2005) was one-quarter Luiseno Indian. He studied in high school with the respected Indian artist Oscar Howe. He later studied with major American artist Wayne Thiebaud in California. Scholder earned an MFA degree from Arizona State University in 1964 and taught at IAIA from 1965 to 1969. In 1972, his work was shown along with T.C. Cannon's at the Smithsonian National Gallery. He enjoyed enormous success in the 1970s and 1980s with books and documentary films made about him. This photograph is believed to have been taken at the 1972 Smithsonian exhibition. In it, Scholder is with Lee Udall, the daughter of Stewart Udall, the US secretary of the interior from 1961 to 1969. (Courtesy of Palace of the Governors Archive, 030601.)

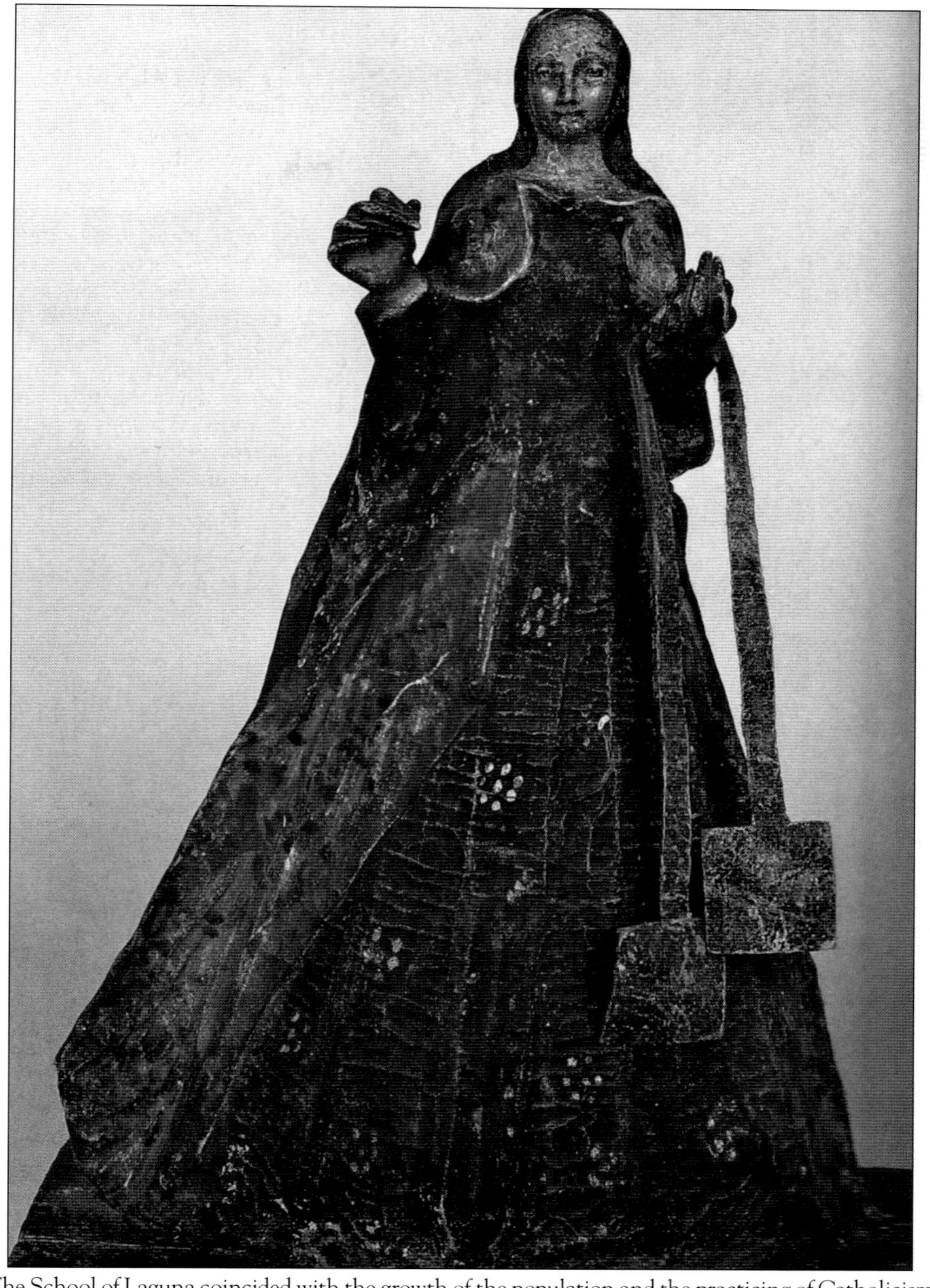

The School of Laguna coincided with the growth of the population and the practicing of Catholicism in the colony. The Laguna Santero (1776–1815) produced altarpieces for two of Santa Fe's churches, the San Miguel Church, in 1798, and the San Esteban de Acoma. This piece is titled *Nuestra Senora de Carmen* and was made in 1795. (Courtesy of the New Mexico History Museum, Larry Frank Collection.)

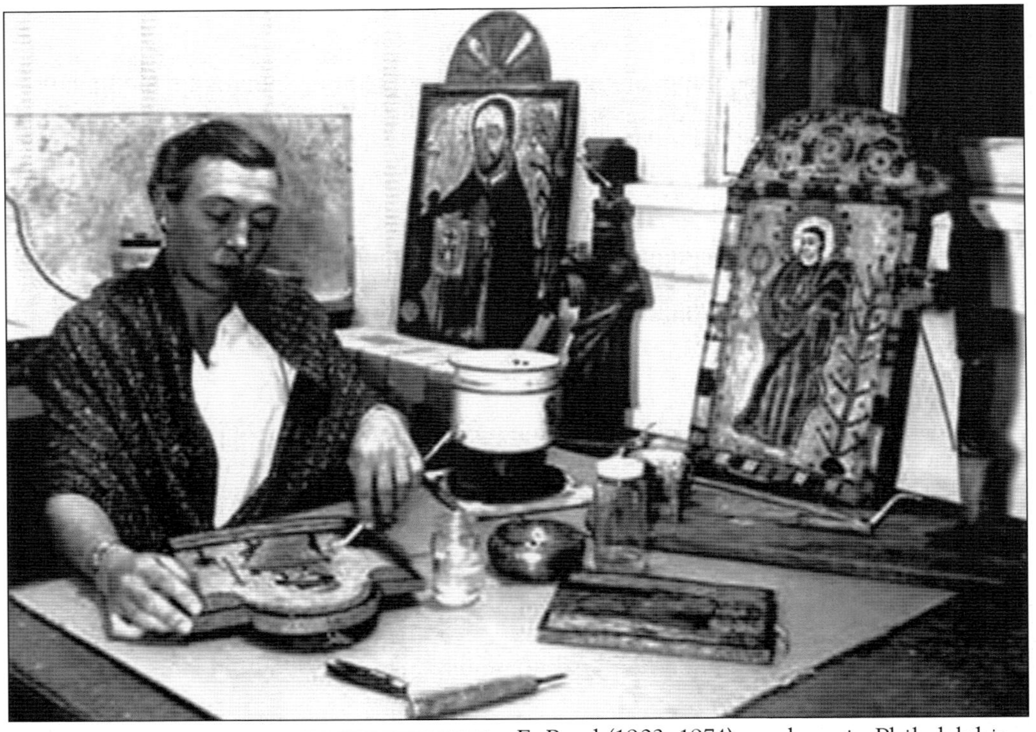

E. Boyd (1903–1974) was born in Philadelphia and attended the Academy of Fine Arts. She studied painting in Paris and traveled in western Europe before moving to New Mexico in 1929. Boyd became interested in New Mexican Santos but found no written material. As part of a federal project, she did watercolor renderings of Santos in churches. Boyd headed the newly established Spanish Colonial Department at the Museum of New Mexico in 1951 and authored an important book titled *Popular Arts of Spanish New Mexico* in 1974. (Courtesy of the Palace of the Governors Archive.)

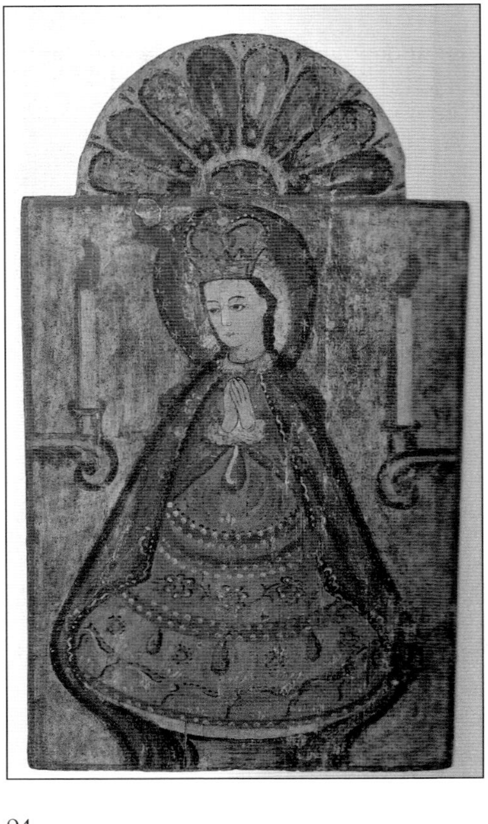

This School of Laguna piece is titled *Our Lady of St. John of the Lakes.* This elegantly balanced composition is a good example of a medium-sized retablo. (Courtesy of the New Mexico History Museum, Larry Frank Collection.)

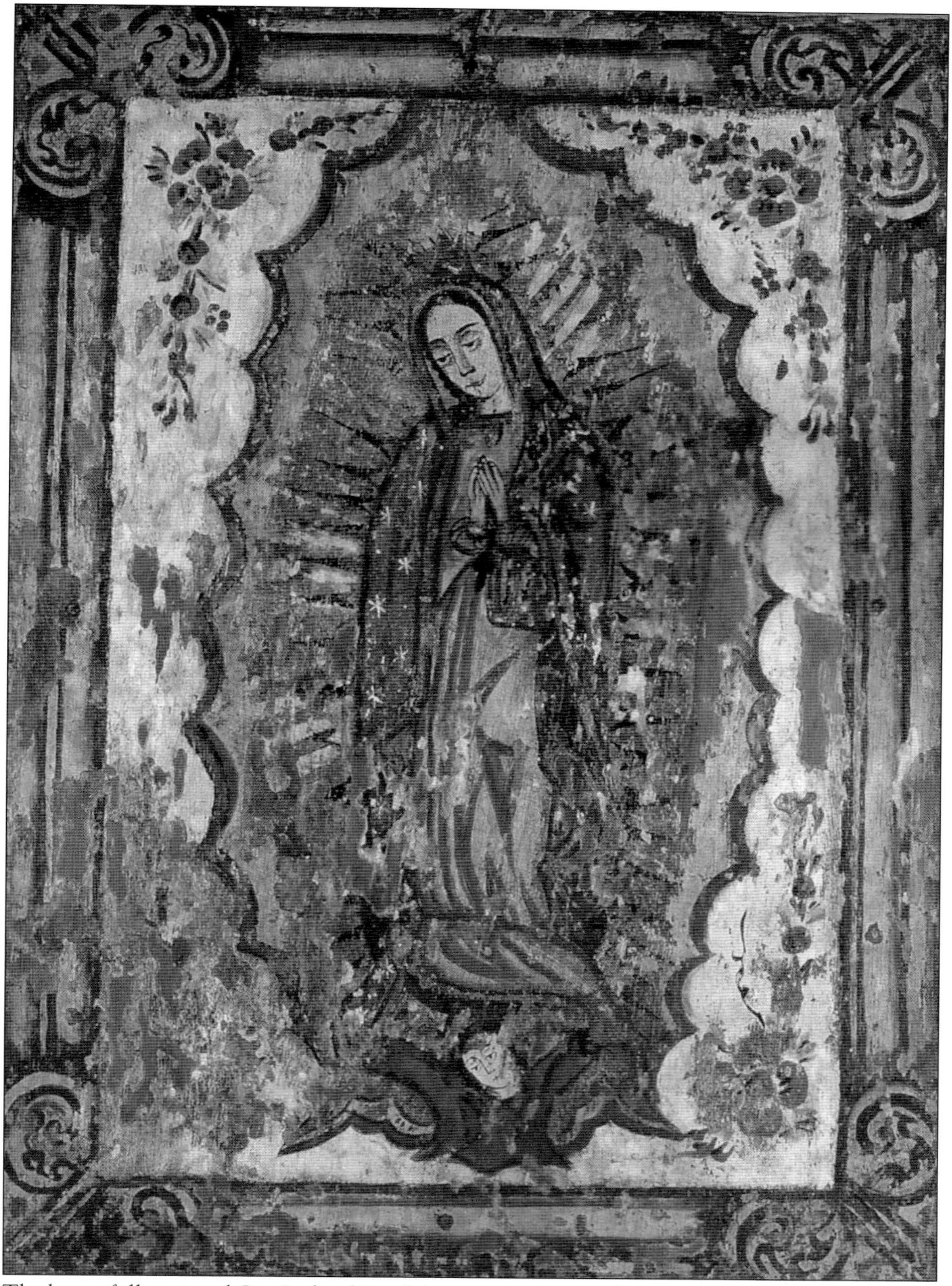

The beautifully painted Our Lady of Guadalupe is seen here with a strong, scalloped edge created by the Laguna Santero (1776–1815). (Courtesy of Taos Historic Museums.)

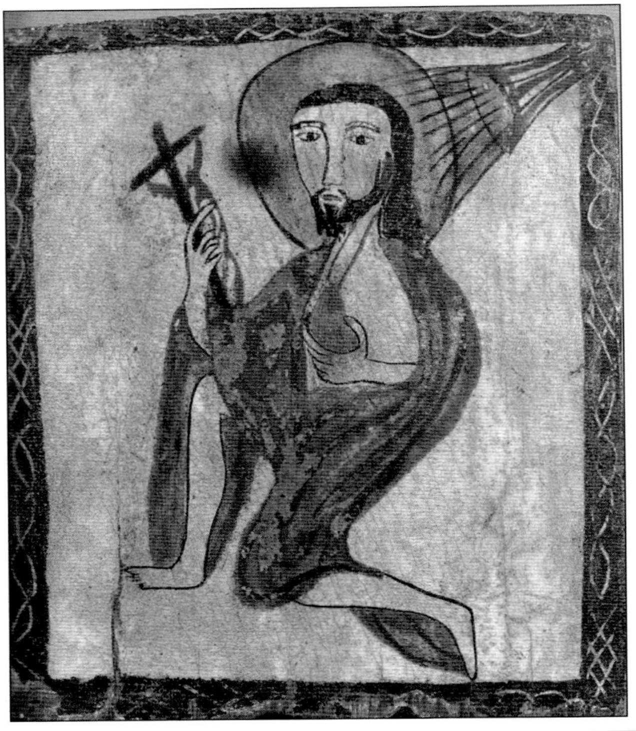

Author/historian E. Boyd named Pedro Fresguis's (1749–1831) previously unidentified bultos and santos. Fresguis, who was born a few miles from the Santuario de Chimayo, where he is buried, was a member of the Santa Cruz Church and had an innovative style that produced a significant number of retablos and a smaller number of bultos. (Courtesy of the New Mexico History Museum, Larry Frank Collection.)

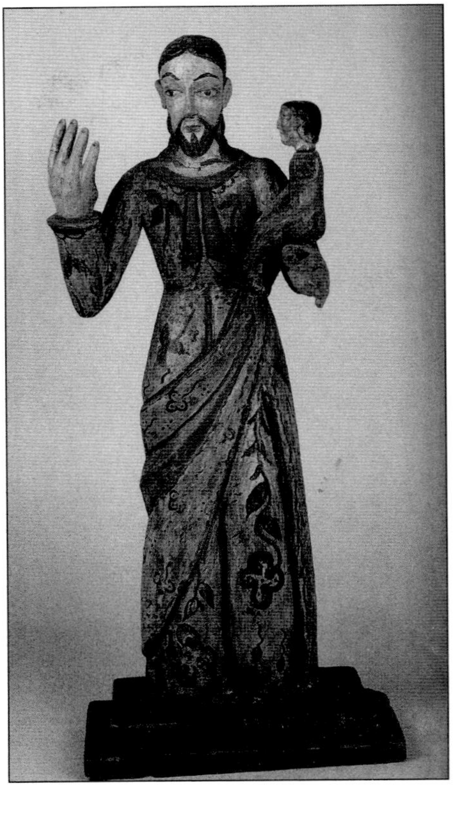

Santo Nino Santero (1830–1860) worked with Jose Aregon, whose style Santero's is most closely related to. Saint Joseph, depicted here, is a powerful but benevolent figure. (Courtesy of the New Mexico History Museum, Larry Frank Collection.)

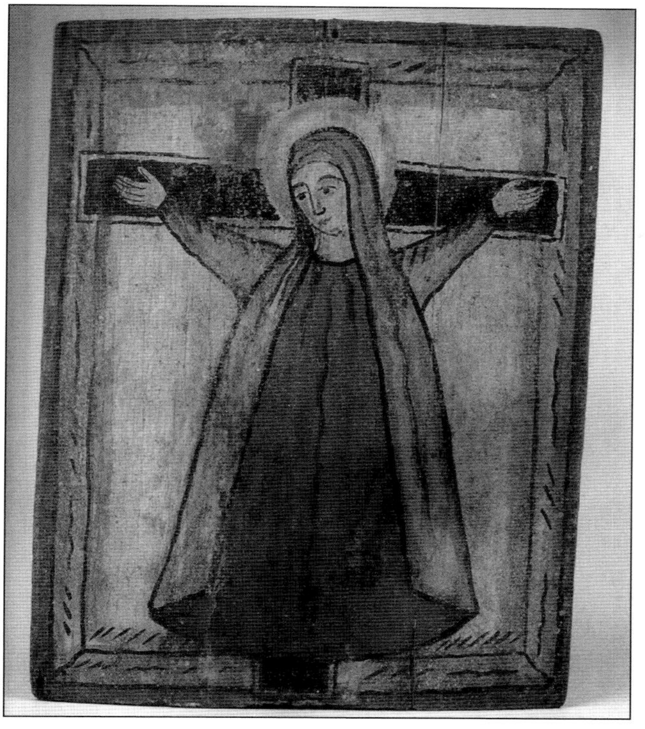

The artist of this piece, titled *Saint Liberta*, is noted as being a follower of Jose Aregon. Saint Liberta is believed to have been the only crucified female martyr. (Courtesy of the New Mexico History Museum, Larry Frank Collection.)

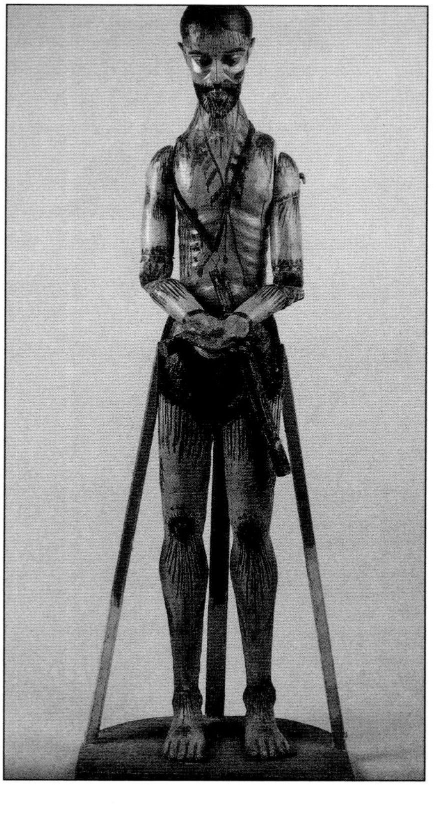

Jose Rafael Aragon (1796–1862) lived in Santa Fe as a young man and worked as a santero from approximately 1820 to 1860. Aragon was very prolific, producing a large number of bultos and santeros and influencing many younger santeros. This large bulto is titled *Our Father Jesus the Nazarene*. (Courtesy of the New Mexico History Museum, Larry Frank Collection.)

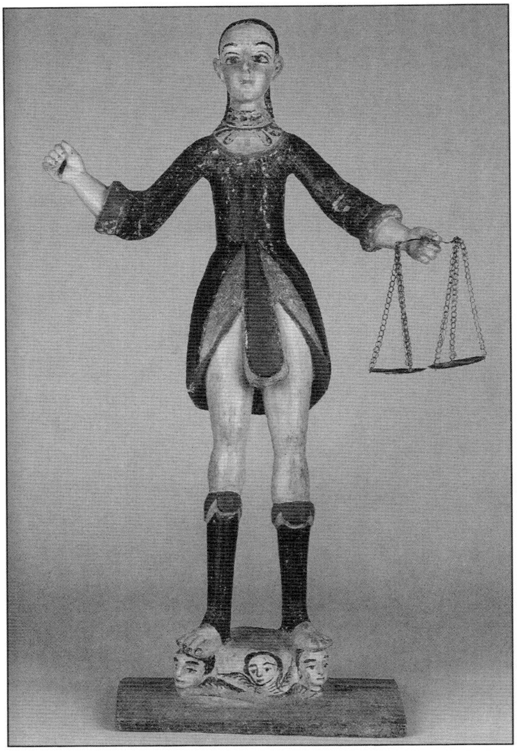

This is another of Aragon's works, a long-legged angular Saint Michael holding a scale and wearing colonial military dress. (Courtesy of the Museum of International Folk Art, Museum of New Mexico, Santa Fe.)

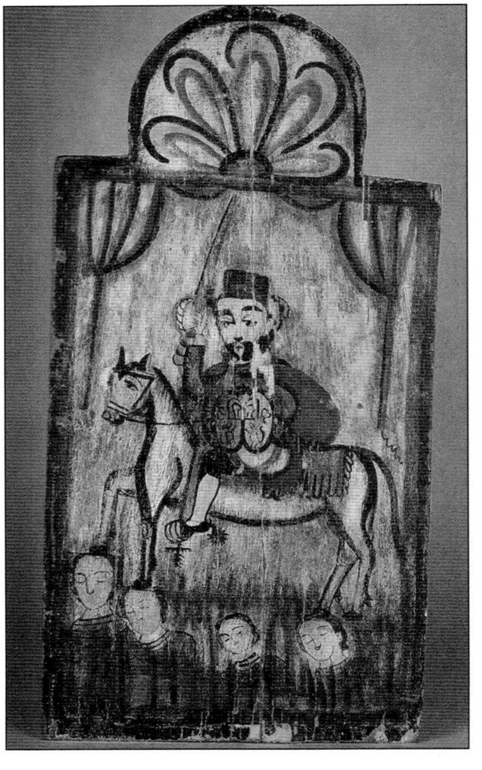

This elongated rectangular retablo by Jose Rafael Aragon, which shows Saint James Matamoros holding a colonial shield and sword, possesses a kind of folk art graphic power. (Courtesy of the Harwood Museum of Art, Taos.)

Jose Rafael Aragon's small but powerful contemplative retablo of the head of Christ is titled *The Holy Face*. (Courtesy of the Harwood Museum of Art, Taos.)

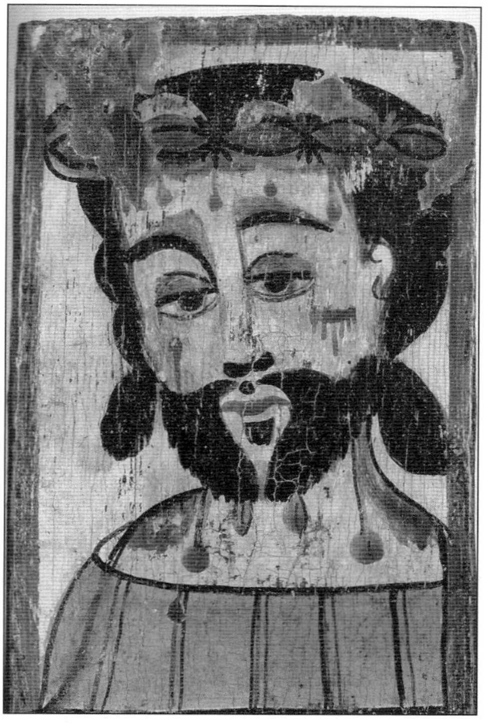

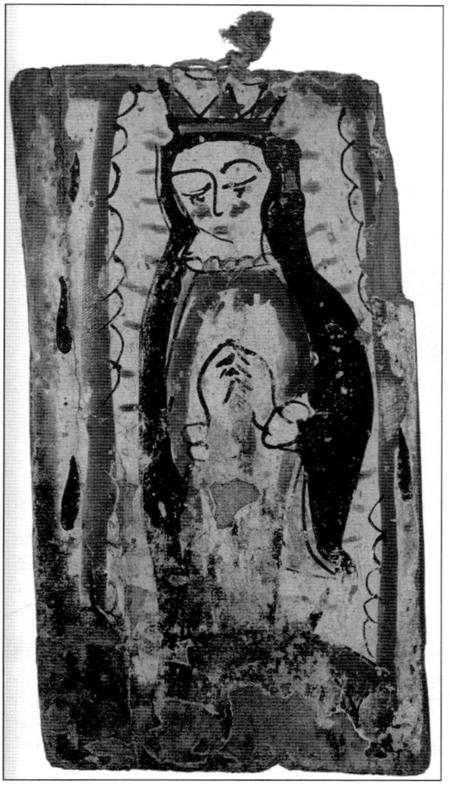

Jose Benito Ortega's (1858–1941) *Our Lady of Guadalupe* is a very small retablo that appears to have been freely and quickly painted, in contrast to the usual detail often found in other retablos. (Courtesy of the New Mexico History Museum, Larry Frank Collection.)

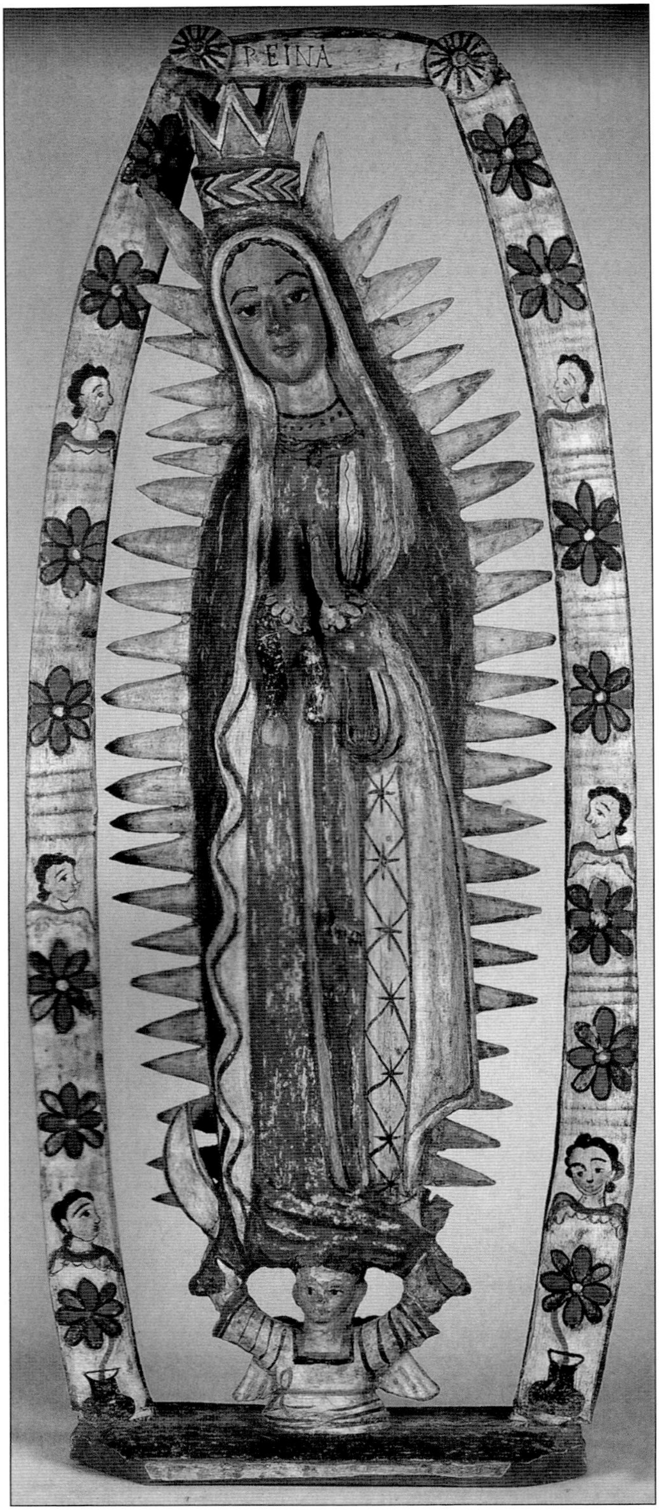

This bultos, titled *Our Lady of Guadalupe*, by Jose Rafael Aragon, is a tall, elegant, expressive, and well-painted carving with an unusual free-floating frame. (Courtesy of the New Mexico History Museum, Larry Frank Collection.)

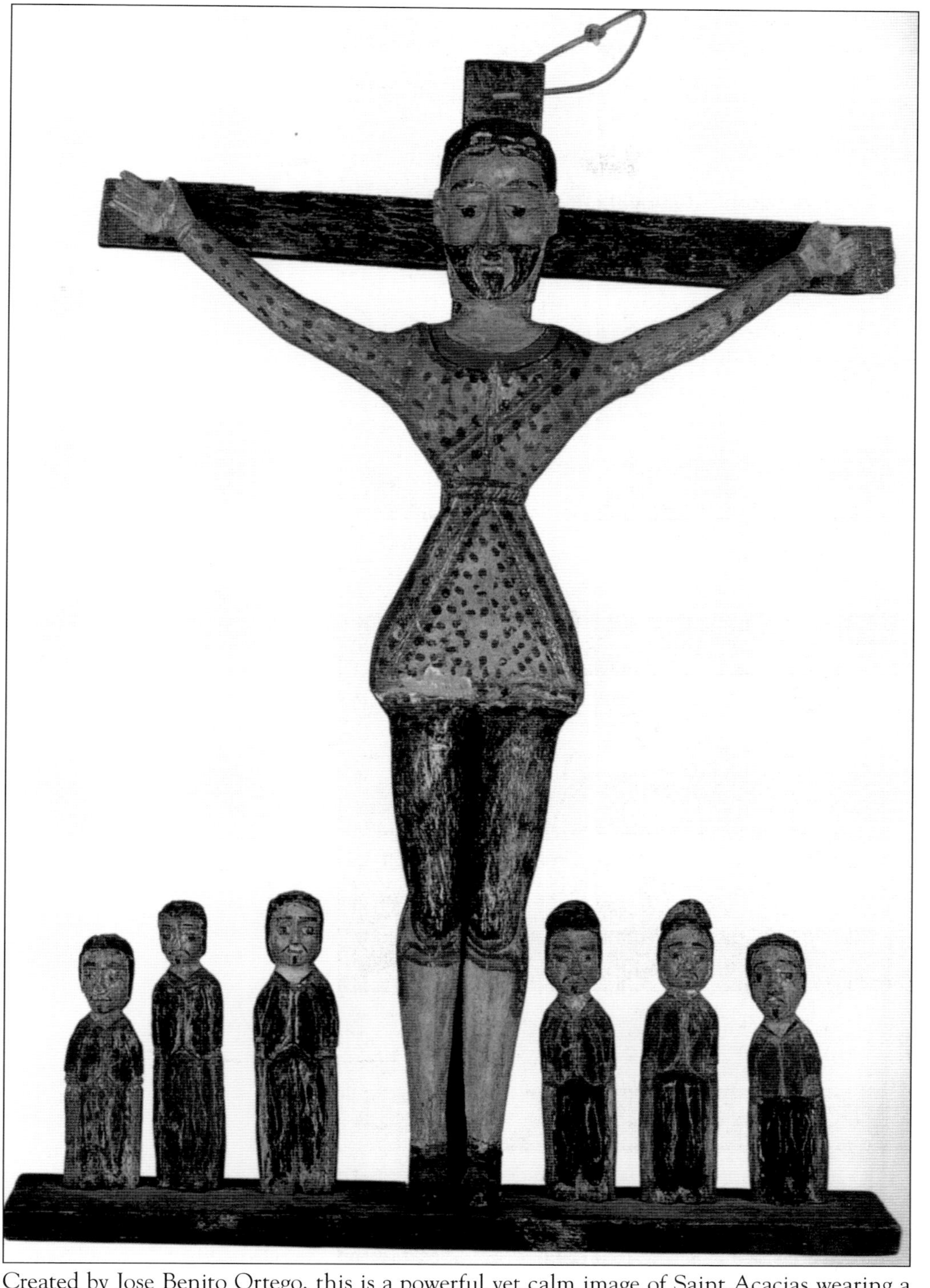

Created by Jose Benito Ortego, this is a powerful yet calm image of Saint Acacias wearing a decorated uniform with a group of smaller attendants. (Courtesy of Museum of International Folk Art, Museum of New Mexico, Santa Fe.)

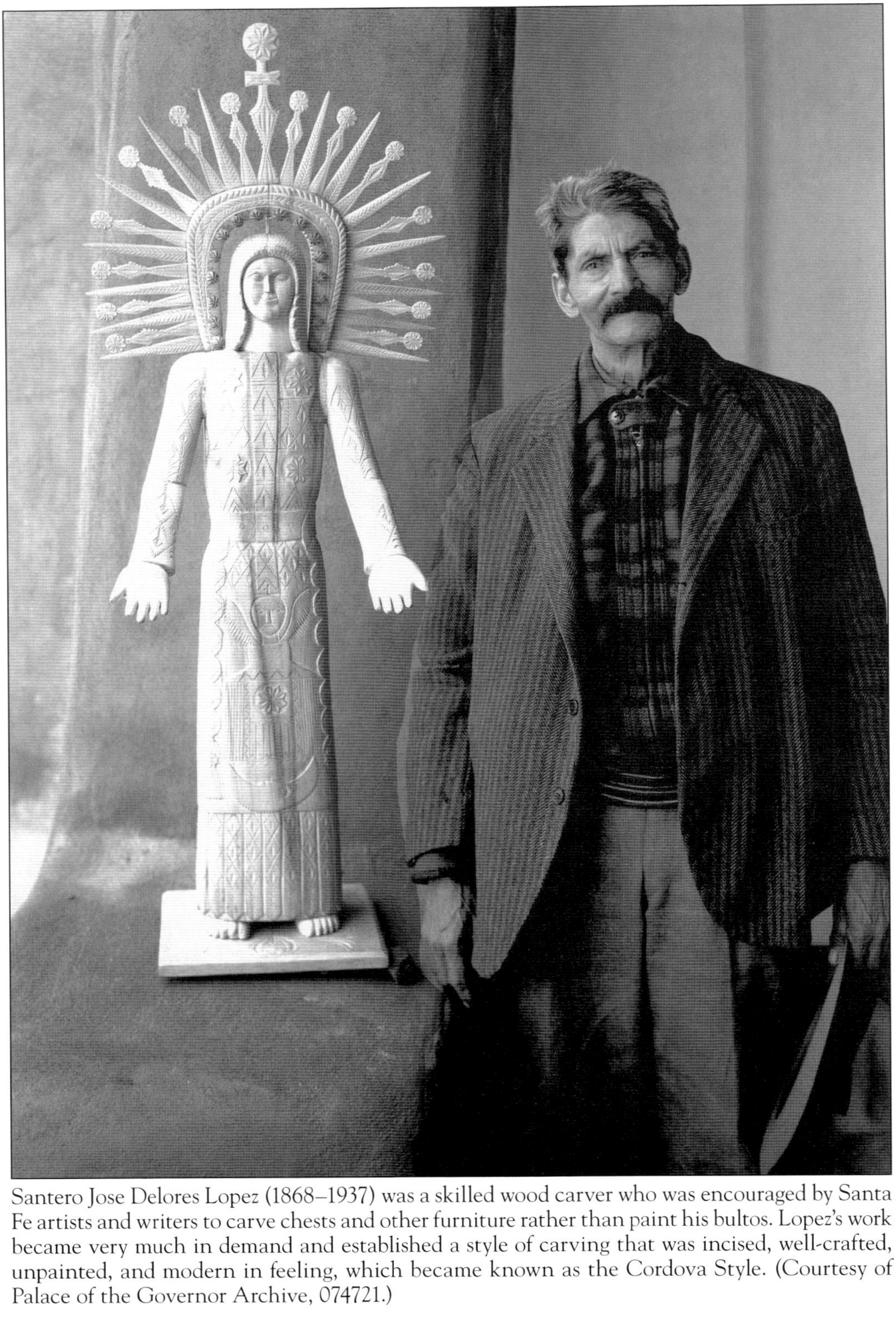

Santero Jose Delores Lopez (1868–1937) was a skilled wood carver who was encouraged by Santa Fe artists and writers to carve chests and other furniture rather than paint his bultos. Lopez's work became very much in demand and established a style of carving that was incised, well-crafted, unpainted, and modern in feeling, which became known as the Cordova Style. (Courtesy of Palace of the Governor Archive, 074721.)

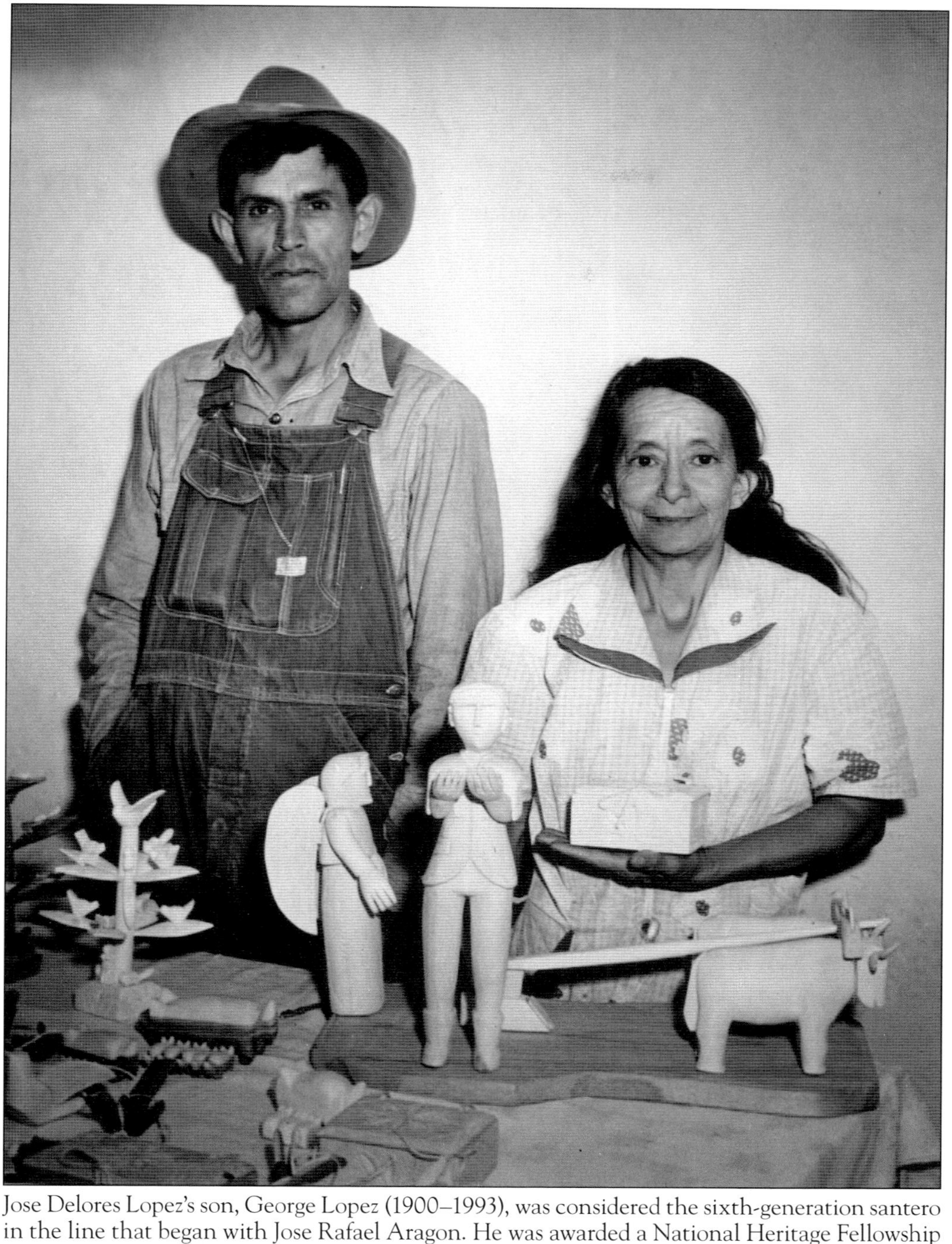

Jose Delores Lopez's son, George Lopez (1900–1993), was considered the sixth-generation santero in the line that began with Jose Rafael Aragon. He was awarded a National Heritage Fellowship by the National Endowment for the Arts in 1982. This photograph shows George Lopez and his wife with a small, carved tablo in the foreground. (Courtesy of the Palace of the Governor Archive, 041710.)

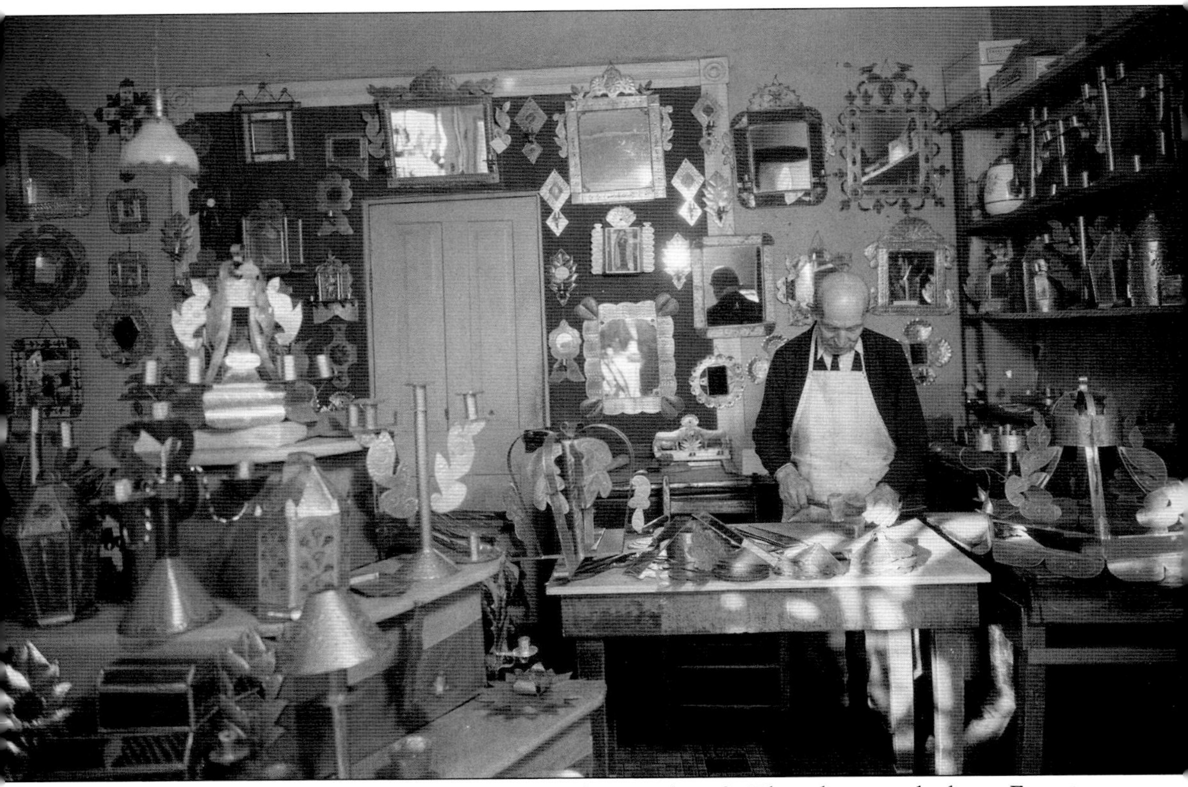

Tinsmithing is a traditional Spanish Colonial art and craft. This photograph shows Francisco Delgado in his studio at 503 Canyon Road in Santa Fe. (T. Harmon Parkhurst Collection, courtesy of Palace of the Governor Archive, 071180.)

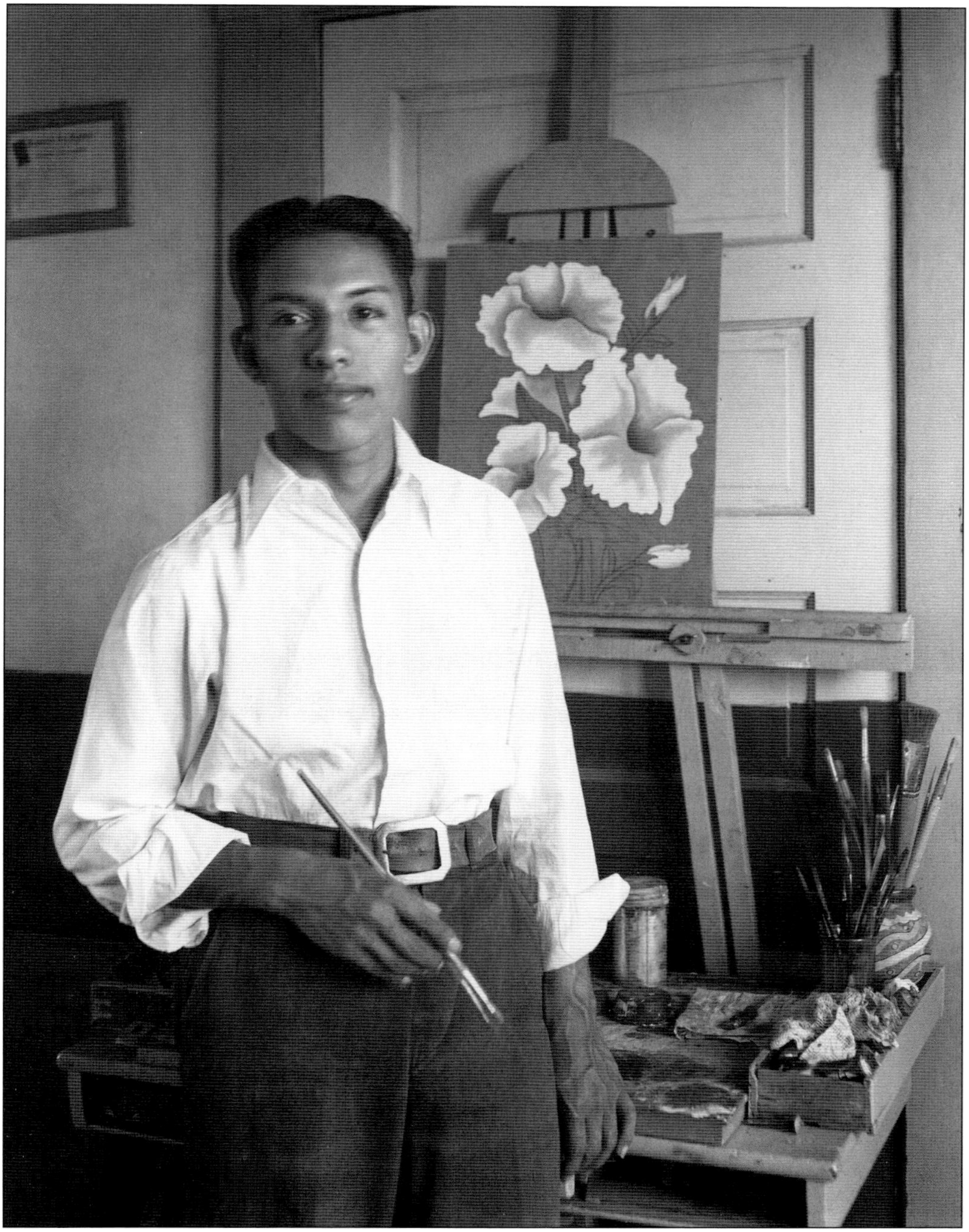

Artist Pedro Cervantez (1914–1987) assisted artist Russell Hunter on the painting of a Works Progress Administration (WPA) mural in 1934. He exhibited New Deal paintings at the Museum of Fine Art in Santa Fe and was included in *Masters of Popular Painting: Modern Primitives of Europe and America* at the Museum of Modern Art in New York City in 1938. One of the first Hispanic painters to receive national recognition, one of his paintings is currently on display at the Smithsonian Museum of Art in Washington, DC. Cervantez served in World War II. (Courtesy of Palace of the Governors Archive, 020401.)

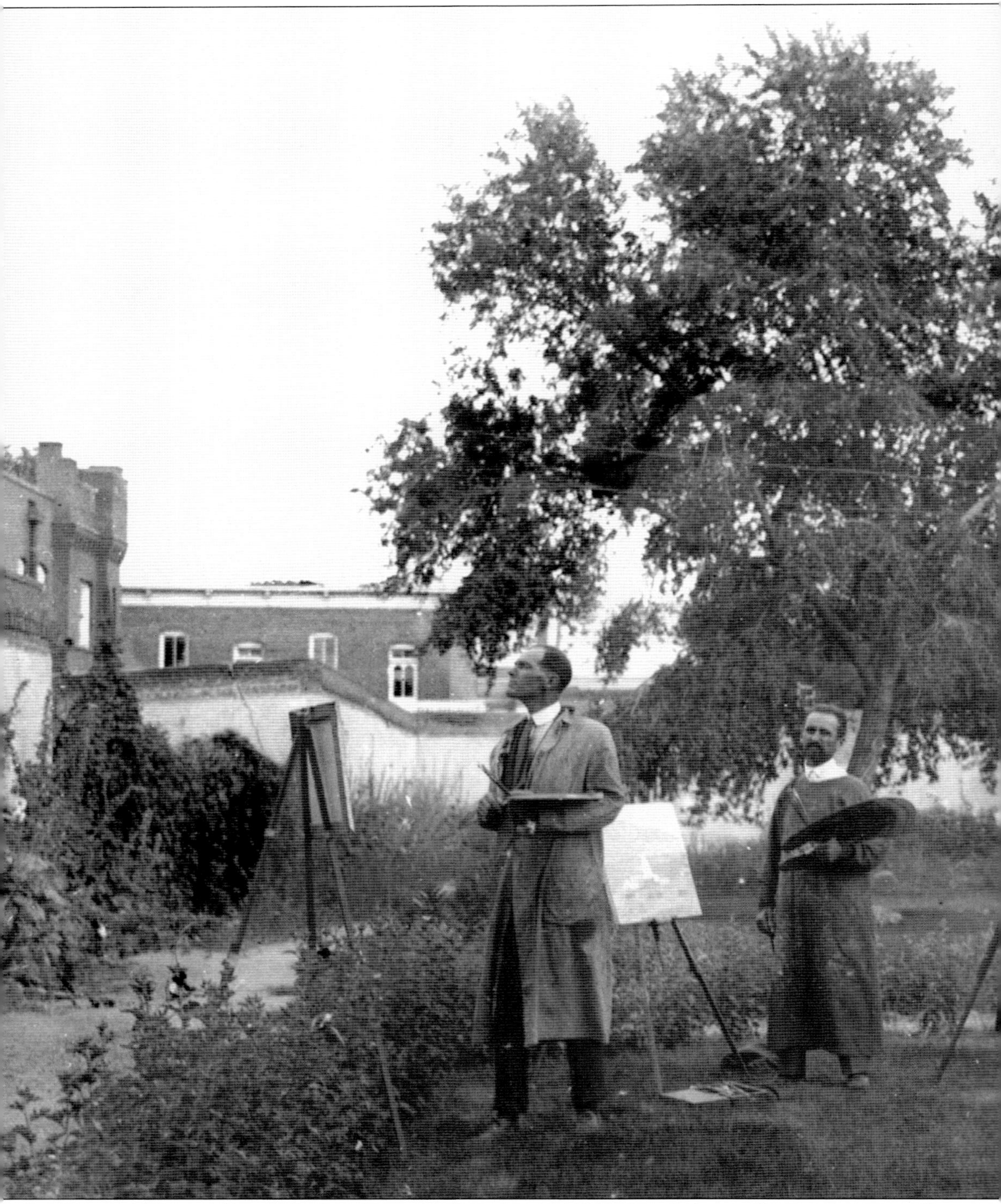

Created by Wesley Bradfield, this 1917 photograph shows, from left to right, artists Kenneth Chapman, Carlos Vierra, two unidentified, and Sheldon Parsons painting in the patio of the Palace of the Governors. Under the directorship of Edgar L. Hewett, many artists who had come

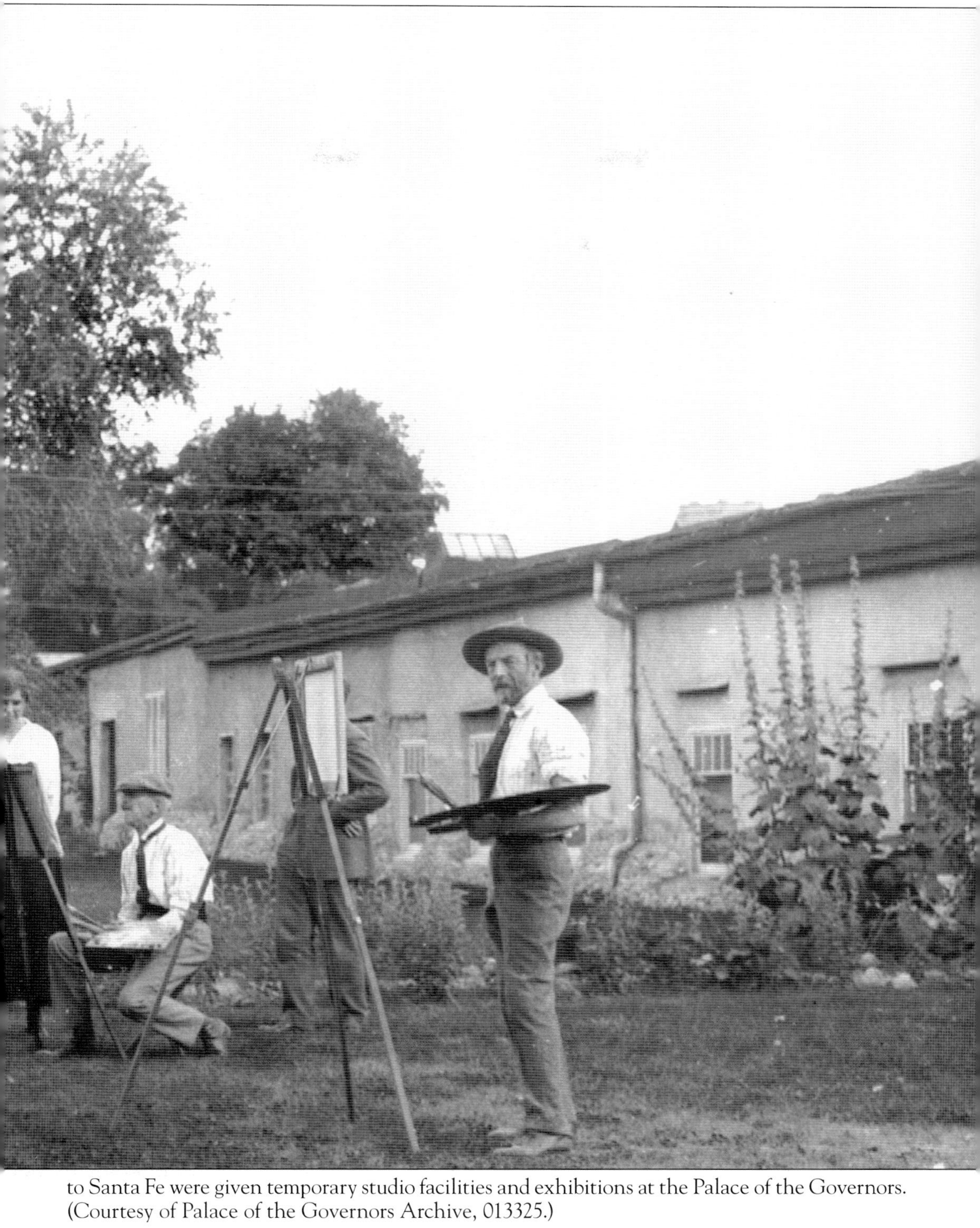

to Santa Fe were given temporary studio facilities and exhibitions at the Palace of the Governors. (Courtesy of Palace of the Governors Archive, 013325.)

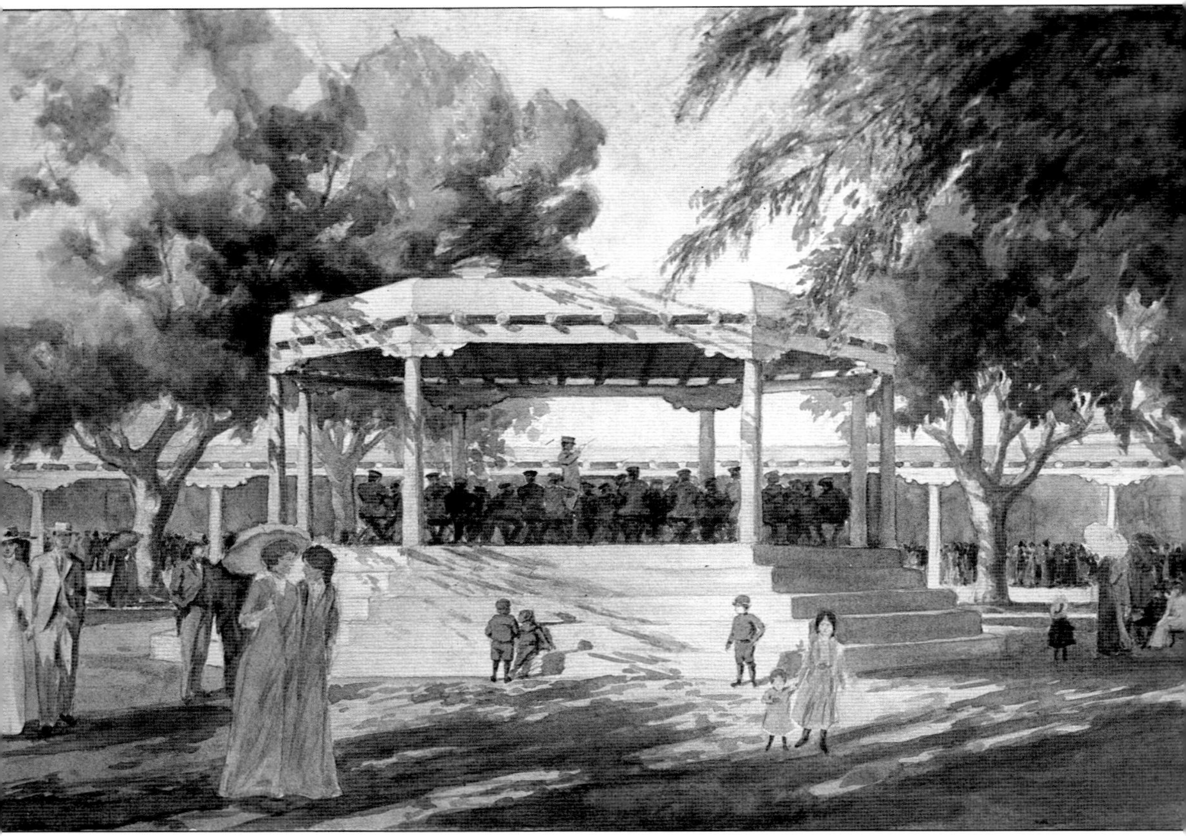

Artist Carlos Vierra, who was instrumental in promoting the new/old Santa Fe style, created this wash of a proposed Plaza bandstand in 1912. (Courtesy of Palace of the Governor Archive, 061464.)

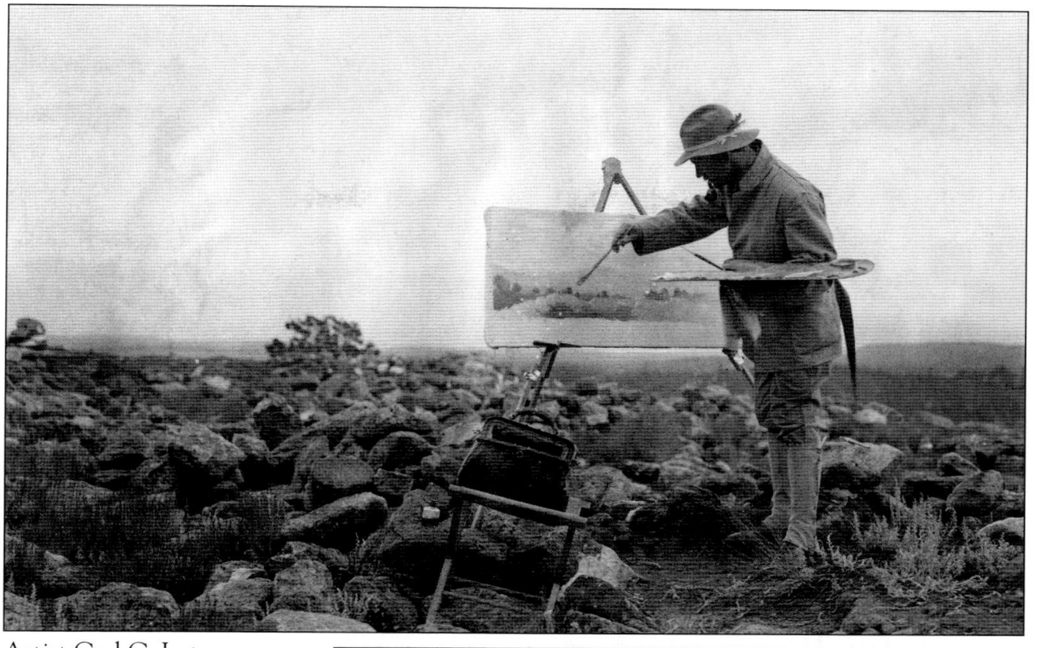

Artist Carl G. Lotave (1872–1924) was born in Sweden and studied in Anders Zorn's studio class in Stockholm. He moved to Kansas, where he lived and taught for a time before coming to Santa Fe. Along with artist G.N. Malm, Lotave organized the first annual Swedish-American Exhibition of Art, which later became known as the Midwest Art Exhibition. The photograph above shows Lotave painting en plein air in Puye, New Mexico. The portrait of Lotave at right was taken by Jesse Nusbaum. (Courtesy of Palace of the Governors Archive, 009972 and 158216.)

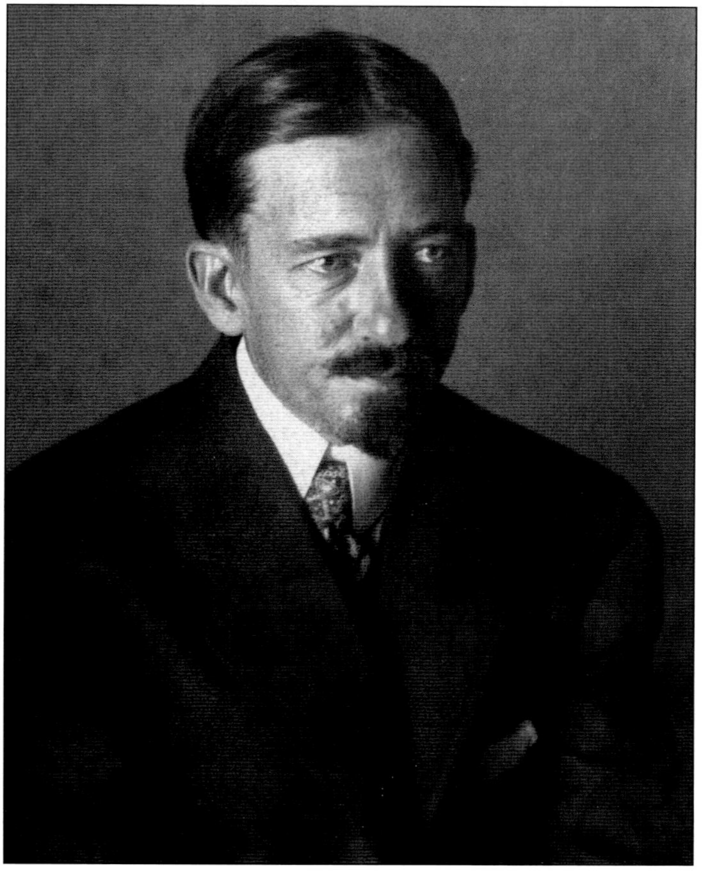

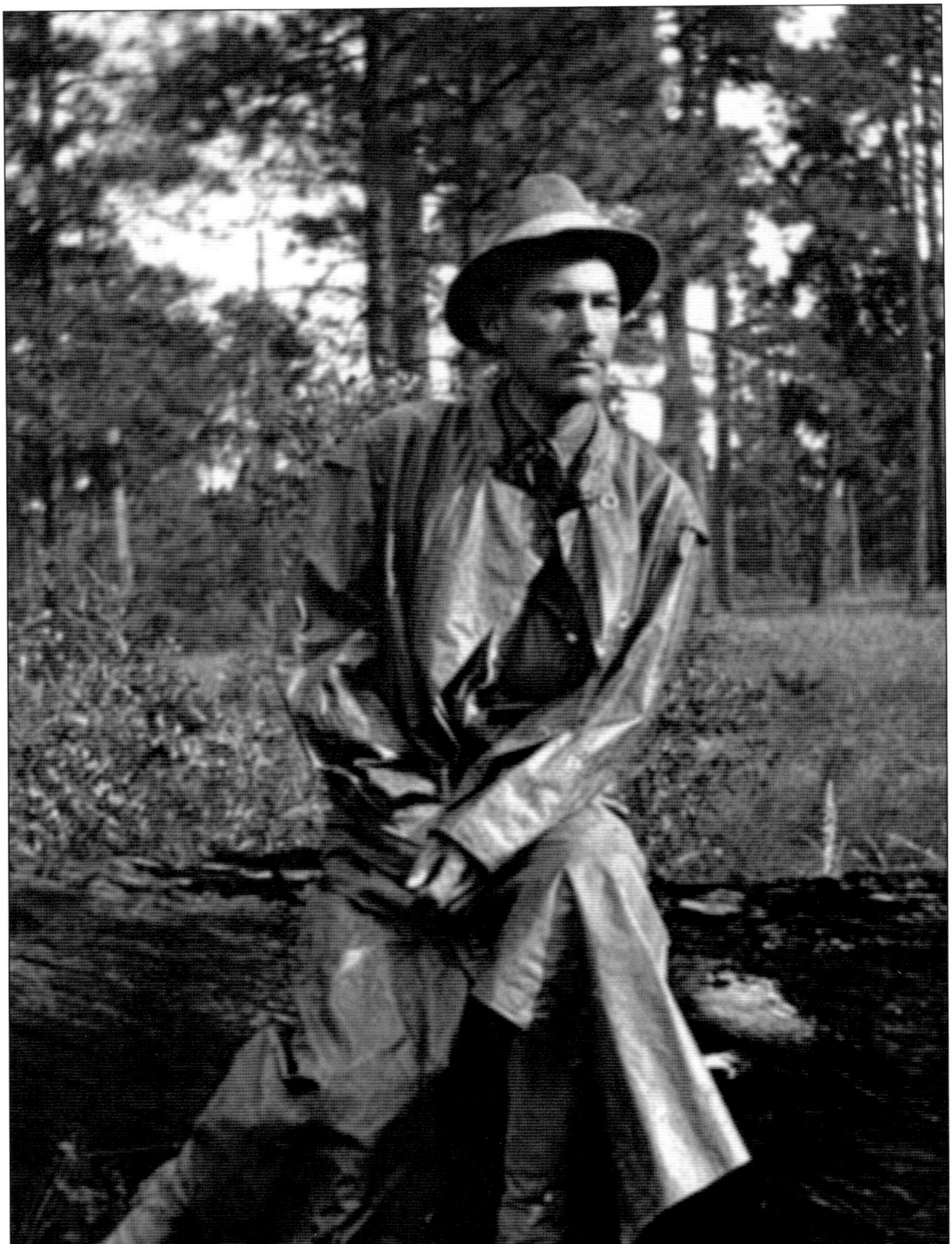

Kenneth Chapman (1875–1958) came to New Mexico to heal his fume-damaged lungs. He was hired by Edgar L. Hewett to work on archeological projects for the Museum of Fine Arts in Santa Fe. An expert in this field, Chapman produced a Pueblo Indian pottery portfolio and cofounded the Indian Art Fund.

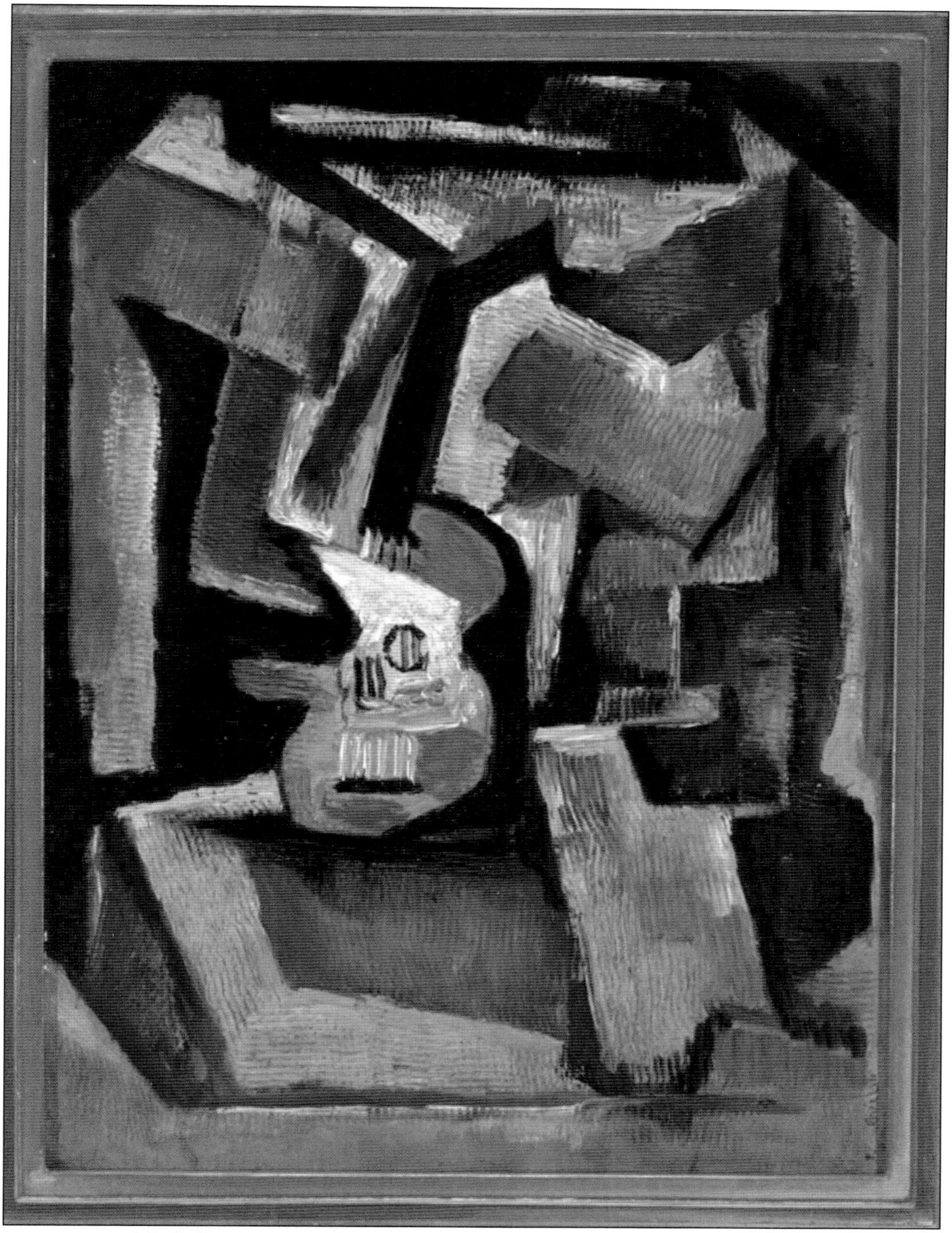

Paul Burlin (1886–1969) was born in New York and attended the National Academy of Art and the Art Students League. His paintings were shown in the historically important Armory exhibition in New York City. He lived in Santa Fe from 1913 to 1920 with his wife, musicologist Natalie Curtis (1875–1921). Burlin enjoyed a long career but began to lose his eyesight in the late 1950s. His last paintings, the *Series of Nine*, were shown at the Museum of Modern Art in New York City in 1971 and at the Pasadena Museum in 1972. (Courtesy of Harwood Museum of Art, Taos.)

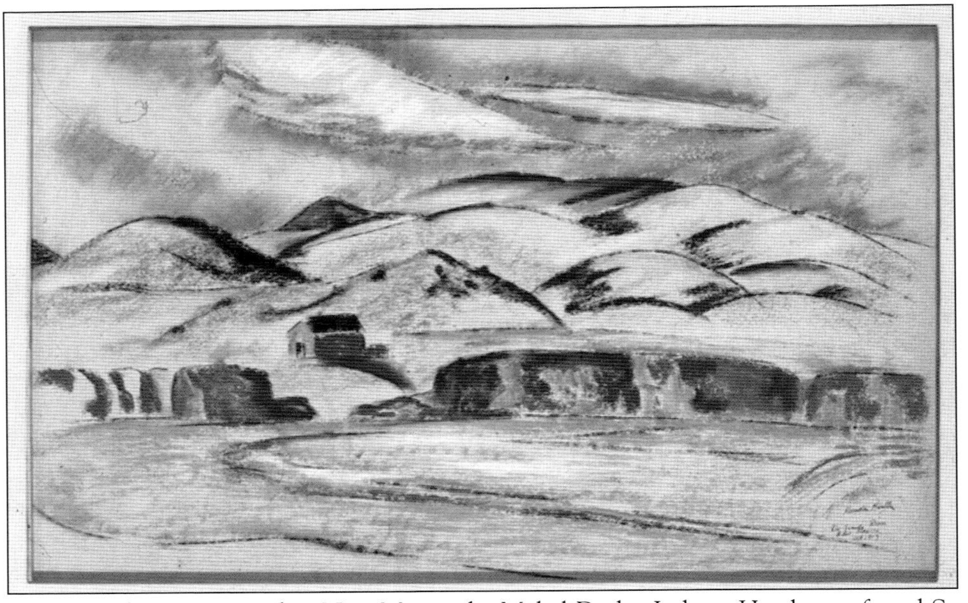

Marsden Hartley was invited to New Mexico by Mabel Dodge Luhan. Hartley preferred Santa Fe to Taos and ultimately moved to Santa Fe. In 1909, Hartley had his first one-man show at Alfred Stieglitz's 291 Gallery in New York City. He continued to show with Stieglitz until 1937 and painted a number of watercolor landscapes en plein air in 1918 and 1919. In later years, he painted New Mexico landscapes from memory. This watercolor landscape is dated 1918. (Courtesy of the Harwood Museum of Art, Taos.)

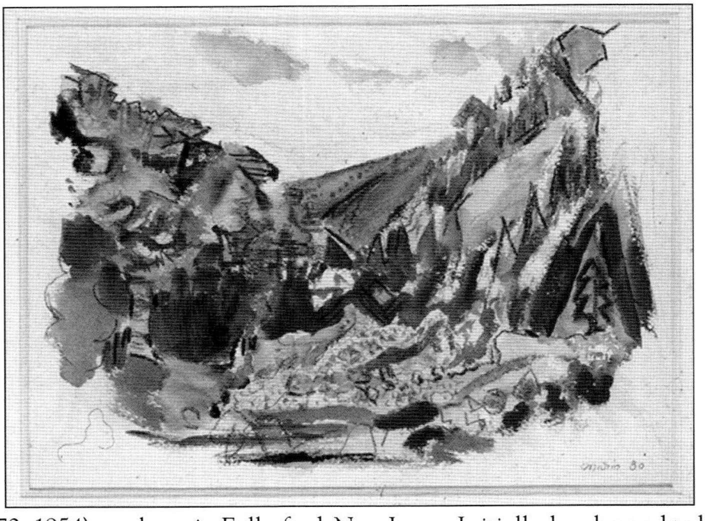

John Marin (1870–1954) was born in Fullerford, New Jersey. Initially, he planned to be an architect, but he attended the Pennsylvania Academy of Fine Arts in Philadelphia, studied with William Merritt Chase, and then went to Paris, traveling throughout Europe. Alfred Stieglitz showed his work in 1909 at the 291 Gallery. It was also shown in the Armory exhibit of 1913. Stieglitz showed Marin's work every year from 1909 until Stieglitz's death in 1946. Marin came to New Mexico to paint in the summer of 1929 and 1930, producing more than 100 watercolors. His work had a large influence on New Mexican artists and was featured in a retrospective at New York City's Museum of Modern Art in 1936. (Courtesy of the Harwood Museum of Art, Taos.)

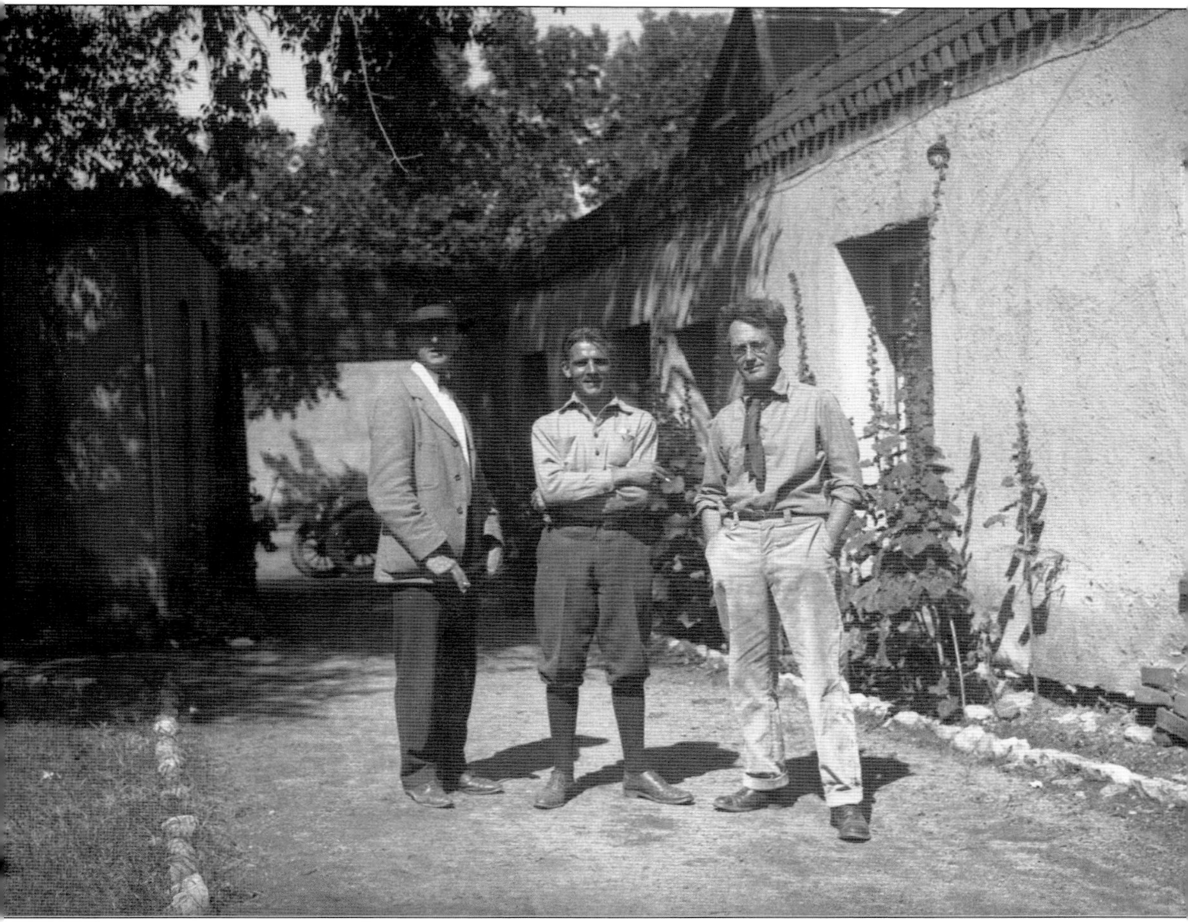

Photographed in 1919 in the courtyard of the Palace of the Governors near the artists' studios are, from left to right, Santa Fe artists Marsden Hartley, Randall Davey, and John Sloan. (Courtesy of the Palace of the Governors Archive, 14232.)

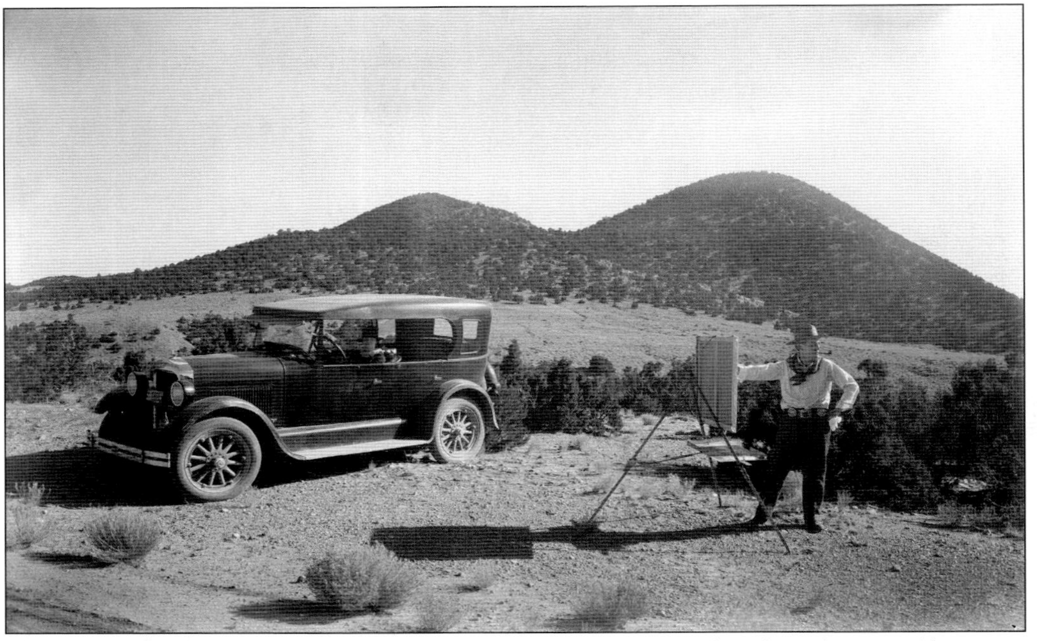

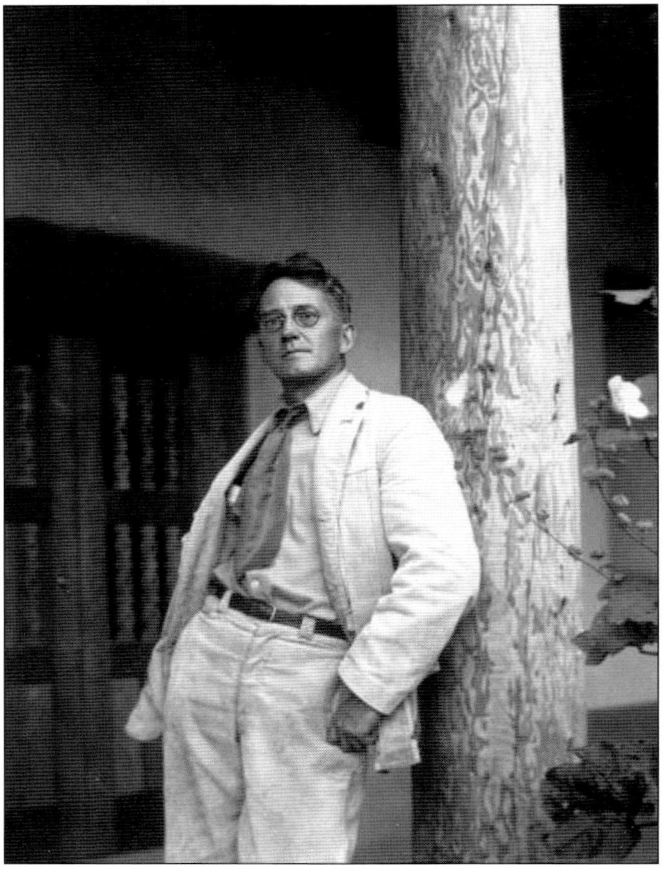

John Sloan (1871–1951) was born in Lock Haven, Pennsylvania, and began as a mostly self-taught illustrator. He attended night classes at the Pennsylvania Academy of Fine Arts, where he met artist Robert Henri and turned to painting. He married Dolly Hall and moved to New York City, where he created illustrations for *The Masses*, a socialist journal. He participated in the 1913 Armory exhibition and was a member of *The Eight* and *The Ashcan School of Realists*. Beginning in 1929, the Sloans lived in Santa Fe for four months of the year for 30 years. Above, John paints outside, and at left, he poses on the portal of the Palace of the Governors. (Above, courtesy of the Palace of the Governors, 028836; left, courtesy of the Palace of the Governors Archive, 030733.)

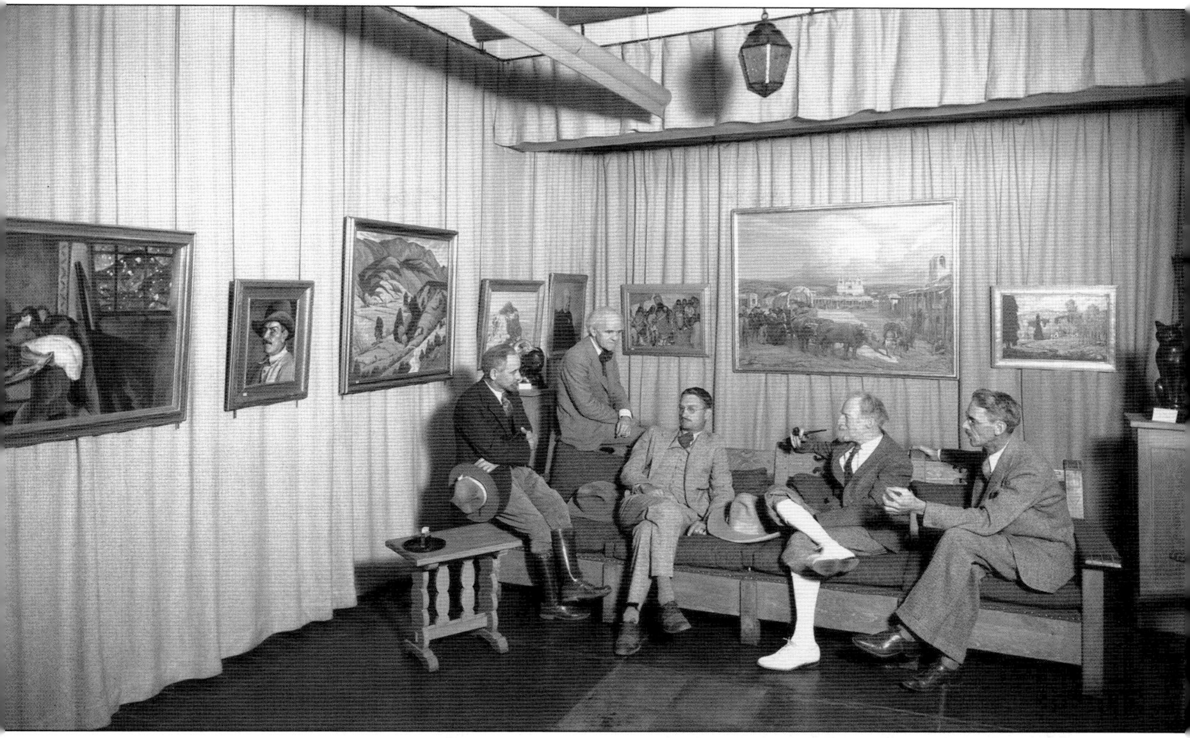

From left to right, artists Carlos Vierra, Gerald Cassidy, Theodore Van Soelen, Sheldon Parsons, and Daus Myers relax at this 1925 art exhibition at the La Fonda Hotel. (T. Harmon Parkhust Collection, courtesy of Palace of the Governors Archive, 019128.)

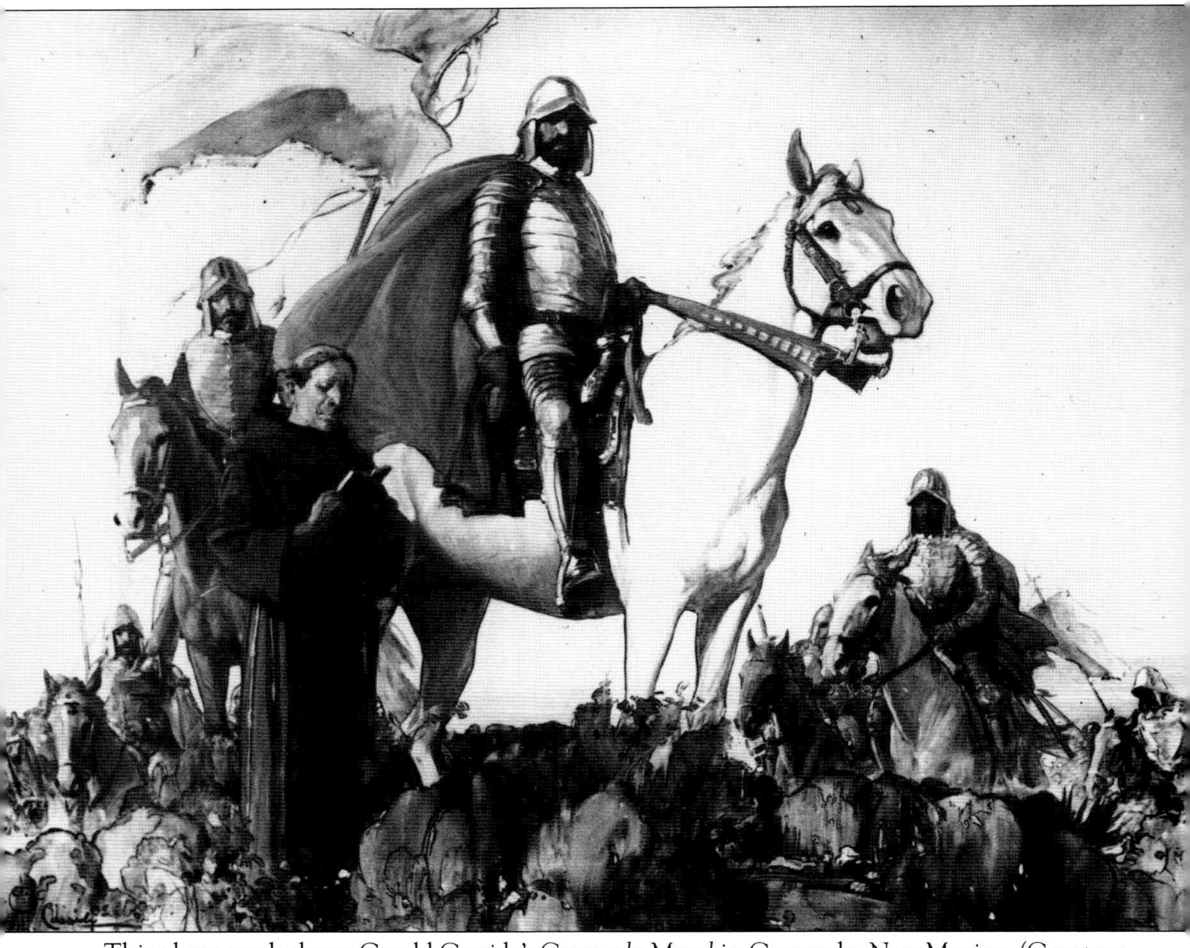

This photograph shows Gerald Cassidy's *Coronado Mural* in Coronado, New Mexico. (Courtesy of the Palace of the Governors, 020206.)

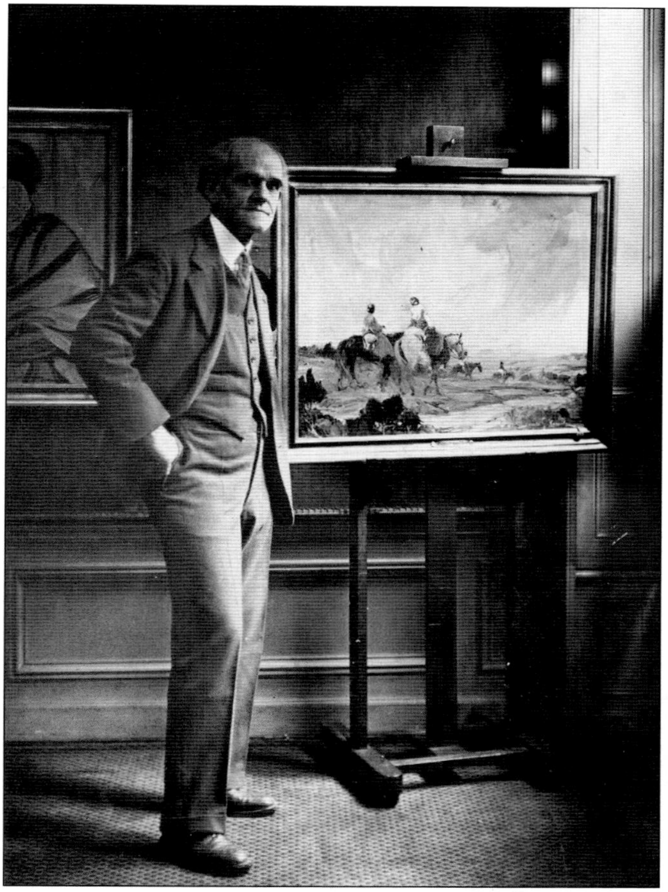

Artist Gerald Cassidy (1879–1934) was born in Kentucky and worked as a lithographer in New York City. He contracted tuberculosis and went to Albuquerque for treatment before moving to Denver to work as a commercial artist. He and his wife, Ina, purchased a home in Taos in 1912, and in 1915, bought a residence at 922 Canyon Road in Santa Fe. Cassidy painted murals in Santa Fe's El Onate Theater. The image below shows the Cassidys outside their Santa Fe home. (Courtesy of the Palace of the Governors Archive, 007121 and 091575.)

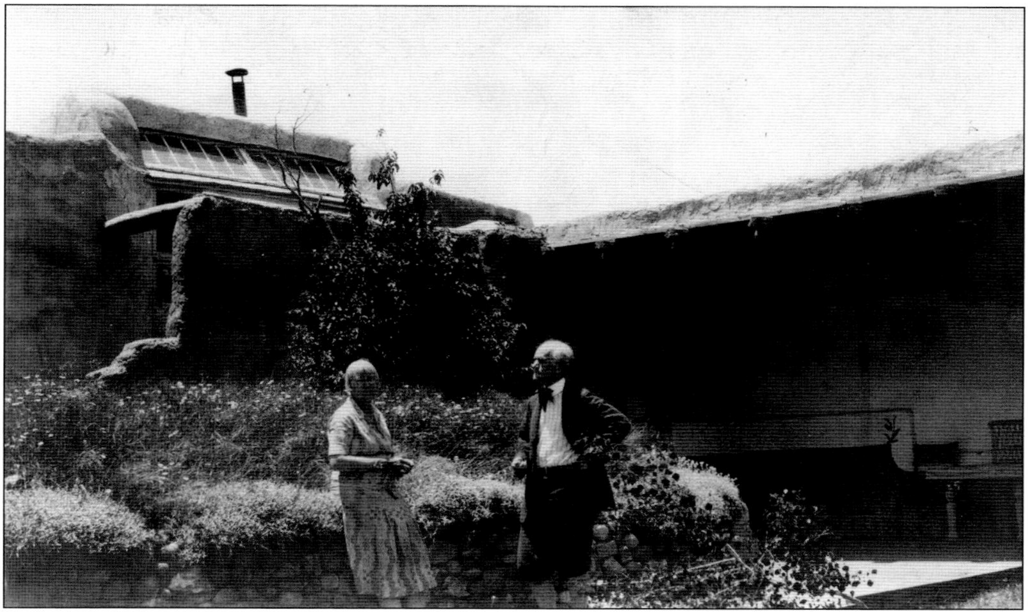

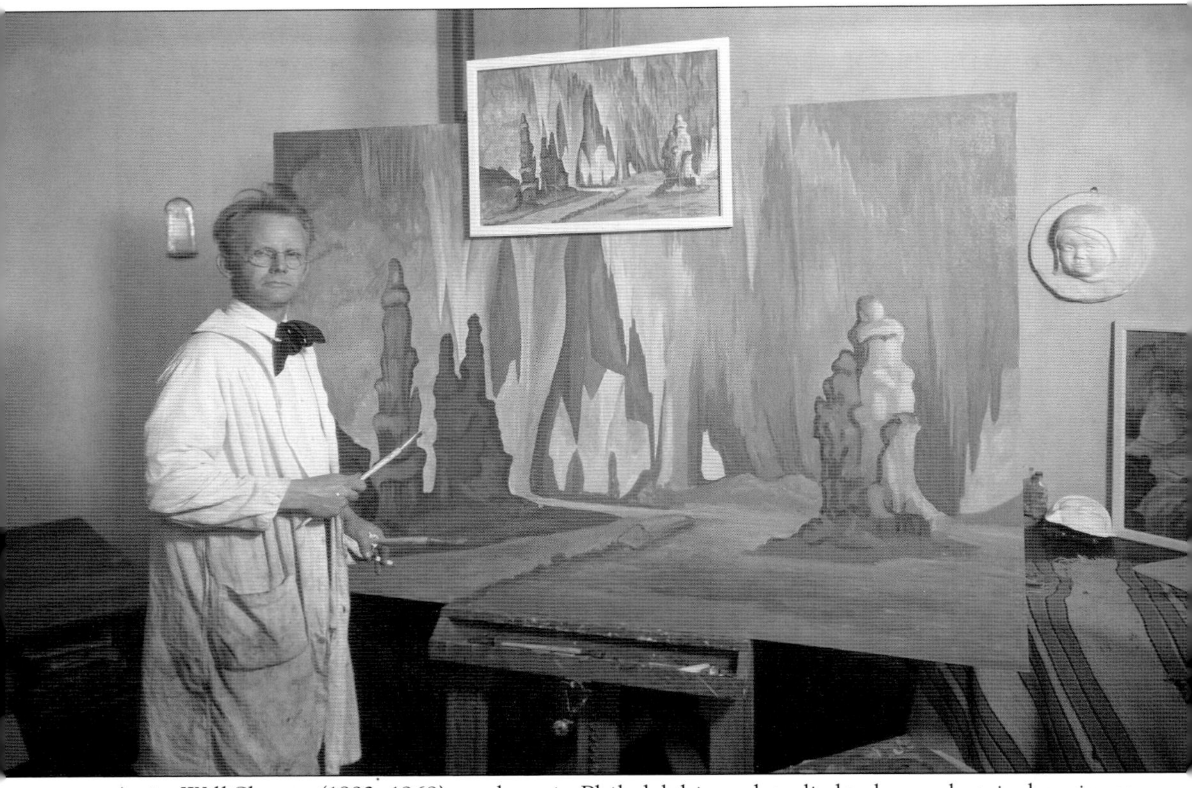

Artist Will Shuster (1893–1969) was born in Philadelphia and studied to be an electrical engineer until he started drawing with an artist friend. After serving in World War I, Shuster contracted tuberculosis and was given one year to live. His doctor recommended trying the dry climate of Santa Fe. He arrived in 1920 and met John Sloan and four young artists who, along with Shuster, would form Los Cincos Pintores (the Five Painters) in 1921. The group exhibited at the Museum of Fine Arts in December 1921. (Courtesy of the Palace of the Governors Archive, 0073983.)

Sheldon Parsons (1866–1943) was born in Rochester, New York. He studied with William Merritt Chase and painted portraits of President McKinley and Susan B. Anthony. Parsons came to Santa Fe in 1913 seeking treatment for tuberculosis and changed his way of painting to a post-impressionist style. His work is still very popular today. (Courtesy of the Palace of the Governors Archive, 007822.)

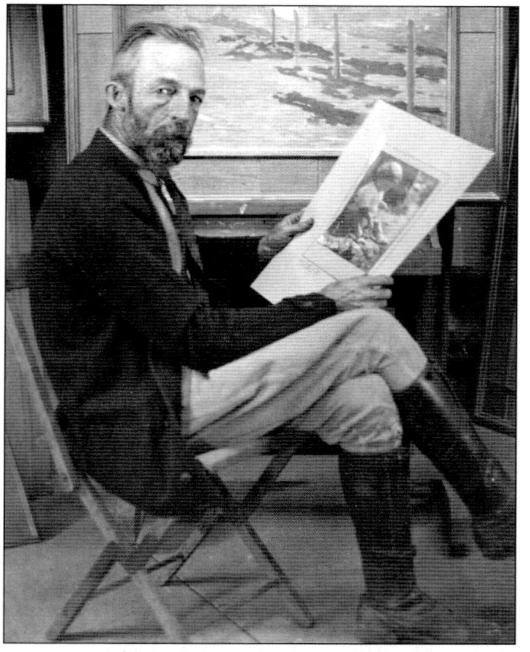

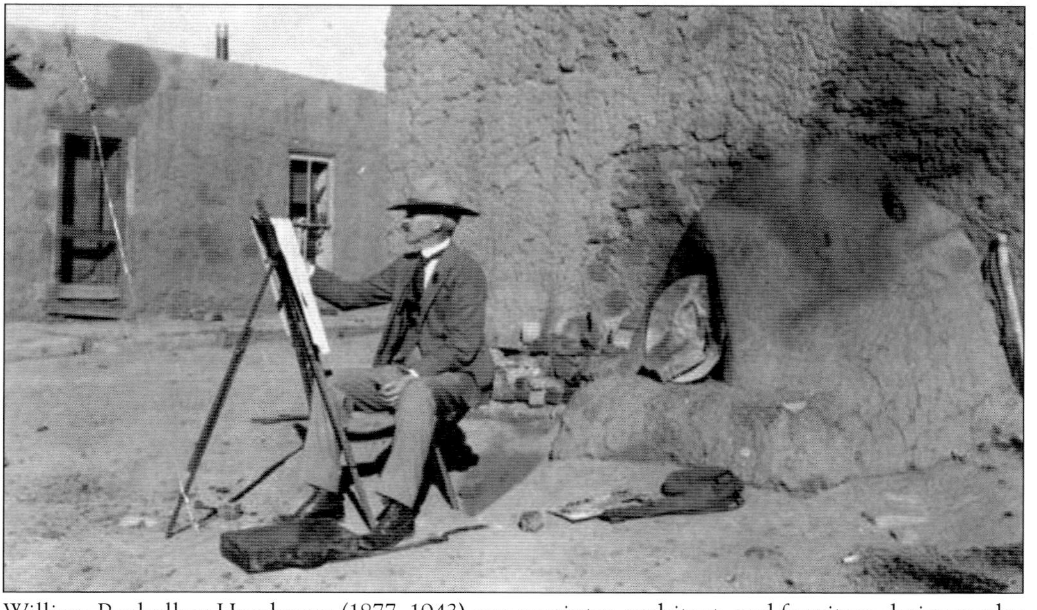

William Penhallow Henderson (1877–1943) was a painter, architect, and furniture designer who was born in Medford, Massachusetts, and studied at Boston's Museum of Fine Arts. Henderson taught at the Academy of Fine Arts in Chicago from 1904 to 1910. In 1905, he married Alice Corbin, an author and poet and the assistant editor of *Poetry* magazine. The couple moved to Santa Fe in 1916 to seek treatment for Alice, who suffered from tuberculosis. In 1925, Henderson and his son-in-law, John Evans, started a Pueblo/Spanish building company, designing and building private homes and public buildings. In 1937, Henderson designed the Navajo House of Religion (now the Wheelwright Museum), and painted six Santa Fe courthouse murals. (Courtesy of the Palace of the Governors Archive, 007318.)

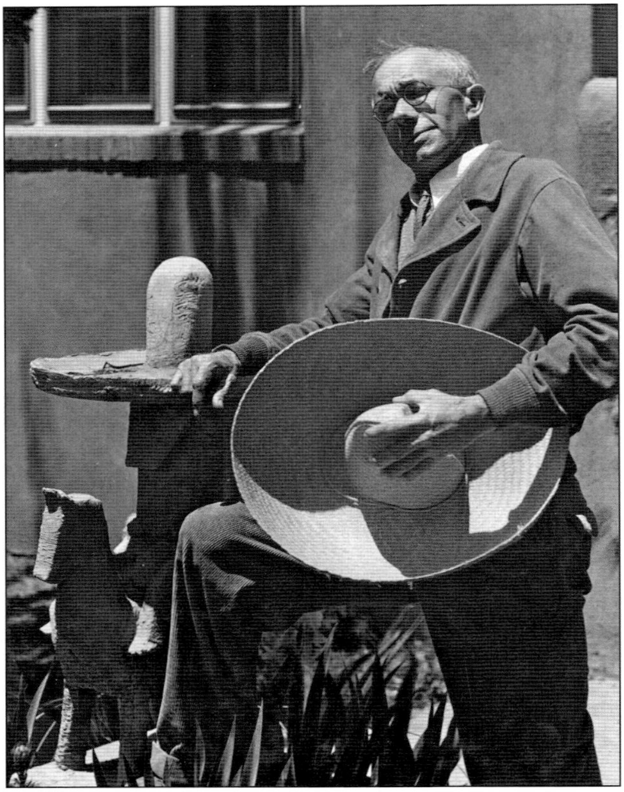

Gustave Bauman (1881–1971) was born in Magdeburg, Germany, and moved to the United States at age 10. He worked at an engraving house and took night classes at the Chicago Art Institute. In 1904, he returned to Germany to study woodblock carving and printing and started making woodcuts back in America in 1908. His large woodcuts were shown at the Panama-Pacific International Exposition in San Diego in 1915. Bauman came to Santa Fe in 1919 and was given an exhibition by Edgar L. Hewett in the newly constructed Museum of Fine Arts. He and his wife settled in Santa Fe, where Bauman produced prints of landscapes, Indian life, and other subjects as well as delightful marionettes for more than 50 years until his death. Below is a woodcut block print announcement of Bauman's 1918 exhibition at the Museum of Fine Arts. At left, Bauman poses in Los Angeles. (Both courtesy of the Palace of the Governors Archive, 092094 and 059739.)

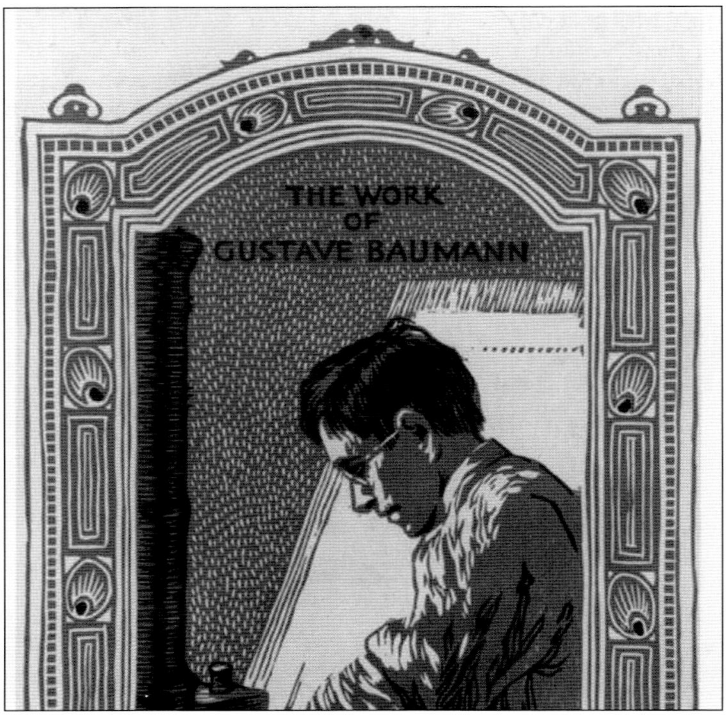

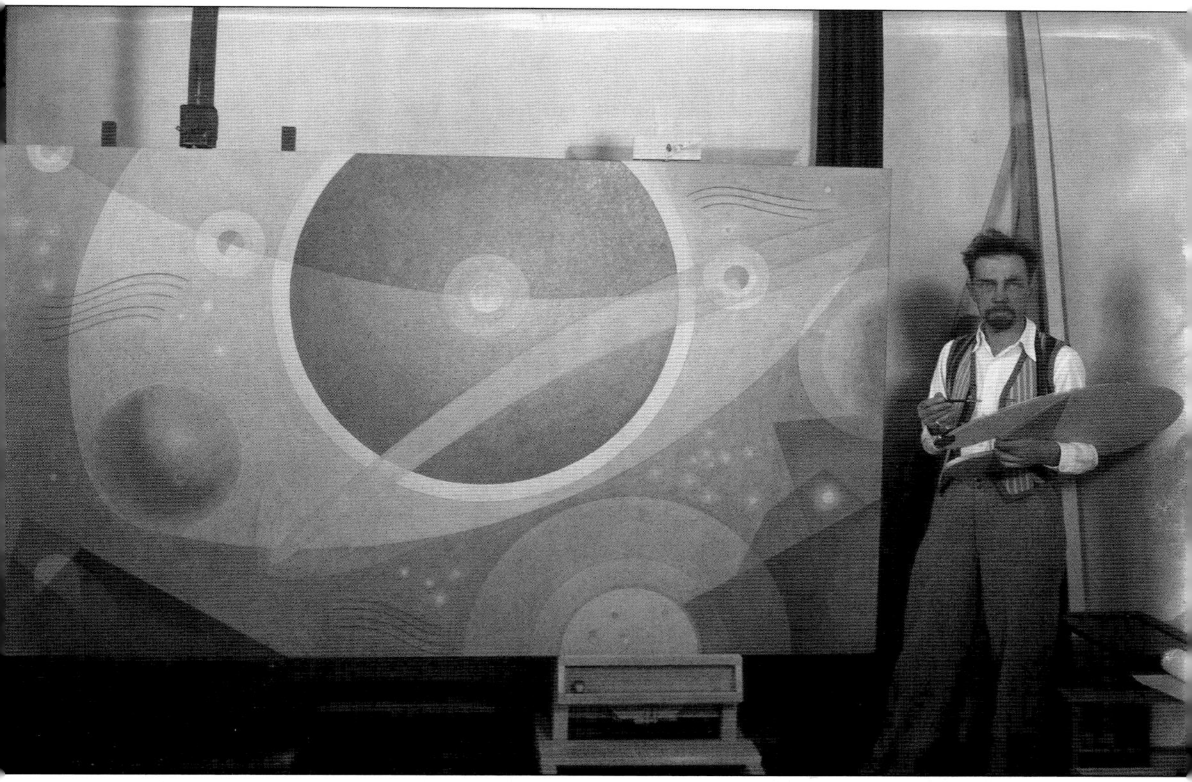

Raymond Jonson (1891–1982) was born in Iowa and grew up in Portland, Oregon. He attended the Chicago Academy of Fine Arts and the Chicago Art Institute, worked as an art director for the Chicago Little Theater, and taught at the Academy of Fine Arts. Jonson visited New Mexico in 1922 and lived in Santa Fe until 1934. He taught at the University of New Mexico in Albuquerque and co-founded a transcendental painting class with Emil Bistrum. The University of New Mexico's Jonson Gallery was established in 1950 in Jonson's home. He is seen here in his studio. (Courtesy of the Palace of the Governors Archive, 073938.)

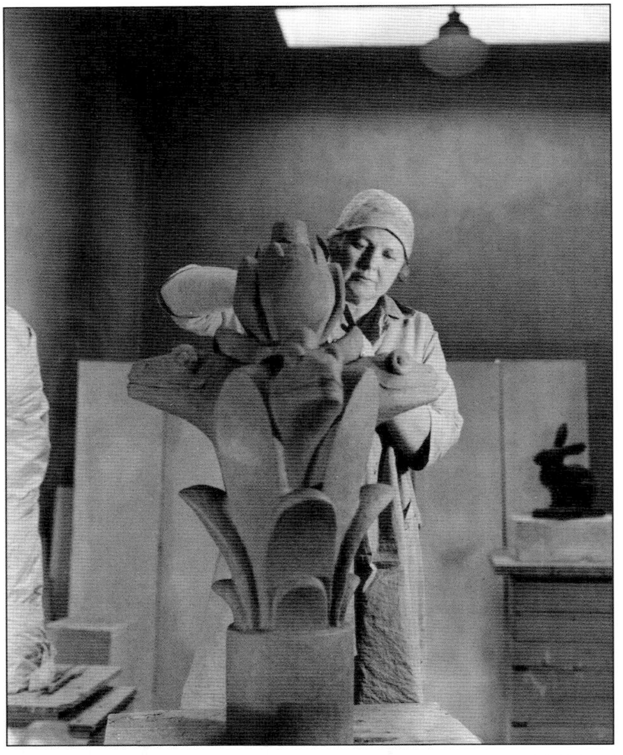

Eugenie Shonnard (left, 1886–1978) was born in Yonkers, New York, and studied at the New York School of Design with Alphose Muncha for three years. She moved to Paris, where she studied with Rodin and his former student, Bourdelle, in 1911 and 1912. Shonnard first visited Santa Fe in 1925 and moved there in 1927. She designed a chapel in Colorado Springs for Frederick Taylor and a bust of Miguel Chavez (below) that was installed at Saint Michael's College. Shonnard worked as a WPA artist and did numerous projects in Santa Fe. She invented a carving material that was lighter in weight and easier to carve. She exhibited in Paris in 1926, at the Museum of Modern Art in 1933, and at the New York World's Fair in 1939.

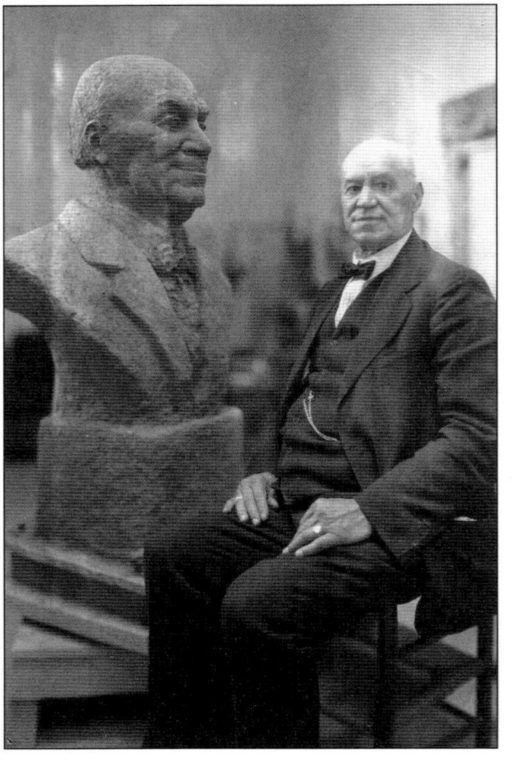

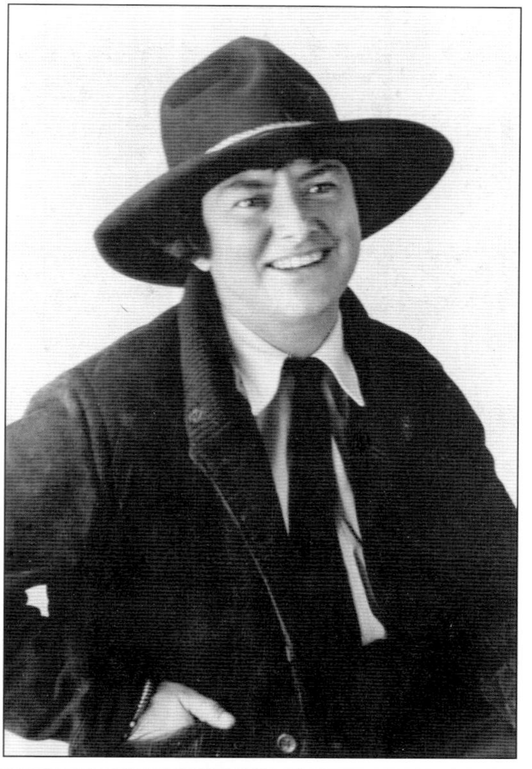

Artist Dorothy Stewart (1891–1955) is shown at right in a c. 1930 portrait and below working on a WPA mural. Stewart studied at the Pennsylvania Academy of Fine Arts, and in France at the American School of Fine Arts. She settled in Santa Fe with her sister, Margrette Dietrich, in 1925. Stewart produced books with multicolored illustrations and painted a mural for Albuquerque's Little Theater. She owned the Canyon Road Hacienda el Zaguan, where she hosted concerts and art events. A number of the rooms in her home are still used as artist's residences by the Historic Santa Fe Foundation. (Courtesy of the Palace of the Governors Archive, 106611 and 019104.)

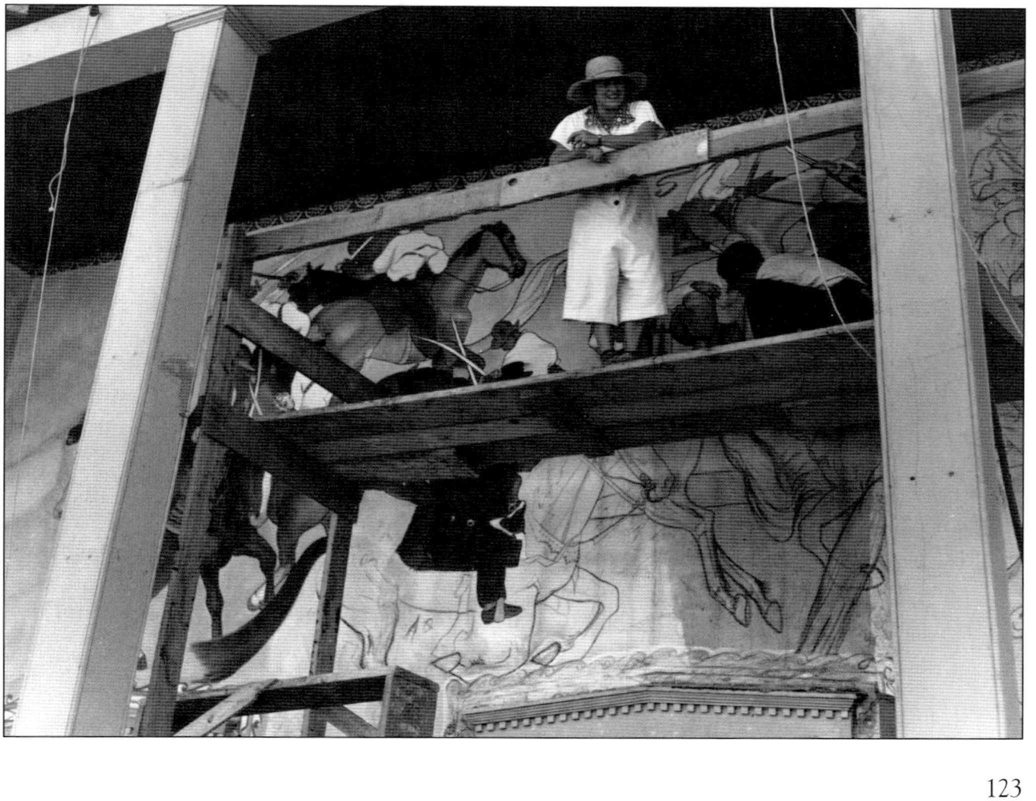

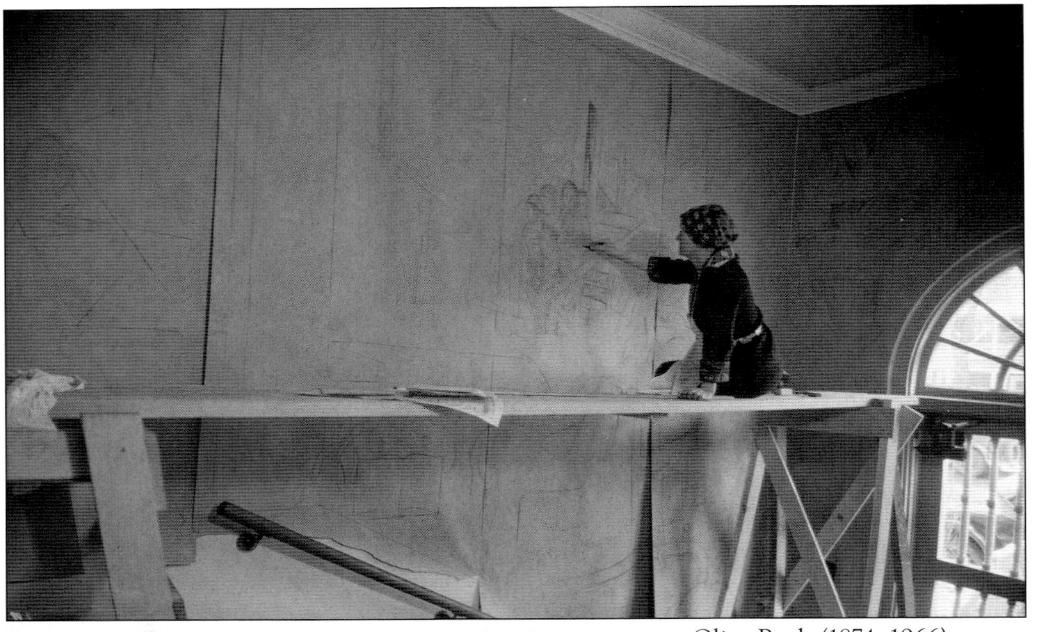

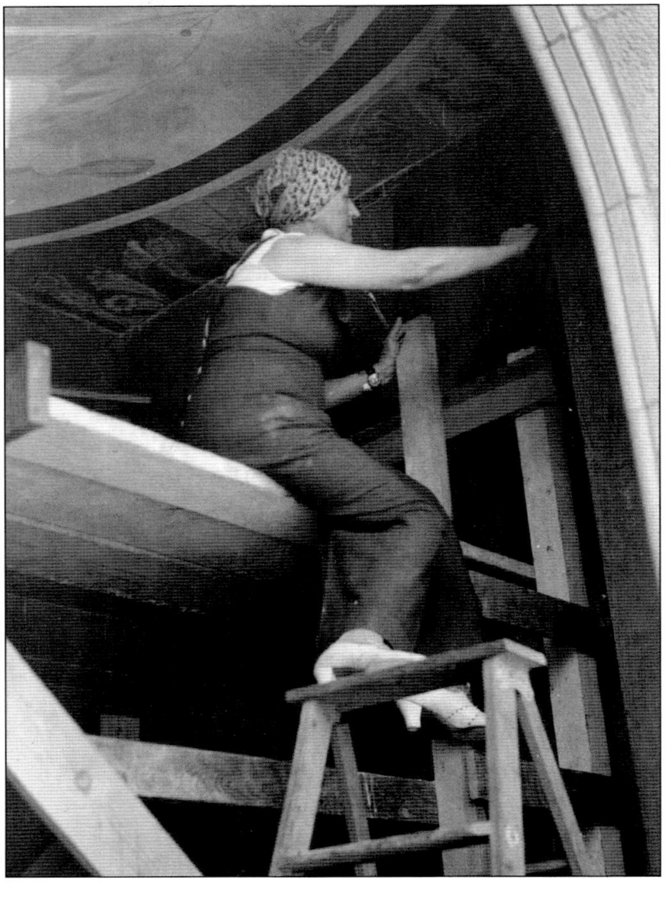

Olive Rush (1874–1966) was born in Indiana and raised as a Quaker. She studied at Corcorron Gallery of Art and at the Art Students League, visiting New Mexico in 1914 for a one-artist exhibit at the Palace of the Governors. Rush moved to Santa Fe permanently in 1928 and painted murals in the public library and post office, and at La Fonda Hotel. She also taught mural painting at Santa Fe Indian School. Rush's former studio and home on Canyon Road is now a Quaker meetinghouse. The c. 1935 photograph above shows Rush painting a mural in Santa Fe's public library. In the image at left, she paints a WPA mural. (Both courtesy of the Palace of the Governors Archive, 019270 and 074015.)

Agnes Simms (1910–1990) is best known for paintings and sculpture inspired by prehistoric rock art, or petroglyphs. She used a batik technique to create a 150-foot mural for a Santa Fe bank. She supported the arts with public events held at her Canyon Road compound. (Courtesy of the Palace of the Governors Archive, 028994.)

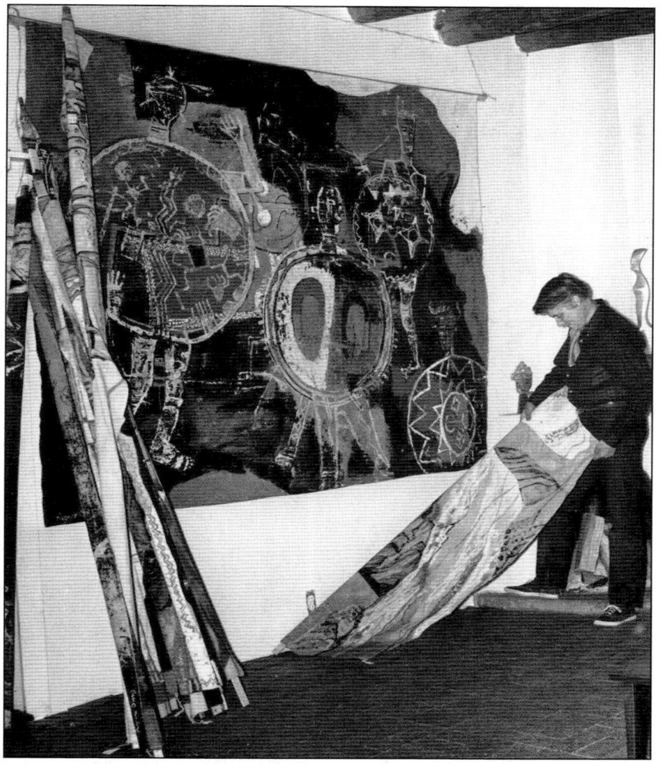

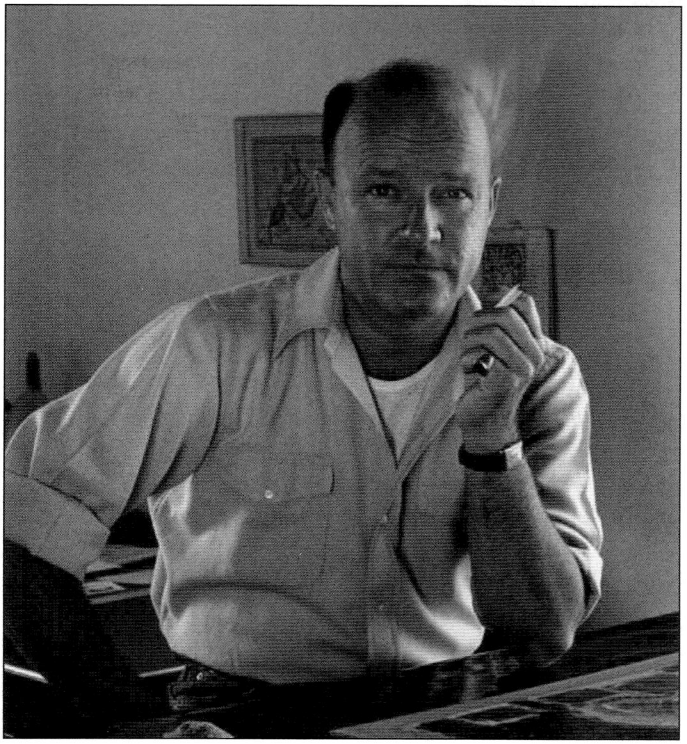

Artist and collector Cady Wells (1904–1954) was born to a wealthy New England family, attending a ranch school in Arizona and private schools in the east. He met E. Boyd in 1932 on a trip to New Mexico and decided to stay. He was first influenced by John Marin's watercolors before developing his own unique style by 1935. Wells's work had a flow and a dark, brooding intensity unlike any other Southwest artist. He built a major collection of bultos and santos and gifted them to the Museum of New Mexico. (Courtesy of the Palace of the Governors Archive, 041698.)

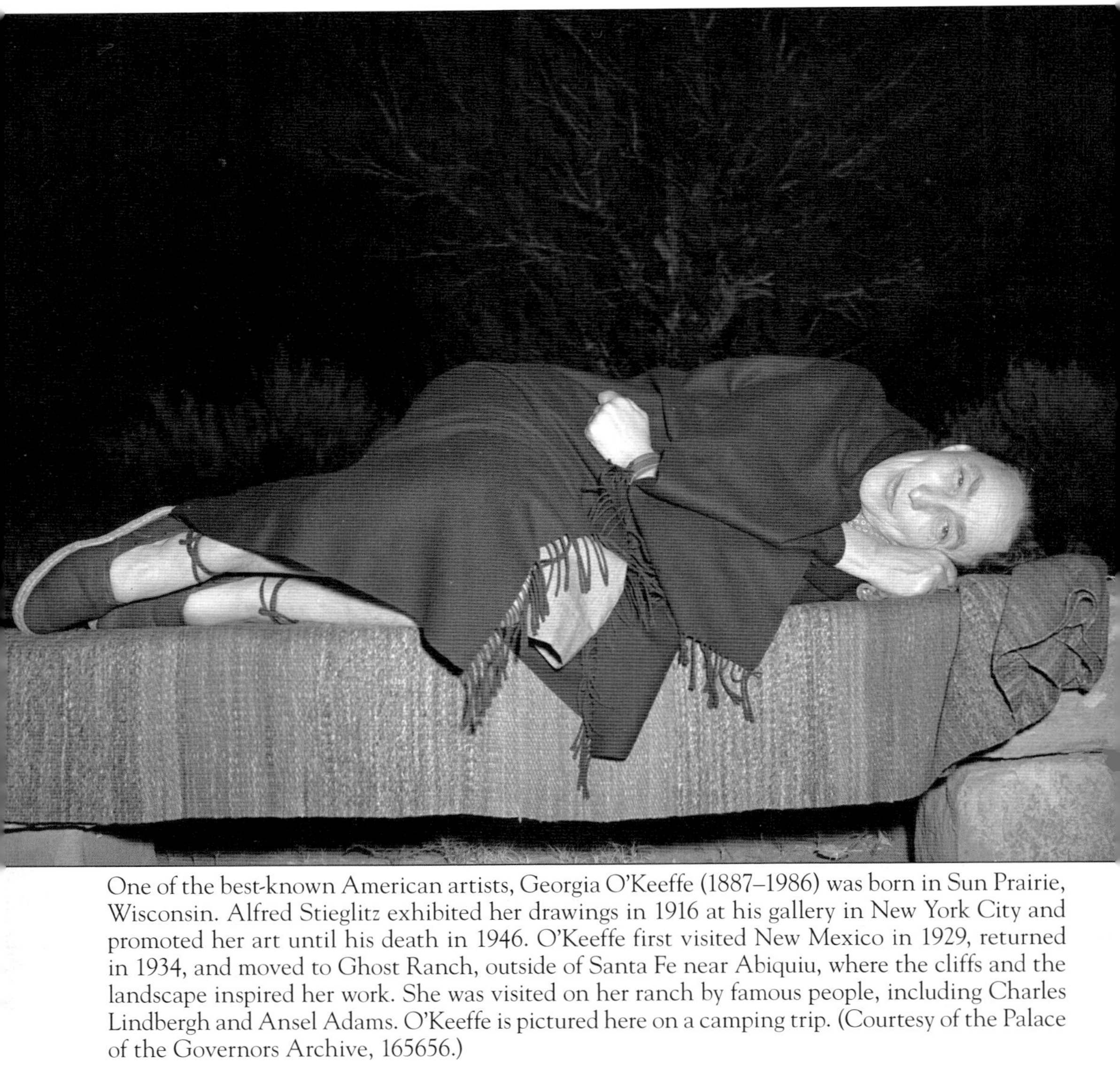

One of the best-known American artists, Georgia O'Keeffe (1887–1986) was born in Sun Prairie, Wisconsin. Alfred Stieglitz exhibited her drawings in 1916 at his gallery in New York City and promoted her art until his death in 1946. O'Keeffe first visited New Mexico in 1929, returned in 1934, and moved to Ghost Ranch, outside of Santa Fe near Abiquiu, where the cliffs and the landscape inspired her work. She was visited on her ranch by famous people, including Charles Lindbergh and Ansel Adams. O'Keeffe is pictured here on a camping trip. (Courtesy of the Palace of the Governors Archive, 165656.)

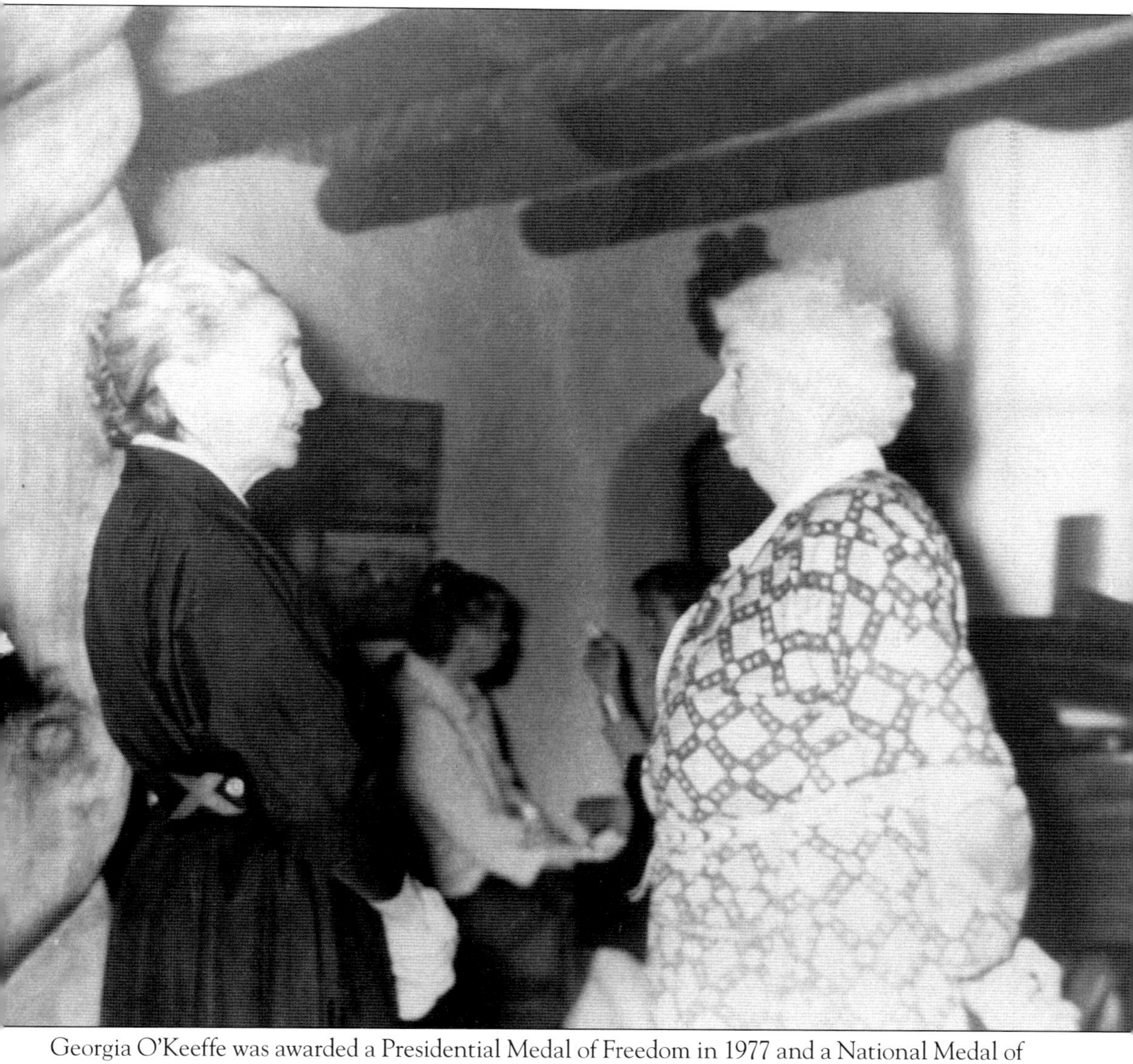

Georgia O'Keeffe was awarded a Presidential Medal of Freedom in 1977 and a National Medal of Arts in 1985. The Georgia O'Keeffe Museum in Santa Fe has changing exhibitions of her work along with that of other artists. She is seen here speaking with Lady Dorothy Brett at Brett's birthday party. (Courtesy of the Harwood Museum of Art, Taos.)